Praise for Carolyne Aarsen and her novels

"*Twin Blessings* is another delightful romance by Carolyne Aarsen sure to bring a smile to your lips."
—*Romantic Times BOOKreviews*

"Ms. Aarsen's refreshing characters learn to forgive, love and hope in this pleasing tale."
—*Romantic Times BOOKreviews* on *The Cowboy's Bride*

"Carolyne Aarsen writes with tender empathy and a true understanding of the struggles her characters endure in *A Family-Style Christmas.*"
—*Romantic Times BOOKreviews*

"A spunky heroine keeps the story fun while a warm romance brews at just the right temperature. You'll be glad to read *Finally a Family.*"
—*Romantic Times BOOKreviews*

CAROLYNE AARSEN

Twin Blessings
&
Toward Home

Published by Steeple Hill Books™

STEEPLE HILL BOOKS

ISBN-13: 978-0-373-65130-6

TWIN BLESSINGS AND TOWARD HOME

This edition published by arrangement with Steeple Hill Books.

www.SteepleHill.com

Printed in U.S.A.

CONTENTS

Books by Carolyne Aarsen

Love Inspired

Homecoming
Ever Faithful
A Bride at Last
The Cowboy's Bride
**A Family-Style Christmas*
**A Mother at Heart*
**A Family at Last*
A Hero for Kelsey
Twin Blessings
Toward Home
Love Is Patient
A Heart's Refuge
Brought Together by Baby
A Silence in the Heart
Any Man of Mine
Yuletide Homecoming
Finally a Family
A Family for Luke

*Stealing Home

CAROLYNE AARSEN

and her husband, Richard, live on a small ranch in Northern Alberta, where they have raised four children and numerous foster children, and are still raising cattle. Carolyne crafts her stories in her office with a large west-facing window through which she can watch the changing seasons while struggling to make her words obey.

TWIN BLESSINGS

When I consider your heavens, the work of your fingers, the moon and the stars which you have set in place, what is man that you are mindful of him and the son of man that you care for him?

—*Psalms* 8:3–4

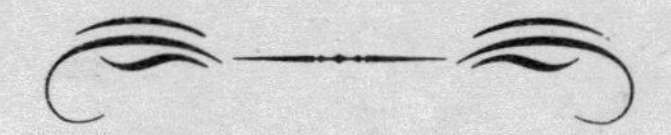

To Richard and my kids.
Always helpful and supportive.
Always enthusiastic and encouraging.

Chapter One

The sun was directly overhead.

Logan's vehicle was headed south. Down the highway toward Cypress Hills—oasis on the Alberta prairie and vacation home of Logan Napier's grandfather and parents.

Logan Napier should have been happy. No, Logan Napier should have been euphoric.

Usually the drive through the wide-open grasslands of the prairies put a smile on his face. The tawny landscape, deceptively smooth, soothed away the jagged edges of city living. The quiet highways never ceased to work their peace on him, erasing the tension of driving in Calgary's busy traffic.

Usually, Logan Napier drove one-handed, leaning back, letting the warm wind and the open space work its magic as he drove with the top of his convertible down.

Today, however, his hands clenched the steering wheel of a minivan, his eyes glaring through his sunglasses at the road ahead. In his estimation a single man moving up in the world shouldn't be driving a minivan. Nor should a single man be contemplating seven different punishments for ten-year-old twin nieces. And his mother.

All three were supposed to be neatly ensconced in the cabin in the hills. He was supposed to be coming up for a two-week holiday, spending his time drawing up plans for a house for Mr. Jonserad of Jonserad Holdings. If he was successful, it had the potential to bring more work from Jonserad's company to his architecture partnership.

Instead his mother had just called. She was leaving for Alaska in a day. Then the tutor called telling him that she was quitting because she wasn't getting the support she needed from Logan's mother. Each phone call put another glitch in his well-laid plans.

He hadn't planned on this, he brooded, squinting against the heat waves that shimmered from the pavement as he rounded a bend. Logan hit the on button of the tape deck and was immediately assaulted by the rhythmic chanting of yet another boy band, which did nothing for his ill humor. Every area of his life had been invaded by his nieces from the first day they came into his home, orphaned when their parents died in a boating accident.

Grimacing, Logan ejected the tape and fiddled with the dials. How was he supposed to work on this very important project with the girls around, unsupervised and running free?

How were they supposed to move on to the next

grade if they didn't have a tutor to work with them? And where was he supposed to find someone on such short notice? It had taken him a number of weeks to find one who was willing to go with the girls to Cypress Hills and to follow the studies their previous teacher had set out.

Glancing down, Logan gave the dial another quick twist. Finally some decent music drifted out of the speakers. He adjusted the tuner then glanced up.

He was heading directly toward a woman standing on the side of the road.

Logan yanked on the steering wheel. The tires squealed on the warm pavement as the van swung around her.

He slammed on the brakes. The van rocked to a halt, and Logan pulled his shaking hands over his face.

He took a slow breath and sent up a heartfelt prayer, thankful that nothing more serious had happened. He got out of the van in time to see the woman bearing down on him, a knapsack flung over one shoulder.

Her long brown hair streamed behind her, her eyes narrowed.

"You could have killed me," she called, throwing her hands in the air.

"I'm sorry," he said, walking toward her. "Are you okay?"

"I'm fine. You missed me." She stopped in front of him, her hands on her hips, her dark eyes assessing him even as he did her.

She was of medium height. Thick brown hair hung in a heavy swath over one shoulder. Her deep brown eyes were framed by eyebrows that winged ever so slightly, giving her a mischievous look. Her tank top revealed tanned arms, her khaki shorts long, tanned legs. Bare feet in sandals. Attractive in a homegrown way.

"What were you doing?" she asked.

Logan blinked, realizing he was studying her a little too long. Chalk it up to loneliness, he thought. And he must be lonely if he was eyeing hitchhikers. "Just trying to find a radio station," he said finally.

She shook her head, lifting her hair from the back of her neck. "Checking the latest stock quotations?"

In spite of the fact that he knew he hadn't been paying attention and had almost missed her, Logan still bristled at her tone. "Why were you on the side of the road?" he returned.

A few vehicles whizzed by, swirling warm air around the two of them.

"Thumbing for a ride." She let her hair drop, tilted her head and looked past him. "I suppose you'll have to give me one now, since you've almost killed me and then made me miss a few potentials."

She didn't look much older than twenty and about as responsible as his nieces. He wasn't in the mood to have her as a passenger, but he did feel he owed her a ride.

"I didn't almost kill you," he said, defending himself. "But I am sorry about the scare."

"So do I get a ride?"

Logan hesitated. He felt he should, though he never picked up hitchhikers as a rule.

"I won't kill you, if that's what you're worried about." Her lips curved into a smirk. "And I won't take your wife and kids hostage or try to sue you for taking five years off my life."

"I don't have a wife and kids."

"But you have a minivan."

Logan frowned at her smirk and decided to let the comment pass. He wasn't in the mood to defend the necessity of his vehicle to a complete stranger, not with the sun's heat pressing all around. "Look, I'm sorry again about what I did. But I'm running late. If you want a ride, I'm leaving now."

He didn't look to see if she had followed him, but she had the passenger door open the same time he had his open.

"Nice and cool in here," she said, pulling off her knapsack. She dropped it on the floor in front of her and looked around. "So, what's a guy like you need a minivan for?" she asked, as Logan clicked his seat belt shut.

"What do you mean, a guy like me?" Logan frowned as he slipped on his sunglasses and checked his side mirror.

"Near as I can see, I figure you for an accountant," she said, glancing around the interior of the van. "Laptop in the seat, briefcase beside it. All nice and orderly. Someone like you should be driving a sedan, not a van."

"Do you usually analyze the people who pick you up?" Logan asked as he pulled onto the road, regretting his momentary lapse that put him in this predicament. He had things on his mind and didn't feel like listening to meaningless chatter.

"I need to. I hear too many scary stories about disappearing women."

"So why take the chance?" He glanced at her, and in spite of his impression of her, he was struck once again by her straightforward good looks.

"Sense of adventure. The lure of the open road." She shrugged. "That and the free ride."

"Of course."

"Okay, I detect a faint note of derision in your voice," she said with a light laugh. "If you're an accountant, I would imagine that there isn't a column in your life for freeloaders."

Logan didn't deign to answer that one.

She waited, then with a shrug bent over and pulled a bottle of water out of her knapsack. Twisting off the top, she offered some to him. "Some free water as payment for my free ride?"

He shook his head.

The woman took a sip and backhanded her mouth. Out of the corner of his eye he could see her scrutiny.

"To further answer your previous question about taking chances," she continued. "I have to admit that I don't see you as a threat."

Logan only nodded, unwilling to encourage her. He didn't really want to talk. He preferred to concentrate on his most recent problem.

"You've got the briefcase, which could be hiding a murder weapon," she said, as if unaware of his silence, "but I'm sure if I were to open it, it would be full of paper. Probably the financial section of the newspaper, folded open to the stock market. Let's see, what else," she mused aloud, still studying him. "A calculator, some sort of computerized personal organizer, a variety of pens and pencils, a package of chewing gum, a manual of one type or another and business cards, of course. Lots of business cards. Murderers don't usually carry that kind of thing. But my biggest clue that you're not a murderer is this." She held up the tape that had fallen out of the tape deck. "I don't think boy bands singing 'oh baby, baby, you are a little baby, you baby' is what a would-be murderer would listen to." She stopped finally, turning the tape over in her hands. "Of course, listening to it might drive you to murder."

In spite of the minor annoyance of her chatter, Logan couldn't stop the faint grin teasing his mouth at her last statement.

"Ah, Mr. Phlegmatic does have a faint sense of humor," she said, lifting her bare feet to the seat and clasping her arms around her knees.

"This Mr. Phlegmatic would prefer it if you buckled up," he said finally.

"And Mr. P. talks," she said with a saucy grin. But to his surprise she lowered her feet and obediently buckled up. "So what do you do when you're not running over women on the side of the road?"

Logan shook his head in exasperation. "Look, I already apologized for that," he said with a measure of asperity. "I don't make a habit of that anymore than I make a habit of picking up hitchhikers."

"Well, for that I'm grateful. And of course, very

grateful that I don't have to worry about not reaching my destination."

"And where, ultimately, is that?" he asked.

"The next stop on this road," the woman said with a laugh. "The Hills."

"That's where I'm headed, too."

"That's just excellent." She beamed at him, and Logan felt a faint stirring of reaction to her infectious enthusiasm.

He pulled himself up short. This woman was definitely not his type, no matter how attractive she might be. He put his reaction down to a melancholy that had been his companion since he and Karen had broken up.

A gentle ache turned through him as he thought of Karen. When Logan was awarded sole guardianship of his nieces, Karen had decided that the responsibility was more than she could handle. So she broke up with Logan. At the time he didn't know if it was his pride or his feelings that hurt more. He still wasn't sure.

"So what's your name?" he asked, relegating that subject to the closed file.

"Sandra Bachman. Pleased to make your acquaintance, Mr. P."

Logan decided to leave it at that. He wasn't as comfortable handing out his name. Not to a total stranger.

She smiled at him and looked at the countryside. "Do you come here often?"

Logan glanced sidelong at her, realizing that she wasn't going to be quiet. Ignoring her didn't work, so he really had not choice but to respond to her. "Not as often as I'd like," he admitted. "I work in Calgary."

"As an accountant?"

"No. Architect."

"Ooh. All those nice straight lines."

Logan ignored her slightly sarcastic remark. "So what do you do?"

Sandra lay her head back against the headrest of the car. "Whatever comes to mind. Wherever I happen to be." She tossed him another mischievous glance. "I've been a short-order cook on Vancouver Island, a waitress in California, a receptionist in Minnesota. I've worked on a road crew and tried planting trees." She wrinkled her nose. "Too hard. The only constant in my life has been my stained glass work."

"As in church windows?"

"Sometimes. Though I don't often see the finished project."

"Why not?"

"Been there, done that and bought the T-shirt. Not my style."

Sandra Bachman sounded exactly like his mother—always moving and resistant to organized religion.

"Do you go to church?" she asked.

"Yes, I do," he said hoping that his conviction came through the three words. "I attend regularly."

"Out of need or custom?"

He shook his head as he smiled. "Need is probably uppermost."

"A good man." Again the slightly sarcastic tone. In spite of his faint animosity toward her, he couldn't help but wonder what caused it.

"Going to church doesn't make anyone good anymore than living in a garage makes someone a mechanic," he retorted.

She laughed again, a throaty sound full of humor. "Good point, Mr. P."

She tilted her head to one side, twisting her hair around her hand. "You have a cabin in Elkwater?"

Logan nodded, checking his speed. "It's my grandfather's."

"So you're on holiday."

"Not really."

"Okay, you sound defensive."

"You sound nosy."

Sandra laughed. "You're not the first one to tell me that." She gave her hair another twist. "So if you're not on holiday, why are you going to a holiday place?"

"I have to meet my mother." *And try and talk some sense into her,* Logan thought. If he could convince his mother to stay, he might win a reprieve.

"So she's holidaying."

Logan glanced at Sandra, slightly annoyed at her steady probing. "My mother has her own strange and irresponsible plans," he said.

His passenger angled him a mischievous glance, unfazed by his abrupt comments. "I sense tension between your mother's choice of lifestyle and yours."

"That's putting it kindly. My mother has a hard time with responsibility."

"Surely you're being a little hard on her? After all, she raised you, didn't she?"

Logan held her dancing eyes, momentarily unable to look away, catching a glimmer of her enthusiasm. She tilted her head again, as if studying him, her smile fading.

Her expression became serious as the contact lengthened.

She really was quite pretty, Logan thought. Possessed an infectious charm.

He caught himself and looked at the road, derailing that particular train of thought. This young woman was as far from what he was looking for as his mother was.

"So why are you so defensive about your mother?"

"Why do you care? I'll probably never see you again."

She lifted her shoulder in a negligent shrug. "Just making conversation. We don't need to talk about your mother," Sandra continued, biting her lip as if considering a safe topic. "We could talk about life, that one great miracle."

"Big topic."

"Depends on how you break it down." She twirled a loose strand of hair around her finger. "What do you want from life?"

Logan wasn't going to answer, but he hadn't spent time with an attractive woman since Karen. He found himself saying, "Normal. I yearn for absolutely normal." He wasn't usually this loquacious with a complete stranger and wondered what it was about her that had drawn that admission from him.

"Normal isn't really normal, you know," Sandra replied, braiding her hair into a thick, dark braid. Her dark eyes held his a brief moment. "Sometimes normal makes you crazy."

Logan gave her a quick look. "Now you sound defensive."

"Nope. Just telling the truth." She dropped the braid, and it lay like a thick rope over her tanned shoulders. "So what's your plan to get your normal life?"

"That's an easy one. I'm picking up my nieces, who are staying with my mother, who wants to scoot off to Alaska for some strange reason. Then I'm taking my nieces back home to Calgary. And that's as close to normal as I'm going to get."

The woman's smile slipped, and she looked straight ahead. "Nieces?" she asked quietly. "As in two?"

"A matched set," Logan replied. "Twin girls that have been a mixed blessing to me."

She tossed him a quick glance, then looked away, as if retreating. She folded her hands on her lap, lay her head against the backrest and closed her eyes. The conversation had come to an end.

Logan wondered what caused the sudden change this time. Wondered why it bothered him. Wondered why he should care.

He had enough on his mind. He concentrated on the road, watching the enticing oasis of Cypress Hills grow larger, bringing Logan closer to his destination and decisions.

Finally the road made one final turn and then skirted the lake for which the town of Elkwater was named. Sandra sat up as Logan slowed down by the town limits.

"Just drop me off at the service station," Sandra said.

He pulled up in front of the confectionary and gas station and before he could get out, Sandra had grabbed her backpack and was out of the van.

"Thanks for the ride, Mr. P.," she said with a quick grin. "I just might see you around."

Logan nodded, feeling suddenly self-conscious at all that he had told her, a complete stranger. He wasn't usually that forthcoming. "You're welcome," he said automatically. She flashed him another bright smile then jogged across the street.

Logan slowly put the car in gear, still watching Sandra as she greeted a group of people standing by the gas pumps, talking. She stopped.

Logan couldn't hear what she was saying but could tell from her gestures that she was relating her adventures of the day. They laughed, she laughed and for a moment Logan was gripped by the same feeling he had when she had first smiled at him.

He pulled away, shaking his head at his own lapse, putting it down to his frustration and, if he were to be honest, a measure of loneliness. Sandra Bachman was a strange, wild young woman, and he'd probably never see her again.

A few minutes later he pulled in beside a small blue car parked in front of a large A-frame house with a commanding view of Elkwater Lake.

"Oh, Logan, my darling. There you are." Florence Napier stood on the porch of the house, her arms held out toward her only son.

As he stepped out of the car to greet his mother, Logan forced a smile to his lips at his mother's effusive welcome. It always struck him as false, considering that when he and his sister were growing up, Florence Napier seldom paid them as much attention as she did her current project.

"Come and give us a kiss," she cried. Today she wore a long dress made of unbleached cotton, covered with a loosely woven vest. Her long gray hair hung loose, tangling in her feathered earrings.

Her artistic pose, Logan thought as he dutifully made his way up the wooden steps to give her a perfunctory hug.

"I'm so glad you came so quickly, Logan. I was just packing up to leave." Florence tucked Logan's arm under hers and led him into the house. "I got an unexpected call from my friend Larissa. You remember her? We took a charcoal class together when we lived in Portland. Anyhow, she's up in Anchorage and absolutely begged me to join her. She wants to do some painting. Of course I couldn't miss this opportunity. We're hoping to check out Whitehorse and possibly Yellowknife, since we're up there anyway."

Logan didn't care to hear about his mother's itinerary. He knew from his youth how hectic it would be. He had more important things to deal with. "Where are Brittany and Bethany?"

Florence wrinkled her nose. "Upstairs. Pouting. I told them you would be taking them home since that dyspeptic tutor you hired decided to quit." Florence shrugged, signifying her inability to understand the tutor's sudden flight.

"Diane has left already?" Logan had to ask, was hoping and praying it wasn't true.

Florence's shoulders lifted in an exaggerated sigh. "Yes. Two days ago. I've never seen a woman so lugubrious."

Logan pulled his arm free from his mother, glaring at her, his frustration and anger coming to the fore. "I talked to her when she phoned me. She told me that you never backed her decisions."

Florence looked at him, her fingertips pressed to her chest. "Logan. That woman's goal was to turn my granddaughters into clones of herself."

"Considering that she came very well qualified, that might not have done Bethany and Brittany any harm."

Logan's mother tut-tutted. "Logan, be reasonable. They're young. It's July. They shouldn't have to do schoolwork. I moved you and your sister all over the country, and it never did you any harm."

"Not by your standards," Logan retorted. For a moment he was clearly reminded of Sandra.

Lord, give me strength, give me patience, he prayed. *Right now would be nice.* "They were also both earning a 45% average in school," Logan said, struggling to keep his tone even. "It was only by begging and agreeing to hire a tutor to work with them over the summer that they won't have to repeat grade five. If they don't finish the work the teacher sent out and if they don't pass the tests she's going to give them at the end of the summer, they will repeat grade five."

A quick wave of Florence's hand relegated his heated remarks to oblivion. At least in her estimation. "My goodness, Logan. You put too much emphasis on formal education." Then she smiled at him. "But don't worry. I'm fully cognizant of your plans and I've already had the good luck and foresight to find a tutor for the girls. Imagine. She lives right here in Elkwater."

"Really? And what are her qualifications?" Logan was almost afraid to ask.

"She has a Bachelor of Education from a well-respected eastern university. With—" she raised an index finger as if to drive her point home "—a major in history."

"And what is this paragon's name?"

"Sandra. Sandra Bachman."

So now what are you going to do? Sandra thought, dropping her knapsack on her tiny kitchen table. She pushed her hair from her face and blew out her breath in a gusty sigh.

She was pretty sure the man who had just dropped her off was the same Uncle Logan that Bethany and Brittany were always talking about. After all, what were the chances of two men having twin nieces living in Elkwater?

From the way the girls spoke of him she had pictured the mysterious uncle to be a portly gentleman, about sixty years old, with no sense of humor.

The real Uncle Logan was a much different story. Tall, thick dark hair that held a soft wave, eyebrows that could frown anyone into the next dimension, hazel eyes fringed with lashes that put hers to shame. His straight mouth and square jaw offset his feminine features big time.

The real Uncle Logan was a dangerous package,

she thought. Dangerously good-looking, if one's tastes ran to clean-cut corporate citizens like accountants. Architects, she corrected. She knew from the girls that Uncle Logan was an architect. She bet he had a closet full of suits at home.

Sandra shuddered at the thought. Her tastes never ran in that direction. If anything, they went in the complete opposite direction of anyone remotely like her father, the epitome of conventional and normal that Logan wanted so badly.

Suppressing a sigh, Sandra slipped into the tiny bedroom and quickly changed into the clothes she had planned to wear for her third and what could possibly be final day on the job. She was tempted to stay away, knowing that losing her job was inevitable, given the way Logan was talking in the car on the way up here, but she had made a deal with Florence Napier. And Sandra held the faint hope that Florence might come through for her.

The walk to the Napier cabin only took ten minutes, but with each step Sandra wondered at the implications for her future. She needed this job to pay for the shipment of glass that would only be delivered cash on delivery. Trouble was she only had enough cash for a few groceries and not near enough for the glass.

At one time she'd been a praying person, but she didn't think God could be bothered with something as minor as a desperate need for money to pay bills.

As she rounded the corner, she saw Logan's van parked beside Florence's car, and her step faltered as she remembered what the girls had told her about Uncle Logan.

A tough disciplinarian who made them go to church every Sunday whether they wanted to or not. A man who kept them to a strict and rigid schedule.

A shiver of apprehension trailed down Sandra's neck at the thought of facing Logan again. This time as her potential boss. A boss she had smart mouthed on the way here. Why had she done it? she thought.

Because he was just like her father, she reminded herself. Though Sandra knew she would never dare be as flippant with Josh Bachman as she was with the formidable Logan Napier.

The front door of the cabin opened, and Florence stepped out carrying a garment bag. She lifted her head at the same moment Sandra stepped forward.

"Oh, Sandra. Hello, darling. We've been waiting for you." Florence set the garment bag on the hood of her little car and flowed toward Sandra, enveloping her in a hug. "The girls were wondering if you were even coming today."

"I'm sorry." Sandra made a futile gesture in the direction of Medicine Hat. "My car. I brought it in for a routine oil change but they found more trouble with it."

"Goodness, how did you get here?"

Sandra caught her lip between her teeth as she glanced at Logan's minivan. "I hitchhiked."

"That's my girl," Florence said approvingly. "Innovative and not scared to accept a challenge." Florence smiled, but Sandra sensed a measure of hesitation.

"So, where are the girls?" Sandra didn't know her status, but she figured it was better to simply act as if she still had a job.

Florence laid an arm over Sandra's shoulders, drawing her a short distance away from the house. "There's been a small complication, Sandra," Florence said, lowering her voice. "The girls' uncle came here. Unexpectedly." Florence laughed as if dismissing this minor problem.

Sandra gave her a weak smile in return. "And what does that mean?" As if she didn't know. Staid Uncle Logan would hardly approve of a smart-mouthed hitch-hiking tutor, regardless of her reasons.

"I think we're okay, but you will have to talk to him."

"Haven't you talked to him yet? Haven't you told him that you hired me? We had an agreement."

Florence tossed a furtive glance over her shoulder, and that insignificant gesture told Sandra precisely how much influence Florence had with Uncle Logan.

None.

Florence looked at Sandra, her hand resting on Sandra's shoulder. "It would probably be best if you spoke with him. Told him your credentials, that kind of thing."

Sandra looked at Florence, whose gaze flittered away. "Okay. I will. Where is he?"

"He's in the house. He's unpacking, so I think that means he'll be staying at least tonight." Florence turned, giving Sandra a light push in the direction of the house. "You go talk to him. You'll do fine."

"Thanks for the vote of confidence," Sandra muttered as she faced the house. She took a deep breath and walked purposefully toward the cabin. Up the stairs, her footsteps echoing on the wood, and then she was standing at the door.

She knocked, hesitant at first, then angry with her indecisiveness, knocking harder the second time.

The door opened almost immediately, making Sandra wonder if he had been watching to see if she would come to the house.

Logan stood framed by the open door. He looked as conservative as he had when he picked her up. Khaki pants, a cotton button-down shirt. All he was missing was a pair of glasses and a pocket protector.

"Hi," she said with a forced jocularity. "You know who I am. Now you know what I am."

Logan wasn't smiling, however. "Come on in, Sandra. We need to talk."

Sandra knew that though she may have weaseled a smile out of him this afternoon, she probably wouldn't now.

Chapter Two

As Sandra walked past him, Logan caught his mother's concerned look. But Florence stayed where she was.

He wasn't surprised that his mother didn't come rushing in to support the person she had hired. Confrontation wasn't Florence's style.

Logan closed the door quietly and turned to face Sandra. She wore a dress with short sleeves. Demure and much more suited to a teacher than the shorts and tank top she had on this afternoon. She had tied up her hair earlier into some kind of braid, finishing the picture.

"Are the girls around?" Sandra asked, her hands clasped in front of her.

"They're upstairs, I think. They haven't dared to come down yet." Logan rested his hands on his hips as he studied her. She was as pretty as before, but definitely not the type of girl he wanted teaching his flighty nieces. They needed an older, stronger influence.

"Do I pass?" she asked suddenly, her brown eyes narrowed.

Logan held her gaze. "I'm sorry to tell you this, Sandra, but you don't have a job. The girls and I are heading back to Calgary tomorrow."

"I thought they were staying here for the summer."

"They were." Logan put emphasis on the last word. "But their antics and those of my mother have proved to me that they are better off in Calgary where I can keep a close eye on them." It wasn't what he wanted at all, but he certainly wasn't going to leave them with someone like her.

"Your mother hired me to teach the girls for the rest of the summer. We had an agreement."

Logan heard the contentious tone in her voice but wasn't moved by it. "I'm the legal guardian of these girls, and I'm the one who has to make decisions that I think are best for them. Not my mother."

"And you wouldn't consider letting the girls stay and having me tutor them?"

Logan shook his head. His nieces had spent enough of their life living around unsuitable people when their parents were alive, carting them around from boat race to boat race. It had taken him a couple of months just to get them into a normal household routine, let alone a schoolwork one. The last thing he wanted was for all his careful and loving work to be undone by someone whose character he knew precious little of. A woman whose first impression was hardly stellar.

"So you're dismissing me out of hand." Her voice

rose ever so slightly. "Without even considering my credentials as a teacher."

"What references do you have? Have you ever worked as a teacher since you graduated?"

"No, I haven't."

"So what have you done?"

Sandra said nothing, and Logan couldn't help but remember her casual comments about work as they had driven here.

"I'm sorry, Sandra," he said. "I have to make a judgment call in this situation."

"Does this have anything to do with the fact that I was hitchhiking this afternoon?"

Logan didn't know what to say. Should he tell an untruth or be bluntly honest?

She laughed shortly. "I can't believe this. I'm perfectly qualified…." She let the sentence slide off.

Logan's shoulders lifted in a sigh as he shoved his hands in the pockets of his pants. "I didn't interview you, Sandra. I had chosen another eminently qualified tutor…"

"I have a Bachelor of Education degree," Sandra stated. "With a major in history and a minor in English. Nothing wrong with that, I'm sure."

Logan bristled at her tone. "I have my nieces' well-being to consider, besides their education."

Sandra held his steady gaze, then her eyes drifted away. "I see." She darted another angry look his way. "Then I'll be on my way." She strode past him and out of the house.

Logan watched her go, fighting a moment's panic.

It would solve so many things if he were to let the girls stay with Sandra. He was in the middle of a hugely important project and he needed all the free time he could get.

But common sense made him keep his mouth shut. Common sense and an innate concern for his nieces. They needed stability and a firm hand. Something that had been sorely lacking in their life.

And, when he was younger, his own.

Logan spent his teen years moving from school to school, dragged across the country by parents searching for the elusive perfect job.

Education wasn't taken seriously in this branch of the Napier family, and as a consequence Logan and his sister Linda's schooling suffered. Always behind academically, Logan dedicated every spare moment to catching up, to striving to get out of the rut his parents seemed willing to flow along in. Then, when Logan was in high school, his father died and Florence Napier was forced to settle down for a while.

During this time Logan pulled himself out of the endless routine of constant movement. He applied himself to finishing high school and going to college. Six years ago he graduated with his degree and was much happier than he had ever been during his aimless childhood.

However, Linda, the twins' mother, had been caught up in the same ceaseless wandering, hooking up and marrying a man who raced speedboats for thrills and the occasional cash prize. An aquatic cowboy who didn't know where his own parents were. Brittany and

Bethany were headed in the same direction until a tragic accident claimed Logan's sister and her husband's life. To his mother's surprise Logan had been named not only guardian but also executor of the small estate the girls had inherited.

Bethany and Brittany's arrival changed everything in Logan's life, but he was determined to do right by them. To take care of them. To make sure that any influence in their life was positive and stable.

A young woman like Sandra Bachman was not the kind of person he wanted tutoring these impressionable young girls.

With a sigh and another quick prayer, he turned to the next task at hand.

"Okay, girls. You can stop listening in and come down."

Two heads popped above the blanket draped over the balustrade of the loft. Both blond, both cute, both looking slightly chastened.

Brittany, the bolder of the two, bounced down the stairs as only a young girl could and landed in front of him, her hands tucked in the pockets of her very baggy white pants. Bethany followed a few paces behind, looking a little more subdued than her counterpart.

Brittany lifted her shoulders, looking genuinely puzzled. "So I guess you came here earlier than you figured. Are you sure you don't want to stay for a while?"

Logan shook his head slowly, as if for emphasis. "I have a special project I need to work on. You know work? The thing that keeps you in those ridiculous clothes?" He pressed his lips together, frustrated at the anger that had surged to the fore. But today had not been a good day, and right now he was all out of magical patience.

Brittany slowly tilted her head as if searching for some kind of answer.

Logan didn't wait for her to find it. "You and Bethany had better hustle yourselves back upstairs and start packing. We're leaving for Calgary tomorrow."

"What?" The word spilled out of both girls' mouths at the same time.

"We can't go now… You promised… You said we'd stay here all summer." Their sentences tumbled over and through each other.

"We've only been here a couple of weeks," Bethany wailed.

Logan glanced at the more docile of the pair, and he felt the hard edges of his anger blur. "Sorry, hon. You guys had your chance and you blew it. We're going back."

"We didn't know it was a test," Brittany cried, her blue eyes glistening.

"It wasn't a test," Logan growled, trying manfully to face down the tears that spilled down both their cheeks. "I don't want to stay here, your grandmother has decided to chase some dream, and you chased off your last tutor, so you have to come back with me."

"But why can't Sandra teach us?" Bethany sniffed, wiping away her tears with the back of her hand. She sat down on the lowest step, still sniffling.

Logan sighed, plowing his hand through his hair. He

could feel himself wavering and knew he shouldn't. He could deal with upstart contractors and rude co-workers, but his nieces' tears always unmanned him.

"Because I don't think she is capable. That's why."

"But we had hoped to stay. We haven't been here since Mom and Dad..." Brittany's voice broke, and she sat beside her sister, pressing her hands against her face, unable to finish.

Logan's heart melted completely. It had been eighteen months since the girls' parents were killed. This summer was the first time they had come back to this place where they and their parents would often stop by on their way to the next destination. It was one of the few constants in their childhood.

It had been difficult enough for him to lose his sister. He couldn't imagine how hard it was for them to lose both parents. And now he was going to take them away from the one place they had fond memories of.

He sat on the step between the girls and put his arms awkwardly around their narrow shoulders. "Oh, sweeties," he said, stroking their arms, wishing he knew exactly what to say. Brittany leaned against him, sniffing loudly.

"Can we stay just for a little while?" Brittany murmured.

Logan considered his options as he drew her close. He had counted on staying here and working for a couple of weeks anyhow. It would take at least a couple of days to find another tutor, even if he did leave tomorrow. Which meant he would be stuck with two cranky girls in a condo in Calgary.

Hold your ground, he reminded himself. *Don't let them think all they have to do is cry and they can get their way.*

But while the rational part of his mind argued the point, his shirt was getting damp from his nieces' tears. Tears that he knew were genuine.

"I suppose we could stay here for a little while." He relented, ignoring a riffle of panic. He had three weeks to brainstorm an idea for a house, do a drawing and create blueprints, then another week to build a model of the idea.

The biggest hitch in all of this was that he didn't have an idea.

You don't have time for this, the sane part of his mind said.

"For a little while? Really?" Bethany lifted her head as a tear slid silently down her cheek.

Logan sighed, bent over and dropped a light kiss on her head. "Yes, really."

He was rewarded with a feeble smile.

"Thank you, Uncle Logan," Bethany said, wiping her cheeks as she sat up.

"But I need your help." He tried to sound stern. "No fooling around. Just do what I ask."

"So that means no schoolwork?" Brittany asked.

Logan sighed. "No. It means I'll have to help you with it until we get back to Calgary. I'm going to start looking for a tutor right away."

Brittany's face fell. "And what about Sandra?"

"I told you already, she is not teaching you. And I'm not going to talk about it while we're here."

He almost missed the glint in Bethany's eye as she glanced at her sister. But as she looked at him, her blue eyes guileless as ever, he figured he must have imagined it.

"And there's no way I could get an advance from you?" Sandra bit her lip as she heard what she knew she would. The restaurant would absolutely not give her a dime until she delivered twenty lamps as promised. She knew that, but thought she would give it a try. "Thanks, then. No, there's no problem. I have other resources," she lied. She hung up the phone.

"I'm not going to worry, I'm not going to worry," Sandra muttered as she grabbed her sweater and slipped it over her shoulders. Trouble was, try as she might, she couldn't stifle the panic that fluttered in her chest.

After months of work and inexpert marketing, she had gotten the first break with her stained glass work. A restaurant in Calgary had ordered twenty lampshades. If they liked her work, she had a good chance to make more for some of their other locations.

Trouble was she was desperately short of money. The unexpected move here from Saltspring Island in British Columbia had cut into her meager savings. She had one month's rent paid on the cabin, and Cora, her friend and roommate, was nowhere to be found.

Working for Florence Napier had been the blessing she had been looking for.

And now that was over, too. Her broken-down car wouldn't even allow her to work in Medicine Hat.

Sandra took a deep breath, then another, hoping the

mad flutters in her heart would settle once she started on her usual evening walk.

Outside, the sun's penetrating warmth had softened and a faint breeze wafted off the lake.

Sandra paused, letting the evening quiet soothe her.

Except it didn't.

She buttoned her sweater and started down the street toward the boardwalk that edged the beach and followed the lake. Her steady tread on the boards echoed hollowly, creating a familiar rhythm.

What to do, what to do, what to do.

Phone home?

The thought slipped insidiously through her subconscious. She let it drift a moment, then pushed it ruthlessly aside.

Phone home and hear how useless she was? Phone home and hear, "Why don't you do anything constructive with that education degree I paid so much money for?"

Sandra shivered, even though it was warm. Conforming was the way things happened in her home. Conform and you get to come along on promised trips. Conform and your education will be paid for. Conform and Father would deign to talk to you. Sandra conformed,trying in vain to live up to the expectations of a father who was never satisfied. She got her degree, and as soon as she could, she fled. All the way to Vancouver Island.

Five years and a hundred experiences later, Sandra's flight from conformity had washed her up here, in Cypress Hills, a four-hour drive from where she started, flat broke with a roommate who had flittered off again.

The evening breeze picked up a little, riffling the

water and teasing her hair. Sandra sucked in another breath and squared her shoulders. She wasn't going to give up. Not yet.

She ambled along the boardwalk, her arms wrapped around herself. Life was still good, she thought, raising her face to the unbearable blue of the Alberta sky. She was still alive and still free, and no one could put a price on that.

"Hey, Sandra."

Sandra lowered her head, wondering who had called her. She looked around and saw Bethany and Brittany sitting on a bench, swinging their legs.

"Hey, yourself." She walked over, happy to see these two very rambunctious girls. "You out on the town tonight?"

Brittany glanced at Bethany, then at Sandra. "Yup. Uncle Logan is buying us an ice cream."

"Then I'd better leave you alone." The last thing Sandra wanted was to come face to face with Logan only half a day after being fired by him.

"Here you are, girls." Logan's deep voice sounded behind her, and Sandra whirled.

Logan looked up and halted, his expression unreadable. "Hello, Sandra," he said, his steady gaze flicking to his nieces and then to her.

"Don't worry," she said crisply. "I haven't had a chance to really corrupt them yet."

Logan said nothing as he handed the cones to the girls. "Why don't you take a walk, Bethany? Brittany?"

The girls giggled and scampered down the beach toward the water.

"I don't think we have anything more to say to each other, Mr. Napier," Sandra said, wrapping her sweater around her. She forced herself to meet his hazel eyes and not to be moved by his casual good looks. A man who wore khaki pants to the beach, whose hair never looked messy, who drove a minivan was exactly the kind of guy her father would love. A conformist. Stifling.

Logan's gaze was steady as he slipped his hands into his back pockets. "I'm sorry that you lost the job—"

"You made me lose the job, Mr. Napier."

"Fair enough. I'm just sorry that it didn't work out."

"It didn't work out because you chose not to let it," Sandra snapped. "You've got your own ideas about who and what I am—"

"I got my ideas from what you told me."

"And based on that you know who I am?"

"Based on what you told me, I'm making a guess." Logan rocked slightly on his heels, still watching her with that unnerving gaze. "I don't think I'm too far off. I have my nieces to think of."

Sandra tried not to get defensive, but she couldn't help it. Everything about him seemed to condemn her out of hand. "Implying that I'm not going to contribute to their well-being."

"Why does this matter so much to you?"

Sandra wasn't sure. It was more than needing the job. Maybe it was because Logan personified the very thing she had been running from, and his judgment stung her pride. Maybe it was because even after spending a couple of days with Brittany and Bethany she was getting attached to the two girls who had lost so much.

Or maybe it was panic at the idea that she had tried to live her life on her own and losing even this small job proved to her the magnitude of her failure.

But Logan didn't need to have one more thing to judge her by. Didn't need to know precisely how close to the bone she was living right now.

"It doesn't matter," she said quietly, turning away. She took a few steps down the boardwalk, then heard Logan call her.

She didn't want to turn but couldn't stop herself.

"Yes?" she asked, forcing a casual tone to her voice.

"Nothing," he said, lifting his hand as if in surrender. "I'm sorry."

Sandra just nodded and walked on.

"So now what are we going to do?" whispered Brittany as she and Bethany huddled beside each other on the floor of their bedroom. Their lights were out. Below them, they could hear the faint tapping of Uncle Logan's computer keys.

"I thought for sure he would like her," Bethany said wistfully. "And now we have to leave."

Brittany flapped her hand. "So, we'll just have to go ahead with Plan B, I guess."

"What was Plan B?"

Brittany giggled. "Same as Plan A."

"But Plan A was to get Mrs. McKee to leave."

"I was just kidding. But we have to get him and Sandra together again. Just think how cool it would be to have her living with us. I mean Uncle Logan's nice, but…" Brittany shrugged, lifting her hands as if to say, "You know what I mean."

And Bethany did. "He's just not a lot of fun."

"And I'm not going to give up," Brittany insisted. "Not this quick."

Chapter Three

Logan got up from his computer, stretching his arms above his head. It was a nuisance working with this tiny screen when he was used to a much larger monitor at work, but in a pinch it sufficed.

He cocked an ear, listening, but it sounded like the girls had finally drifted off to sleep.

Logan sighed. He had spent most of the day on the phone and still hadn't found a tutor for the girls. No teacher was willing to work for the summer, and no organization had any tutors available.

He saved his work then rubbed his weary eyes. He hadn't gotten as much done as he had hoped between phone calls and trying to concentrate over the girls' chatter. He couldn't catch the concept he aimed for. The Jonserads' vague ideas of light and space were difficult to translate onto a computer screen or paper. It was just a house, but the project was significant. Pass this test and other buildings put up by Jonserad Holdings would be his to design.

Condos, office buildings and gated complexes for senior citizens who didn't want to have to face uninvited children.

A concept Logan could entirely sympathize with.

Logan rubbed the kinks out of his neck and dropped into his recliner. With a sigh he glanced at the clock. Midnight. He knew he should go to bed. *Later,* he thought. *I just want to close my eyes for a few seconds.*

A muffled thump jerked him awake. He sat up, confused and disoriented. The clock struck one.

"Must have fallen asleep," he muttered. Yawning, he got up and stepped into his shoes, not bothering to tie them. He trudged up the stairs to check on his nieces, the tips of the laces ticking on the floor.

Carefully, so as not to wake them, he eased the door open and squinted in the half gloom at the beds.

He frowned at the lumpy outlines of his nieces. They looked odd. A faint breeze riffling through the open window caught his attention. Then he saw the chair. He pulled back the blanket on one of the beds and found rolled-up towels.

Logan stifled an angry sound and spun around. He ran out the door, stepped on a shoelace and promptly hit the hard floor chest first.

Groaning, angry and frustrated, he took the time to tie his laces, then jumped to his feet and took off. His ribs hurt, but his anger fueled him.

Sandra lay back on the prickly grass, pulling the blanket just a little closer around her. The utter quiet was broken by the occasional wail of a coyote in the night, answered in time by another. From horizon to horizon, stars were flung across the velvet black of the sky. Over the crest of the hill behind her lay Elkwater, its few lights faint competition for the glory overhead.

"I see you, Cygna," Sandra whispered, reaching up to trace the cross of the constellation. From there she moved to the brightest stars. "And you, Deneb and Vega and Altair." She let her hand drop and smiled as her eyes drifted over the sky, unable to take in its sheer vastness.

"When I consider the heavens, the works of Thy hands, the moon and the stars which Thou has ordained…" Sandra spoke the words of the Psalms aloud and shivered at how easily they came back to her. She had spent the past few years avoiding the God Who had made all this. Austere, judgmental and demanding.

She had last heard that quote from Brittany and Bethany the night they had sat out here looking at the stars. Sandra was working on astronomy with them, and what better way to study than to actually see it. So, with Florence Napier's blessing, she had taken the girls out late at night to look at the stars.

Bethany and Brittany. Sandra's satisfaction broke as she thought of the girls and, right on the heels of that, of their uncle. His offhand dismissal of her had touched an old wound. One initially opened by her father. She sighed, wondering what it was going to take to finally rid herself of the constant presence of her father's disapproval.

"Hey, Sandra." The sound of young voices drifted to her and she sat up, looking around.

Then she saw the vague outline of two girls running up the hill. They materialized beside her and dropped down to the grass, panting.

"What are you girls doing here?" she asked, looking past them. She expected to see Logan looming out of the dark. "You're supposed to be in bed."

Brittany shrugged her comment off as she caught her breath. "We need to talk to you. Uncle Logan wants us to go to Calgary with him."

"I know that. He told me. And I don't suppose Uncle Logan knows you're here?" Sandra asked.

In the dim light she saw the girls exchange a quick glance.

Bingo.

"Listen, your uncle already has his own opinion of me, and it isn't what I'd call supportive." Sandra put an arm around each of them. "So if he finds you here, my feeling is he's going to be a little underwhelmed by the whole situation."

The girls giggled.

"Don't worry about Uncle Logan," Brittany said airily, waving a hand as if dismissing her six-foot-two-inch relative.

Sandra didn't think Logan could be gotten rid of that easily. "It's not a good idea to sneak out at night. What if he checks your beds and you're gone? He'd worry."

Brittany and Bethany exchanged another quick glance as if puzzled over this phenomenon. "Our mom and dad never worried when we snuck out at night," Brittany said.

"We didn't even need to sneak."

"Well, I think Uncle Logan is a little different."

Brittany sighed. "He's different, all right. He can barely cook."

"He's learning," Bethany replied in her uncle's defense. "He makes real good pancakes and sausages."

"Sausages aren't hard. Even our mom could make them," Brittany retorted.

"They're hard. You can burn them real quick if you're not careful," Bethany answered, leaning forward to see her sister better. "Uncle Logan doesn't burn them much."

Sandra tried to picture Logan standing in front of a stove, cooking. The thought made her smile, as did Bethany's defense of him.

Brittany turned to Sandra again. "Can't you help us stay? Could you hide us or something?"

Sandra almost laughed at that. "No. I will not hide you, although I will miss you."

"Will we see you before we go?"

"When are you leaving?" Sandra asked.

"In a couple of days."

"I'll probably be on the beach a few times. But I'll be moving on once my car is fixed. I can't stay around here if I don't have a job." Sandra felt a clutch of panic at the thought. A prayer hovered on the periphery of her mind. A cry for help and peace. She shook her head as if to dismiss it. God was a father, after all. Distant, reserved and judging.

She got up and pulled the girls to their feet, giving them each a quick hug. "We'll see each other soon. But now I want you to get back to the house."

They hugged her, their arms clinging. And again Sandra wondered at their upbringing that they grew so quickly attached to someone they barely knew.

"Go. Now." Sandra gave them a little push and watched as they walked down the hill, going a different way than they had come.

"Bethany, Brittany." Logan's voice, muffled by distance, drifted toward them from another direction.

The girls glanced at Sandra who fluttered an urgent hand at them, then they turned and ran down the shortcut.

"Bethany, Brittany, I know you're up there," Logan called, coming closer.

Sandra winced at the tone of his voice, wrapping her blanket around herself. "He does not sound amused," she whispered, bracing herself as she turned to face him.

Logan's heavy step faltered when he saw who stood on the hill.

"Hey, how's it going?" she asked, adopting a breezy attitude as Logan made it to the top of the hill.

He stood in front of her. Loomed would be a better word, she thought, looking at him in the vague light.

Don't step back. Don't show fear, she reminded herself.

"It's not going good. Where are my nieces?"

Sandra's spine automatically stiffened at his autocratic and accusing tone. "And why do you suppose I would know where they are?"

Logan's hands were planted on his hips, his feet slightly spread, as if he were ready to do battle. Sandra stifled a mixture of fear and admiration at the sight. "Because I'm pretty sure they snuck out to meet you."

It was his tone more than what he said that sparked her temper. That and the remembrance of how he looked down his nose at her the day she had come to teach the girls. The day he had picked her up on the road. "Oh, really?" she asked, her voice hard. "And I suppose I encouraged that?"

He said nothing, and each beat of silence made Sandra fume even as his scrutiny made her feel uncomfortable. His silence and his pose reminded her of intimidating sessions with her father as she struggled to explain herself to him once again. To explain how once again she had failed the great Professor Bachman.

But she was a big girl now. And men like Logan—men like her father—didn't bother her as easily as they used to.

"Your nieces aren't here," she said and turned away from him. The conversation was over.

"I saw their bedroom window open," Logan said, his voice quieter. "I saw a chair under the window."

"Which means what?" she asked, turning to face him. "I'm sure if you were to go down to your house right now you'd find them in bed."

Logan seemed to consider this. "If I talk to them I'll get the truth out of them," he said confidently. "I always do."

"You might. If you push." Sandra wasn't about to either enlighten or lie to him. But some part of her felt sorry for the girls and the confusion of moving from their parents' home to an uncle they had known only briefly. She tried to choose her words, advocating for two girls who, underneath their flighty natures, felt lost and afraid of the future. "I know that if you push children, you can end up pushing them into a lie." She shrugged. "Sometimes you have to choose the battles you want to win."

"You're not defending my nieces, are you?" Logan asked.

In the darkness Sandra couldn't tell from his expression if she had imagined the faint note of humor in his voice.

She lifted one shoulder. "Not really. I just know they really like being here in Cypress Hills. The freedom and the memories, I guess."

"The memories I'll grant them. But they've had enough freedom in their life."

Sandra sighed at the harsh note. "Their parents loved them. Surely that speaks for something."

"It was a strange kind of love, as far as I'm concerned."

Sandra couldn't help but bristle at his comment, memories from her own upbringing clouding her judgment. "What's better? Pushing and forcing your will on them? It's like trying to hold water, Logan. The harder you squeeze, the less control you have."

"You don't understand," he said simply.

"I do, though. I understand far too well."

Logan's eyes seemed to glitter in the dark, and Sandra knew she had overstepped her bounds. But she wasn't going to let him bully her.

"Be careful with them, Logan," she added quietly,

sorrow tinging her voice. "They may be spunky, but they're also just young girls."

Logan was quiet a moment. Then without another word he stepped back, turned and strode down the hill before Sandra could say anything more.

She watched him go, frustrated and confused by him all at the same time. He was bossy, and yet his concern for his nieces touched a part of her that she hadn't paid attention to in a while.

With each step Logan took away from Sandra, his confusion grew. He knew for a fact the girls had been with her. She hadn't said anything, though, and he suspected she was protecting the girls from his wrath.

In spite of his irritation with her, he had to smile. She was concerned about the twins, he gave her that much. He wasn't surprised that Brittany and Bethany were so taken with her. She had a fun sense of humor.

But he had to think of the girls, he reminded himself.

For a moment he yearned for the time when he didn't have the responsibility of two young girls. Young girls were scary enough to take care of outside of the house. Inside, it was chaos and confusion.

He hated chaos and confusion. Had lived with it all his life.

He didn't know what he was going to do if he found the girls in their beds as Sandra had intimated. He couldn't very well accuse them of something he hadn't any true proof of, even if he was the adult in the situation.

Give me wisdom, Lord, he prayed as he had most

every day since the girls had dropped into his life. *Give me courage and strength and patience. I don't always know what to do.*

In spite of his confusion, he couldn't help but smile at Sandra's assessment of the situation.

Choose the battles you want to win.

The advice was sound, and he figured it could save him a lot of headaches.

"C'mon, Bethy, it's not that hard. Look, you have to line the numbers up and multiply them." Logan stifled the urge to grab the pencil out of his niece's hand and do the problem himself.

"I can't do it, Uncle Logan. Not when you yell." Bethany frowned at him, chewing on her pencil. "Sandra never got that mad at us."

"Just try it the way I showed you," he said, glancing at Brittany, who quickly looked at her own work. He got up to check it, hoping she at least had understood him.

"No, honey. Look…" He pulled the paper toward him. "You have to make sure that you carry the numbers when there's more than one digit." He showed her and pushed the paper back.

Brittany looked at him, frowning. "What do you mean carry the numbers? Sandra did it better."

"And I suppose she walked on water, too," he muttered.

Logan recognized he wasn't a patient teacher, but he also knew he wasn't too difficult to understand. He knew exactly where his two innocent nieces were leading him. Down the garden path directly to Sandra Bachman's door. Trouble was, after the past few days, he was wondering if maybe he shouldn't just give in.

Yesterday morning, for a few bright and shining moments, he had felt in charge. The girls had come downstairs as if waiting for him to jump on them. Instead he had said nothing, and they seemed confused. They also seemed wary and docile. Logan had felt pretty good.

But the moment of triumph lasted only as long as it took him to get them started on their work.

He was behind on his own work and clinging by his fingernails to the end of his proverbial rope. He still hadn't found a tutor, and each moment he spent with the girls kept him away from his project.

He sighed, looking at the girls as if hoping for one last chance. But they only held his steady gaze, their soft blue eyes unblinking.

So what did he have to lose?

He remembered his condemnation of Sandra and wondered what her reaction to him would be.

Was he being wise? His opinion of her hadn't really changed.

But her comments on how to discipline the girls had lingered. In spite of some of her strange opinions and in spite of her lifestyle, she seemed to have an intuition and basic understanding of how to deal with his nieces. She did have a degree, after all. She couldn't be as flighty as she seemed.

If he hired Sandra it could buy him some time. Time to find a tutor, time to finish his project. It would only be temporary, he reminded himself.

"Okay, let's get this over and done with," he grumbled, walking to the phone. "What's her phone number?"

Brittany and Bethany rattled it off in unison while Logan punched in the numbers, praying that this was the right decision.

He just didn't have a lot of options left to him.

Sandra knocked on the door of the Napier cabin, smoothed her skirt with her hands, adjusted her shirt and then got mad at herself for doing so. She wasn't going to be nervous, she told herself. Logan was just an uptight person who had changed his mind. Nothing personal.

But when Logan opened the door, she stiffened. She couldn't help feeling defensive, remembering comments he had made the night he had gone looking for his nieces. When he had called her a couple of minutes ago, her first impulse had been to tell him that she was no longer available.

But pride was something only people with money could afford. So she accepted. They laid out the terms and rate of pay, and now she was here, facing a slightly disheveled Logan Napier.

He stood in the doorway, looking at her in that assessing way of his. "Thanks for coming so quickly," he said. "I appreciate it."

A smart answer died as Sandra gave him a closer look.

His dark hair looked like he had been running his fingers through it, and today he wore jeans and a T-shirt.

Not quite as put together as when she had first met him. In fact, he looked worn out. In spite of their moments of antagonism, Sandra felt a gentle softening toward him.

"The girls are in the kitchen, trying to figure out how to cross multiply," he added with a heavy sigh.

Sandra frowned. "They know how to do that."

"I thought so, too." Logan smiled a mirthless smile. "But it seems to have slipped their minds since you stopped working with them. Amazing coincidence."

"Must be the air," she said with a careful lift of her eyebrows, acknowledging his attempt at reconciliation.

"Must be." Logan stepped back, allowing her to enter. "Just come with me a moment. We need to go over a few things before you start."

Sandra swallowed, toying with the idea of asking him for an advance. As she followed him through the cabin, she decided against it. She didn't need to reinforce his idea that she was a freeloader. She'd have to get along as best she could until she'd worked for at least a week, she thought, following him into his office.

"I need to emphasize that this job is only temporary," he said with a piercing look. "You shouldn't have too much trouble with that."

"Just like every other job I've held," Sandra couldn't help but add.

Logan didn't even blink. He looked her straight in the eye. "Then this should work out just fine for you."

Sandra felt a shiver of animosity. But she knew she couldn't indulge in her usual antics. Like it or not, Logan was her boss, and her situation here was tenuous.

She swallowed her pride and nodded. "I better get to it, then," she said quietly.

"I'm going to be working in the bedroom down here. If you need anything." He looked at the papers he was organizing on his drafting table.

Feeling dismissed, Sandra bit her lip and walked out of the room, angry that she had ever seen him as helpless. About as helpless as a grizzly, she thought.

Then she walked into the kitchen to be greeted with shouts of happiness and hugs from the girls. It helped to negate some of her anger at Logan. But not totally dissipate it.

Logan pulled out another sheet of paper, his frustration growing. He had an idea in his head of how he wanted the Jonserad house to look. He could close his eyes and just about picture it, but always when he put pencil to paper, the thoughts wouldn't translate.

He stretched his neck and glanced out the window. He saw a family walking down the road. Mom and Dad were carrying a picnic hamper between them, beach towels slung over their shoulders. Two young boys ran ahead, carrying inflatable beach toys. Off for a day of sun and water, he thought with a slight pang of jealousy.

But he had work to do, and so did the girls. They had spent enough of their childhood running around carefree. They really needed to work.

And so did he, if he wanted the project, he reminded himself.

As he picked up another pencil, he heard the sound

of muffled laughter. Then Sandra's laugh pealed out, stifled to a giggle. What humor could they possibly find in doing math?

It sounded as though they had moved from the kitchen to the main room. What were they doing there? He got up to check when things got very quiet.

The girls were sprawled on the living room floor. Brittany was chewing on a pencil while she frowned at a problem she worked on, and Sandra lay on the floor between them, quietly explaining something to Bethany. Her hair hung like a shimmering curtain over her shoulder. With an impatient gesture she pushed it back, exposing the fine line of her jaw, her smiling mouth.

Logan caught himself staring at her. Attractive or no, he wasn't too sure about her teaching arrangements. "Shouldn't you girls be sitting at a table?" Logan asked.

"I suggested that we move to a place that's a little more comfortable," Sandra said, sitting up.

Logan frowned at her quick reply. "I can't see that you'll get much done laying all over the floor."

Bethany's and Brittany's heads shot up, and Sandra motioned to the girls to go back to their work as she got up.

"Can I talk to you a moment, Mr. Napier?" she asked.

"Sure."

Sandra walked past Logan to his office. Momentarily taken aback, he couldn't help but follow.

Once inside the room, Sandra turned to face him. "I understand your concern about the girls and I appreciate that. But I think I need to establish something right from the beginning. This job may be temporary." She paused, glancing at him through narrowed eyes. "But I'm their teacher and I'll decide on the teaching methods."

Logan scowled, uncomfortable with how quickly she took charge. "I guess I need to make something clear, too, Miss Bachman. I'm their guardian and I'm the one who hired you," he countered.

Sandra crossed her arms as if ready to face him down. "That's correct. But you came to me, I didn't come to you. You recognized that I have abilities and training, and in order for me to do my job, I need you to just let me do it."

"And if I don't like your methods?"

"Then I guess you'll be teaching them on your own." Her deep brown eyes held his. She tipped her head ever so slightly. "Just like you were doing when you called me."

Logan swallowed, fighting down the urge to tell this snippy woman that she could leave. He'd been in charge of his nieces for a year and a half without any outside help, thank you very much. He didn't appreciate being told to back off and let someone else take over.

However, as she had so diplomatically pointed out, teaching the girls on his own wasn't working, and he didn't have any alternative available to him.

He couldn't give up so easily. Not with her. "That sounds like a threat, Sandra Bachman."

She shook her head, smiling lightly. "No threat, Logan Napier. Just setting out boundaries."

Logan had to regain some ground. He forced himself to smile. "Just so you realize, these girls need to go back to formal schooling in September. They won't be able to lay on the floor in their classroom."

Sandra's smile stiffened. "Formal school." She laughed lightly. "It never ceases to amaze me that curiosity and adventure manage to survive formal education."

Logan wondered if he imagined the caustic note in her voice. "That's an interesting comment, coming from you," he said, testing her. "Formal education gave you a degree, even though you don't seem to be doing much with it."

Sandra straightened, her eyes narrowed, and Logan knew he had stepped over an invisible boundary. "I'm teaching your nieces with it, Mr. Napier," she said. "And I had better get back to it." She tossed him a look that clearly told him the subject was closed, and with a swish of her skirt, she left.

Logan felt momentarily taken aback at her abrupt exit. He hoped he had made his point with her, though he wasn't sure how he came out of that little skirmish. Sandra was a puzzle, that much he knew.

And a puzzle she would stay, he thought. As long as she was teaching his girls, he would keep his eye on her, but her private life would remain private as far as he was concerned.

He went to his computer and dropped into the chair. As he struggled with a plan that was finally coming together, he couldn't help but pause once in a while, listening to the husky tones of Sandra's voice as she patiently explained the vagaries of mathematics.

Later he heard Sandra telling the girls what she wanted them to work on that evening. He got up and wandered into the living room, ostensibly to establish his so-called parental involvement.

"Work on the rest of chapter four in your math books," she said, writing on a piece of paper. "And I want you to go over some of the history material."

"But history is so boring," Brittany said with a pout. "Especially this stuff."

"History is just a story that you have to discover," Sandra said.

Logan could see from Brittany's expression that she wasn't convinced.

"Hey, a lot of the history you are studying happened right here." Sandra chucked Brittany lightly under the chin. "In Cypress Hills."

"Really?" Brittany didn't sound like she believed Sandra.

"Fort Walsh was an important place in the late eighteen hundreds. And it's part of Cypress Hills Park," Sandra explained. "On the Saskatchewan side."

"Could we go there?"

"That would be a good idea, but I have no way of bringing you there." Sandra lifted her hands as if in surrender. "Sorry."

The girls turned as one to Uncle Logan. He recognized the gleam in their eyes and knew what was coming.

"You could give us the van, Uncle Logan," Brittany said with an ingenuous smile.

Logan shook his head. "Now why did I know you were going to say that?"

Brittany shrugged, a delicate movement that would one day drive some young boy crazy. "I don't know."

He wasn't going to look at Sandra but couldn't stop himself. She held his gaze, her own slightly mocking.

"I don't have time to bring you," he said.

"Uncle Logan," Brittany said. "You have to."

"I think your uncle Logan is too busy working to come with us, Brittany," Sandra said with a lift of her chin.

Logan couldn't help but pick up the challenging note in her voice.

"Not all of us have the luxury of doing what we want, Miss Bachman."

"Oh, yes, we do. It's all in what we choose to give up to do what we want. You've chosen to sit inside and work instead of enjoying the wonderful outdoors."

"I've chosen to try to make a living," he said with a short laugh.

Sandra held his gaze for a split second, then looked away, a faint grin teasing her mouth. "If that's what you want to call it."

Logan was about to defend himself, to explain how necessary this project was, when a faint niggling doubt wormed its way into his subconscious. He remembered seeing the family going to the beach this morning. He thought of the project he wasn't having much luck putting together. Maybe some time off with the girls would be good for him.

And, he reasoned, he could keep an eye on Sandra

Bachman. After all, the girls were his responsibility, and she had only been teaching them for a short time.

Brittany sensed his hesitation and jumped on it. “So, are you going to come with us, Uncle Logan?”

“Please, Uncle Logan?” Bethany added her entreaty.

He looked at the two girls and wondered if there was ever going to come a time that he wouldn’t give in to them.

“I could do that,” he said, careful to make it look as if his capitulation came at a price. “If Ms. Bachman doesn’t mind,” he added as a concession to Sandra.

“Seeing as how Ms. Bachman doesn’t own a set of working wheels, Ms. Bachman doesn’t mind at all,” Sandra said, finally looking up from the paper she held. “As long as Mr. Napier is willing to work with me.”

Logan recognized the challenge and rose to it. “I believe in being diplomatic, Ms. Bachman.”

She smiled. “Ah, yes. Diplomacy. The art of letting people have your own way.”

Logan couldn’t help the smile that tugged on his mouth at her snappy answer and decided to let it go. He sensed that he would be the loser in a verbal battle with Sandra.

“So set a time and we’ll be ready to leave,” he said.

“First thing tomorrow morning,” Sandra replied. “I’d like to go before it gets too hot.”

“We’ll be ready.”

As the innocuous words were tossed back and forth, Logan stifled the faint dart of pleasure at the idea of spending time with Sandra. He was only coming along to supervise. That was all.

Chapter Four

"So how did you like a taste of Whoop Up Country?" Sandra asked as they left the stockaded fort known as Farwell's Trading Post.

"Hot," Bethany said, fanning herself with a brochure.

"Can you imagine what it was like in those days when no one had air-conditioning?" Sandra asked with a laugh. She lifted her hair from her damp neck, wishing she had worn it up.

"You girls would have roasted in those long dresses they had to wear in those days," Logan added.

The girls groaned in sympathy.

"Men didn't have it a whole lot better," Sandra added, glancing at Logan's short-sleeved shirt. "You look a lot cooler than Farwell, owner of the trading post. Or how about those poor Mounties in their red serge. Hot, hot, hot."

Heat waves shimmered from the ground, attesting to how warm it really was. The short grass crunched under their feet as they walked toward the tour bus.

"I can't imagine how the grass even grows here, it's so warm." Brittany poked the ground with her toe.

"This grass is very high in protein," Sandra explained. "The buffalo survived quite nicely on it. That's how Fort Benton, in Montana, got started. It was a fur and buffalo robe trading post stuck in the middle of buffalo country. From Fort Benton, traders for both furs and whiskey ended up taking the Whoop Up Trail into Canada where there was nothing but trouble. No law, no rules. People did what they wanted."

"So how did that stop?" Bethany asked.

Sandra paused, looking at the hills. So peaceful, it was hard to believe that at one time the fear-filled cries of Lakota Indians rang through these hills. As she retold the story of the Cypress Hills Massacre, she tried to inject a feeling of humanity—putting a human face to the story—into what was often mere facts and history. She could feel the girls looking first at her, then at the hills. Even Logan listened intently as she spoke.

The silence that followed her story told her she had done her job.

"After the massacre the Canadian government sent the Northwest Mounted Police, later known as the Royal Canadian Mounted Police, to this area. They started out from Manitoba and ended up in Fort Benton to replenish their supplies and get some information on the massacre. When they came to the place Fort Macleod is now, the whiskey traders had taken off. Knew the Mounties were coming." Sandra winked at Brittany, relieving the heavy atmosphere her sad story had created. "Knew the Mounties always get their man."

She answered a few more questions the girls had, trying each time to work in some pertinent information. She knew that history told was one thing but history experienced meant much more.

She also knew that history, even when told in an entertaining manner, was only interesting for a short period of time.

"I guess we should head back to the main fort now," she said, noticing the shuttle bus pulling into the parking lot.

Bethany and Brittany hurried toward it.

"Hey, girls. Slow down," Logan called, but the girls didn't hear. Or pretended not to.

"Relax, Uncle Logan," Sandra said with a grin at how protective he was. "They're not going anywhere we aren't."

"Maybe, but it's still too hot to run."

Sandra frowned. "My goodness, Logan, they won't melt. From what they told me, they've been in warmer climates than this."

Logan's gaze sliced sideways, then back. "They told you about their parents?"

"Just a little."

She waited to hear something, anything, more, but he didn't offer any information. Merely stepped aside so Sandra could get on the bus.

Without looking at Logan, Sandra walked to an empty seat directly behind the girls and sat down. To her surprise, Logan sat beside her.

Brittany and Bethany glanced back and immediately moved to the front, but Logan stayed where he was.

She wanted to ask him more about the girls' parents but didn't think that he would be very forthcoming.

But with each lurch of the bus, Sandra grew more self-conscious, more aware of him sitting silently beside her. He said nothing, did nothing, but Sandra felt every time his elbow brushed hers, each time a hole in the road threw her against him.

She pulled herself closer to the side of the bus and away from him, turning to stare out the window.

The bus stopped, and the girls were the first ones out. By the time Logan and Sandra got out, the girls were waiting for them, full of good cheer. "Can we have some ice cream, Uncle Logan?" Bethany asked, tipping her head coyly. "Pretty please?"

Logan was already digging in his pocket. He pulled out a bill. He glanced sidelong at Sandra, his dark brows pulled together in a light frown. "These girls have an insatiable appetite for ice cream. Do you want one?"

Sandra shook her head. "No, thanks."

"I'll wait out here for you then," Logan said, handing the bill to the girls. "And I expect to see the change."

Brittany and Bethany flashed him demure smiles, shared a grin and ran into the building.

Without looking at Logan, Sandra turned and walked up the hill overlooking the valley, then sat down, determined to put some space between her and Logan.

But to her surprise, Logan followed her and sat beside her. She pulled her knees up, wrapping her arms around them. She resented the awkwardness he created in her, and she tried not to let it show.

The best defense is offense, she thought.

"So, you aren't chafing to get back to your work," she said, her heightened reaction to him giving her voice an unexpected bite.

Logan leaned back, resting his weight on his elbows. He looked over the valley below them. He seemed surprisingly at ease.

"I can do this," he said, tucking his chin on his chest. "Even though I do need to get back to work."

"Ah, yes. Uncle Logan the upwardly mobile man." Sandra couldn't stop the little gibe. It seemed better to put him on the defensive rather than to look at him and notice the faint wave to his hair, how it curled over his ears.

The way his sudden smile eased the harsh line of his features.

"Do you ever run out of smart remarks?" he asked.

"I think life is too serious to be taken seriously," she replied.

Logan let out a short laugh. But he didn't answer her question.

Note to self, she thought, biting her lip. *No more smart comments. At least not to Logan Napier.*

She wasn't usually this flip. Usually she could carry on a normal, intelligent conversation, but Logan's calm self-possession touched a nerve.

At any rate, she had better learn to put a curb on her tongue if she wanted to stay in Logan's good graces and keep this job.

She looked over the sweep of the valley. The hills here were softened, smoothed by the wind that swept across the open plains of Montana and Saskatchewan and sifted around this oasis in the prairie. She sighed lightly, waiting for the utter peace of the place to slowly soothe the tension she felt sitting beside Logan. But try as she might, she couldn't ignore his strong presence.

And he seemed content to just sit, saying nothing.

Once again, his silence unnerved her. In spite of her resolution, she sought to find something, anything to ease the discomfort he created.

"So how long have the girls been living with you?" she asked, resting her chin on her knees.

Logan plucked a blade of grass, twirling it between his fingers. "About a year and a half."

"Did they come right after their parents died?"

Logan nodded, still looking away.

"That must have been difficult," she said quietly.

"It was. At first. I think kids grieve differently than adults do. They dive in deep and hard, but they come out of it quicker. Their sadness is different…." Logan stopped, twirling the grass faster.

"Different than what?" Sandra prompted.

He looked at her then. "Different than adults, I was going to say."

"Their mother was your sister, wasn't she?" Sandra asked, holding his steady gaze, wondering at their relationship.

"She was my only sibling. Flighty. Strange. But still my sister."

For a moment Sandra envied him even that. "How did you get along?"

Logan pushed himself to a sitting position. "Pretty

good. When I was younger we depended heavily on each other. We switched schools so many times the only person we knew in school was each other."

"Your parents traveled that much?"

Logan laughed, but it held no humor. "Endlessly. Every few months we would pack up and be gone again. My father died a while ago, but my mother still travels a lot."

Sandra sighed, thinking of her upbringing. "Sounds kind of neat."

"I'm sure to you it would," Logan said dryly. He got up, held her gaze a moment, then looked down the hill.

"Here come the girls," he said, brushing off his pants.

And once again Sandra felt as if she had been weighed and found wanting.

And once again it bothered her.

Chapter Five

Logan watched as the girls dawdled up the hill toward them. He was about to call to them when they suddenly turned and ran to the visitors' center. He started off after them.

"What are they doing?" he heard Sandra ask as she caught up to him.

Logan knew all too well what they were up to and decided it would be better if everything was out in the open.

"My dear nieces can't stand the idea that I don't currently have a girlfriend," he said dryly, glancing at her. "They're avoiding us because they have grand visions of playing matchmaker."

Sandra laughed.

To his chagrin, Logan felt deflated at her reaction. "What can I say," he said, wishing he had her quick, glib tongue. "They're young."

"Some day they'll grow up, Logan Napier."

Logan sighed. "I pray for it daily."

"Do you?"

He turned, looking fully at her. "Yes. I do."

Sandra's gaze flicked sideways then back. "I remember you said that you go to church."

"Why does that always come out with a faint note of mockery?" he asked as he reached the sidewalk at the bottom of the hill.

"Like I told you before, I'm not a church person."

"Why not?" He stopped, turning to face her. He wanted to know more about this part of her life. After all, she was teaching his nieces.

"It's full of hypocrites," she said airily.

"That's the oldest excuse in the book."

Sandra's dark brown eyes met his, unable to conceal the sparkle that lit at his challenge. "What book?"

"Pardon me?" Logan asked.

"What book is that the oldest excuse in? Is there a book somewhere full of excuses? And if there is, how do you know it's the oldest one? What if it's the newest?" Sandra threw out the questions one after the other, a smile curving her lips.

In spite of his exasperation with her, Logan laughed. "I'm not even going to start a battle of words with you," he said. "But I will challenge your hypocrite comment. You have to admit that using that excuse is pretty lame. There are hypocrites in every organization. Where there are people, there are failings."

Sandra cocked her head as if thinking. "Okay. I'll concede that point. Begrudgingly," she added, pointing a finger at him. "Don't want to let you off too easy."

"So why don't you go to church?" Logan asked.

"I believe in God, Logan. Just in case that's what you're really wondering. I just don't believe that church fills any need of mine. I prefer to worship God in nature."

Logan felt a stab of disappointment. He didn't know what he had hoped for, but her answer brushed away some faint hope he had harbored. A hope that didn't really have anything to do with his nieces' well-being. "But nature doesn't tell you of the need for redemption, Sandra," he replied quietly.

Sandra's answer was a dismissive shrug.

Right then the girls came out of the building, pretending surprise to see Logan and Sandra.

"Let's look at the rest of the site," Sandra said, forestalling any recriminations or feeble explanations.

The girls followed Sandra while Logan lagged behind, listening as she explained the history of Fort Walsh.

"Later, in the nineteen forties, the RCMP purchased this site and set up Remount Ranch to breed and raise their horses. They also raised and trained the horses for the Musical Ride here."

"I've heard of the Musical Ride," Logan said. "But what exactly is it?"

"A riding display developed from traditional cavalry drills. It's very impressive. I believe 32 horses and riders are involved."

"We saw that," Bethany offered. "In Texas. At a rodeo. It was awesome. Those black horses. And the riders in those neat red coats."

Logan wasn't surprised at that. Linda and her husband traveled enough different places, they were bound to have crossed paths at one time or another with the RCMP's Musical Ride.

The rest of the tour went fast. To her credit, Sandra could tell when the girls' interest waned, and would quickly move on to the next place. They walked through barracks and living quarters, then took a picture by the flagpole in the center of the fort. Logan operated the camera, smiling as Bethany and Brittany crowded right up beside Sandra.

He looked through the lens and adjusted the zoom lens, bringing the little group in closer. Sandra looked up, smiling, and Logan couldn't suppress the tug of attraction. Sandra's open smile suffused her entire being and made him want to laugh along with her.

He snapped the picture, recognizing Sandra's beauty and at the same time realizing that any man would be attracted to her. And that was all he felt, he reminded himself. Just a basic recognition of her appeal. He didn't have the time or the inclination to take anything further from there. Not with someone like Sandra.

The drive back was quiet. Both girls slept in the back seat, which meant, Logan thought with a sigh, that they would be awake and giddy for most of the evening. Looked like he wasn't going to get much done tonight.

Sandra didn't say much. Just looked ahead, her expression serious. Logan couldn't help but glance at her once in a while, wondering what she was thinking.

Logan wondered if his comment about church had made the usually loquacious Sandra Bachman retreat into silence. He doubted it. Someone as self-possessed as Sandra wasn't the kind of person to be intimidated by someone else's opinion.

But her silence made him feel uncomfortable. As they neared Elkwater, she picked up her knapsack, fiddling with the zippers and buckles.

"Just drop me off at the gas station," she said as he made the long turn into the town.

"Tell me where you live and I'll drop you off," Logan said.

"No. Please. I want to go for a walk. Maybe even a swim," she said with a forced laugh, pushing her hair from her face.

Logan slowed and stopped at the gas station as she had requested. "Are you sure you don't want me to bring you to your house?" he asked once again, feeling most unchivalrous.

"No. Thanks. I really want to walk." She glanced at the girls, who were still sleeping, their cheeks flushed with the heat and the sun. "Say goodbye to the girls. Tell them I'll see them on Monday."

Logan nodded, bending over as Sandra got out of the van. She paused, holding on to the door, and glanced at him. "Thanks for driving us to the fort," she said. "I had a good time."

"You're welcome. I learned a lot today," he said with a quick grin. "Thanks for that."

"Nice to be able to put my expensive education to some use," she returned. "Have a good evening." She turned and walked away, her skirt swaying.

Logan knew he should drive away. Knew he shouldn't be watching Sandra, shouldn't be allowing his basic attraction to her good looks take over his common sense.

But he had enjoyed the day with her, and even though part of him disapproved, he had to laugh at her quick tongue, her pert responses. Once again he smiled at some of the things she had said.

Then he glanced at the girls, dismayed to see Brittany awake and looking at him with frank interest.

"What are we waiting for, Uncle Logan?" she asked, her voice radiating innocence.

"Traffic," he replied, deadpan. Then, without a second glance, he drove to their house.

Sandra pulled out her last sheet of ruby glass, setting it carefully on the light table. With a felt pen she marked the places she would cut, working with the striations and the patterns inherent in the glass.

She smiled as she envisioned how the completed lamp would look, how the light would play through it.

So far she had enough glass for one lamp and a few pieces left over for a second. She had hoped to pick up her glass shipment, still sitting in a warehouse in Medicine Hat. But she would have to wait until she got her first tutoring paycheck. It surprised her that Logan was willing to pay her more than Florence had offered. Of course, he could probably afford it, she reasoned.

She didn't know how long the job would last, but so far she calculated that if she worked one more day, she would have enough money to pay for the glass. Three more days would pay for her car, and four more days would earn a few more groceries that would last until the lamps were finished.

A small thrill of excitement fluttered through her at the thought of completing the lamp and what the job represented. Money earned on her own and maybe, perhaps, the beginning of a new career.

For now, it looked as if she would be able to prove her father wrong, after all. Her life was finally coming to a place of her own choosing.

She pulled out the patterns for the petals of the flowers, and as she laid them on the glass, she happened to look out the window.

If she angled her head slightly, she could see the front door of the church in Elkwater. She had never attended. As she had told Logan, her preferred place of worship was up on a hill, away from other people. Alone and away from the harsh expectations she'd grown up with.

But today she caught herself looking at the church more than once as she worked. Wondered what kind of people went. Wondered if they sang any of the traditional songs that were sung in her church.

She hadn't been to church since she left home five years ago. She had thrown off the stifling expectations of her father, and church attendance was one of them.

She'd been in Elkwater for four months, and only in the last two had she started eyeing the church.

And that was mostly because Cora, her good friend and fellow traveler, had left again.

If anyone could talk her out of going, Cora could, Sandra thought, looking at the glass she was preparing to cut. She and Cora had been through a lot together. California, Minnesota and at the end, Hornby Island and Henri Desault.

Sandra shivered. Henri was too vivid a memory still. She wouldn't be in the financial pickle she was in if it wasn't for Henri and his smooth talking. A consummate salesman, she thought, curling her lip in disgust. She set the pattern on the glass, tracing it with quick, decisive strokes as if trying to eradicate the memory.

She had spent time with Henri. Had dated him and thought she'd found someone who cared about her. Who accepted her without expectations. Then one day she let him see the stained glass work she did in her spare time. Time she'd eked away from the mindless day jobs she needed to pay for her supplies. She'd planned on selling her work when she had enough inventory built up. The money was going to finance her working full time on her own.

Henri knew a place to sell her stuff and promised her more money than she could get peddling at craft fairs and local markets.

She had fallen for his charm, his smooth talk, and in no time, seven of her best pieces of work had been taken and sold. She had trusted him to return. Trusted him to give her the money.

She hadn't seen a penny from Henri. Nor had she seen Henri again.

At that low point in her life, Cora came up with the brain wave of moving to Alberta.

Sandra had fought the move. Anywhere in Alberta

was too close to Calgary and home. But the thought of staying alone was even more depressing.

So she gamely packed up her little car with the few things she and Cora owned. They worked their way through the Fraser Valley, then across Alberta to Medicine Hat. There they found an ad for a small furnished house for rent in the town of Elkwater. It had an extra room for Sandra to set up a studio of sorts. Sandra sold a few pieces, and through that got the order for the lamps.

Now Cora was gone, with a promise that as soon as she returned, they would head south to California. But the longer Cora stayed away, the less sure Sandra was of leaving. In fact, it seemed that in the past six months, Sandra's dissatisfaction with her life had grown.

She missed belonging somewhere. And whether she wanted to admit it or not, she missed belonging to someone.

She glanced out the window. A movement at the church made Sandra pay closer attention. The doors opened and a few people walked out.

She wasn't going to watch, she thought.

But she couldn't stop herself from looking. Bethany and Brittany bounced out of the church, their facial expressions exaggerated as they chatted with each other. Sandra smiled and kept looking, wondering.

And there he was. Behind them, hands in the pockets of his eternal khaki pants, came their uncle Logan.

He was smiling, looking relaxed, at peace.

Sandra felt a mixture of envy and a lift of pleasure as she watched him. He was good-looking, she had to concede. He had the potential to be a lot of fun, if only he'd drop the fussy, protective-uncle shtick he insisted on maintaining.

He paused, looking back to say something to a young woman who caught up to him. She wore a beige shift. Neat. Elegant. Uptight, Sandra thought a bit cattily.

Logan's smile grew as he spoke to the woman. He lifted his hand and touched her shoulder lightly. It was almost avuncular, but for the first time in many years, Sandra felt a distinct dig of jealousy at the gesture. Around Sandra, Logan was either uptight, thinking she might lead his nieces astray, or he was scowling, thinking she might lead his nieces astray.

He was worse than some of the parents she had met while student teaching.

Yet she couldn't keep her eyes off him as he talked to the woman.

She wondered who she was. Friend? Girlfriend who had come up for a visit?

Sandra took a deep breath, as if cleansing away the coil of strange emotions, and concentrated on tracing exactly twelve petals on the glass. She made a mistake and rubbed it out with a tissue then glanced out the window again.

But Logan, the woman and the girls were gone.

She felt momentarily bereft. Left out. She didn't belong to that little group. She was here in her rented house. They were out there, heading to Logan's spacious cabin.

This was enough, she told herself.

She capped her pen, dropped it on her worktable and headed to the beach, open spaces and other people.

"I'd love to go for a walk." As Karen stood, she addressed the girls, who were laying on the floor, playing a board game. "Are you coming, Brittany and Bethany?"

Logan saw them exchange a quick look, and it wasn't kind. He knew they would say no. They had never really liked Karen.

"We'd love to," Brittany said, getting up. "Wouldn't we Bethany?"

Bethany nodded, smiling at her uncle, who looked at both his nieces, his eyes narrowed. Why the sudden change of heart?

"We'll clean the game up after, Uncle Logan," Brittany said, smiling at him.

They were up to something. He knew it. He angled his body away from Karen. He shot them both a warning look that he knew Karen wouldn't see.

They quickly glanced down, and he knew the message was sent and understood. Behave.

He turned to Karen with a forced smile. "Shall we go?"

The afternoon sun warmed Logan's shoulders as they walked in silence to the lake.

Logan was still trying to absorb the shock he had felt when Karen showed up unexpectedly on his doorstep this morning.

She had been passing through, she had said. Stayed overnight in Medicine Hat. Logan's partner told her where he was. She thought, since she was in the neighborhood, maybe she would stop in and see how Logan and the girls were doing.

Brittany and Bethany stayed close by as they walked, as if unwilling to give Karen and Logan the space they always gave him and Sandra.

"Your partner, Ian, tells me that you've got an important project due," Karen said, breaking the silence.

Logan nodded. "I'm submitting it on spec. A few other architects are submitting plans, as well. If the client likes what I've done, we have a good chance at more work." He bit his lip, thinking of the project that just wouldn't obey. He'd never had this hard a time coming up with ideas. Nor had so much been riding on one project, he reminded himself.

"I heard it was the Jonserads that you might be doing this work for." Karen angled him a questioning glance. "They're a pretty big company. Family business."

Logan nodded. He didn't need the reminder.

"My parents know the Jonserads," she added coyly. "If you want, I could put in a good word for you."

Logan stiffened at the suggestion. All his life he had worked for everything he had. Nothing had come easily. He had managed without anyone's help, and he was proud of that.

"Thanks for that, Karen. But I would just as soon earn the job based on my own merit." He smiled at her to ease the harshness of his words. But he could tell from the suddenly brittle smile that she was hurt.

"The girls seem to be settling down," Karen said with forced brightness as she wrapped her sweater around herself.

Thankfully Brittany and Bethany had gone a little ahead, talking and laughing.

"It's taken a bit of doing, but it's coming along." Logan slipped his hands in his pockets, squinting against the glare of the sun off the lake. He wondered again why Karen had come.

They arrived at the boardwalk that led partway around the lake. Karen's steps slowed. She was letting the girls get even farther ahead.

"I know my coming here is a surprise," she said quietly, looking straight ahead. "I'm sure you thought, after I broke up with you, that you'd never see me again."

Logan said nothing, letting her do all the talking. Their break had caused him a measure of pain, but in retrospect, he realized that his pride had hurt more than his feelings.

"This is a little awkward for me." She sighed and stopped, turning to face him, lifting her exquisite face to his. Her short blond hair framed her features perfectly, emphasizing her delicate cheekbones, the fine line of her chin. Logan recognized her beauty almost as an afterthought. Which surprised him, considering that at one time he'd been attracted to her.

"I realized how much I missed you, Logan," she continued, her soft green eyes holding his. "When the girls came, I made a rash decision. I see that now."

"It was a while ago, Karen," he gently reminded her. Eighteen months, to be precise, he thought.

"I know. That's what makes this so awkward." She smiled at him, tentatively reaching out to him. "I tried to date other guys. I thought I could forget you." She shrugged her dainty shoulders, wrapped by her finely knit cardigan. "I couldn't."

Logan nodded, wondering how to extricate himself from this situation. Karen might have been yearning to try again, but he had no inclination to renew the relationship. Not with his work and his nieces occupying most of his time.

Where were those girls when he needed them?

As if on cue, he heard Brittany call, "Uncle Logan, look who we found."

He glanced up with a grin of relief that faded when he saw their reluctant escort.

Sandra Bachman.

Brittany had one of her hands, Bethany the other, and they were pulling her along the boardwalk.

The girls stopped in front of Karen and Logan, looking at Sandra like they had just snagged a prize.

"She was coming this way already," Bethany said, bestowing an angelic smile on Logan.

"I was just heading home, actually," Sandra said. The soft breeze coming off the lake teased her loose hair, made her long flowing skirt sway. She looked soft, deceptively gentle. Logan couldn't look away.

Her dark eyes flicked over Karen, then to Logan, one eyebrow quirking when she noticed his regard.

Covering up, Logan turned to Karen. "I should introduce you to the girls' tutor, Sandra Bachman. Sandra, this is…Karen."

Karen seemed to catch his momentary hesitation over her official title, but recovered and put on a polite smile, extending her hand to Sandra.

"Nice to meet you," Karen said smoothly.

Sandra shook her hand, her gaze assessing. "Likewise," she said, one corner of her mouth curling into a smile.

Logan braced himself for one of Sandra's comments, but she said nothing more.

"So the girls must keep you quite busy," Karen said.

Sandra glanced at each of the girls. "They're a challenge that I try to rise to every day. But I think we're making some progress."

Karen murmured a vague response, then looked at Logan, as if expecting him to end this conversation.

But Logan knew what faced him if he was alone with Karen again. He didn't feel inclined to reopen the topic of Karen and her feelings on their relationship.

"Out for some exercise?" he asked Sandra, slipping his hands in his pockets, projecting the image of someone with nothing better to do than chat up his nieces' tutor.

"No, just a walk," Sandra replied with a sparkle in her eye. "I get enough exercise just pushing my luck."

Logan couldn't help his answering grin. "And here I thought you were the kind of person who would spend hours in aerobic classes."

Sandra waved that comment away. "I'd sooner spend my money on chocolate fudge sundaes than pay someone to put me through pain."

"If you've experienced pain while doing aerobics, that could be the fault of your instructor," Karen informed her.

Logan glanced sidelong at Karen, feeling a faint flush of shame at how completely he had ignored her.

"Could be," Sandra agreed, her grin fading as she looked at Karen. "Or it could be that I just wasn't doing things right." Sandra took an abrupt step back, and Logan recognized the first movement toward departure. The quick glance at her watch was the second.

He didn't want her to go.

"It's been nice meeting you, Karen," she said, formal. Polite.

Karen smiled in return.

But the girls weren't happy. "We just got here. You can't go now, Sandra," Brittany wailed.

Sandra laid a hand on each of their shoulders, still grinning. "I have two legs, and in spite of not taking aerobics, I can walk quite well. No 'can't' about it."

"Then you shouldn't go," Bethany corrected, grabbing Sandra's hand.

"And shouldn't is a moral imperative, Bethany." Sandra tapped Bethany's nose. "I'm on my day off, so I'm not under any obligation to follow it."

Logan couldn't help but smile at the word games Sandra so easily indulged in. But it was better for all concerned, himself included, if they kept their relationship arm's-length.

"Let's go, Bethy, Brit," Logan said, hastening the separation. "We shouldn't waste Sandra's time."

In spite of his reflections, he couldn't help another glance in her direction and was disconcerted to see her looking at him, as well, her expression serious.

Then, with a quick wave and a toss of her head, Sandra was striding down the boardwalk toward the beach, her hair and skirt swinging in time with her steps.

"So, that's the new tutor," Karen said, a prim note in her voice. "She seems very…vivacious."

Logan's only acknowledgment of Karen's statement was a curt nod. As he glanced at Karen, he couldn't help comparing the two women. Sandra's dark eyes, dark hair and wide smile. Karen's light hair, clear eyes and composed manner.

Shaking his head, he pushed the thoughts aside. Karen had come to church. Sandra hadn't. That should be comparison enough for him.

Karen stayed until late afternoon. She coerced the girls into a board game, talked with Logan about friends they had in common.

But when she drove away and he came into the cabin, he felt worn out and was thankful to be alone again.

"You're not going back to her, are you?" Brittany asked as soon as he stepped into the house. She lay on the couch, Bethany on the recliner. Both had their eyes fixed on their uncle.

Logan looked at his more outspoken niece, weighing his words. "That's not for you to say, Brittany," he replied firmly, recognizing the need to set personal boundaries. "Karen is a good person, and at one time we had a strong relationship."

"Why did she come back?"

"She just came for a visit." Logan wasn't going to delve into the real reason. Given the girls' antagonism toward his former girlfriend and their not so subtle cheerleading for Sandra, he figured the less they knew, the better.

Brittany gave her uncle a knowing look. "I bet she wants you back."

Logan was taken aback at Brittany's perceptiveness.

"I've seen the way she looks at you," Brittany said smugly. "What do you think, Bethany?"

Bethany gave a hesitant shrug. "I don't know."

Brittany snorted. "Of course, you don't know. She liked *you.*" Brittany looked at her uncle. "I think she wants you back."

"And I think you've said enough, Brittany," Logan chided, walking past her to the kitchen. "Seeing as how you're so full of advice, you can help me make supper tonight."

But as they ate, the girls' words reinforced what he already knew. Karen was sweet, kind and shared the same faith.

She just didn't hold the appeal she once had. Her soft green eyes and her pale blondness seemed pallid.

Pallid compared to Sandra's heavy brown hair and dancing eyes.

Chapter Six

Logan added a few more flourishes to his drawing and stood to have a better look.

His first impulse was to throw it in the garbage.

His second was to rip it up.

Then throw it in the garbage.

He wasn't exactly sure why he didn't like it, just that it looked like every other house in Calgary right now. Boxy and choppy with cluttered rooflines.

"Uncle Logan, we're done with the dishes." Bethany stood in the doorway of his office looking especially demure.

He nodded absently.

"Can me and Brittany ask you a favor?"

Logan frowned and turned, giving his niece his full attention. "Since when do you girls ask if you can ask?"

Bethany lifted her hands and shoulders at the same time, signaling complete incomprehension.

"So, what is it?"

"Well, it's Grandma's birthday pretty soon, and me

and Brit want to make her a present to give to her. We wanted to give her something real special and we had a good idea."

"And what's the point of all this?" Logan asked, stifling a yawn.

"Well..." Bethany hesitated, pressing her fingers together as if in supplication. "We thought it would be fun to make a stained glass sun catcher. Sandra said she would help us."

Logan shouldn't have been surprised. Since Sunday, the girls had been jockeying to visit Sandra each evening, and each evening he firmly said no.

"It would make a real cool present for her," Bethany added.

"You girls just don't quit, do you?" he said, shaking his head.

Bethany looked the picture of innocence, and once again Logan went through all the reasons they shouldn't go to Sandra's. She was their tutor, not their friend, and it was important to teach them the difference. She was much older than them and probably not a whole lot wiser, in spite of her degree. He didn't like them hanging around with her. Period.

Although the last was becoming harder to justify. He had given her the responsibility of teaching his nieces, and in spite of their differing over her methods, the girls were understanding their work.

Brittany joined Bethany. Reinforcements, he thought wryly. "Come to add your two cents?" he asked her, his hands on his hips.

"We thought it would be a good idea to go," Brittany said, ignoring his rhetorical question. "This way you could have some more time alone to work on your project." Her eyes skittered to the drawing on his board, and her face fell. "Are you done?"

Logan didn't even bother to give the rendering another second of his attention. He sighed. "No, I'm not. I thought I was, but I don't like it."

Brittany walked to the drawing and held it up. "It looks okay," she said. "But not your best work."

Logan bit back the quick smile at Brittany's authoritative tone. She glanced at him, perfectly serious. "Looks like it's back to the drawing board."

"I guess."

"So you'll want some more quiet time," she added.

Logan couldn't stop his smile. "You're more than just a pretty face, Brittany," he said, his voice full of admiration. He knew exactly where she was headed.

"Maybe we should visit Sandra and she can help us with Grandma's birthday present so you'll have the house to yourself for a while."

Logan held their innocent gazes and against his will he had to admit that he was beat. He raised his hands as if in surrender. "Okay, okay," he said with a suppressed sigh. He crossed his arms over his chest and looked first at one, then the other. "I will bring you girls there and come and pick you up at exactly nine o'clock. Sharp. No excuses."

"Okay," they said in unison.

"Can we go now?" Bethany asked.

Once he had caved in, he couldn't think of a reason.

* * *

Logan glanced at his watch. Eight-eighteen. Still too early to go and get the girls. When he had dropped them off at Sandra's place, she'd been cool and reserved. Just as she'd been when she came to work with the girls during the day. They spent as much time outside as possible, as if avoiding him. They went for short walks into the hills and came back giggling and laughing. When, out of curiosity, he asked her what she was doing, she told him, but her tone was defensive. He didn't like it.

Sighing, he picked up his pencil, made a few halfhearted doodles and glared at the result. This project was slowly losing its appeal, even though he couldn't put it out of his head. Sure, it would be nice to get the Jonserads as clients, but this project was starting to consume him. He found no joy in it. And, he reminded himself, it wasn't even a sure thing.

He got up from his makeshift drawing board and wandered to the living room.

He tried to analyze the peculiar restlessness that had gripped him since Sunday. He was sure it wasn't Karen. When she left he had felt relief more than anything. But she was a reminder to him of what he had once had. A girlfriend. Someone who cared that he was spending his entire holiday on a project when he really should be sitting at the beach with his nieces.

She was also a reminder of his one-time freedom and the chance to make choices for himself. No responsibilities other than his own.

Since the girls had come into his life, he felt a keen pressure to provide for them, to make sure that they had food and clothes and that their schoolwork was done. To supervise them and to seek out their best interests.

He thought of Sandra again and begrudgingly realized that with her the girls were enthusiastic and did their work. He wondered what they were doing right now.

A quick glance at his watch showed him that precisely sixty seconds had passed. He dropped into his recliner and, pushing the papers he had been reading aside, he reached for his Bible. Yesterday was the last time he had read it, and in his current frame of mind, he needed the comfort he knew he would find there.

Leafing through the pages, he found the Psalm he had often read to the girls when they first came. Psalm sixty-eight. "Sing to God, sing praise to His name, extol Him who rides on the clouds—His name is the Lord—and rejoice before Him. A father to the fatherless, a defender of widows, is God in His holy dwelling. God sets the lonely in families, He leads forth the prisoners with singing."

Logan smiled as he read the familiar words. When the girls came to his home, they were lonely, grieving and afraid. They knew him, but just in passing, and now they were living with him.

Bethany and Brittany had been comforted by the words and comforted by the faith they were slowly discovering each day.

A faith he tried to nurture wherever possible. He had found a Christian school they could attend. He took them to church, got them involved in the youth group.

Each day he tried, in his own inadequate way, to show them God's love.

So how did someone like Sandra fit into their lives? She didn't go to church, though she professed a faith in God. How wise was it to let her teach girls who were still struggling in their own faith?

Logan's second thoughts made him close the Bible and get up. It didn't matter what time he had told the girls he was going to pick them up, he was leaving now.

The streets of Elkwater were quiet as he made his way to Sandra's place. From a distance he heard the insistent boom of a stereo. Probably some teenagers whooping it up on the campground, he figured. He felt sorry for the campers. At least he didn't have to contend with that, because they owned their own cabin.

The lights were on in Sandra's house, and he realized that the music he had thought was coming from the campground was coming from Sandra's stereo.

He knocked on the door, knowing it was futile over the noise. So he let himself in.

When he had dropped the girls off, Sandra had been sitting outside reading, so he hadn't gone in. He stepped into the house, curiously glancing around at the array of mismatched furniture, the books piled on every available table. It was neat, sort of, yet with a lived-in and comfortable feeling. The lighting in this part of the house was warm, created by the jeweled glow of two stained glass lamps—a tall standing lamp hovering behind a well-worn chair and a table lamp across the room. Sandra's creations, he presumed.

"Hello," he called, staying in the entrance. The

music was coming from a room off the living room. He waited, then Bethany popped her head around the corner.

"Oh, hi, Uncle Logan," she called.

"Don't sound so excited to see me," he returned with a grin.

The music was turned down, and Sandra appeared behind Bethany, glancing at her watch.

"I know. I'm early," he said. "I just thought I'd see what the girls were up to."

"Checking on me?" Sandra asked with a petulant tilt of her eyebrows.

"Nope, just bored."

Sandra angled her head toward the room they had come out of. "Come in, then, and see what they've been doing."

Logan forced a smile, wondering again why she was so cool in his presence. Wondering why he didn't like it.

He followed Sandra into a brightly lit room, watching as she walked to the stereo and turned it down more.

"Sorry about that. The girls brought some CDs. I told them they could play them while we worked." She shoved her hands in the back pockets of her jeans, tossing her hair behind her shoulders. "It's Christian music, in case you were wondering."

Logan felt the defensiveness in her attitude. He was at a loss as to what caused it. "That's fine," he said quietly.

The girls were bent over a table, pretending not to

watch Logan and Sandra. Logan walked to them, glancing over their shoulders. All he saw was an array of pieces of glass, some edged with what looked like thin strips of copper. "So what is this?"

Brittany looked at Sandra. "I'll make lemonade and you tell Uncle Logan what we're doing. You know it better anyway." She turned to her sister. "C'mon, Bethy, lets go."

The two girls fled. Logan shrugged in Sandra's direction, hoping she understood what the girls were up to. "I guess it's up to you," he said with a forced smile.

Sandra blew out her breath and walked to his side, keeping her distance, as if reluctant to come too close. "They're making a sun catcher. Here's the pattern." She pointed out a stylized black-and-white sketch of an iris in an oval frame. "They have to trace the pattern pieces on the glass and then cut them with this cutter." She held up a small, pencil-shaped object. "After grinding the edges they have to foil each piece. Then dab kester on it to get rid of the finish. After that they solder it together."

Logan nodded, pretending to understand.

Sandra glanced his way, and their gazes meshed. She curled one corner of her mouth, showing the first semblance of a smile since Sunday. "You don't have a clue what I'm talking about, do you?"

"I got foiled by the foil."

She held his gaze, and her smile grew. "I see."

So once again she explained the process, showing him how the individual pieces of glass were wrapped in foil that was sticky on one side. "You have to make sure you go all around and that you give enough foil on each side of the glass," she explained, showing him.

Logan stepped a little closer, ostensibly to see what she was showing him. But as he did, he caught the faint scent of her perfume—light, fresh and lingering. It caught him unexpectedly. Made him pause and breathe a little more deeply.

"Once all the pieces are wrapped, you have to lay it out in the same shape as the pattern," she continued, oblivious to the reaction she had elicited in him. "This is when you need the kester, a type of acid, to get rid of the finish on the foil so that the solder can stick to it. I don't have the soldering iron plugged in because we're not ready yet." She reached across the table, picked up a small project she had been working on and set it in front of Logan without looking at him.

He glanced at her hands, stained and marked with small white scars. From handling glass, he presumed. Hands that carefully handled the piece she held.

"This is what it should look like when it's done. The solder should lie in a nice, neat bead on both sides of the work. It gives the same effect as lead but without the weight."

"Can I?" Logan reached out for the sun catcher she was holding, and with a shrug Sandra handed it to him. Their fingers brushed each other, sending a peculiar riffle up his arm at the contact.

He forced his attention to what he held, astonished at how small some of the pieces of glass were, how intricately she had cut them and put them all together. When he held it up to the light, it was as if it came to life.

"This is amazing. I'm guessing you did the lamps in the living room, as well."

She nodded, stepping back from him, taking that beguiling scent with her.

"Do you do other work besides this?"

"I've done some windows. But I use lead for them. A slightly different process."

"For homes?"

"No. Churches."

Logan couldn't resist. "Oh. For those hypocrites," he teased.

She held his gaze, smiling. "It's all for the glory of God," she returned.

Logan didn't look away. Didn't want to. He felt his smile fade as he tried to delve into her deep brown eyes, tried to find something solid, something serious behind her flippant facade.

"And do you think He's glorified?" he asked quietly.

Sandra looked away, then shrugged. "I guess you'll have to ask Him sometime," she said.

Logan recognized the retreat and decided to leave it at that. "Do you support yourself doing this?"

Sandra rolled her shoulders in answer. "I don't have high needs. But I've got a contract with a restaurant in Calgary to supply them with some lamps. I'm pretty pleased about that."

"Have you started on them yet?" He laid the piece down and glanced at her again.

She shook her head. "I've been busy with the girls…." She let the sentence drift off as she retreated one more step. "I should see how they're doing."

Logan watched her go, wondering once again at her sudden reticence.

"Tastes just about right," Sandra said, taking a sip of the lemonade the girls offered her. "Why don't you get your uncle Logan and tell him that it's ready?"

Bethany ran out of the small kitchen as Brittany set out four cups. "Do you have any cookies?" Brittany asked as she filled the cups. "They would go really nice with lemonade."

"No. Sorry." Sandra flashed her an apologetic grin. "I'm a little low on cookies right now." Low on groceries, period. Thanks to Cora, who consumed gallons of lemonade, she at least had lemonade crystals.

She bit her lip as she stirred the lemonade, wondering if she could work up enough courage to ask Logan for an advance.

And what would he think of her if he found out how tight things actually were for her? These days, her idea of a seven-course meal was stopping outside the restaurant in town and taking a deep sniff.

Luckily utilities were included with the cottage rent, which had been paid in advance, or the roof over her head might have been iffy, as well. Logan's low opinion of her would sink if he knew the particulars of her financial situation.

She had tried to tell herself that what he thought of her didn't matter. But after meeting Karen—after seeing a perfectly put together woman who probably phoned home once a week, who attended church with Logan and the girls, who probably never had an unsuitable boyfriend—Sandra had spent the past few days feeling less confident than normal.

Which was annoying, of course. Self-confidence wasn't something Sandra usually lacked.

She looked up as Logan and the girls came into the kitchen.

"Why are you still stirring that?" Bethany asked.

"It takes a lot of stirring," Sandra said quickly to cover up. "I'm hoping to carbonate it." She grinned, then put out the four cups and motioned for everyone to sit down.

"Can we go back and work on the sun catcher?" Brittany picked up her cup and tugged on her sister's arm with her free hand.

Sandra glanced at Logan, who was sitting down. His face didn't change expression.

"I think you girls can stay here with us," he commented, taking a sip of his lemonade.

"Well, we want to get it done." Brittany gave Bethany's arm another tug. Without looking at Logan, they left.

Sandra gave Logan a forced grin. "Well, here we are. Alone again." Goodness, she thought. If that didn't sound like a proposition. She felt like smacking herself on the forehead.

"Sorry about that." Logan scratched his forehead with his index finger as if trying to puzzle out his nieces. "Tact isn't a word that comes to mind when one thinks of Brittany and Bethany." He sighed lightly. "I'd like to think that they might be a little less subtle, but I guess I misplaced that part of the training manual."

Sandra couldn't help but smile at his deprecating humor. "You've done well with them. In spite of missing parts of the course."

Logan looked at her as if puzzled by her compliment. "Thanks, I think."

His moment of vulnerability was surprisingly captivating. In spite of her resolve to keep her distance from this man, she found she wanted to reassure him. "Really, Logan. They're nice girls, and I know they think very highly of you."

Logan's deep hazel eyes met and held hers. His face relaxed, a shifting of his features, and Sandra felt herself drawn to him. Unable to look away.

"That's good to know," he said, taking a sip of his lemonade and setting the cup down. "There are many times that I feel like all I'm doing is damage control. Just trying to catch up. That's life, I guess."

"Life is hard. You get the test first, the lessons later," Sandra mused, quirking him a grin.

He angled his head, as if to look at her from a different perspective. "You always have a quick comeback, don't you?"

"Mind like a steel trap," she quipped, uncomfortable with his scrutiny. "Except it's rusty and illegal in most parts of the country."

Logan didn't respond, merely leaned his elbows on the table as he continued to look at her. "So what makes you tick, Sandra Bachman?" He held up his hand as if to stop her. "Okay, that was giving you a wide-open opportunity. Let me try that again with a more specific question. How did you get here? To Elkwater?"

Sandra wondered at his sudden interest. Wondered what he would say were she to tell him the facts of her life. Facts that would only reinforce his opinion of her.

She looked at her cup, ran her thumbnail along an old scratch in the plastic and decided to be honest. His opinion couldn't get much lower, she figured. "I came here from Vancouver Island. Actually, Hornby Island. Cora, the woman I rent this house with, and I met up there. We both decided we'd had enough of the life there and wandered around until we stumbled on this place."

"What did you do on Hornby Island?"

"Stained glass work. Like I'm doing now."

"Did you make a living at it?"

Sandra pressed her thumbnail a little harder into the scratch, biting her lip. "Sort of."

"Do you enjoy it?"

Sandra hesitated. She had. At one time. It was something new and interesting. And totally different from what her father would approve of.

The thought plucked at her with nervous fingers. Was that her only reason for doing it? To make her father angry?

She dismissed the questions and their nugget of truth.

"I like it," she admitted. "Usually."

"Just like? Is there anything you love doing?"

Sandra frowned at him. "What is this? Part of my ongoing interview?"

"Maybe," Logan admitted. "But I'm also curious."

He caught her eye as he leaned forward, as if inviting her confidence.

Sandra felt an ache grow. In spite of their earlier antagonism, she sensed his interest and wondered again about Karen.

"I like doing a lot of things," Sandra admitted, not moving from her position.

"Why didn't you ever use your teaching degree?"

Sandra glanced at him. Logan's mouth curled at one corner in a smile that created a dimple in his cheek.

She tried to find the words to explain the heavy weight of responsibility that dogged her all through school, through college. The feeling that no matter how hard she tried, she never measured up. Would Logan, with his easygoing upbringing, even have the faintest notion of how debilitating the unceasing expectations of her parents could be?

She thought of Florence Napier, remembered comments Logan made about his upbringing and what he wanted for his nieces. She remembered Florence's laissez-faire attitude.

He wouldn't understand, she thought.

"Teaching wasn't what I really wanted to do," she said, settling on a mundane answer as she leaned back in her chair.

"You're good at it."

"Thanks. But two girls as opposed to a whole classroom of kids..." She shrugged. "Not my style, I'm afraid."

"Why not?"

Sandra felt herself stiffen at the tone of his question. "Not everyone is cut out for that kind of thing."

"Meaning?"

"Routine. Schedule. The same thing every day."

Logan held her gaze, his expression unreadable. "That's not your style," he replied quietly.

"No, it isn't," she answered with a little more force than the comment required.

"What would be your ideal job, then?"

Sandra looked away, pulling the corner of her lower lip between her teeth. She wasn't sure. She had spent so much time figuring out what she didn't want to do that she hadn't formulated a clear plan of what she did want. The past few years had been a whirl of trying and discarding.

"I'm sure your girlfriend Karen is the kind of person who has her life all figured out. I'm not like that."

Logan tipped his eyebrows. "She's not my girlfriend."

Why did that simple statement ease a small measure of the loneliness that had gripped her on Sunday?

"I...I'm not sure what my ideal job would be," Sandra said quickly, looking away. "I haven't found it yet."

"That's too bad, Sandra. I think you have a lot of potential."

Then, taking a final sip of his lemonade, he got up. He set his cup down, hooked his thumbs in the tops of his pants pockets, one corner of his mouth caught between his teeth. He looked as if he wanted to say something else. "Thanks for the lemonade." He tilted her a halfhearted grin and went to the back room to get the girls.

Sandra hugged herself, watching him go, wondering why she had said what she did. It was as if she was determined to keep him at arm's length.

And she should. *He's an architect,* she reminded

herself. *A secure, solid, hardworking architect who lives for schedules and routine.*

A man who took good care of the women in his life—his nieces, his mother.

A man who probably would never do to Karen what Henri had done to her, she thought with a faint feeling of remorse.

And in spite of his comment about Karen, a man who would be out of her life once they all went back to Calgary, she reminded herself. She and Logan moved in different circles. Only for this moment had their lives intersected.

The girls gave her noisy goodbyes as they left. Logan ushered them out the door. In the doorway he turned to face her. "Thanks for working with them tonight." Still holding on to the door, his eyes met hers.

Once again, Sandra had that peculiar feeling of an intangible allurement that tightened between them, drawing her toward him.

She looked away and nodded. Her only reply.

The door closed, and Sandra was alone again. As she heard the girls' excited chatter and Logan's deep voice fading away, it was as if the house had grown smaller, emptier.

Restless, Sandra got up, went to the stereo and turned it up. Unfamiliar music spilled out of the speakers. Bethany's CD, Sandra remembered. She was about to turn it down but was stopped by the music. Upbeat and catchy. She found herself tapping her fingers against her leg in time to the beat.

The singer sang the words with an absoluteness that

Sandra would once have dismissed as narrow-minded, but the sincerity in her voice kept Sandra from turning the song off.

In the lyrics of the song Sandra heard a call back to the faith of her youth, a call to come and worship Jesus as Lord, a challenge that one day every tongue would confess God, every knee would bow.

Sandra felt a shiver of apprehension followed by a pressing of guilt and sorrow as the music swelled, built in intensity, the singer drawing Sandra in.

She felt a touch of God's hand. Just like she did when she was outside, when she looked into the heavens and knew for certainty that the vastness and the order she saw there didn't come through happenstance.

She hit the power button and turned the music off. Standing alone in the empty room, Sandra closed her eyes as the now familiar loneliness washed over her.

Home, she thought. She wished she could go home.

But that was out of the question.

"He hasn't kissed her yet," Brittany whispered to her sister, setting the plates on the table.

Bethany spun around, still holding the utensils she had pulled out of the drawer. "How do you know?"

Brittany glanced over her shoulder and tiptoed to the door. But Uncle Logan was still in the shower.

"I watched them last night. They were just sitting and talking." She shook her head in disgust. "This is taking forever."

Bethany carefully set the knives beside the plates Brittany had laid out. "We just have to wait, I guess."

"I wish I knew if that Karen was going to come back."

Bethany shuddered. "She really likes Uncle Logan. I wish she'd leave him alone."

"Well, I don't think he likes her much. He never even held her hand when they were walking."

"So we have to keep getting Sandra and Uncle Logan together," said Bethany with a sigh. "We don't have much longer."

"Good morning, girls," Logan said from the doorway, toweling his wet hair. "You're up bright and early."

Brittany threw Bethany a guilty look, wondering if Uncle Logan had heard what they said. She looked at him, smiling, hoping he didn't. "Just thought we'd get up early so we can do some schoolwork."

Logan paused, holding the towel, looking at Brittany as if he didn't quite believe her. "You're doing homework in the morning?"

Brittany nodded. "Sandra gave us a contest. She said if we get our work done by tonight, she was going to take us out to look at the meteor shower." She stopped. "Oops. I wasn't supposed to tell you."

"You weren't?" Logan hung on to his towel, his dark eyes flicking over one, then the other twin. "Why not?"

"I think it was a secret," Brittany said, biting her lip.

Logan nodded once, then left.

"Do you think he was mad?" Bethany asked, her eyes wide. "He sounded mad."

Brittany shrugged. "I hope not. Otherwise Sandra might get in trouble with him again."

* * *

Logan stood by the window watching as Sandra came up the road to the cabin, her knapsack slung over one shoulder, her hands shoved in the pockets of her faded blue jeans. She wore her hair back, tied in a heavy braid that hung over one shoulder.

She looked much younger than he knew her to be. More like an older sister of his nieces than their tutor.

Mentally he compared her to Karen, whose clothing was always up to date, polished.

Once he had envisioned Karen as a potential wife, the perfect complement to an up-and-coming architect.

But after seeing Karen on Sunday and spending time with her again, he knew that even though she seemed more than willing to come back to him, he wasn't ready to take her. Nothing in his circumstances had changed. He still had the girls, and she still wasn't comfortable around them.

Whereas Sandra had an ease and naturalness that he admired, in spite of questionable characteristics that he didn't. Like keeping tonight's excursion a big secret from him.

As Sandra came up the wooden sidewalk to the cabin, Logan stepped away from the window hoping she hadn't seen him. When she knocked on the door, he was already there, opening it for her.

She looked taken aback at the sight of him, then recovered. "Hey, there. How are you?" she asked, stepping past him. "The girls ready for another day of education?"

Logan nodded, wondering how he was going to approach her. It seemed that just as one thing was resolved between them, something else came up.

He decided to go straight to it.

"Brittany told me about your plans to see the meteor shower tonight."

Sandra nodded, shrugging her knapsack off her shoulder. "That's right."

"She said that you had asked her not to tell me. I'd like to know why you don't think I need to be consulted about this."

Sandra let the knapsack drop with a muffled thud and looked directly at him, all traces of good humor vanished. "Is this going to go on until I'm done, Logan Napier?" she asked, her voice chilled. "This constant questioning and mistrusting and wondering if I'm good enough?" She began pulling books out of her backpack, her movements jerky with anger. "I'm taking my job with them very seriously." She slammed a book on the table. "I'm not some heathen that is determined to turn your nieces astray. They're learning things and I'm doing a good job." Another book joined the first with a heavy thump. She threw a fistful of pencils on the table.

Logan watched her sudden spill of anger, heard the indignation in her voice. It seemed out of proportion to what he had asked her, and for a moment he wondered what was behind her anger. He forced his mind to the topic at hand.

"You have to admit, Sandra, I have a right to know what's happening," he said quietly, leaning against the door. "All I ask is that you let me know."

Sandra's gaze flew to his, her dark eyes snapping with suppressed indignation. She blinked, then looked at the books on the table. "I'm sorry," she said, straightening them, tidying the pencils. She took a slow breath, pulling her hands over her face as if to erase the anger he had seen etched there a moment ago. "I told Brittany not to say anything so that I could ask you. I wasn't trying to hide anything from you. I was going to ask you last night, but I forgot."

She stood by the table, looking straight ahead, avoiding his gaze. "I'm sorry that you thought that of me."

Logan felt a flicker of guilt mixed with sympathy for her and wondered once again at the mystery that eddied around her. He walked to her side and gently laid his hand on her shoulder, feeling the warmth of her skin through the thin T-shirt she wore. "I'm sorry, too, Sandra," he said. "I guess I just jumped to the wrong conclusion."

"You seem to do that often." She looked at him, her chin up.

"I know." Logan squeezed her shoulder. He told himself it was his way of apologizing, but he enjoyed the brief contact too much for that. He had to resist the urge to let his hand linger, to toy with the hank of hair that lay inches from his hand.

He stepped back, momentarily shaken by his feelings.

"So when do you plan on doing this?" he asked, hoping his voice sounded normal.

"I thought we could go out tonight." Sandra angled

him a quick look over her shoulder. Their eyes held a moment, and Logan found himself unable to break the brief contact.

"I was going to walk to the hill behind your cabin. There's a better place farther along, but it's not within walking distance." She returned his smile, and Logan felt a faint twist in his midsection.

He nodded, picking up on her vaguely worded hint. "In other words, you need a vehicle."

She nodded, then to his surprise said, "But you can come along if you want."

"That would be nice," he said, their gazes still locked.

Then she looked away, breaking the insidious connection, leaving Logan to wonder if she was as shaken at the contact as he had been.

Chapter Seven

"Why did you ask him to come?" Sandra muttered to herself, hunching her shoulders deeper in the light jacket she had thrown on. She strode down the darkened streets to the Napier cabin. "He's pushy and he'll only criticize what you do." But even as she tried to list all the reasons she shouldn't have asked Logan along, she knew there were deeper reasons. Reasons she didn't want to delve too far into for fear of making them too real.

She was becoming attracted to Logan Napier.

Sandra stopped, biting her lip as she considered her position. She could cancel. She could turn around and change her mind. It was, after all, one-thirty in the morning. Surely they wouldn't mind missing out.

But Sandra had promised the girls this event as a reward for all their hard work during the week, and they were looking forward to it with an amazing amount of enthusiasm. She didn't think girls the age of Bethany and Brittany would be interested in meteor showers.

Asking Logan along had been a silly impulse. This morning, when he had put his hand on her shoulder, it was as if every nerve in her body swung like a compass needle toward his touch.

She couldn't imagine why one simple gesture from a guy like Logan could turn her knees to jelly.

But it had, and afterward, when she could analyze it, she knew that spending time with him was just playing with fire. He wasn't her type—he'd drive her crazy in a week. And if she fell in love with him…

"Whoa, whoa, now you're really jumping the gun," she said. She shook her head as if to dislodge even the faintest mote of the previous idea.

Sandra bit her lip, still hesitating. Then, laughing at her foolishness, she walked on. Logan was here temporarily. Once he was gone, her life could go back to, well, whatever it should be.

She bounded up the steps and knocked on the door of the darkened house. No answer. A quick glance at her watch told her that she was right on time.

Just as she was about to knock again, the door opened, and the light in the cabin was turned on, throwing out rectangles of golden yellow on the lawn.

Framed by the door, backlit by the light in the cabin, stood Logan.

His hair was unkempt, and whiskers stubbled his firm jaw, accenting the slight indentation in its center. His eyes were bleary with sleep. He was dressed, however, in a wrinkled T-shirt and jeans. No khaki pants tonight.

"Hi there," he said, his voice still husky from disuse. Sandra felt a peculiar little thrill at the sound.

"I'm not early, am I?" she said quickly.

Logan yawned, scratching his chin. His fingers rasped over his whiskers. "Nope." He glanced at Sandra, blinking. "How do you manage to look so perky at this ridiculous time of night?"

Sandra shrugged, warmed at the offhand compliment. "I don't need much sleep."

Logan yawned again. "Lucky you. Well, come in. The girls are just getting ready."

Sandra stepped inside. Logan closed the door behind her and ambled toward the kitchen.

He stumbled, muttered something under his breath and stood for a moment, glaring at the offending table.

Sandra stifled a laugh at the sight and was rewarded with a bleary look from Logan.

"Sorry," she said, with a quick shrug of her shoulders.

"I somehow doubt that," he replied. But his grin belied the gruffness of his voice.

"We're ready to go," Brittany called, stepping out of the kitchen.

"So am I," Sandra said. "Now we just have to get your uncle Logan ready."

She glanced pointedly at Logan's bare feet. He stared at her as if he didn't understand, then looked down. "Oops. Sorry." He yawned again, trudged to his bedroom and came back a few minutes later holding his shoes.

Rubbing his eyes, he sat in the nearest chair, dropped his shoes on the floor and stared into space.

Sandra waited for him to put his shoes on. But he didn't move.

"Logan?" she asked, taking a step nearer. She glanced at the girls, who merely lifted their shoulders in puzzlement.

"Hey, let's get going." She reached out, grasped his shoulder and gave it a little shake.

He blinked, then, looking at her, smiled. It was a smile with no reservation, a smile that held no hint of his usual asperity. "Hi, Sandra," he said, his voice husky, lowered to an intimate level. Then, to her surprise, he lifted his hand, resting it on hers. His hand was large, engulfing hers, his fingers warm as they lightly caressed her own.

Sandra swallowed as her heart rate jumped. She pulled her hand back as if burned. "Logan? Are you awake?"

He blinked, frowned, then blinked again, and Sandra realized with a beat of disappointment that he hadn't been.

"What's up?" he asked, looking around, puzzled, completely unaware of what had just happened.

"It's time to go," Sandra said stiffly, grasping her knapsack strap with both hands.

"Okay." He nodded and slipped on his shoes. As he bent to tie them, Sandra looked away, directly into the smirking faces of the twins.

"Well, girls," she said briskly, covering her confusion, "get your things together and we'll leave."

"We have everything, Sandra," Bethany said, still grinning.

"Good. That's good." Sandra took a step back as Logan stood up and blinked. He looked at her as if seeing her for the first time. A frown wrinkled his forehead then he shook his head lightly and turned away.

"I'll go start the van," he said, slipping on a denim jacket.

Sandra nodded. She avoided meeting his eyes, wondering if he had truly forgotten what he had done.

The drive through the hills would have been silent if it had depended on Logan or Sandra to make conversation. Fortunately the girls had more than enough to talk about. They asked Sandra questions about what they were going to see, even though they knew.

"I can't guarantee we're going to see a lot of meteor activity," Sandra said as Logan parked the van at the top of the hill on a graveled turnout. "But from what I know, this is an ideal time."

"One-thirty in the morning is anything but ideal," Logan muttered, getting out of the van.

"Hey, you didn't have to come." Sandra angled him a quick glance.

In the reflected glow of the van's headlights, Sandra caught his eye, and she once again remembered the feel of his hand on hers. She looked away.

"C'mon, girls, get the stuff we'll need and then we can get this show on the road," she said.

Sandra pulled her sweater closer around her. The daytime temperatures were hot, but in the open prairie, the middle of the night was always cool.

"Where do you want us to be?" Logan asked, carrying the blanket that Sandra had taken along.

"I'd like to go just beyond the gravel. The hill is open

to the south, and I'd like to face that direction." Sandra led the way, the beams from the van illuminating her path through the brush.

They came to an open hillside, protected from a faint breeze by the trees that fanned out on either side.

"Perfect," Sandra said with satisfaction. "Okay, girls. Lay out your bags right here."

"I'll go and shut off the van's headlights," Logan offered, handing Sandra the blanket. Her eyes were still semiblinded by the van's lights, so she couldn't see his expression. He waited a moment, then turned and left.

"Here, girls, help me lay out this blanket," she said to the girls, pulling herself into the moment. *Concentrate, concentrate,* she thought.

She wished she hadn't asked him along. It was going to be an awkward event.

"We remembered our flashlights and pens and paper," Bethany offered as they laid the blanket out.

"Good for you. I'm hoping we'll see a lot of meteors right now."

A rustle in the bushes brought her senses to alert, then she realized it was Logan coming back from the van, and she felt even more tense.

Her eyes were slowly becoming adjusted to the dark, and she felt a sense of déjà vu. Remembered another time he had materialized out of the darkness.

Sandra turned quickly to the girls and sat on one edge of the blanket, indicating that they were to sit beside her.

"What is the name of the meteor shower we're going

to watch?" she asked, putting on her teacher's voice as she tried not to notice Logan sitting down just a few feet away.

"The Phoenicids," both girls replied.

"Good. So why are we up this early in the morning to watch them?"

"Because the moon is gone now," Bethany said, stifling a yawn. "And the sky is as dark as it is going to be."

"And what is the moon called?"

Silence greeted that question.

"The moon," Brittany said, puzzled.

"A gibbous moon. Another word for the shape of the moon." Sandra pulled out her book of star charts as she spoke. "And what's another reason we're up at this ridiculous time?"

Silence again.

Sandra was disappointed that they hadn't remembered what she had shown them this afternoon. It didn't speak well for her training, and some perverse part of her was trying to show Logan what a good teacher she was.

Then Brittany rescued her. "I think I remember. Is it because we're facing the same way the earth is traveling in the orbit?" Sandra could hear the question in her voice. "You said something about snow and snowflakes and driving."

"Very good." Sandra felt a surge of relief. "If we're facing in any other direction, it's like looking out of the back window of a van during a snowstorm. You'll see some meteors, but not as much as if you're in the front of the van. Right now we're heading into the meteor shower, like a van into a snowstorm." She went on to show the girls where in the sky was the best place to look. Flashlights came out, and they bent over the book.

"Uncle Logan, come and see, too," Brittany ordered. And Uncle Logan obediently got up from his side of the blanket and looked over Sandra's shoulder.

She tried to concentrate on what she was showing the girls, but all her senses were alert to his presence behind her.

Luckily it was dark, and the girls were bent over the book, pointing out the constellations.

"Okay, get out your pens and paper and be sure to notice where you see meteors, how long you see them and keep a note of the time between them."

The flashlights were shut off, and the little group was plunged into darkness.

Slowly, as Sandra's night vision righted itself, she could better make out the figures of the girls lying down on the blanket beside her and Logan, who sat behind them.

She hugged her knees, looking at the sky. She knew she was going to get a sore neck if she stayed in this position, but she was certainly not going to lie down. Not with Logan so close behind her.

"There's one," Brittany said, pointing up.

"Mark it down," Sandra prompted. "But try to write without the flashlight so your eyes don't have to get used to the dark again."

She heard their pens scratching on the paper.

"So how did you know when the shower was coming?" Logan asked from behind her.

"Earth intersects these meteoroid swarms at about the same relative time and place each year," Sandra said confidently, clutching her knees. She was on familiar territory here.

"And where does the name come from?"

"When we cross one of these swarms, the meteors seem to come from a common point of origin, known as a radiant. This regular shower is named after the constellation from which it seems to originate."

He was quiet again. Then he got up and stretched out on the other side of Brittany. Sandra ruthlessly suppressed a twinge of disappointment. Crazy. That's what it was.

Or maybe just plain loneliness, another voice said.

Sandra pressed her chin against her knees, staring at the stars that went directly to the horizon, meeting the faint outline of the hills that sloped away from them. Sitting outside under the stars always made her feel vulnerable and philosophical.

The lines of her life had, of late, not fallen in pleasant places. She thought that her hard-won freedom would have given her a sense of satisfaction. Instead it was as if each move was a move away from something rather than a move toward something.

She glanced past the girls at Logan, who lay on the blanket, his hand under his head. He seemed to know what he wanted and how to go about getting it. In spite of his interference, or maybe because of it, she realized that he was a concerned uncle. She wondered how many of the men she had met in her life would willingly take in two young girls, thereby risking their own freedom.

She sighed lightly, her gaze falling on the girls who were watching her watching Logan.

She looked away.

"How many have you seen, Bethany?" she asked, disconcerted that they had caught her staring at their uncle.

"Four already."

"Good for you." She lay back, watching the sky, reminding herself of the reason she was here. The girls first and foremost.

"The stars sure are peaceful," Logan said quietly. "Unchanging. Always the same. Amazing."

A few moments before, Sandra might have agreed with him, but her reactions to him left her feeling edgy.

"Actually they aren't," she contradicted. "Out there are colliding neutron stars, gamma ray bursts, black holes. All kinds of noise and confusion."

"What's a gamma ray?" Bethany asked.

"A powerful form of light. More energetic than a microwave or X-ray. Like the difference between humming and screaming." She stopped herself, knowing she was spouting off. Knowing that if she kept talking she would end up talking above the girls' heads.

"Can you see gamma rays?"

"No. Not with the naked eye."

"Then what's the point?" Bethany asked.

"I think God made some things just for His own pleasure," Sandra said. "We can't even see the tiniest amount of all the stars and galaxies He made, but He still made them."

"You believe in God?" Bethany asked.

"Of course, I do." Sandra wondered where that question had come from and wondered if that explained part of Logan's reserve with her. "How can you look up at all of this and not believe that it was created by God?"

"Cool."

"Really cool." Brittany sat up, shivering. "I'm cold, Sandra. I want my sweater." She stood and grabbed her sister's hand. "C'mon, Bethy, I'm scared in the dark. You come with me."

Sandra could see Logan lift himself onto his elbow. "Do you want me to come?" he asked.

"No. That's okay, Uncle Logan." As they walked through the bushes, Sandra could hear faint giggles and wondered what they were up to.

But Logan lay down, seemingly unconcerned.

"You seem to know a lot about astronomy," he commented.

Sandra shrugged, sitting up. "When I graduated from high school, my first choice was to go into that field."

"Why didn't you?"

Sandra hugged her knees. "My parents wanted me to study something that would give me a job at the end. And since they were paying for my education…"

"You took teaching." Logan finished the sentence for her.

"Bingo."

She heard as much as saw, in her peripheral vision, Logan sit up, leaning on one elbow again. "Why didn't you go ahead? On your own?"

She thought back to that time. To the daily confrontations she had with her father over her education, her mother hovering, always the peacemaker. Except there never was any peace to make between Sandra and her father. There was always something to fight about. Her clothes, her friends, her marks. Always something that didn't measure up.

The memories dredged up old feelings of inadequacy. She turned to Logan, finding her own questions. "Did *you* go it on your own?"

Logan laughed lightly. "Absolutely. I paid my own way. I got where I did by the grace of God and my own hard work."

"With no help from your parents?"

"Sandra, you know what my mother is like. We lived hand to mouth as long as I can remember. One of the benefits of living a free and easy life."

Sandra pulled her lip between her teeth as she thought of her financial situation, also the result of the free and easy life Logan spoke disparagingly of. "Money isn't everything," she said softly, trying to find some feeble way of justifying her choices.

Logan was quiet. In the dark, all she could see of him was the gleam of his eyes, then a flash of white as he grinned.

"Is that the best you can do, Sandra? 'Money isn't everything.' I expected better."

She couldn't stop her answering smile. "Sorry. I must be a little off my form tonight."

Logan sat up and faced her, sitting cross-legged. "So what made you interested in astronomy?"

Thankfully he had found another topic. Talking about her parents always created a mixture of guilt, anger and frustration.

"I guess I was drawn to the vastness of this universe. The fact that there is so much dark interspersed with so much light. That during the day, light is stronger, then in the evening, darkness wins out."

"But even in the darkest night, like now, there's light."

"And Jesus said, 'I am the light of the world,'" Sandra quoted softly.

"How about this one from Job. 'What is the way to the abode of light? And where does darkness reside?'"

Sandra paused, letting the words take root. "I've never read that before. That's beautiful."

"It's from God's mighty challenge to Job, asking him who he possibly thinks he is." Logan moved closer, creating an intimacy. "You know your Bible, Sandra, yet you claim to not need God."

"I've never made that claim," she said quietly, her heart stepping up its rhythm at his nearness. "I just don't feel that I need to restrict myself to worshiping Him in church."

"Those hypocrites," he said, his voice holding a faint teasing note.

"I only said that once."

"But you meant it?"

Sandra shrugged. She didn't know what she meant anymore. Didn't know what she needed. Since she left home, her life had lost a center, a focus. No one had challenged her on her faith until now. Until the girls. Until Logan.

"What do you really want from God, Sandra? From life?"

"Why do you want to know?" she countered, uncomfortable with his probing questions. He sounded like her father.

"I'm not sure," he whispered. To her utter surprise, he took her hand in his, stroking her fingers. "I'm not sure at all."

She looked at their connected hands, knowing she should pull away, yet unwilling to. It had been so long since she had allowed any man to get close to her. That the first man since Henri should be someone like her father…

She stopped that thought, knowing that in spite of some similarities, it wasn't really true.

"You don't like answering questions, do you, Sandra," he said, letting go of her hand.

"I've answered enough in my life," she retorted.

To her relief, Logan leaned back again, creating a distance. "From who?"

"My father."

"What was he like?"

Sandra sighed as the conversation came full circle. "I don't talk about my parents much." In the first place, none of the people she had lived with or spent time with since she left home had ever asked her about them. Second, each time she thought of them she faced a combination of emotions. Guilt and sorrow.

She suddenly realized that they had been alone a while. As she and Logan had been talking, she had heard Bethany and Brittany's faint giggling, but it had been quiet for some time now. "Where are the girls?"

Logan didn't seem too concerned. "I'm pretty sure they're not far. Brit, Bethy, where are you two scalawags?" he called.

But all that came back was silence.

Logan got to his feet, and as he did, he held out his hand to Sandra to help her up. The gesture was casually intimate. It bespoke of established relationships and had a chivalry that Sandra had never seen before.

She couldn't stop herself from putting her hand in his, from allowing his to grip hers as he pulled her to her feet.

As soon as she was upright, however, she pulled her hand free and walked down the path, through the shrubs and to the road to the van.

The girls weren't there, either.

"Brittany, Bethany," Logan called, turning around.

He sighed, plowing his hand through his hair. "I guess we'll have to go looking for them." He turned to Sandra. "Get in. I suspect they're just down the road."

Sandra quelled the nervous jumping of her stomach. Logan didn't seem worried. She was sure he had been through enough other things with the girls that this was simply another event.

But she couldn't stop her feelings of concern about the girls as she got into the van.

Logan lifted his hand to turn the key in the ignition. "Did I take the keys out?" he asked, turning to Sandra.

"Not that I remember," she replied.

He turned on a light on the dash that illuminated the interior of the van, then bent over to look. "Didn't drop them, either." He sat up, glancing sidelong at Sandra. "I suspect my dear little nieces took them."

"So what do we do?" she asked.

"We could wait."

"Or we could start walking," Sandra offered quickly. The idea of sitting in the confines of the van felt too intimate to her.

"Okay. We walk," he agreed.

Logan got out and Sandra followed him, relief mingled with a tiny niggling of regret.

Chapter Eight

Logan clenched his fists at his sides, anger mixing with shame at what his nieces had done. They had gone too far this time.

"Can you figure which way they went?" Sandra asked.

"I'm guessing toward town." Logan bit down on his anger at the girls, hoping he was right. It could be a long night out here trying to find them if they decided they didn't want to be found. He stifled a flash of worry. Nothing had happened yet. He would find them.

Though Logan's eyes were accustomed to the dark, it was still slow walking down the road. Thankfully it was fairly wide, and the trees were more sparse at the top of the hill the road followed. Sandra was quiet, and Logan didn't know what to say.

Except to apologize for his nieces.

"I'm sorry about the girls," he said. "I keep hoping that one day they'll settle down and make some wise choices."

"It's okay, Logan. They're only ten, and I don't mind walking."

"Well, I do. I own a van. A nice van that works really well. I just hope they haven't lost the keys to it."

"I'm just glad they didn't try to start it. Brittany told me they used to drive their parents' van once in a while."

Logan snorted. "I'm not surprised. Linda and August let those girls do everything."

"Is that why you're so protective of them?"

Logan slipped his hands in his pockets as he walked along, considering his answer. "I've had to be. Their parents didn't always make the wisest choices."

"Do you mind telling me a little more about them?"

He hesitated.

"I think it would help me, if I'm going to be teaching them, to know what their family life was like," Sandra prompted.

"I suppose you're right," he conceded, glancing sidelong at her. She had gently probed before, when they were at Fort Walsh, and he had put her off. But now he knew she was as concerned about the girls as he was and as caught up in their schooling.

"My sister Linda used to flirt with every boy in sight," he said, searching for the right words, the right phrases. "Mostly it didn't matter because in a few months we would be moving to the next place my father wanted to go." He paused. His family's failings could still embarrass him, even in front of someone who lived almost the same lifestyle. "We were in one town longer than a few months, and my sister had been chasing a couple of boys around, playing one against the other. One was a good friend of mine, one of the few I ever got to know. He ended up in the hospital because the other guy beat him up. Linda thought it was funny. Worse than that, my mother thought it was a real honor that two guys would fight over her daughter. My dad, as usual, wasn't around." He shook his head, remembering the rage that flowed through him that day. His sister didn't seem to care. "Then she got married. Had to, by the way. But things didn't change much. Commitment wasn't in her vocabulary. I know she left August at various times, hoping to find herself. Sometimes she took the girls, sometimes she didn't. My nieces grew up seeing that."

"Did their parents love the girls?"

Logan blew out his breath as he considered Sandra's question. "In their way, I suppose they did."

"Then at least they had that."

Logan glanced sidelong at her. He couldn't see her expression very clearly in the dark, but he detected a note of wistfulness in her voice.

"What was your childhood like?"

She had managed to find out things about him, but he still didn't know much of her.

She lifted her face to the dark sky as if looking for help there. "This isn't part of my ongoing interview, is it?"

"No. But it is a way of making conversation while we're walking down this road," he said.

"A way of getting to know each other?"

Logan considered that. "Partly." He wasn't sure how

deeply he wanted to get involved in Sandra's life. Yet on the other hand, she intrigued him. That and something deeper, more elemental. Something he had never experienced with a woman. "What was your father like?" he asked, fighting the direction of his thoughts.

Sandra wrapped her arms around herself as she seemed to consider her answer, as well.

They were so careful with each other, thought Logan. Each waiting, measuring, wondering how the other would judge them.

Sandra drew in a deep breath. "I guess the best way to describe my father is to call him the original guilt trip cruise guide. Even when I followed his lead and did what he wanted, I still felt as if I had completely disappointed him. Or my mother. So I did what any girl did who had spent most of her life trying to please a man who couldn't be pleased, and jumped ship."

Logan heard what she was saying and realized that while she had stated a basic conflict, she still hadn't told him much. "You do that often, don't you," he stated, glancing at her again.

"Do what?" She stopped, looking back.

Logan turned to face her, his hands still in his pockets. "Use words and figures of speech to give the idea that you're making conversation, that you're telling people something without really saying anything."

"Don't tell me you didn't understand what I was saying," she said, sounding slightly testy.

"I understood that he had expectations of you that differed from what you wanted. That's not so unusual. I understood that you didn't get along with your father. Neither did I. But you've really not told me anything."

Sandra sighed, looked away and then back again. "What do you want to know?"

Her eyes were two dark smudges, but as he stepped closer, he could see them glowing with a banked light. "I guess I'm only going to find out what you want to tell me, but I'd like to know more than that."

"Why?"

Her question hung between them, a whisper in the dark. He wasn't sure. Wasn't sure of the heightened feelings that resonated between them.

She was the complete opposite of everything he had ever wanted, but he couldn't stop the attraction he knew was growing between them. He wondered if she felt the same.

Then she turned and began walking, and he got his answer.

He caught up to her, but they said nothing more, the space between them greater than before.

Logan squinted through the dark, wondering how far the girls might have walked, wondering if they were okay. Hoping and praying that nothing had happened. The silence between him and Sandra was uncomfortable, and for the first time in a while, he missed the girls' chatter.

He heard Sandra cry out, and from the corner of his eye saw her stumble and fall heavily to the ground.

"Sandra, what happened?" He rushed to her side, dropping beside her. "Did you break something?"

"No, no," she gasped, clutching her knee. "I twisted my knee."

He didn't know first aid. Didn't know what to do. So he knelt beside her, helplessly watching as she pulled in one slow breath after another, her head pressed into the dirt as she moaned softly.

"What can I do? Let me help you."

She took in another labored breath and clenched her teeth. "Just wait. Just wait," she gasped.

Logan touched her shoulder, curved his hand around her to make some kind of connection, offer some kind of assistance.

Then she carefully lowered her leg.

"I think it's okay now," she said slowly. She tried to get up and would have fallen again. Logan caught her this time. Again she cried out, clutching his arm.

"Not so quick, Sandra," he said, holding her. "Take it easy."

"I need to get up. To keep moving." Her words were a thin thread of sound. Logan could tell she was in a lot of pain.

He slipped her arm around his neck and supported her as she struggled to her feet. Then, taking a few more slow breaths, she straightened.

"I'll be okay now," she said, pulling her arm back.

But Logan kept his other arm firmly clamped around her waist. "No, you won't."

She tried to take a step and faltered. Her breath hissed through clenched teeth.

"Take it easy, Sandra," he said quietly, holding her close to his side, supporting her easily.

"It's an old injury," she explained between breaths. "I tore ligaments last year."

Logan winced in sympathy. When he was a teen he'd strained ligaments, and he could vividly remember how much that hurt.

"I'll be okay," she added.

"No, you won't, and stop trying to be so tough," he reprimanded, his anger building. If the girls hadn't stolen the keys, this wouldn't have happened. Again he felt guilt and remorse over Sandra's pain.

"I think you should wait here while I try to find out where the girls are," Logan said, stopping.

Sandra looked at him, and in spite of the pain he knew she must be suffering, she managed a smile. "I think maybe I better stay with you. For the girls' sake."

In spite of his irritation, Logan managed to laugh.

"You're probably right," he said. "But this walking isn't going to be good for your knee."

"Truly, I need to keep moving a little bit, otherwise it will stiffen up on me."

Logan was surprised at how upbeat she sounded. She was tough, he had to give her that.

"Let me help you. We'll head to the van." He placed her arm across his shoulders again, holding on to her hand. To his surprise, she didn't object.

She took a step and leaned heavily on him as she took the next one.

Logan wanted to protest again, but he knew Sandra wasn't going to stop because he told her to. So he held her even closer.

He caught the scent of her hair. A faint night breeze

teased strands of it, tickling his face in an altogether too pleasant way. Sandra didn't say anything, and Logan couldn't.

Their progress was slow, and periodically Logan would call out for the girls. Yet, as he held Sandra close to him, as his hand curved around her waist, he couldn't stop the insidious hope that he wouldn't find them quite yet.

"Where do you suppose the girls are?" Sandra asked, clinging to him.

Her voice sounded strained, as if she was fighting the pain. The tightening of his hand was an automatic, defensive gesture. To his surprise and pleasure, she didn't pull away.

"My guess would be they are either hiding a few minutes away from here or following us and too scared to show their faces," he said.

In the darkness her eyes glowed. She blinked and half turned. Logan shifted his weight. Then, instead of being side by side, they were face to face.

He held her eyes, felt his reason drifting away the longer they stayed facing each other, silent. It seemed the most normal thing, then, to lower his head.

Her faint protest brushed his lips, then faded as their mouths met and held.

A slow warmth spread through Logan as he held her closer, as he murmured her name against her lips. Her hands clung to his shoulders, her fingers pressing into him as she stood pliant in his arms.

Logan ignored the voice of reason that warned and chided. The voice that reminded him how little he really knew about Sandra. That reminded him of all the unknowns that swirled around her transient life.

But he couldn't keep the voices silent forever.

Reluctantly he pulled back. Lowered his hands.

Kissing her was a mistake, Logan told himself even as disappointment sifted through his rationalizations. Withdrawing was the right thing to do.

Logan repeated these words over and over again as Sandra turned and started hobbling away from him.

He caught up to her and was about to slip his arm around her again to support her.

"I don't need your help." Her voice sounded strained as she pushed his arm away.

Logan felt torn as he walked alongside her. Helping her had put him in this predicament. Yet he couldn't very well let her do worse damage to her knee.

"You shouldn't be walking," he said finally. "Why don't you sit down and wait while I try to find the girls."

Sandra didn't acknowledge his comment with words but moved to the side of the road and carefully lowered herself to the ground, still not looking at him.

Logan wished he could find the right words to ease the strain that had sprung up between them. Wished he could go back and erase the kiss they had shared.

Do you? Really?

His thoughts mocked him as he remembered the feel of her lips, the warmth of her arms. For a moment he had felt as if all was right with his world. As if all the frustrations of the past few months were but minor irritations that could be dealt with.

As long as he had Sandra.

Logan shook his head, as if to dislodge the enticement of those thoughts.

"Just stay here," he said gruffly. "I'll try to find the girls."

A rustle in the bushes ahead made him look up. In the darkness all he could see was two vague patches of white. They moved and then came slowly closer.

Bethany and Brittany.

"We're here, Uncle Logan," they said, voices subdued.

Logan clenched his fists at his side, took a deep breath and prayed for patience. He wanted to lash out at them for the pain they put Sandra through. For the situation they had created with their silly game.

"I think you had better give me the keys," he said quietly.

Brittany dug in the pockets of her shorts and pulled out a ring of keys. Their faint jangle was the only sound in the tense stillness that surrounded the four of them.

"You stay right here with Sandra. I'm going to get the van."

He knew they heard the suppressed anger in his voice because without a word they drifted to Sandra and sat beside her. They each took one of her hands. A silent plea for forgiveness. They glanced at Logan again.

Logan glared at them, knowing they couldn't make out his expression in the dark. But they felt his anger, because they quickly looked away.

He spun on his heel and marched up the hill, hoping

his anger wouldn't make him fall and injure himself. That would just finish things off, he thought.

In a matter of minutes he was back in a swirl of dust that eddied in the headlights.

By the time he had his door open Sandra was standing, leaning on Brittany and Bethany as she hobbled to the van.

Logan opened the passenger door and held out his hand to help her in, but she ignored it.

The trip to Elkwater was made in absolute silence. A dozen comments ran through Logan's mind as he drove, but all of them sounded apologetic, which would be insincere, or encouraging, which would be wrong.

He got to Elkwater and slowed down.

"I should take you to the hospital," he said. "Get your knee looked at."

"No. It's not that bad," Sandra replied, her tone nonchalant.

"But you could have done some major damage to it. Especially if you've hurt it before."

Sandra shook her head, still not looking at him. "All the doctor is going to do is tell me that I have to stay off my foot and put a tensor bandage on it. I'm not going to go all the way into town just to find that out."

Logan couldn't help but glance behind him at his nieces. They were still looking suitably subdued, and he was sure they felt bad about what had happened to Sandra, as well.

He would deal with them later. Right now his main concern was for Sandra.

"I don't like this, Sandra. I don't think leaving it

alone is such a good idea. It could get worse during the night, and then what?"

Sandra waved his comments away as they drove closer to her home. He still didn't like the idea of leaving her alone, but she was an adult and capable of making her own decisions.

He parked the van in front of her small home and was out and beside her van door before she could even get it open. In the dim glow of the streetlights, he could see the lines of pain etched on her features as she tried to get out on her own.

"Sandra, please. Don't be stubborn about this." He caught her by the shoulders and turned her to face him. "Let me take you to the hospital."

Sandra smiled. "Thanks for your concern, Logan. But truly, the only thing a doctor is going to do is poke around and twist it to see if I've torn anything, which really hurts. Then he's going to give me a prescription for painkillers, which I can't get filled until the next morning because there's no pharmacist on duty at two in the morning in a place the size of Medicine Hat."

What she said sounded reasonable. Yet Logan still felt the twist of guilt and the niggling feeling of wanting to do something to help her.

"You can walk me to the door, though, to make sure I don't fall again," she said.

Logan held out his arm, sensing that she wouldn't be comfortable with their previous arrangement. With another smile at him, she leaned on him as they walked. Logan couldn't stop himself from covering her arm, her skin soft under his hand. "Watch this step," he cautioned, leading her carefully around a large heave in the sidewalk.

Once again Logan found himself conscious of her beside him. Found himself pulling her a little closer than necessary. The fact that two pairs of eyes were watching them from the back of the van helped keep him from repeating the mistake he made on the hill a while ago.

"Where's your key?" he asked as they made it up the front step of her house.

"It's not locked," she said, reaching over and opening the door.

"That's not a good idea, Sandra. This is the best way to get robbed."

He felt Sandra's shrug, her way of dismissing his concern, as they stepped into the darkened house. "I don't have much worth stealing," she said, fumbling for the switch just inside the door.

The room was lit by the jewellike glow of the stained glass lamps. "I don't know about that," Logan said, his eyes caught by their soothing glow. "Those lamps must be worth a lot."

"Maybe," Sandra said. "But not too many people are buying them. A thief might have a hard time fencing them." She let go of his arm as she lowered herself onto the couch, carefully lifting her knee.

Logan bit his lip, loath to leave her. "How do you figure on getting to bed?"

"I just might stay here for the night. I can keep my leg elevated that way."

"Do you have any ice I can put on it? I'm sure that would help if there's any swelling."

Sandra shook her head as she lay back on the couch. "No. I'm fine, Logan. You should get those girls to bed."

Still he couldn't leave, guilt and an indefinable emotion he didn't want to explore keeping him beside her.

"Do you have anything I can get you for the pain?"

Sandra smiled at him. But it was a gentle smile, warm and friendly. Logan felt the curl of attraction and had to stop himself from moving toward her. He dismissed his feelings as the natural protectiveness of a man with a defenseless woman.

A defenseless, wholly appealing woman, he amended, his eyes following the curve of her smile, the dark spill of her hair over her shoulder.

Go now, he told himself. *She doesn't need or want anything from you right now.*

But still he lingered.

"Don't worry about working tomorrow. Me and the girls will figure something out." He slipped his hands into his back pockets, rocking on his heels. "I feel so bad about what happened."

"It was just an accident, Logan." Sandra raised herself on one elbow. "And please, don't come down too hard on the girls. They're young. What they did was wrong, I know, but I don't think they knew precisely what they were doing." Her dark eyes were full of concern.

Logan bit back a harsh reply, disagreeing with her. The girls knew exactly what they were doing, only the consequences had been greater than they realized. But he sensed, in Sandra's plea on behalf of Brittany and Bethany, something more than a simple defense of their actions.

"Please, Logan?" she repeated.

"I'm not going to beat them and lock them in their rooms with a ration of bread and water, if that's what you're worried about," Logan assured her. "I know they feel pretty bad about what happened. But I do have to make them see that there are consequences to their actions. Make them see that they have to think about that before they do something even more foolish."

Sandra nodded and leaned back, her brow smooth as if what he said had reassured her. "You're a good uncle to them, Logan. I hope they appreciate it."

Her unexpected compliment softened the defense he had been building against her ever since that misguided kiss in the hills. He found that he couldn't look away. Didn't want to look away.

Her expression grew serious. He saw the faint lift of her throat as she swallowed.

Then she turned her head and closed her eyes. "You better go, Logan."

He went to the door, knowing she was right. Yet just before he closed the door behind himself, he couldn't stop from looking at her one more time.

But her eyes were still closed, and as Logan shut the door behind him, he wondered what she was thinking.

Chapter Nine

Sandra listened to Logan's steps as he walked down the sidewalk. Then the sound of a door closing, an engine starting.

Sandra blew out her breath forcing away the memories of Logan holding her, the concern in his voice, the touch of his mouth on hers…

"Stop right there," she said aloud. "Get ready for bed."

The hot flashes of pain centered on her injured knee pushed everything else out of her mind. She slowly lowered her leg, pushed herself up and caught her balance. It took her a few minutes to get to the bathroom, to down the last two painkillers she had and find the tensor bandage to wrap around her knee.

Her movements were awkward and fraught with pain as she got into bed. She turned off the small bedside lamp and settled back, waiting for the painkillers to take effect.

Fifteen minutes later, she painfully rolled onto her

side. Instead of sleep bringing its blessed memory loss, it was as if the loneliness of the dark pressed in on her. A loneliness made all the sharper because of what she had shared just an hour ago with Logan.

Don't go there, she warned herself. Going back to that moment was a mistake. For both of them.

So why did it feel so wrong to dismiss him? He wasn't the man she had been looking for all her life. In fact, Logan was the exact opposite of what she wanted.

But what do you want? she asked herself. *Someone like Henri who lives free and easy then stiffs you? Do you enjoy living hand to mouth, spending more time avoiding what you don't want instead of figuring out what you do?*

Her words accused her, underscoring the dissatisfaction that grew with each wrong decision, each stumbling mistake she made in her life. She had left her home, her father and his unceasing expectations, hoping to find an elusive peace.

Peace I leave with you; My Peace I give you. I do not give to you as the world gives. Do not let your hearts be troubled and do not be afraid.

The words that drifted through her mind were familiar, safe. Words from her past. Words she had heard and read many times. She wasn't exactly sure where in the Bible they were found, she only knew they were words of comfort.

So what did they mean to her?

Sandra rolled carefully onto her back again, wincing at the pain in her knee. Unbidden came memories of other times she was in bed, hurting or sick. Her mother's hand on her forehead. A cup of juice or soda on the bedside table.

The gentle weight of her mother's body as she would sit on the mattress, lightly stroking Sandra's head.

Sandra stifled a cry at the memory. Her mother had been Sandra's defense, her refuge. But she was gone. Sandra pressed her hand against her mouth as she looked around the room. How had she come here, to a rented place and short of money?

Running away. Leaving the heaviness of expectations she could never meet. Leaving the constant disapproval of a father who always wanted more than she could give.

Honor your father and your mother, so that you may live long in the land the Lord your God is giving you.

She had tried, Sandra thought, remembering the commandment laid out in Exodus. She had tried to live up to their expectations until she knew she would crumple under the weight of those expectations unless she could flee and find herself.

Memories of her parents began to intermingle with thoughts of Logan. She wondered why he had kissed her. Sandra knew what Logan thought of her. He disapproved of her lifestyle, of her choices. Not that she should care. He wasn't her type.

Then why did she feel so right in his arms? Why had she felt safe with him?

Sandra closed her eyes as her thoughts became muzzy. With a light sigh, she released all her concerns and let her mind wander.

But her last thoughts were of Logan.

His arms around her, holding her close.

Peace.

"I'm going to go to Sandra's now," Logan said, standing over his nieces. They sat at the dining room table, papers scattered around, their heads bent, looking properly contrite. "I'll be back in about twenty minutes and I'll expect that you'll have those problems Sandra gave you done by then."

He had taken them into town early this morning to pick up a pair of crutches, but as soon as they came home, he put them to work.

Brittany glanced at him, then her eyes flicked away. In that brief look Logan saw sorrow and regret. Logan felt a flutter of sympathy for them. What they had done was silly, but if Sandra hadn't hurt herself, their actions would only have been a nuisance. And what did they know of responsibility. They were only ten. Most of their lives had been spent with parents who would merely laugh at what had happened last night.

Logan steeled himself against those thoughts. The girls had to learn consequences, and feeling sorry for what happened in the past was only part of it.

"Is Sandra going to come and teach us today?" Bethany asked in a small voice.

"It all depends on her," Logan said. "She might be able to walk using these crutches."

Brittany set her pencil down, folded her hands demurely on her lap. "Are we going back to Calgary after you see Sandra?"

"I don't know, Brittany." He had thought of it. But

he still hadn't come up with a plan for the Jonserad home he was satisfied with. He had phoned Ian, his partner, who didn't sound too eager for Logan to come back. He suspected that had more to do with Ian angling for a long vacation once Logan was back.

He wasn't going to tell the girls this. Better they didn't know. And it would also be better if they didn't know what had happened last night between him and Sandra.

The memory teased him, dancing on the edge of his consciousness. He had tried to forget it, but in every weak moment images of Sandra returned.

It was a momentary lapse, he reminded himself, pulling his thoughts to the present.

"Are you going to stay at Sandra's for a while?" Brittany asked, her expression guileless.

But Logan knew better and sensed more than heard the hopefulness in her voice.

"I'm going to bring the crutches to her and then I'm coming straight back." He held Brittany's eye and decided to bring things out in the open. "And I know what you girls were doing last night and what you've been trying to do ever since you met Sandra."

Brittany blinked as her mouth drooped. "What were we doing?" she asked, a false innocencecoating her words.

"Brittany, I may be older than you but I'm not dumb. I've seen the movies you've seen, too. I know all about young girls who think they can play matchmaker for their unsuspecting uncles or fathers or brothers or whatever hapless male ends up in their life. That's what you girls were doing last night."

Brittany's eyes grew wide as her shoulders slumped in defeat. "No, Uncle Logan. We weren't trying to do that at all." She tossed her sister a look of panic-stricken appeal. "Were we, Bethany?"

But of the two of them, poor Bethany was blessed with an overabundance of conscience, and she couldn't look her uncle in the face. She concentrated fiercely on her work, her pencil making dark marks on the paper.

"Don't try it again," Logan warned, his hands resting on his hips as he stared Brittany down. "I'm sure Sandra is a wonderful person, but she just isn't my type. We're leaving here, she's leaving here, and we'll probably never see her again."

Brittany blinked, licked her lips and looked down, defeated.

Logan waited a beat, as if to press the point home, then he turned and left.

But as he walked toward Sandra's house, he couldn't help but think that his stern words were directed as much to himself as to the girls.

He'd tried all morning to pass off the protective feeling he had toward Sandra. How she'd felt in his arms.

Get a grip, he reminded himself. He was acting as silly as any of the young boys he saw on the beach every day, flirting with the girls they met, feeling safe in the transitory nature of summer flings.

As he had told Bethany and Brittany, the reality was he was going back to Calgary, and Sandra was…

He wasn't sure what Sandra was going to do, and he suspected she didn't know, either.

Sandra was sitting outside in a dilapidated beach chair when he came up the winding street to her house. He should have phoned, he thought. Should have warned her he was coming.

But as he watched her, he was glad he caught her unawares.

She lay with her head back, a smile teasing her lips. Her hair hung loose, lustrous in the bright sun. One leg was up on a chair, a tensor bandage white against her skin. She wore shorts and a loose top that set off her tanned skin and dark hair.

Logan's steps slowed as he watched her, a part of him captivated by her beauty, his more practical part taking in the strings hanging from the side of the lawn chair, her faded and worn shorts. She was a woman who rejected all the things important to him. Stability. Home. Family.

He pushed those thoughts aside. He didn't want to think about that. Didn't want to think about anything, really. For a brief moment, he was tired of being responsible and making sensible decisions. For a moment, he envied Sandra's relative freedom.

"Hey there," he said, forcing a light tone to his voice as he came nearer.

Her head jerked up, her eyes met his, and time became nothing.

The reality of their kiss from last night hovered between them, as real as the breeze that fanned their cheeks. Logan couldn't help but look at her mouth, wondering if she was thinking of it, as well.

"Hey, yourself," she said finally, breaking the

contact. She bent her head over her bandage, fussing unnecessarily with it. “I’m sorry I couldn’t come this morning.”

“I didn’t expect you to.” He walked to her side and set the crutches beside her chair. “I brought you these. Since you wouldn’t go to the doctor, I figured we could at least follow his advice.”

As Sandra looked up, her smile spread, transforming her face. “So you’ve appointed yourself my doctor as well as my conscience.”

Logan shrugged her comment aside and glanced around. He found a plastic lawn chair nearby and pulled it closer. Ignoring the dust on the seat, he sat down.

“How did you sleep last night?” he asked, leaning forward, his elbows resting on his knees, hoping he sounded more restrained than he felt.

She waggled her hand in front of him. “So-so. I kept waking up when I had to roll over. But the knee is already much better.”

“Are you sure you don’t want to see a doctor?”

Sandra laughed, pushing her hair from her face in a casually graceful gesture. “I’m sure. It would be a waste of time.” She glanced at the crutches. “So don’t tell me that you come equipped to cover all contingencies?”

“I went into town this morning with the girls to pick them up for you.”

Sandra tilted her head slightly, as if studying him from another angle. “You what?”

“You heard me.”

She quirked her lips in a half smile, tucking her hair

behind her ear. "I did, but I can't believe you went through all that trouble for me."

"The girls figured the sooner you were mobile, the sooner you could come back to teach them." As soon as he said the words, he realized how they sounded. Brittany and Bethany had nothing to do with him getting her crutches.

Her smile slipped, and Logan knew that she understood the implication, as well. "I see." That was all she said. Then she lowered her leg and reached down to pick the crutches up. "Well, I guess the sooner I get used to these things, the quicker I can go back to work."

"There's no rush, Sandra," he said quietly, still feeling guilty, wishing she would smile at him again. "I wasn't trying to tell you that you have to come back right away."

Sandra didn't reply. She stood, fitted the crutches under her arms and made her way down the sidewalk and back again. Logan stood, ready to catch her if she fell, almost hoping he could come swooping to her rescue again. But she made it on her own, handling the crutches with confidence.

"They work and they fit good." She glanced at him, then away. "I guess there's no reason I should stay moping around here, is there? We can leave right away."

Logan felt a twinge of disappointment. He wasn't quite ready to go back to the twins and share Sandra with them. In spite of his previous self-castigation, he would have liked to spend a few moments with her. Just the two of them.

He wasn't sure what he wanted from her. He only

knew that no matter how he scolded and reminded himself of her unsuitability, being with her only a few moments brushed all those objections away as easily as cobwebs.

"I have a few notes I wrote down from last night," Sandra said, shaking her hair and glancing at him. "Would you mind getting them for me? They're on the low table in the living room."

"Gladly done," he said.

Logan stepped inside her home, unable to keep from looking around. The house looked as shabby as it had before. The furniture was poor, though he knew none of it belonged to either Sandra or her roommate.

He sighed, knowing he shouldn't judge Sandra by her lack of possessions, but her house reminded him clearly of his upbringing. How his parents had so often decried material possessions and said they didn't matter. In his walk with God he had discovered that his parents were right, but somehow they had forgotten the responsibility they had to their children to at least provide them with some of the basics.

Logan thrust the memories aside even as he was thankful for the equilibrium they gave him. The reminder of how empty other life choices can be.

The papers Sandra wanted lay in a neat pile on the table. As he bent to pick them up, he absently glanced at the pad of paper beside them.

"Dear Dad, I hope you are well. I need..." That was all that was written across the top of the pad in flowing handwriting as delicate as lace. "I need..." what? Money? Help?

Logan felt a flush of guilt, knowing he shouldn't have read it. Brief and unfinished the note may be, but the words were meant for someone else. Did she write her father often requesting help? How convenient for her, he thought with a flush of anger.

He turned away. It was none of his business. Sandra had never told him much about her father and he doubted she ever would. Their lives weren't that intertwined.

Sandra was waiting outside. "Good. You found them." She flashed him a bright smile. In spite of what he had remembered in her house, he couldn't stop his reaction to her. Angry with himself, he looked away.

"I'll carry these for you," he said.

"Thanks. I appreciate it." She didn't seem to notice anything as she started toward his cabin. Logan slowed his steps to match hers.

"So what nefarious punishment did you dream up for the girls?" she asked.

"They wanted to come with me to bring the crutches, but I wouldn't let them. I'm hoping you will put them through their paces."

"Thanks. I get to be the heavy."

Logan wanted to be able to come back with a witty reply, but then he made the mistake of looking at her. A mischievous smile lit her mouth, her eyes seemed to twinkle, and memories of their last time together slipped into his mind. As he held Sandra's animated gaze, he wondered if she was thinking about last night, as well.

Several times he wanted to bring up what happened, but he didn't know how to broach the subject. Didn't know if it was something he should apologize for or if he should simply act as if kissing his nieces' tutor was a casual way of saying thanks.

"Sandra, I want to talk about—"

"No, you don't," she interrupted him. She quickened her pace, the rubber tips of the crutches making soft clumping sounds on the sidewalk. "And neither do I." She sounded defensive, almost angry.

She *was* thinking about last night, he realized.

So he said nothing. She said nothing. And the rest of the trip to his cabin was made in a reproving silence.

The girls welcomed Sandra with cries of apology and a few tears. Sandra forgave them, and in a matter of minutes they were all seated at the table in the main living area. Logan waited a moment, watching, then he retreated to his room, hoping and praying inspiration and forgetfulness would come to him.

Four hours and six cups of coffee later, he had managed to come up with a reasonable design. Not exceptional, but he was realizing that exceptional was beyond his capabilities. A depressing thought.

He pushed himself away from his drafting table and stretched to work the kinks out of his back. All day, he had had a hard time concentrating on what he was doing. Part of his attention had been on his work, but most had been on the subdued chatter coming from the other part of the cabin. Sandra's deep voice, counterpointed by the hushed sounds of the girls, seemed designed to create a minimum of annoyance.

He got up, and the moment he entered the living room, three pairs of eyes shot to his.

He felt like a dictator surveying the troops. "At ease," he joked, coming to stand beside Bethany. "How's it going?"

"Good, Uncle Logan," she said with forced brightness, her gaze going to the book in front of her.

Logan glanced at Brittany, who averted her eyes, then at Sandra. But she didn't look away. Her head was angled in a purely defensive gesture, and he didn't like it.

"I'm going to get supper going," he said, striving for a nonchalant tone to break the tension that held everyone in thrall. "Would you like to stay, Sandra?"

"Yes, please stay for supper," Brittany said.

"You can't cook for yourself with your leg so sore," Bethany added.

Sandra smiled at the girls, but Logan could see her wavering. *Probably thinks I'm going to attack her again,* he thought.

"I think the girls are right," he said quietly, adding his voice to theirs. "And if they help me, it will be their way of letting you know how sorry they are."

He caught Bethany's aggrieved look, but a quick frown from him erased it from her face. "Good idea, Uncle Logan," she said meekly.

Sandra's gaze skittered over his face, then away. "Okay. I won't say no to a meal I don't have to cook."

"Great. Are the girls done?" Logan asked.

"Brittany can go. Bethany just needs a few minutes to finish up what she's doing."

Logan nodded to Brittany, who still looked far from pleased. They'd have to have a little talk while peeling potatoes, he realized.

Sandra bit her lip as she watched Logan walk out of the room, Brittany trailing behind him. She should have refused supper, she thought. Especially after what happened last night.

It still hung between them, that stolen kiss. She didn't know why it should have had such an impact on her, but it had. For a moment she had had this utter feeling of rightness.

Of peace.

Then, on the way here, she knew Logan wanted to talk about it. To dissect it.

To apologize and erase it.

She didn't want him to and had cut him off. It might have been better for both of them if they had simply discussed it as mature adults.

She looked around the cozy cabin and sighed. She shouldn't stay. No matter how nonchalant she wanted to be about Logan, undercurrents swirled around them each time they were together. She wasn't sure of her footing anymore, of where she wanted to be.

But the thought of going to her empty cabin to sit with her leg up didn't measure up to the dangerous appeal of being with Logan in a more relaxed setting.

She was playing a dire game, she warned herself as she gathered Brittany's work. And worst of all, she knew it.

It was just that she was so tired of being alone. The past week had been more enjoyable than she had imagined. Working with the girls and seeing their faces light up when they understood something she had been trying to tell them was more fulfilling than anything she had done since graduating from school.

How ironic that she ended up enjoying the very thing she had been running away from.

"I'm done, Sandra." Bethany closed her book, and Sandra's attention was drawn sharply to the young girl.

"Good. You can go and help your uncle."

Bethany nodded and slipped out of her chair.

Sandra finished cleaning up the papers and books, listening all the while to the sounds coming from the kitchen. The low rumble of Logan's voice patiently explaining what had to be done. The clank of pots on the stove, water running. A question from one of the girls. Logan explaining again.

Sandra felt a sharp pang as she listened. The only time her father had ever been in the kitchen was to get a glass of water from the fridge. She couldn't imagine her father doing what Logan was doing right now.

She didn't want to compare Logan to her father, but she couldn't help it. Every man she had met in the past five years had been measured against Josh Bachman. The closer they were to him, the quicker she ran in the other direction.

So she ended up with someone like Henri, who was about as far removed from her father in temperament as a cocker spaniel was from a Doberman. But thanks to Henri and his scheming, she was stuck in this town, trying to find a way out of the economic hole she had dug for herself.

But she didn't want to think about that now.

Tomorrow will worry about itself. Each day has enough trouble of its own.

The familiar words drifted into Sandra's consciousness. She knew they were from the Bible. Her mother used to quote them time and time again.

She stacked books neatly in a pile and carefully maneuvered her leg around the table to get to her feet. The crutches were definitely a help, she thought as she worked her way to the kitchen. Once again, she was thankful that Logan had gone through the trouble to get them for her. Of course, as he said, it was only because of the girls, but she still appreciated it.

"Do you need any help?" she asked, pausing in the doorway.

Logan glanced over his shoulder, smiling at her.

"No. I think we can manage."

Sandra felt the all too familiar jump of her stomach at the sight of his smile. "I'm feeling a little guilty sitting in that room without doing anything," she added.

"Well, we're a little cramped in here right now, but you can keep us company. Sit yourself down by the table if you want." Logan angled his chin toward the dining nook.

Sandra worked her way around the counter where the girls were chopping up the fixings for a salad. They glanced quickly at her. Each flashed her a smile and then went back to work.

Sandra was amazed at how reserved they were. In fact all afternoon they had been very cooperative and quiet. Not at all their usual selves. Sandra wondered what Logan had told them to create such meekness.

She carefully lowered herself in the chair, laying the crutches on the floor beside her. As she looked up she caught Brittany's cheeky grin. Her careful wink.

And she realized that the girls may be down but not out.

She glanced at Logan again and for a moment felt sorry for him and the responsibility of these two rambunctious young girls.

At that moment he chanced a look her way.

It was just a casual turning of his head, a quick glance. He was stirring a pot.

But as their eyes met, his hands slowed, she swallowed, and it was as if everything around them slipped away. As if there were only the two of them, and nothing else mattered.

Chapter Ten

"Now it will be easier to make a circle when we pray," Brittany said brightly, holding out her hand to Sandra.

Logan set the pan of spaghetti carefully on the table then sat down between Bethany and Sandra. He tossed Brittany a warning glance, but she had already bowed her head. Bethany had his hand, and he had no choice but to hold out his other hand for Sandra.

Without looking up, she laid hers in his. Her fingers were cool and soft, and as Logan closed his hand over hers, he felt the tiny ridge of a scar.

He couldn't stop the faint tremor of his heart at the fragility of her hand in his.

Then he, too, bent his head to pray, forcing thoughts of Sandra aside as he asked God for a blessing on the food. He prayed for his mother, for the girls. After a heartbeat of silence, he prayed for Sandra. Silently, he prayed that he could keep his senses around her, but out loud he prayed that she would be kept in God's care and that her knee would heal.

As soon as he said amen Sandra slid her hand out of his. The girls began chattering, asking Sandra what kind of dressing she wanted on her salad, how much pasta.

They were attentive and gracious hostesses, and Logan was pleased with their behavior.

But all through supper, Sandra avoided his gaze. As if that moment just before supper was ready hadn't happened.

But Logan didn't have to speak. The girls filled in all the dead air with their chattering. Logan didn't know how, after spending most of their days with Sandra, they could have much more to say to each other, but they managed.

After being prompted by the girls, Logan obediently told Sandra about the condo they lived in.

"It's right on the Bow River and has a huge balcony," Bethany added.

"And Uncle Logan said if he gets the Jonserad project, then we might be able to buy a house with a yard." Brittany looked at Logan as if for confirmation.

He nodded, realizing that for the moment he was superfluous.

"What is the Jonserad project?" Sandra asked, her gaze glancing off Logan's.

"It's a home I'm designing for an older couple."

"He's got some really good ideas," Brittany said, scraping the last of the spaghetti off her plate. "Can I show her, Uncle Logan?"

"No. I don't think that's necessary. I'm sure Sandra isn't interested." Logan gave Brittany his I'm serious look, and thankfully she backed off.

"You know that Uncle Logan doesn't like anyone to see what he's working on," Bethany added, chiding her sister.

Logan caught Brittany discreetly giving Bethany a reproving poke and chose to ignore it. He couldn't be refereeing them all the time. And sometimes he couldn't blame either of them. Bethany had a tendency toward self-righteousness, which often antagonized Brittany's fractious side.

"Are you done, Brittany?" he asked, holding her gaze.

She nodded.

"Then you and Bethany can clear up the dishes and wash up."

"If we do that, can we get some ice cream for dessert?"

"I don't think it would be a good idea for Sandra to try to walk on the beach with crutches," Logan said, glancing at Sandra.

"You could stay here with her and we could get it." Brittany made the offer brightly.

Logan stifled a sigh, knowing exactly where Brittany was going with this. In spite of his warnings, the girls just didn't give up. But he had to confess that he didn't mind the idea of being alone with Sandra again, either.

"Okay. But first the dishes."

The girls moved faster than Logan had ever seen. In a manner of minutes and without any arguments whatsoever, they had the table cleared, the dishes done and the counters wiped as clean as a surgeon's table.

Brittany hung up the dish towel while Bethany sidled up to Logan and leaned against him. Logan smiled and slipped his arm around her waist. Her head came just past his shoulder. He turned to look at her, and for a moment he wondered how long it would be before she stopped these spontaneous shows of affection.

"Can I have the money for ice cream, Uncle Logan?"

"I should have known better," Logan said, tickling Bethany. She pulled back, giggling. "Here I thought you were being all sweet and nice because I'm such a great guy."

"You are," Bethany said, still laughing. "But we don't have any money for the ice cream. And you do."

Logan hitched himself sideways, pulling his wallet out of his pants pocket. He slipped a few bills in Bethany's hand and winked at her. "I want a chocolate swirl, dipped with sprinkles," he said. Then he turned to Sandra. "And what about you?"

"Just vanilla is fine," she said with a smile in Bethany's direction.

"I expect to get the change back," Logan called as Bethany spun around and the girls bolted from the room.

"You will, Uncle Logan." Brittany's words drifted back and were cut off by the dull slam of the wooden screen door.

It was as if the entire house had deflated.

Logan turned to Sandra, smiling, as he sat across from her. "Amazing how quiet it gets when they're gone."

Sandra wasn't looking at him. Instead she was toying with a flower petal that had fallen from the wildflower arrangement in the center of the table. "They sure listen well to you," she said quietly.

Logan searched her features, wondering if her words commended or condemned.

"At times they do," he replied, watching as she carefully unfolded the small blue petal, her movements unhurried. He wanted to find out more about her even as he questioned the wisdom of it. They were going to be parting ways, and when they did, it would be to their own separate lives. Better if he kept things superficial.

"Do you want to sit outside while we wait for the girls?" he asked. "It's so nice this time of the evening."

"Sure." She gave him a polite smile and pushed her chair back. Logan handed her the crutches, helping her to her feet.

Once again they were facing each other, Logan's hand on her arm. Once again Logan felt awareness arcing between them, real and tangible.

But this time reason ruled, and he took a quick step back from her.

Sandra led the way, and Logan followed. Once on the deck, Logan made sure she had an extra chair for her leg. He sat down, stretching his legs out in front of him.

In spite of the undercurrents that had flowed between them a few moments ago, he felt a curious peace drifting over him.

It had been a long while since he'd had a woman over for supper. It had been entirely pleasant to see the girls interact with Sandra. In spite of their constant maneuvering to get him and Sandra together, Brittany and Bethany didn't seem as calculating around Sandra as they did with Karen. With Sandra it was as if they had found someone they could connect with, someone they were comfortable around.

"I'm surprised you let the girls go get ice cream."

Logan glanced sidelong at Sandra, aware that he had been quiet for a while.

"I thought you would have had them locked in their bedrooms with bread and water," Sandra continued, her eyes flicking to his then away.

Logan had to laugh. "I'm not very creative when it comes to thinking up punishments. They did have to work pretty hard on their math once we were back from town, but I couldn't think of anything else. They feel pretty bad about what happened."

Sandra nodded, acknowledging his comment, and the conversation lagged. He wondered how to say what he really wanted to. They were alone, and it would probably be their last chance until he and the girls left for Calgary. He wanted to clear up what happened last night. Wanted to let her know that he wasn't in the habit of kissing just any woman.

And what had it meant to you? He rubbed his forehead as he glanced sidelong at Sandra.

She was staring straight ahead, twirling a strand of hair around her finger.

He didn't know what to say to her.

"What school will the girls be attending in the fall?" Sandra asked finally.

"McIntyre Elementary."

Sandra nodded, giving her hair another twist. "I imagine you'll be looking for another tutor once you go back to Calgary?" Her tone was perfectly reasonable, businesslike almost, which made her comment seem even more stark.

"I've got my secretary in Calgary still looking for me." He couldn't imagine that she would have much more success finding anyone now than she had before Logan had been forced to ask Sandra.

"And if you don't find someone?"

Logan bit back a sigh. "I don't want to think about that." He didn't. Because if he did, he knew he would be asking Sandra if she would be willing to come and tutor the girls.

And he knew, in spite of his attraction toward her, that would be a mistake. It was as if he had to remind himself again and again of his responsibility to his nieces. What they did last night showed him more clearly than ever the need for stability in their lives. If Sandra did come to Calgary, how long would she stay, given her employment record?

"And what are your plans once we leave here?" he asked, almost afraid of her answer.

"I have that lamp order to work on, and from there—" she shrugged "—I'll have to see where the wind blows me." She released the strand of hair she'd been playing with.

Logan felt a stab of disappointment. He should have known that.

He thought of the letter she'd started to her father. "Do you see your father often on your meanderings around the country?"

Sandra stiffened, then lowered her hand to her lap. "I keep in touch with him."

Dear Dad, I need... The beginning of her letter came back to him. "Have you seen him lately?"

Sandra's gaze flicked to him. She seemed curious and defensive at the same time. "I haven't seen him for five years. When I told him I wasn't going to teach, he told me to leave. Told me not to bother coming back until I had a real job. I don't think what I'm doing now would constitute a real job."

Beneath the cool delivery of her words, Logan couldn't help but catch a note of pain.

"Do you miss him?"

Sandra threw him an angry look, but then like a deflating balloon, she sank back in her chair. "My dad and I were never close," she said abruptly. "My mother and I did more together than he did."

"And where is your mother?"

Sandra looked away, then at her hands twined in her lap. "My mother died when I was in my third year of college."

Logan felt himself grow absolutely still. He had always assumed that her mother was still alive.

He watched her nervous movements, felt a wave of pity well up in him.

He said nothing, sensing that more would come if he waited.

Listened.

"They haven't kissed yet." Brittany pulled behind the corner of the empty cabin beside Uncle Logan's. She looked at Bethany. "What are we going to do?"

Bethany bit her lip. "We can wait a few more minutes but we have to get the ice cream soon or Uncle Logan is going to think we're scheming again."

Brittany sighed and looked at her most uncooperative uncle. "At least they kissed each other once already."

Bethany giggled at the memory. "And we prayed together tonight. That's a good thing."

Brittany nodded. "Well, we can't wait too much longer. We should go."

Sandra sat back in her chair, looking past the cabins to the lake beyond.

It had been a long time since anyone had asked her about her family, and even then it was just in passing. Cora usually was discussing how to make her next fortune and flitted in and out of Sandra's life like a moth.

Now, after knowing her only a few weeks, Logan was asking her about her mother.

Sandra drew in a slow breath as memories of her mother, like pages of a photo album, flipped through her mind.

"My mother was always my last line of defense," she said softly, breaking the long silence.

"What do you mean?"

Sandra chanced a glance at Logan, wondering what he would think, wondering if he would really understand. Suddenly, she wanted him to. Wanted him to be able to see what her youth had been like.

"My dad had high expectations of me. My mother did, too, but she was more realistic. With my father it was as if all the plans he'd had for four children were put on the one he did have. Me." Sandra ran her finger up and down the arm of her chair. "He'd go over my homework every night with me, and if it wasn't right, I'd have to do it again. My social life was well guarded, as well. Only certain friends, and they all had to come from church."

She stopped, remembering the confrontations and the struggles.

"You said your mother was your defense," Logan said quietly.

Sandra nodded, smiling. "My mother was more pragmatic. She'd invite over a few of the neighborhood kids once in a while. When Dad was gone at conferences, she'd rent frivolous videos. She tried to create a balance when she could, but my father was very domineering. As I got older she knew they hadn't raised a genius, so she could usually get my father to tone his expectations down. By grade nine, when he realized I wasn't going to be a physicist or an engineer, he was willing to settle for mere professor. My mother talked him into letting me become a teacher." She laughed, but it wasn't a happy sound.

"Did you want to?"

Sandra shrugged. "I never had a chance to figure out what I wanted. My dad told me, and when I was younger I listened. Then I became a teenager, and everything changed."

She stopped, staring straight ahead at nothing, her mind's eye going back to the many confrontations they had over her clothes, her friends, her studies. Anything and everything.

"But you finished your degree."

"I was programmed to." She tried for lighthearted but missed the mark. "Finish what you start," she continued. "So I did. After Mom died, Dad started pushing again. Started pulling strings to make sure that I got just the right kind of job in just the right kind of school." Sandra closed her eyes, rubbing her forehead with one finger as if erasing a memory. "The daughter of Josh Bachman wasn't going to get just any old job. I wanted to do things on my own, but he wouldn't hear of it. I was going to quit, but thank goodness a friend talked me into staying. Told me that I might never know when my education would come in handy. She was right." She angled her head to look at him. "Because here I am."

Logan sat back slowly, as if absorbing this new information. "And when you left, you stopped going to church."

Sandra's mouth lifted in a faint smile, and she slanted Logan a quick sidewise glance. "You don't give up on that, do you?"

"I guess it's because God doesn't give up on you, either."

Things were getting heavy, Sandra thought. She remembered the evening in her cabin. After Logan and the girls had left. The compelling music. The faint touch of God's hand.

Sandra tilted her head, forcing herself to make a light comment. "I suppose this is where you are going to tell me that if I go to the church of my choice, I will find the God Who doesn't give up on me."

Logan moved in his chair, pulling it closer. Sandra found she didn't mind. Didn't mind his concern or the fact that he so easily spoke of things she hadn't discussed with anyone in a long time. "Church is one place to find God," he said quietly.

"Nature is another," she countered. "And I like the God I find in nature much better."

"Same God."

"Not the way I've seen it. Church is stifling and restrictive. I mean, look at the whole idea. Ten commandments read each Sunday. All a bunch of don'ts." She spoke the words with a little more force than necessary. As if she was trying to convince herself, she thought.

"The freedom of discipline."

"Pardon me?"

Logan smiled lightly, a dimple winking at her from one corner of his mouth. "There's freedom in rules."

"Okay, that begs an explanation." Sandra adjusted her leg on the chair ahead of her, wondering what Logan meant. "And I think you can give me one."

Logan shrugged, looked down as if gathering his thoughts. "Freedom isn't always as freeing as you think. I can do what I do because I had the discipline to stick with what I was doing. I didn't learn that from my parents."

"I did," she said softly. "Nothing so wonderful about it."

"Are you doing what you want?"

Logan's question wound itself around her heart, slowly pulling up her self-doubts, her moments when she understood that her freedom hadn't been exactly freeing. "I thought I was," she said quietly. "I really thought I was."

"So what happened?"

"I think I lost my way," Sandra said, fiddling with the material of her skirt, unable to meet his eyes. "I was the one with all the chances, all the support, and here I am, floundering. You who had to figure it out yourself, you know what you want."

"It's in how you start, Sandra. You started with a no. No to God, no to your family. That doesn't take you far. Doesn't take you anywhere, if you don't know what you are going to say yes to. God says yes to us. Our life with Him isn't just a list of do nots. It's freedom within discipline. I am where I am because I said yes to God's yes. I knew what I wanted better than what I didn't want."

Sandra felt a deep sadness overwhelm her. She didn't want to examine her life anymore. "I told you about my parents," she said, forcing herself to sound bright, cheery, carefree. "Tell me more about yours."

Logan held her gaze, his hazel eyes steady on hers. "My parents raised Linda and myself to be free. We were allowed to do what we wanted. But it went both ways, because so were my parents. Like I said, there were times we didn't have enough to eat because my parents were exercising their own freedom. Which, in turn, restricted what Linda and I could do. I only started feeling truly free when I went to school. When I disciplined myself to learn something." He looked at Sandra, holding her gaze, his expression serious. "When I gave my life to God and let Him make the decisions in my life. And when I did that, I felt such perfect peace and perfect freedom."

A feeling of shame coursed through her at Logan's words. At one time, in spite of her antipathy to her father, she had a childlike faith in God. Had trusted Him to take care of her, much as she had trusted her parents to take care of her. She'd never had to worry about where her food or clothing was going to come from.

She thought of the decisions she had made in the past. She had made mistakes and had regretted some of them. She had spent so much time figuring out what she didn't want, she wasn't so sure anymore what she did want.

For the first time since she left the home she felt so stifled by, she yearned for the very things she had been spending all these years avoiding.

Security. Commitment. Love.

But she wasn't ready for them yet.

"But to go to church means to conform to what other people expect. To be exactly what they expect. Don't tell me that's freedom," she replied.

"My freedom in Christ has little to do with how other people see me," Logan said quietly, clasping his hands between his knees. "When I gave my life to Christ, I could stop trying to think I had to live for other people's expectations. I only had to please Him."

"And follow His commandments. Heavy responsibility."

"That's a response. A response of gratitude. Didn't you ever do something just out of love? Just because you were so thankful for what you got?"

Guilt surged through her. She thought of the degree her father had paid for. The degree he had kept reminding her of. "I've not always had the chance to be thankful. Usually I was told I had to be before I had a chance *to* be."

Logan nodded. "I'm starting to understand."

"What? Me or my life?"

"Both, I think." He smiled at her, but then the sound of the girls finally returning caught their attention.

They had taken an inordinately long time to return, thought Sandra, wondering if this was part of the schemes Logan had alluded to.

"Hey, Uncle Logan, Sandra. We got your ice cream."

Sandra welcomed the intrusion.

"Great, and you got just what I wanted," Logan said as they clomped up the stairs.

Brittany handed Logan his ice cream, her eyes flicking between them, a speculative gleam in her eye.

Sandra knew the truth of what happened between her and Logan would disappoint them mightily.

Yet as she took her ice cream from Bethany, she realized that while on the surface not much had happened, in reality much had.

Logan was getting closer to a part of her she'd not shown to too many people.

It made her vulnerable. It gave him power over her.

She wasn't sure what to think of it all.

Chapter Eleven

Sandra finished her cone and knew it was time for her to go home. So far the evening had been altogether too pleasant. Too much like a normal family, she thought, looking at the girls sitting at her feet.

She felt a wave of love and compassion for them as she thought of her mother. They had lost their mother at such a young age, they would only have a portion of the memories Sandra had.

Sandra wiped her fingers on the napkin Logan had provided as she glanced at him. She felt a flush warm her neck as she realized he had been watching her.

Again she couldn't look away. Again she wondered about this man. Wondered why he managed to make her talk about things she had never spoken about to anyone since she left home.

"I think the phone is ringing." Bethany cocked her head as if listening.

"I'll get it." Brittany surged to her feet and ran into the house, the door slapping on its frame behind her.

"It's for you, Uncle Logan." Her voice echoed from inside the house.

As Logan got up, Sandra couldn't help but wonder if maybe it was Karen.

None of your business, she chided herself. She glanced at her watch and knew it was time for her to go home. She had been here long enough.

She'd wait until Logan came back, then she'd leave, she decided. This whole scene was getting too domestic.

Logan came back, a frown creasing his forehead.

"What's the matter, Uncle Logan?" Bethany asked.

"That was Ian. My partner. There's been a problem with one of the projects we've been working on. I need to go back to Calgary. So that means you girls will have to come with me."

"No, Uncle Logan. Not yet," the girls cried.

Sandra felt her heart take a slow pitch downward.

She caught herself. Why should it matter to her? She couldn't look at him—wouldn't let him see that she felt anything at all.

But she could no more stop her eyes from darting to his than she could stop the spin of the earth on its axis.

Logan's gaze flicked from the twins to her, stopping, his lips pressed together as if displeased.

Did he want to stay?

Sandra pushed the thought aside. Of course he didn't. He had to get back to work. To making money.

"Can we please stay?" Brittany jumped to her feet.

Bethany was right behind. "We'll be good. We will. We'll listen to Sandra."

They clung to his hands, pleading.

"We can stay here. Sandra can stay with us." Brittany glanced at Sandra as if to confirm what she had said.

Sandra gave a noncommittal shrug, her eyes averted. She wasn't about to get caught up in this.

Logan sighed lightly, and in her peripheral vision she saw him plunge a hand through his thick hair, rearranging it. "I don't know, girls."

Sandra chanced a quick glance at him, and her eyes once again locked with his. She could see the question in them.

Don't do it, don't offer to stay. Keep your life separate.

But she was spending most of her day with these girls anyhow. What difference would a few evenings in the cabin make?

All the difference. You'll be giving them one more part of your life, the insidious voice in her head continued. *And then you'll be waiting for Logan to come back. Getting caught up with someone who's temporary in your life.*

"Sandra could stay with us, and take care of us," Bethany said quietly. She looked over her shoulder at Sandra. "Couldn't you?"

Sandra felt herself wavering as she met Bethany's soft blue eyes. "I don't know," she temporized, unwilling to say a flat-out no.

"Would you come back, Uncle Logan?" Brittany joined in the fray.

"I could." Logan spoke slowly, looking at Brittany.

He took a slow breath, then looked at Sandra. "Would you be willing to stay?"

Sandra swallowed, glanced at the girls who were looking at her, their glances imploring her to consider it.

For their sake she should do it. If she didn't, Logan would have to take them to Calgary, and then he might decide to stay there. She wasn't quite ready to let the girls go yet.

That's not what it is, and you know it. It's him you don't want to let go of. Don't do it.

"Okay," she said quickly, as if taking her time answering might make her listen to the other voice in her mind. The reasonable one. "I'll stay with the girls."

They rushed to her side, throwing their arms around her. "Thank you, thank you. You're the best," they cried.

A peculiar warmth suffused her at the girls' enthusiastic thanks. At the feel of their arms holding her tight. Their hair was sun-warmed and smelled of shampoo. *Is this what it's like to have children?* she wondered. *Being held and thanked for doing so little. Giving part of myself away and getting all this back?*

"I think Sandra might like to breathe for a bit," Logan said dryly.

The girls pulled back, grins splitting their faces, and Sandra knew she had done the right thing. The easiest thing would have been to say no. To see them leave with Logan. And watch the three of them move out of her life.

She didn't want to think about that. Didn't have to. For the next few days, she was still a part of their lives.

The reality of her situation was she had nowhere else to go. And until she paid for the shipment of glass, nothing else to do.

She wasn't ready to have Logan move out of her life so quickly. So unexpectedly. This way she could prepare to say goodbye.

"Well, I'd better get ready," Logan said, his thumbs slung in the belt loops of his pants. "Bethany, Brittany, I want you to get the guest bedroom ready for Sandra."

The girls grinned at each other and ran off, their excited giggles trailing in their wake.

"Well, you've just made two girls extremely happy," Logan said when the screen door had slapped shut behind them.

Sandra glanced at him and smiled. "It doesn't seem to take much," she said.

Logan's expression grew serious as he held her gaze. "I know how much it means to them to stay here," he said quietly. "It's been a crazy kind of holiday for them, what with catching up on schoolwork and all. But so far it's been working out okay. Thanks to you. I have to confess I had my reservations about you, but I want to thank you for making their schoolwork so interesting for them."

His words, his eyes holding hers, even his stance created an intimacy that felt so right, so real, Sandra had to catch herself from reaching out to him. From making a connection more tangible than the one they already shared.

Shocked and surprised at the feelings he elicited in her, Sandra looked down, fumbling for her crutches.

"I should go," she muttered, her heart pounding in her chest. "Tell the girls I'll see them in the morning."

In her awkwardness she dropped one of the crutches. Logan knelt beside her chair and picked it up.

"I'll walk you to your cabin," he said quietly as Sandra surged to her feet.

"That's fine. I'll be okay. It's not far. I'm used to the crutches." Her words tumbled out, mirroring her confusion. What was this man doing to her? Kissing her, complimenting her. Looking at her with those hazel eyes that made her forget all the differences between them.

Making her wonder if maybe, just maybe…

Sandra wrapped her hands around the crutches, squeezing them as if squeezing these ridiculous thoughts out of her mind.

"Thanks again for supper." She chanced a quick grin at him, wishing, praying for the composure she used to have around him.

"You're welcome, Sandra. I'm glad you could come." He slipped his hands in his pockets, as if he were waiting.

Then, with what she hoped was a nonchalant smile, Sandra started out, her crutches pounding a hollow beat on the deck.

Logan was right behind her as she navigated the stairs.

"I told you, I'll be okay." The words came out harsher than she had intended, but Logan didn't seem too perturbed.

"I'm sure you will, but I just like to make sure." And

once again she was stumping along the street, Logan right beside her.

"I'll probably be gone tomorrow and part of the day after. I'm sure I can get the business finished by then," he said quietly.

"And after that?" Sandra couldn't stop the question. She needed to know.

"I had initially figured on staying here for two and a half weeks and then taking the tutor I had hired back to Calgary with me. But I'm going to have to make different plans."

Sandra said nothing, knowing his plans didn't include her.

Spending time with Logan and the girls this evening had been more than pleasant. For the first time since her mother had died, Sandra had felt as if she was in a home, rather than a house.

For the first time in a long time she found herself attracted to a man who created a feeling of rightness in her.

She pushed the dangerous thought to the back of her mind. She had no right entertaining any kind of thoughts about Logan. They were too far apart in outlook, in attitude.

But should that matter?

They got to the door of Sandra's cabin. She thought he would leave then, but he opened the door for her and followed her inside.

The door closed behind him, and she turned to thank him again, disconcerted to see him standing directly in front of her. She had to tip her head back to look into his eyes. His deep, searching eyes.

"Thanks for bringing me home," she said, wishing she felt as nonchalant as she sounded.

"Just wanted to make sure you didn't hurt yourself," Logan said, smiling at her. "How's the knee?"

"It's fine."

"Really?"

"Well, there's no sense whining about it. The more you complain, the longer God lets you live."

Logan's smile widened at her flippant remark. "I guess you are feeling okay."

Sandra couldn't help but smile back. "Sorry. It's my defense mechanism," she admitted.

"I know." Logan's eyes held hers as the smile slowly faded from his mouth. He laid a warm hand on her shoulder, his fingers curling around it. "Are you sure you're going to be okay?"

Sandra wasn't sure at all. Not with the way he was looking at her right now. She couldn't stop her hand from reaching out to him. Resting on his chest.

Her heart climbed up her throat and then stopped when Logan lowered his mouth to hers.

Her crutches clattered to the ground as her arms slid around his neck. He was holding her, supporting her.

His hand tangled itself in her hair as he murmured her name against her mouth. Then a light sigh escaped his lips as he gently pulled away. He rested his forehead against hers. Sandra couldn't focus on his face. It was just a pale blur, his eyes two dark smudges.

"What's happening here, Sandra?" he murmured, his thumb stroking her neck.

Sandra didn't trust herself to respond. She didn't

know herself. She had never felt this way with anyone. Ever. She had tried to tell herself again and again that Logan wasn't her type.

After this evening, however, standing within the safety of his arms, none of that mattered. Being with him felt good and true and right.

Logan dropped a light kiss on her forehead and drew back. Without a word he bent, picked up her crutches and handed them to her. "I better go," he said quietly, his forefinger tracing a light line down the side of her face.

Sandra was surprised at the feeling of deprivation that washed over her when he lowered his hand. Surprised at how incomplete she felt without him. It seemed an overreaction to such a simple thing. But she knew that between her and Logan, things weren't so simple anymore.

"Do you mind coming by at seven tomorrow morning? I want to get an early start" He slipped his hands into his pockets, still watching her.

She shook her head, hoping her voice sounded steadier than she felt. "I don't mind at all."

He smiled, and to Sandra it was like seeing the sun peeking through storm clouds. "I'll see you then."

And on that mundane comment, he walked out the door, leaving behind a distinctly bemused Sandra.

Sandra rolled over in her bed, glancing at the clock. Four o'clock. What had woken her? Her knee felt fine.

There it was again. A rustle, then the thunk of the kitchen door closing. Sandra sat up, her heart thudding in her chest, adrenaline coursing through her. Someone was trying to break in.

Then she heard a tuneless whistle, followed by a muttered question.

Cora was back.

Sandra eased herself out of bed and grabbed her crutches. She stumbled through the darkness toward the crack of light that appeared under her door.

Cora was standing in front of the fridge, one hand on the door, the other rooting through the precious few groceries Sandra had bought with the advance Logan had given her.

"Hey, Cora. What's up?" Sandra asked.

Cora whirled around, her hand pressed to her chest. "Sandra. You scared the living daylights out of me." Then she grinned at her friend. "What do you have to eat?"

Sandra helped Cora put a sandwich together. Cora made a pot of coffee, and they sat at the table.

Sandra found out that Cora hadn't found a job yet. "So I guess it's either head out east or maybe welfare," she said with a casual shrug.

"I thought we were going to try to make our own way in this world. Without help."

"My skills aren't appreciated," she mumbled around a mouthful of sandwich. "Hey, how's the stained glass business? You must have gotten some money."

Sandra explained what had happened as Cora finished the sandwich and made another. Sandra stifled a stab of annoyance at her friend's nonchalant attitude and how easily she helped herself to food that Sandra had paid for.

"I need some money for rent, Cora," Sandra said, crossing her arms on the table. This time she wasn't going to let Cora finesse her way out of paying her share.

"Well, if you're making money, then it's cool."

"No, it isn't cool, Cora. You owe me for gas on the way out here and rent for two months." Sandra frowned. "By the way, how did you get here?"

Cora held up her thumb with a grin. "Beats walking." She took another bite of her sandwich and jumped up. "Hey. Got some pictures."

And for the next half hour, the rent was conveniently forgotten. Sandra was regaled with stories of where Cora had been and some crazy notion of moving to the island where she could make a fortune growing ginseng. But as Sandra listened, she realized that where once she would have been entertained, she found that she grew annoyed with Cora's pipe dreams. Cora never managed to stay with anything longer than six weeks before she got impatient because the money didn't come in fast enough. Then she'd be off to the next thing.

"So, you gonna come?" Cora leaned forward, an expectant gleam in her eye. Sandra sat back, flipping through Cora's pictures, melancholy settling on her. At one time the idea of packing up and leaving might have created a sense of expectation and adventure, but now she knew different.

The excitement of the change would die down, and the new venture wouldn't live up to the high expectations, and Cora would start chafing. It took time to make money, and it never came easy.

"No. I'm not coming." Sandra handed the pictures back with a wry smile.

"Are you nuts?" Cora grabbed the pictures, shaking her head. "This is a great opportunity. The big chance."

"Yah. Just like selling my stained glass to Henri was a great opportunity. I'm still trying to get over that one."

"Okay. Tactical error. But at least you made some money. C'mon. It'll be fun. I mean, what's keeping you here?"

Sandra didn't want to tell her. Didn't want to share the fragile feelings that she knew had as much future as Cora's newest big chance did. "I've got this stained glass job to do," she said instead.

"And after that, why don't you come?"

Because you'll be somewhere else by then, Sandra thought. "I don't know what I'll do. Maybe get a job in Medicine Hat until I get other commissions."

"Don't be an idiot. You'll die of boredom. Like you always do." She looked at Sandra with a knowing smirk. "And I hate to burst your bubble, but you haven't really made as much money cutting glass as you thought you would."

Sandra shrugged Cora's comment away, knowing it for the truth. She swallowed a bubble of panic at the thought of trying, once again, to find out what she really wanted to do. Would she be able to work a steady job as she so casually mentioned to Cora?

But the other side of the coin was Cora and dreams and plans that never, ever came to fruition. Cora and scrimping and being forced to make bad decisions. All this for the sake of preserving a freedom that was illusionary.

And Sandra knew she didn't want to go back to that lifestyle. Not anymore.

"Anyhow, I'm going to bed," Sandra said, getting slowly to her feet. "I have to work tomorrow."

"I just got back," Cora grumbled. "Phone in sick. We need to catch up."

Sandra looked at her friend, remembering many times she had done just that. Sandra was the only one of the two who ever held down a traditional job, and Cora had always encouraged her to skip work. But this job was different. Brittany and Bethany were counting on her. She wasn't going to let them down.

"No. I'm going to work. I'll see you when I'm done."

Cora licked her fingers. "Maybe you will, maybe you won't."

Sandra held her friend's gaze, then shook her head. "If I don't, take care of yourself." Then she turned and hobbled to her bedroom. As she settled in the bed, she realized that not once had Cora asked her what happened to her knee.

"Here's where I'll be staying." Logan handed Sandra a piece of paper. "This is the number of the condo, this one is the office's."

He looked at her bent head as she glanced at the paper. She wore a long skirt today. The same one she had worn the first time she had come here, he realized.

"Thanks. I'm hoping I won't need this," Sandra said,

glancing at him. She gave a little hop and pinned the paper to the bulletin board that served as a message board beside the fridge. Logan had to catch himself from reaching out to make sure she didn't fall.

He'd had to stop himself a number of times this morning from supporting her, helping her up the stairs. It was as if he was looking for an excuse to touch her, to make sure she was real. To show himself what happened last night and the night before that wasn't just loneliness, but emotions that might, just might, have a future.

He glanced at the clock. He had to get going, but he was loath to leave. Ian's timing really stunk, yet at the same time being away from Sandra might be just what Logan needed to put her into perspective.

"Will you be back for supper tomorrow night?" she asked, tossing her hair from her face as she turned to him, resting on her crutches.

Logan shook his head, a wistful tenderness engulfing him. He couldn't stop himself this time and reached out to gently stroke a strand of hair from her face. He didn't want to go, he thought with a sudden yearning as his fingers drifted down her cheek.

He drew in a deep breath, as if to dispel the notion, then dropped his hand and took a step back.

He really needed some time out, he thought, shaken by his reaction to her.

"I'm not sure when I'll be back tomorrow, but it will be later on in the evening."

Sandra nodded, looking down. He waited a moment, as if willing her to look at him, but she kept her eyes resolutely on a point beyond him, just below his shoulders.

He turned and caught a glimpse of two heads quickly withdrawing from the doorway and knew the girls had been spying on them. The thought disconcerted him. If they had seen that slight interaction between him and Sandra, no telling how far their imaginations would run with it.

But there was nothing he could do about that now.

He affected a casual air and sauntered into the main living area. "You girls listen to Sandra, now," he said, holding their gaze. "I don't want to hear about any funny business while I'm gone."

They shook their heads, watching him with shrewd eyes. "We'll be good," Bethany said, giving him a quick hug.

Logan returned the hug, rubbed Brittany's hair and with a quick wave he left.

But as he drove away, he wondered how he would feel about Sandra on his return.

Chapter Twelve

"Why can't we go to the beach now?" Brittany looked up at Sandra, her tone wheedling, her eyes wide with innocence.

"Because we're not finished yet. That's why." Sandra pushed the textbook toward Brittany and opened it again.

"But we can work on this tonight. Uncle Logan isn't here," Bethany added.

"That's no excuse." Sandra frowned at the more docile of the twins, surprised at the disgruntled attitude that had come over her since Logan had left. "You still have to get the day's work done."

Brittany let out a sigh like a gust of wind. "We've been working all year already. Now we have to work all summer. It's just not fair."

Sandra could sympathize. And a few weeks ago, she might have sided with the girls. However, after spending two weeks with them she noticed they both had a tendency to put off what they could.

Logan had been correct. They needed to learn a measure of self-discipline.

The thought of him made her heart wobble. In every quiet moment the memory of his kiss, of his light touch this morning came back with a rush of wonderment and concern. Why was he doing this? And why was she letting it happen? They were worlds apart, yet something drew them together. Something as elemental as loneliness and as basic as a few kisses.

But Sandra knew it was more.

"We could work really hard tomorrow and get it done then," Brittany continued, taking Sandra's momentary lapse in concentration as assent.

Sandra pulled herself back with a jerk, castigating herself for woolgathering. She was acting as silly and as abstracted as a young woman in love. As if she hadn't learned a few hard lessons in that department.

"No, Brittany," she said, hoping she sounded firm. "Once a person starts procrastinating, you're never done."

"But this stuff is boring, and I thought you told us that life should never be boring."

Sandra felt an unwelcome jolt as her words came back to her. "Well, guess what?" Sandra said with a wide grin. "Sometimes I'm wrong. And you are going to find that finishing something boring can make you feel good about yourself. Now let's get back to work."

Both girls let out sighs, and Sandra had to stifle hers. It was a struggle each day to make their lessons not only relevant but interesting. As a result the girls seemed to think that Sandra was there more to entertain than to teach them.

What had made her change her view?

Logan had, Sandra thought. Logan as well as Cora. After spending time with Logan and the girls, Cora was such a contrast. It was as if she saw her friend clearly for the first time. And by doing so, got a look at herself and where she might be headed.

Brittany shut the book Sandra had pushed her way. "I thought that when Uncle Logan left you would be easier on us," she said with a pout.

"Well, you were wrong," she said with a quick grin. "Now back to work."

The rest of the day didn't go much better. By the time supper was over and the dishes were finally done, Sandra had gained a new appreciation and respect for Logan.

She also realized that the girls were far better behaved around him than around her.

She went through another struggle to get the girls to bed at a decent time. But finally they were cleaned up and tucked into their beds.

"Are you going to do our devotions with us?" Bethany asked, her hands folded demurely across her chest.

Sandra glanced at the book that lay on the bedside table between the two girls. "Sure," she said with a nonchalance she didn't feel.

Today had been enough of an epiphany, she thought as she picked up the book. She wasn't sure she needed any further reminders of how wrong her life had been.

But she settled on Bethany's bed, paging through the book until she found the bookmark. At the top of the page was the Bible verse. She read it out loud, a slow ache building at the words from Psalm 90.

May the favor of the Lord our God rest upon us; establish the work of our hands for us—yes, establish the work of our hands.

And what had her hands done that God could establish? she wondered as she paused to swallow past the thickness in her throat. At one time it wouldn't have mattered as much to her, but a different reality had permeated her life.

Logan and his solid trust in God.

Logan and his penetrating questions that had worn down her defenses against people just like him. Logan and the easy way he spoke to God.

"Aren't you going to read?" Bethany asked, sitting up.

Sandra took a deep breath to still her fluctuating emotions and nodded. But the devotional piece hit her even harder than the verses did. It spoke of God-given talents and responsibilities to use those talents. A year ago she might have scoffed at what she read. But the past year had been difficult. Her pride had struggled with her conscience and her knowledge of God.

She finished the piece then listened to the girls' prayers. They prayed for their grandmother, for their uncle Logan and thanked the Lord for the day. Listening to their confidently spoken requests, she harkened back to the time in her life when she would list her own requests with a simple faith that God would take care of her.

And He had.

She just hadn't done much with what He had given her, she realized as she got to her feet.

"Can you kiss us good-night?" Brittany asked as Sandra turned off the bedroom light. "Uncle Logan always does."

With a forced smile Sandra hobbled to the bed, bent and gave Brittany a gentle kiss on her forehead. As she looked at the young girl, her heart warmed. She did the same for Bethany.

"Sleep tight, girls," she whispered, a feeling of completeness surging through her.

Sandra paused in the doorway, looking at the girls, but in her mind she saw Logan's tall form bent over the beds. Her heart flipped, and a curious ache squeezed her heart. Did these girls know how fortunate they were? Logan, who took such good care of them, could just as easily have handed the responsibility to their grandmother.

And then where would they be?

Traipsing around Alaska waiting for inspiration, that's where. Falling even further behind in their schoolwork. She had always maintained that formal education was overrated, but thanks to her education, she had a paying job.

Something she'd not had in a while.

The next day the girls weren't quite as rambunctious, but they still tested her. Sandra had her hands full, keeping them focused and under control.

Lunchtime drifted by, and for the rest of the afternoon, Sandra found herself tensing each time she heard a vehicle. She was waiting for Logan, she realized, catching herself glancing out the window for what must have been the fifth time in an hour.

The afternoon dragged on leaden feet. When they were done they went for a quick swim. Supper was simple. Leftovers from the night before.

They were just finishing the dishes when Sandra heard the faint purr of a vehicle pull up to the front door, then stop.

"Uncle Logan is home," the girls called. They ran out of the kitchen, their dish towels fluttering to the floor in their wake.

Sandra's heart gave a curious lurch, her hands felt suddenly cold, and she had trouble swallowing.

Logan was home.

She bit her lip and pressed her eyelids shut, squeezing away the errant emotions. Logan was her boss. The uncle of her students. Straitlaced and narrow-minded.

Then why had she missed him? Missed his slightly hovering presence, the way he could dominate a room just by standing in the doorway. Missed the way his hazel eyes could hold hers, draw her in.

Pulling herself together, she carefully bent to pick up the towels the girls dropped, making sure she didn't bend her knee. Fitting the crutches under her arms, she followed the girls to the doorway.

"Hey, Uncle Logan," they called waving at him.

"Hey, yourselves," he returned.

Through the open door, over the shoulders of the twins, she watched as he got out of the van and tossed his sunglasses onto his seat. He was wearing a suit, which sat easily on his shoulders. A dark tie cinched the collar of his white shirt, giving him an austere air.

Sandra felt a heaviness in her chest where her heart was. Unreachable, that's what he was. In another world and another place that she had been running away from. A place she couldn't go back to. Not without getting pulled into the vortex of past expectations.

Logan reached into the back, pulled out his suitcase and strode up the walk toward them.

"So how have you been doing?"

Bethany was the first to reach his side, slipping her arm easily through his. "We did all our work."

Brittany was on the other side, relieving him of his suitcase. "And we finished supper. Did you have some?"

"I ate already." He tousled their hair and pulled them close to him, dropping a kiss first on Bethany then Brittany's head.

And Sandra felt a sharp stab of jealousy at their easy rapport. At how nonchalant the girls were about the affection Logan so quickly bestowed on them.

They walked up the stairs and came to a stop in front of Sandra.

She got a smile that did nothing for her composure and a faint wink that made her cling to her crutches in surprise.

"Hi there, Sandra. How are you?"

Simple words. Words she had heard so many times, but hearing Logan speak them gave her a peculiar thrill.

"I'm okay."

"And your knee?" He glanced at her crutches, then at her face, his eyes holding hers just as she remembered.

"It's okay, too."

This was scintillating conversation, she thought wryly, but somehow she couldn't conjure up a humorous comment, a snappy quip. She felt as tongue-tied as any teenage girl in the presence of her crush.

"I'll just go change," he said with another grin. He gave the girls a quick hug and left.

Sandra and the girls settled into the main room, leaving the recliner for Logan.

He was back in record time, his suit replaced with faded blue jeans and a T-shirt.

The heaviness in Sandra's chest drifted away at the sight of his casual clothes. This was a more approachable Logan.

He dropped into the recliner and let out a gusty sigh as he raised the footrest. "Oh, it's good to be off the road," he said, closing his eyes.

The girls sat perched on the edge of the couch, their eyes darting warily from Sandra to Logan, as if looking for any sign that their work had not been in vain.

It hadn't, thought Sandra, with a peculiar hitch in her chest. Being away from Logan and then seeing him again had created a shift in her perception of him, in her feelings toward him.

And don't forget the kisses.

Sandra felt her cheeks flush. She didn't want to feel this way, knew it shouldn't happen. Her and Logan. They were just too different.

And yet…

She glanced at him and caught his steadfast gaze. It was as if his eyes could see what she didn't want to acknowledge.

Her attraction to him.

"Did you finish what you needed to?" she asked, aware that the twins weren't going to contribute to this conversation at all.

Knowing them, they were probably planning their escape so Logan and Sandra could be conveniently alone.

"It went okay." Logan's deep voice, now familiar, seemed to surround her.

Sandra didn't know how to respond to that. She glanced at the twins again, but they were determinedly quiet.

"Girls, maybe your uncle would like something to drink?"

Brittany jumped up and grabbed her sister by the arm. "Some soda or orange juice?" she asked as she pulled Bethany toward the kitchen.

"Orange juice," Logan said with a wry grin.

The girls left, and Logan and Sandra were alone.

They glanced at each other and then away. Sandra scrabbled through her mind, trying to come up with something, anything.

Logan sat up and lowered the footrest.

Sandra swallowed as he got to his feet. What was he going to do?

"Here's your orange juice, Uncle Logan." Bethany came into the room, concentrating on the glass of juice in her hands. She looked up, her steps faltered and she almost dropped the glass. She set it carefully on the end table beside Logan's recliner and darted a quick look over her shoulder. "I think I'm tired," she announced.

Brittany came up behind her with a plate of cookies and frowned at her sister. Then her glance ticked over Logan and Sandra, and she nodded. "Me, too. I think we should go to bed."

"I just got home," Logan said, biting one corner of his lip.

The barely subdued sparkle in his eye showed Sandra he knew the girls were up to their usual tricks. And the grin that slowly spread across his face showed her he didn't seem to mind one bit.

"You and Sandra can come and tuck us in, if you want."

Sandra caught Logan's helpless look. "I guess, if Sandra wants."

But Sandra remembered last night too clearly. And because of her changing feelings toward Logan, she wasn't too sure she was ready for another reminder from the Lord in the form of the twins' evening devotions.

"I'll just stay here," she said. "I should leave pretty soon, anyhow."

Logan held her eyes, his expression softening. Her heart gave a funny little quiver, and she looked away. This was getting ridiculous, she thought, pleating the material of her loose skirt as he went upstairs.

She should leave right now. Things had already gone further than she could deal with.

She heard water running and the faint rumble of Logan's voice, the excited voices of the girls. Then a cry of dismay, and Logan was speaking again.

She wondered what he had to tell them. Wondered what they might find to complain about this time. She really had to go, she thought. Whatever was building between her and Logan, if indeed anything was, it was a waste of time. He was leaving next week and she at the end of the month. Her rent was paid up until then, and after that she had to come up with a new plan. But what?

She didn't know what was supposed to come next.

"Well, I think the girls are settled for the night," Logan said, coming down the stairs. "They said they were very tired." He stopped in front of Sandra, his thumbs slung in the front belt loops of his pants. "What do you think?"

Sandra looked at him, the banked gleam in his eye quickening her pulse. "I think that they are very choosy about which reality they are going to select."

"I just hope they don't select sneaking out again."

"Well, I'm here. And I was the one they were sneaking out to see." Sandra forced a smile to her face as the memory of that night came crashing back.

"That night seems like a long time ago instead of just a couple of weeks," he said softly.

Sandra felt a fragment of fear shiver through her.

He was right. In the past few days much had changed, and yet nothing had. She was still a temporary fixture in his life, and he in hers.

The atmosphere was beginning to feel charged, and

Sandra was eager to dispel it, yet not so eager to go home just yet.

"The girls were telling me about your project—that you were having some difficulty with it. Did you get it done?"

Logan shook his head, dropping to the couch beside her. He lay his head back and laced his fingers over his stomach, his mouth pursed in a wry grin. "Nope. Just can't seem to get it." He rolled his head to face her. "But I've decided I'm not going to obsess over it. If I get it I get it, if I don't..." He lifted his hands off his stomach in a gesture of resignation. "God has never failed to take care of me yet."

Sandra reached for sarcasm, her best defense against the rash of feelings this man brought out in her. "My goodness. Full speed ahead to prosperity, and Logan Napier is going to let a chance for fame and fortune slip through his fingers."

Logan shook his head lightly, laughing. "You know me better than that."

His voice was low, almost caressing, and Sandra felt all the unraveling ends of her life slowly become whole in his presence.

"Yes," she agreed. "I do." She looked away. "But I'd still like to see the drawings you've been working on."

Logan sighed. "Okay. You asked for it." He pushed himself from the couch and left. He soon came back holding a sheaf of papers. "I've been fooling with a number of ideas, but I can't say I'm really thrilled with any of them." He shuffled through the papers and gave Sandra a quizzical glance over the top of them. "You realize I'm making myself totally vulnerable to that sharp tongue of yours by doing this."

Sandra held his gaze and gave him a careful smile. "I'll be gentle," she said.

Then he gave her the papers, and she felt as if something fine and delicate had shifted between them.

He sat beside her as she went through the sheaf of papers. Sandra was impressed with his expertise. Somehow the drawings she saw didn't mesh with the straightforward image Logan presented.

"So, what's wrong with them?" she asked, turning back to the first page.

Logan took the pages from her and studied them, his elbows resting on his knees.

"They look like every single house in Calgary, that's what."

Sandra angled her head as if to get a better look. This brought her closer to Logan. Fine shivers danced up her arm at his proximity.

"Not really." She temporized and cleared her throat. "What do these people want?" *Keep the topic safe,* she reminded herself.

"They want it built into the hill so that you can only see part of it when you come onto the yard." Logan showed her another view, and Sandra had to keep herself from catching her breath. Even though it was just lines on paper, she could see that this was going to be an impressive home.

"I'm going with flying buttresses between these pillars to hold back the lateral load. There's going to be a lot of concrete because the soil is quite sandy."

Sandra nodded, trying to look knowledgeable, but when Logan glanced sidelong at her, his smile told her she wasn't succeeding.

"Anyhow, it looks cold and austere and I don't know how to soften it." Logan shuffled through the papers once more, slowly shaking his head. "If the Jonserads had a clear idea of what they wanted, it would be easier. Mrs. Jonserad kept talking about light and air and space, and all Mr. Jonserad wanted was a room he could smoke cigars in."

Sandra's laugh bubbled up. "So she needs the space to get rid of the cigar smoke."

"I guess." He scratched his head.

Sandra gently tugged on the top piece of paper. "Do you mind?" she asked, holding out her other hand for the pencil she knew Logan always carried in his pocket.

He gave it to her, and with another quick glance to him for permission, she took his initial rendering and squinted at it. Then she turned it sideways and held it up. She looked at it from all possible angles.

"What about if you soften this part of the house?" she asked, pointing with the pencil at the front entrance. "Put in a curved window."

"It wouldn't work with the other lines," Logan said, leaning closer. "I've done the math."

"Oh, you and your math," she chided with a light smile. "You have to learn to let go and let your creativity flow."

"You sound like my mother."

"That's good. She's a very creative person."

"A lackadaisical person." Logan huffed.

"She wasn't always wrong, you know. As I said before, she raised you, and you turned out just fine."

Logan grinned. "You think?" He turned serious. "You may be right. But I know I am, too. Your father wasn't all wrong, either."

Sandra held his gaze, sensing the seriousness of the moment. But she couldn't hold his eyes. She looked at the drawing. "It would work if you repeated the idea here." She drew a few quick strokes on each end of the house.

"That looks good. But from a construction viewpoint, it would be a nightmare to work in. Raises the costs substantially without enough aesthetic gain." He held out his hand, and without a word, she handed him the pencil. He made a few corrections.

"How about this?" She took the pencil, but as she drew, she poked a hole in the paper. "Oh, no. I'm sorry."

"No, no. Don't worry," Logan reassured her. "Let's go sit at the table. It'll be easier."

They moved and continued working, bouncing ideas off each other. Sandra didn't have the first clue about architecture or construction. When Logan started talking about sheet pilings, rebar and angle of repose she was lost.

What she did recognize was the energy flowing between the two of them as slowly the rendering began to change.

Logan grew excited, nodding as she made suggestions.

He got a fresh pad of sketch paper and started over again.

"I wonder if a stained glass window would work in here," Sandra suggested. "Mrs. Jonserad did mention that she wanted to work with light."

Logan angled her a sly, sidewise look. "A little plug for your own business?" he teased.

Sandra shrugged, feeling her face warm. "Maybe. But I like the idea."

"I do, too." Logan pursed his lips as he considered it. "That could work. If we go with a modern concept to echo the basic design of the house."

Logan made a few quick lines, grinning as he did so. "This is great," he enthused, the front view of the home taking shape as he sketched. "Look, I think this would work." He finished and laid the paper down, as if to have a better look at it. Then he slung an arm over Sandra's shoulders. "Wow. I'm really impressed."

Sandra let him pull her against him, allowing them this moment of closeness. Just a few moments, she promised herself, letting his warmth and strength fill the empty spots of her life. She closed her eyes as if to concentrate on the moment, to store it in a place where she might take it out later on. When Logan was out of her life.

Then, just as she was about to pull away, Logan shifted his weight and with his free hand cupped her chin.

Her eyes flew open in time to see him lower his head. Then his face became a blur as his lips touched hers, warm and inviting. Sandra couldn't stop her hands from slipping around his neck, her fingers from tangling themselves in his thick hair. She knew she should pull away, stop this, but her lonely heart, her empty soul hungered for all she knew Logan was and all she knew he could give her.

Logan touched his lips to her forehead, her hair.

She bent her head and slowly lowered her hands. A careful withdrawal.

Logan sat back, his hands toying with her fingers. "Now what, Sandra?" he asked, his voice husky. "Where do we go from here?"

She couldn't answer his question because she didn't know. She had only known him a few weeks, but tonight she had felt a connection with him that was as old as the earth.

"I thought being away from you for a few days would help put things into perspective," Logan said, his thumb tracing a path across the back of her hand. He looked at her then, his gaze direct, unyielding. "I didn't expect that I would miss you."

Once again Sandra couldn't look away, and once again she didn't want to.

He had missed her.

Why did those simple words from this particular man make her heart sing? They shouldn't, she reminded herself. She shouldn't be letting herself get caught up in this man and his life. They were too different. She didn't know what she wanted, whereas he knew exactly where he was headed.

It would never work.

Chapter Thirteen

Logan stared at Sandra's bent head and wondered what was happening to him.

He slipped his thumbs over Sandra's hands again, his mind arguing with his heart. Nothing had changed in their lives. They had merely gotten to know each other better.

Yet he knew—sensed that Sandra felt a dissatisfaction with her life. He remembered something she had said just before he left—"I lost my way."

He thought of what he had found out this afternoon. He knew he had to tell Sandra.

"I, uh, got a message from my secretary." Logan kept his hold on her hands, unsure what to hope for. What to pray for. "She found a tutor for me who's willing to start Monday and work for the rest of the summer."

He felt Sandra's slight withdrawal, the gentle tug of her hands. But he didn't let go. He had more to say.

He looked at her, wishing she would do the same.

"But I was going to ask you if you could come with us to Calgary. If you'd be willing to work for me there."

It was a long shot. Maybe even a dumb suggestion.

All he knew was that it took only a few hours away from her to make him realize how much she had come to mean to him. He wasn't sure where this would go, he only knew that somehow he wasn't ready to let her leave.

"I don't know," Sandra replied, her voice unsteady.

It wasn't what he hoped to hear, but he knew Sandra well enough to know she wasn't going to commit to something like this immediately.

"I have a friend who's away for the month of August on a project. He always told me that if I could find someone to live in his condo, that would be great. You'd have a place to stay and a place to finish your lamps. Maybe even find another job."

He realized he was pressuring her, pushing her into a corner. But he wanted to make sure that all the options and possibilities were laid out before she made a decision.

Sandra looked at him, her eyes holding his in a long look that cut directly to his heart. "I'd like to think about this."

Logan nodded. Of course she couldn't make a decision right away. They both realized the portent of what he was suggesting. "I understand. But I need to tell you that no matter what you decide, the girls and I are leaving tomorrow night."

Another absent nod from Sandra. Then she finally succeeded in pulling her hands out of his. "I should go," she whispered, looking around for her crutches.

Logan picked them up and handed them to her as

she rose. She wouldn't look at him. Wouldn't make eye contact.

He wished there was some way he could understand what was going through her mind.

"You don't have to walk me home," she said, moving toward the door.

Logan ignored that remark as he held the door open for her and followed her into the cool of the evening.

As they made their way to her house, Logan felt as if he'd made himself vulnerable to her by offering her the job. It was like an echo of the approval he kept hoping he would get from his parents for what he was doing.

But what else could he have done? he wondered. He couldn't just leave her. Not after discovering how much he missed her. He gave Sandra a quick sidewise glance, surprised to see her looking directly at him.

"What are you thinking about?" He couldn't help asking.

Sandra smiled lightly, then looked ahead. "I'm thinking that those two girls may not have parents, but they are the luckiest girls I've met."

"Why do you say that?"

"Because they have an uncle who looks out for them. Who takes good care of all aspects of their lives. I know that's not how I talked a few weeks ago," Sandra continued, stopping at the end of her walk. She shook her thick hair, glancing at him. "You're a good man, Logan Napier. And you've done a good job with Brittany and Bethany."

Even as her compliment warmed his heart, her words sounded suspiciously like words of farewell. A tying off of loose ends.

In the diffused light of evening, her eyes were like dark smudges in her face. Unreadable and mysterious.

Logan wanted to touch her, to establish some kind of connection, but sensed that this was not the time or place. He would see her tomorrow, he reasoned. She hadn't given him a definite answer one way or the other. He had to bide his time.

And trust.

"Thanks for that, Sandra," he said quietly, rocking on his heels. "And I'll see you tomorrow." He couldn't stop himself from reaching out, brushing his knuckle over her cheek. Then he left.

Sandra watched him go, wavering between calling him back and keeping her mouth shut. His offer of a job was a turning point in their relationship. A change that would take her irrevocably in another direction. Could she go?

Could she stay here when the thought of him and the girls leaving created a dull ache in her chest, a sense of losing something pure and real?

Yet to go with them would mean going back to Calgary, the place her father lived. She wasn't ready for him and wanted to see him on her own terms. She had dreamed so many times of being able to show him that she could make it on her own. That she didn't need the degree he had forced her to get.

She wanted to prove that her choices were valid. That she could finish what she started and make money doing it.

Going to Calgary as the girls' tutor was not what she

had planned. But she knew it could lead to more than she was able and maybe even willing to give Logan and his nieces.

Sandra pushed open the door of her cabin. Cora was draped all over their couch, papers scattered around her. She looked up and grinned as Sandra entered.

"I decided to stay for a couple of days. I need a base of operations for now."

Sandra nodded. *And you needed something to eat,* she thought.

"And how was your day of coaxing young girls into streamlined learning processes?" Cora asked.

"It went well." Sandra sat down in the lumpy chair across from the sofa.

"And I noticed that a very good-looking man escorted you to the door." Cora grinned at Sandra and tucked a pencil behind her ear.

"The girls' uncle. My boss." Sandra said the words as much for herself as for Cora.

Does a boss stroke your cheek when he says good-night? Does he kiss you like Logan did?

Sandra could feel the heat rising up her neck and warming her cheeks at the very thought of Logan. But fortunately Cora was too busy making some notations on one of the papers scattered in front of her to notice.

"So how long are you going to work for him?"

"He and the girls are going to Calgary tomorrow night."

"Hey, did you know that Jane is in Calgary now? I saw her. She said hey and gave me her number." Cora fished in the pocket of her pants and pulled out a card. "If you're going there you can look her up. I think she's looking for a roommate."

Sandra took the card. "I don't think I'm going to Calgary," she said. "He found a tutor there."

Cora pulled a face. "Lousy luck for you, girl. Two jobs lost in one evening."

Sandra frowned. "What do you mean, two jobs?"

Cora got up and handed Sandra a piece of paper with a scribbled message on it. "I took this phone call earlier today."

Sandra read it. Quickly at first. Then once again as the words slowly sank in, heavy and hard.

The restaurant that had requested her lamps had changed ownership. The new owner didn't feel obligated to keep the contract. So he was canceling the order.

Sandra thought of all the materials she had sitting in the little room that served as her workshop. All the money they represented.

The failure this represented. Another job she wouldn't be able to finish.

She carefully folded the paper, futility washing over her like a wave.

You're a failure. Nothing but a failure.

The harsh and painful words her father threw at her as she left home echoed through her mind.

He was right.

"So, what are you going to do?" Cora asked.

Sandra ran her finger along the sharp edge of the paper, wishing Cora was gone. Wishing she was alone.

"I don't know."

"You thought any more about coming with me?"

Sandra looked across the table at Cora, glanced at the papers she had scattered around her. How many times since she met Cora had she seen the same scenario? Cora full of plans and schemes. None of them successful.

And she was no better, she realized.

You started with a no to your family. That doesn't take you anywhere, if you don't know what you are going to say yes to.

Logan's words sifted through her mind. He was so right. Her decisions had been made as responses, rather than as beginnings.

Please, Lord. Show me what I should do.

The prayer was involuntary, but even as she formulated the words, she knew the answer.

"I'm not going," she said firmly.

"What?" Cora stood up, shaking her head. "What else are you going to do?"

"I don't know, but I'm going to figure out my own life." She wasn't quite sure how, she just had a feeling that she had to start making normal plans.

With what? Guidance from God?

Maybe.

Sandra endured an instant of pain at the thought of Logan. At the thought of the girls he was trying to raise to be responsible citizens.

Unlike her.

"I'm going to bed," she told Cora. "I'll see you in the morning."

Cora held her gaze, as if testing her, then with a casual shrug looked away. "Sure thing."

It took Sandra no time to wash up, but as she lay in bed alone, sorrow engulfed her. Sorrow and the haunting reality that once again she had to start over.

Sandra slowed as she came closer to Logan's cabin. This morning she had almost chickened out and written a note.

But last night she had made a decision to make changes in her life. And one of the changes was to face things head-on instead of running away.

Talking to Logan face to face was part of the deal, she figured.

She had gone over every possibility in her mind. Had tried to reason everything out. But it all came back to the fact that the independent life she thought she had carved out for herself was a sham. The news Cora had given her yesterday only underlined the total failure of her plans.

Of her life. And she knew it wasn't fair to Logan to pretend that she had anything to offer him.

Sandra took a slow breath, sent up a quick prayer for strength and worked her way up the stairs. She didn't need the crutches anymore and had decided to bring them to Logan. He knew where they had come from and would probably return them for her.

She raised her hand to knock on the door.

Don't do it, just leave. He doesn't have to know. You'll never see them again.

But she had done enough of that. She knew that she cared too much for him to just walk away. Sandra swallowed a knot of pain that formed in her chest.

Please, Lord, help me get through this.

She knocked on the door, hard. From inside the cabin she heard a flurry of steps and then the twins were at the door, grinning at her with expectation.

"So, you gonna come with us?" Bethany asked.

Sandra smiled at the girls, the knot getting larger. She had truly come to care for these two. Had enjoyed, more than she thought she would, the challenge of teaching them.

"Is your uncle Logan up yet?" she managed to ask, pleased that her voice sounded so normal as she avoided answering Bethany.

"Of course he is." Brittany's voice held a note of surprise that Sandra had to ask.

"I thought he might be sleeping in, that's all."

Brittany rolled her eyes. "As if. I don't think he went to bed at all last night." Then she grinned at Sandra. "But he's not grumpy. Come in."

Sandra limped through the door. *Now what?* she thought. *Sit? Stand? How long is it going to take to tell Logan what I've decided?*

"Hi there." Logan entered the room, a pencil stuck behind his ear, a smile creasing his unshaven face. His rumpled shirt was tucked into faded blue jeans. His feet were bare. The overall effect was a complete contradiction to the very put-together Logan she knew.

His hazel eyes lit briefly as they held hers, then he glanced at his clothes. "Sorry about this. I was busy most of the night." He gestured to her. "Come. I want to show you something."

Against her will, Sandra walked slowly to the room where he worked, the girls trailing behind her.

"Look, I think I got it." Logan was bent over his drafting table, sorting through the papers there. He pulled one out, turned and handed it to her.

Sandra didn't look at him, but concentrated fiercely on the heavy paper she held. The house she saw there took her breath away. Elegant yet welcoming. A harmony of windows and angles softened by a large, half-round stained glass window echoed by two smaller ones flanking it. It was a home as well as a statement.

"It's beautiful," she whispered.

Logan was beside her. Sandra could feel the warmth of his arm as it brushed hers. She felt her eyes begin a dangerous prickling and knew that if she didn't pull herself together she was going to cry.

"I didn't get it right until you helped me," he said quietly, his deep voice beside her creating a circle of intimacy that excluded the girls, who were avidly ignoring the two of them. "I wish I could tell you how much I appreciate it."

Sandra bit her lip, handing him the paper. "I didn't do anything, Logan." She blinked carefully, thankful that no tears escaped. "I just doodled. You're the one with the talent and the ideas." She gave him a weak smile, wishing she could tell him and go. Wishing he wouldn't look at her with those warm hazel eyes that promised so much.

Promised her what she didn't deserve. She was exactly what he had initially said she was, she thought, looking away. Irresponsible and selfish. She had taken an education from her father, and even though she had tried to send him what money she could spare, it would have barely paid the interest on any loan she would have had to take out. She had this job with Brittany and Bethany thanks to that education.

"Look, I've thought about your offer," she said quickly before she changed her mind. "It's great, and I'd love to continue working with the girls...." Her voice faltered, and she took a slow breath, wondering how she was going to tell him. "But I've got other plans and—" she lifted her shoulder in a faint shrug, chancing a quick look at him "—I don't think it would work."

Surprising how thoroughly a face could change expression without moving many muscles, she thought, watching Logan's features alter from open friendliness to reserved animosity.

The girls cried out, but a quick glance from Logan silenced them. He could do that so easily, Sandra thought. He had much better control over the girls than she ever could hope to. He, who claimed to have no stability in his life, had more than she did. And she, who had been raised by dependable parents and put through school, was rootless and drifting. Each thought dismantled the life she thought she had built for herself.

A life with no foundation, she thought with a throb of sorrow. A selfish life built on sand.

What could she possibly give this man?

"What do you mean, you don't think it would work?" Logan asked.

This was harder than she had anticipated. Sandra held his angry gaze, and as usual took refuge in humor.

"You know me," she said lightly. "I'm just here until I can find a really good fast-food job."

"And that's your ambition?" Logan shook his head. "I think I know you better than that."

His unexpected defense almost wore her down. But she knew she had to stay firm. She didn't deserve Logan. Didn't deserve the steady, caring person he was.

"Well, you know what they say about ambition. It's just a poor excuse for not having enough sense to be lazy." She forced another smile, then began walking out the door. She had to go. The longer she stayed, the weaker her resolve.

She knew that something was happening between her and Logan. Intrinsically she knew he wasn't the flirting type. He had kissed her, had held her, and she had responded to him. He was growing more and more important to her.

And so were those dear, exasperating, sweet girls.

But they all deserved better than what she had to offer.

Brittany and Bethany were beside her, hanging on to her, pleading with her. She stopped, wishing they would leave.

"Sandra." Logan said her name. Against her better judgment, she turned to him.

He stood facing her, his hands on his hips, chewing on one corner of his mouth. He laughed, a short, bitter sound. "So this is it? You're just going to walk away? No explanations, no solid reason."

How much had changed, she thought, unable to hold his angry gaze. "When I took this job on I knew it was only going to be temporary." She chanced a quick look at him. "And so did you."

"Yeah. I guess that's true." He shook his head, then laughed again. "I owe you for this week yet," he said. "Let me write you out a check."

Sandra wanted this to be done but also knew that she would need the money he was going to give her, so she waited.

He yanked open a drawer and pulled out a checkbook. He filled the check in and ripped it out of the book, handing it to her without looking up.

Sandra took it, then Logan held out his hands to the girls. "C'mon, Bethy. Brit. Let Sandra go."

Sandra watched them walk to Logan's side. Where they belonged.

Without a look behind her she walked slowly out of the cabin, down the steps and to her home.

She didn't want to think about him. Didn't want to wonder what his opinion of her was. He was out of her life, she out of his.

But as she paused by the door of her cabin, her heart a heavy stone in her chest, she knew she would never forget him.

Chapter Fourteen

"Come on down, girls." Logan called up the stairs. "We're ready to leave."

He and the girls had spent most of the morning packing their clothes, personal items and any groceries they had into the van. He had originally planned to stay another day. To go to church. In some optimistic part of his mind he had hoped he might talk Sandra into coming with them.

He leaned against the stairs' handrail a moment, surprised at the dull ache created by the thought of her. Sandra, as she had told him from the beginning, had her own agenda, her own plans. That he thought she might change had been his fault, not hers.

He took a deep breath and called once more.

Two glum faces appeared at the railing. Déjà vu, thought Logan. Less than three weeks ago the same scenario had been played out.

He could hardly believe it had been that short a time.

Indeed, he felt as if everything in his life had shifted. As if nothing would be the same anymore.

The girls clumped down the stairs, dejection showing in their every movement. The ache in Logan's chest solidified into anger with Sandra at the girls' sorrow. She had let the twins down, as well.

In silence they left the cabin and got in the van. Low clouds dropped a light rain on them as they left. Appropriate weather, thought Logan, as he made the last curve around the end of the lake.

A few cars were ahead of them, driving slowly, held up by a truck pulling a wide load. Logan tapped the steering wheel, anxious to be gone.

"Look, there's Sandra."

Logan's heart jumped in his chest. He peered through the rain to see where Bethany was pointing.

Sure enough, on the side of the road stood Sandra. Hitchhiking.

The story had come full circle indeed.

"Let's pick her up, okay?" Bethany turned a pleading look to Logan, who wondered at the irony of the predicament.

He bit his lip, considering. Ever since Sandra told him she couldn't come with them, a feeling that something wasn't right had nagged at him. She wasn't being forthright. He made a quick decision. He was going to pick her up. Make her tell him.

"Oh, no. Someone else is going to give her a ride," Brittany called.

Sure enough, a car two vehicles ahead of them pulled over. Sandra picked up her knapsack, slung a duffel bag over her shoulder and started walking toward the car. At the last moment she glanced up, her hair sticking in dark strings to her face. She froze, staring at them.

Did he see sorrow in her face or was he just being optimistic? He stepped on the brake.

But then she looked away, got in the car and closed the door. The car drove away.

"Why didn't she come over?" Bethany said, her voice full of pain.

"I guess she has her own plans," Logan snapped.

He stepped on the gas, swung past the vehicle ahead of them. In seconds he was past the truck carrying a mobile home and in minutes a few miles ahead of the car with Sandra in it.

They would forget her, Logan figured. It would take a little time, but the girls would get over her.

And so would he. So would he.

"I'll see you tomorrow, Sandra."

Sandra waved at her fellow cashier as she walked across the parking lot of the grocery store toward her car. She didn't want to think about tomorrow. About coming back here again. She'd only been working at this job for a month, but she was already tired of it. No staying power, she realized. Couldn't stick with anything. Just like her dad said. Just like Logan had implied.

The thought of Logan made her close her eyes and lean against the car in a moment of weakness. Made her wish that one day she would be able to think of him without experiencing this utter sense of loss. This sense that something wonderful and beautiful had been just out of her reach.

She got into her car and started it. The engine turned over the first time, and she made her way home.

Her apartment was a bachelor suite on the third floor, and by the time she trudged up the stairs and down the hall to the door, she could hear the muffled sound of the phone.

She shoved her key into the lock, the ringing galvanizing her into action. Who would be calling her? she wondered as she finally got the door open. She ran to the phone, jerked it off the hook and sucked in a breath, willing her pounding heart to still.

"Hello," she said slowly. "Sandra here."

"Hey, Sandy, it's Jane."

Funny that her heart, still beating so hard, should plummet so heavily with disappointment. "Hi, Jane." She didn't know why she expected Logan to phone. He didn't even know her phone number. Didn't know where she was staying.

"So how's your cashier job?"

"Tiring, boring, exhausting. But it pays bills." Sandra tucked the phone under her chin as she bent to unlace her running shoes. "I'm getting real good at making change," she said dryly as she kicked off her shoes. She sighed lightly as she sank into a nearby chair, glad to be off her feet.

"Have you considered coming to Calgary to work?"

Sandra bit her lip. "I'm not sure."

"I've got a posting listed here for a job you might

be interested in." Jane explained how she pulled it off the bulletin board at the school where she worked as a secretary. "The girl had an accident and won't be coming back. Bad for her, but it might be good for you. I know you're more than qualified for this job, girl."

Sandra hesitated. "I'm not sure, Jane."

"C'mon. Calgary's big enough for you and your father."

Sandra rotated her feet, thinking about going back to a job with no future. A job that paid minimum wage. Too much to die on, not enough to live on. Not on her own.

"I suppose. What's the job?"

"Teacher's aide. And if you get in with this school, I'm pretty sure you could get a teaching job. I know of two teachers who will be quitting in the next year or so."

"Teaching, eh?"

"I know you're thinking about it, Sandra Bachman. From what you told me about those girls, I get the feeling you enjoyed doing that kind of work."

Sandra had connected with Jane when Cora moved out. In no time they had caught up, reestablished their old acquaintence. Sandra had told Jane about Brittany and Bethany. But not about Logan. That still hurt too much.

"I did."

"So why not come down and apply?"

Sandra bit her lip, considering.

"What do you have to lose except a day of work?" Jane insisted.

"I've got a day off coming to me, anyway," Sandra said slowly.

"Think about it. And send in your application, just in case." Jane gave her the address, and Sandra copied it down on the back of a utility bill she had to pay yet. "The money is good, and you can move in with me. That'll save you a few dollars, too."

"I'll think about it," Sandra said. "It'll mean quitting another job, though."

"Oh, c'mon, Sandra. You have other qualifications. No one would fault you for wanting to use them."

"Maybe." Sandra hesitated. She knew she wasn't using her talents properly. And she also knew that avoiding this job just because she would be using the degree her father paid for was being foolish in the extreme. "But I might not get the job."

"Trust me, Sandra. I know who's been applying. They'll be happy to have you."

"I'll send in my résumé. That's all I'll promise," she said slowly. "Take care, and thanks for calling." Then she hung up the phone.

Supper was quick. She heated leftovers from the day before and ate standing against the counter. She looked out the small window that faced west and another apartment block. Thankfully it was fall and the evenings were cooler. When she first moved in, it was still August, and the apartment was like a stifling oven.

Sandra glanced at her watch and yawned. Too early to go to bed. She wandered into the living room, and with a smile picked up the Bible she had set on the small end table that came with the apartment. She'd been reading it more often lately, finding comfort in the pages that were barely worn. Each time she read it she thought of Logan and his solid faith. Each time she read it she wondered if she would ever see him again.

She unwittingly opened the book to the dedication page. Given to her on the occasion of her high school graduation. From her parents.

Sandra traced her mother's signature, her father's. She missed her mother, but in one way Sandra was glad that her mother had been spared knowing what was happening in Sandra's life. Of course, had her mother still been alive, Sandra wondered if she would have left home.

Still holding the Bible, Sandra dropped onto the couch. She turned to the Psalms. She came to Psalm 103. She read, then stopped at verse twelve. *As far as the east is from the west, so far has he removed our transgressions from us. As a father has compassion on his children, so the Lord has compassion on those who fear him.*

Would her father have compassion? Sandra wondered. If she were to show up on his doorstep, would he let her in?

She fingered the pages as she remembered his final words of anger. Telling her she was ungrateful, irresponsible. That she no longer had a home with him. That she didn't need to come back.

So what if she got this job? Would it prove anything to him? Did she even need to?

Sandra felt a sob slip past her lips. A faint cry that

echoed like an empty house. In spite of their angry confrontations, she still loved him.

She bent her head. Covered her face. Then, slowly, haltingly, she began to pray. She'd been doing more of that lately, too. *Give me wisdom,* she prayed. *Show me clearly what I should be doing. Show me how I can fix all the things that are wrong in my life.* She knew what she was doing—working as a cashier—was just another way of putting off what she had to do. She wondered if the phone call from Jane wasn't enough of an indication for her.

She prayed a little longer, praying for her father. Praying for Logan and the girls. It brought them nearer for a moment, and eased her loneliness.

"This is absolutely amazing." Delores Jonserad put down the drawing, shaking her head. "How did you know?"

Logan frowned, trying not to lean forward in the chair he was perched on. "How did I know what?"

"What we really wanted." Delores glanced at her husband, who was staring at the second and third renderings of the house. "Isn't this wonderful, Nathan? Can't you just feel the space?"

"If you want I can give you a visual walk-through on the computer." Logan pulled out his laptop, trying to still the shaking in his fingers. Delores and Nathan Jonserad had chosen three final designs, and Logan's was one of them. He didn't want to look overeager, nor did he want to look unprofessional. So much was riding on this.

Nathan shrugged, laying the papers on the table. "I don't think so."

Logan tried not to let the heaviness of his disappointment show. Having the Jonserads accept his design meant more than just the possibility of more work thrown his way.

He couldn't explain his deep-seated desire to see the plan he and Sandra had designed come to fruition. It was as if it was the only connection he had with the woman who had walked out of his life two months ago. A woman he hadn't been able to forget.

"I like it the best, anyhow." Ignoring his wife's angry glare, Nathan Jonserad took his pipe out of his pocket and polished it slowly, like an apple, on his shirt. "It doesn't make our house look like a museum. Or Tara. Or Green Gables. Like the others." He winked at his wife and put his pipe away. "I think we'll go with your plan. It has a spark of creativity that I haven't seen in any of the others."

Logan wanted to jump up, to cheer, but instead he satisfied himself with a brief clench of his hands and a quick prayer of thanks. "That's wonderful," he said, smiling at Nathan and Delores. "Just wonderful." He wished he could share this with Sandra. Wished she could be here.

He dismissed the errant thought. He had been thinking about her too much because of this project. Each time he saw the design they had created together, he thought of her.

Someday, he would be able to drive along a city street and not have his heart jump each time he saw a woman with a backpack, long brown hair and a jaunty air. Someday he would not wonder how she was doing and where she was.

Someday, but not yet.

Logan leaned back in his seat, glancing at his watch. He was half an hour early, but he was on his way from a construction site and was done for the day.

He crossed his arms over his chest and opened the window to let some fresh air into the van. It was the end of September, and the weather was still balmy and warm. Fall would come soon enough, he figured, and then winter, bleak and cold.

The thought of spending another winter in the condo with the two girls sent a shiver down his back. He really had to go looking for a house with more room. A place with a front and back door, a yard they could play in on warm days.

A slender figure walking past the van caught his eye. Tall, dark hair.

He tapped his fingers on the steering wheel as he laughed at himself. Of course it wasn't Sandra. Just like the woman he'd seen downtown a week ago wasn't Sandra. Nor was the woman who delivered their mail.

He was doing well. This morning was the last time he had thought of her until now.

Then the woman glanced toward the school, stopping.

Logan's heart thudded against his rib cage, and before he could even think, he was out of the vehicle.

"Sandra?"

Her head spun around, her hand pressed against her chest. She turned, her face pale.

"Hey, Logan," she said slowly.

Logan suppressed a light shiver as his eyes traveled hungrily over her familiar features. There were dozens of questions he wanted answered, but he settled for the common, the inane.

"How've you been?"

"Okay. I've been okay." She hugged herself as if chilled. "I've got a job here in Calgary."

"Doing what?" He wanted to know, yet didn't. Probably some other crazy scheme. Just like his mother.

"I'm a teacher's aide." She laughed, a harsh sound. "Surprise, surprise."

"A teacher's aide," he repeated, surprised at the surge of anger her reply gave him. "That's not much different than being a tutor, is it?"

Sandra looked away, but not before Logan caught the brief flash of pain in her eyes.

He felt immediately contrite. It was really none of his business what she was doing. She had every right to turn down a temporary job in favor of a more permanent one.

"What about your stained glass work?"

Sandra flipped her hair back, avoiding his gaze. "I decided to give that up."

"I see." He shouldn't be surprised. How long had his mother managed to stay with anything? Two months? Three?

Was Sandra any different than his mother, after all? For a time, he had thought she was.

He couldn't forget their last night together. Working on the Jonserad plan. The energy that flowed between them. The ideas that flew around. The vitality she created. Before she left, he sincerely thought something was building between them. Had he been so badly fooled by her?

"So, have you heard from the Jonserads?" she asked, breaking the silence.

Logan's eyes snapped to hers. It was as if she had read his mind. "Yes, I have," he said slowly, still looking into her deep brown eyes. He didn't want to be mesmerized by them. But he couldn't look away. Nor did he want to. "They chose our plan."

As Sandra's smile spread across her face, his carefully constructed defenses melted as easily as frost beneath a morning sun.

"Really?" she said. "That's great. When did this happen?"

"About a week ago."

"That's wonderful."

Silence pushed them apart. Logan knew this would be a good time to say goodbye, but he couldn't help but wonder. "So what brings you to this neighborhood?"

Sandra pulled her jacket closer around herself. "I'm living with my friend Jane. She has an apartment a block from here. I would normally be working now, but we had some problems with the plumbing at school. We got let out early and I…I thought I'd go for a walk."

He remembered telling Sandra the name of the girls' school and wondered if her being here was a coincidence. He decided to push things a little.

"You thought you would go for a walk right past Bethany and Brittany's school."

She looked away, a flush creeping up her neck. "Yes."

"Were you hoping to see them?"

She nodded.

"Why?"

"I just wanted to see them." She tossed her hair, hunched her shoulders. "I wasn't going to talk to them. I just wanted to see them."

"So you haven't forgotten about them."

Sandra's laugh was a choked sound, and she glanced quickly down. "No. Not at all."

Something shifted at her admission. "And what about me?"

Sandra still didn't look up. "Unfair question, Logan Napier."

He wondered if his growing optimism made him imagine the pain in her voice. "Sandra, why did you go?"

"Doesn't matter, Logan."

"That's convenient, Sandra. I offered you a job. I offered you a chance to come back with us."

She looked at him then, her eyes pleading. "I couldn't do it. I know what's important to you."

"And what is important to me?"

"Your faith. Your family. Those two wonderful girls."

Logan nodded. "And what's important to you, Sandra?"

She waited, chewing her lip. "I don't know any more."

She sounded desolate, lost. He didn't know what to say.

"How are the girls doing in school?" she asked, changing the subject.

"They're doing quite well." Logan decided to ease off, surprised that she had already shown him as much as she had. Surprised at his emotional response to her. "The tutor I hired managed to help them get caught up even though they didn't work as hard for her as they did for you." That was an understatement. The tutor suffered from constantly being compared unfavorably to Sandra and from a decided lack of imagination and ingenuity. Things Sandra had in abundance. "They rewrote some of the exams and managed a conditional pass. So far they're doing just fine." *They miss you,* he wanted to add. *And I do, too.* But he was afraid if he mentioned that, she would leave. Run away. The original free spirit who couldn't commit herself.

So why was she here, hoping to catch a glimpse of the girls? Why was she still interested in what they were doing?

He felt inexplicably jealous of his nieces.

"Well, I should go," she said quietly, darting him a quick glance.

Logan held her eyes, wouldn't look away.

He felt it again. That peculiar connection, an echo of the energy that flowed between them when they were working on the Jonserad project.

He remembered the times he had held her. Kissed her.

He couldn't let her go just yet.

"Sandra, we need to talk."

"What about?" she asked, looking suddenly wary.

Did he dare push her?

Did he dare let her walk away? Did he want to think about her living somewhere nearby and yet unreachable? He had to take a chance.

"Why did you leave?" he asked again. "Why didn't you come back with me and the girls?"

Sandra looked into his eyes, and he caught a flicker of some unreadable emotion in hers. Sadness? Regret?

"I think I have a right to know, Sandra," he continued.

"What do you mean?"

He paused, one corner of his mouth lifting in a wry smile. He decided he had nothing to lose. If after telling her she turned and walked away, he had only suffered a minor humiliation.

But if she stayed... If he explained...

"I thought I'd be able to forget about you, Sandra. But I can't. I thought this would slowly disappear, but seeing you right now, I feel as if any ground I've gained is completely lost. You're occupying too much of my head, girl." His smile faded. "That's the right I claim."

She closed her eyes, lowered her head. "Please don't talk like that, Logan. I don't deserve any of this."

Her words connected with other words, with memories of what she had told him of her father.

He couldn't stop himself from laying his hand on her shoulder, from making a connection to her, however tenuous. "Come and sit in my van," he said. "Talk to me there." He didn't want this discussion to take place out in the open. He preferred the privacy of his vehicle.

"Okay," she whispered.

Logan walked to the passenger door and opened it for her. Sandra, without looking at him, stepped in.

He watched her as he came around the front of the van, then got in. Logan half turned to face her, one arm resting on the steering wheel. He looked at her, wondering where to start.

Sandra shoved her hands in the pockets of her jacket and sighed lightly. "You wanted to know why I left." Sandra leaned back in the seat, staring straight ahead.

"Yes, if you want to tell me," he encouraged gently.

"I left because I know you and the girls deserve better than me."

Logan's first reaction was to negate, to deny what she said. But hadn't he at times felt the same? Yet even as all his previous judgments of her came back to him, one thing was sure. She was Sandra, and he loved her in spite of—and, if he were to be honest, because of—who she was.

"Sandra, look at me."

She slowly turned her head, her dark eyes wary.

He wished he could be as glib as she could be. Wished he had the right words. "Whatever made you think I deserve better than you?"

She looked away again. "My life and how pointless it really was." She laughed, a harsh, bitter sound. "My father was right, and so were you."

"I don't know if I like being spoken of in the same breath as your father."

"I'm sorry," Sandra said. "You're not really like him, but in other ways you both saw who I really was." She sighed, turning her head to him again. "I was just a coward. Just like you said, my whole life after I left home was concentrated around no. I didn't know what I wanted, only what I didn't want."

"You wanted to do stained glass work, didn't you?"

Sandra shrugged. "I'm not sure. I picked it up on Vancouver Island as something to do. That old work ethic pounded into me by my dad. It paid a few bills here and there." She laughed shortly. "I was lucky I had friends. I thought my big break was that order from the restaurant in Calgary." She took a deep breath. "I never told you how flat broke I was when I first met you. I worked for you only because I needed the money so badly to pay for my glass supplies so I could do the job."

"Did you finish that job?"

"The company that owned the restaurant was taken over, and the new owners canceled the order." She glanced his way again, her mouth curved in a wry smile. "I found out the day you offered that job to me. Losing that order seemed to underline the total futility of my life. I couldn't seem to do anything on my own." She laughed again. "Even this job I got thanks to my friend Jane."

"Do you like the work?"

Sandra smiled then. A smile of warmth and humor. A glimpse of the Sandra he had fallen in love with. "Yes, I do." She looked at him, her eyes holding his. "I also realized I learned something important while I was working for you."

Logan leaned against the door, surprised at her revelations. Sandra was a proud person. To lose what she saw as her independence was certainly a blow for her. "And what was that?"

"That I'd been selfish. That the freedom I worshiped was really a way of avoiding responsibility. The responsibility I owed my father for paying for my education." She shrugged. "When I found out I lost the job, I realized what an illusion my independence had been."

"If you needed work, why didn't you come with me and the girls?"

Sandra fiddled with the zipper pull on her coat. "Because I was ashamed," she said finally. "Because I felt unworthy of you. Of the girls. My whole life, everything I'd spent all those years developing was proven to be just a sham. A joke. Someone playing at being an adult. Someone who took very good care of herself." She blinked, and a bead of silver glimmered in one corner of her eye. She reached up and wiped it away.

Logan wanted to pull her into his arms. To comfort her. But he sensed she had more to say. He wanted to hear it all. To sweep away any misconceptions that had been created.

"I knew of your faith and how sincere it was," Sandra continued, her voice thick with emotion. "I'm still not sure of my own."

"But it matters, doesn't it?"

Sandra frowned. "What do you mean?"

"You know God. Yet I sense you hold back, though you were raised in a Christian home." This was the true barrier to any relationship they might develop.

"Oh, yes. Mandatory church attendance and expectations and all the rest. But no matter what I did, it was never good enough for Dad. Probably not good enough for God." She stopped, giving Logan a wry glance. "Sorry. That sounded whiny. I made my choices. I have to learn to live with the consequences. But lately God and I have been talking more."

Logan couldn't stop himself. He took her hands in his, needing a physical connection with her.

He wanted to tell her so much. All the things he had learned. All the truths he had assimilated and made part of his life. *Please, Lord, give me the right words. Let what I say be from You, not my own puny explanations.*

He could see the struggle on her face. And he prayed that she would see the things that God had shown him.

Redemption. The life-changing power of God. The love of a celestial Father Who loved unconditionally.

Chapter Fifteen

"I went to church last Sunday," Sandra murmured, staring at Logan's hands holding hers.

She felt his tighten, but she still didn't want to look up. It was amazing enough to be sitting with him, to have him expressing concern for her spiritual well-being.

It's more than that and you know it.

But Sandra didn't want to entertain that thought.

"And what did you discover?" Logan's voice was warm, encouraging, soothing away the pain she had initially felt in his presence.

"That I'm a pretty unworthy person." She looked at him, forcing a smile. "I've also been reading the Bible more and discovering the same thing."

"Nothing we do can ever be good enough for God," Logan said softly. "But He loves us just the same. While we were sinners, Christ died for us. Not when we were good. When we didn't deserve it. We can never hope to deserve it. It's a gift. An absolute gift, freely given. Surely you know that."

Sandra lowered her head. "I should. But it's not what I saw as I grew up."

"Sandra, your parents' love was imperfect. But God loves you as you are. Yes, He wants you to be better than you are. Yes, He challenges us to step outside of our lives. But not without His help. Not without His Spirit and His love."

His words surrounded her, gently reinforcing the positive message she had heard at church. That He who made the lily, who flung the stars into space, had made Himself weak and vulnerable for the world. For her.

"You know," she replied softly, "it's so much easier to think I'm unworthy."

"Why is that?" His voice was pitched low, creating an intimacy that drew her closer to him.

"That way I don't have any obligations." She dared to look at him, to lose herself in the depths of his warm eyes. "No expectations. That way I could think I was free."

"And were you?"

Sandra shook her head slowly, feeling a freedom in just admitting this to Logan. "No. I was tied down to trying to outrun my father. How betrayed I felt that my mother had died, leaving me alone with him and his expectations."

"And what about God in your life?"

"I think I was trying to outrun Him, too. But I didn't. He found me."

"Sandra, it means so much to me that you can understand this."

She was fascinated by the sight of his hands holding hers, by his comment. "Why?"

Logan's thumbs moved across her knuckles. "Because I've come to care for you more than I've ever cared for anyone else. I thought I could forget you when you left, but I've thought of you every day since you left twelve weeks ago."

"Twelve weeks and two days," Sandra corrected with a light shiver. She looked at him, dared to make yet one more connection with him.

His hands tightened on hers, then he slowly leaned forward and touched his lips lightly to hers.

Sandra's heart spiraled slowly downward as she sat perfectly still, her eyes drifting shut, her hands clenching his.

Logan drew back slightly and rested his forehead against hers with a sigh light as a wish.

"I haven't been able to forget you, Sandra. I haven't stopped praying for you, wondering what you were doing."

Sandra closed her eyes as a single tear slid down her face, cool and wet on her cheek. She wanted to say so much but couldn't articulate the fullness in her heart. The peace she felt stealing over her as if so much had suddenly become right in her world.

"I couldn't forget about you, either."

Logan kissed her again and again, then drew back, still holding her hands, his smile huge. "I love you, Sandra."

Sandra thought her heart couldn't hold any more happiness. Still she couldn't stop herself. "Logan, I don't deserve…"

He laid a light finger on her lips. "I don't, either, okay? None of us do. Love is a gift."

"Then I have a gift for you, too," she said softly. "I've never cared for anyone like I care for you. I love you, too."

Logan pulled her close, holding her tightly. Sandra's thoughts became inarticulate prayers of thanks. He tucked her head under his chin, still holding her. "I never thought this would happen. Not today," he whispered, stroking her head with his chin. "If ever."

Sandra snuggled as close as she could, her free hand tangling in his thick hair. "I didn't, either." It was wonderful, heaven to be in his arms. She never wanted to move.

"I wonder what the girls will have to say about all this," he said quietly.

Sandra laughed, pressing a quick kiss to his warm neck. "I'm sure they'll take all the credit."

"No doubt."

They were quiet a moment. Logan fingered her hair, sending shivers down Sandra's back. She didn't know if her body could possibly contain the happiness that filled her. She wanted to tell him, but couldn't.

So she simply held him, praying he would understand.

"There's something else we need to talk about, Sandra."

"What?" she murmured, fingering the corner of his shirt collar, feeling an absolute freedom in doing so.

"I'd like to meet your father."

Sandra stiffened and almost pulled away, but Logan wouldn't let her go.

"I take it you haven't visited him yet?"

Sandra swallowed at the softly worded question as new sorrow engulfed her. "No, I haven't," she said quietly. "I tried to call him over the summer, but there was no answer. Then, when I got this job, I thought maybe I could tell him that. But I didn't dare." Her laugh was without humor. "I called him a couple of times after I left home, but he hung up on me. I don't know what I would do if that happened again."

"Have you ever thought of seeing him face to face?"

Sandra pulled back, looking at Logan. "If he won't talk to me on the phone, you surely don't think he'll let me in his house?"

Logan cupped her cheek with his hand. "I'd like to meet him. With you."

Sandra lifted a shoulder, pressing his hand against her face. "How can I tell him we're coming?"

"We could just show up at his place. See what happens."

Sandra couldn't repress a shiver.

"I'll be with you, Sandra," Logan said. "You won't be alone."

Sandra blinked as new tears pooled in her eyes at his words. It seemed too much to comprehend all at once.

"I'm not sure I want to do this to me. To you. My father can be pretty intimidating," she said.

"I want to do this for you, Sandra," Logan replied. "I think whether you want to admit it or not, you miss him."

Sandra sighed, brushing away an errant tear. "I do," she whispered.

"Then I'll pray his heart will be softened when he

sees his beautiful daughter on his steps, just like mine was when I first saw you."

"It was not," she said.

Logan canted his head to one side, as if studying her. "Yes, it was." He grinned. "But then you started talking. And everything changed." He dropped a light kiss on her mouth. "You talk a lot, you know."

She kissed him back. "Not all the time."

His grin widened. "That's a good thing." He pulled her close and sighed. "'Cause I'd hate to have to compete with you and the twins."

Sandra nestled closer to him, her heart full.

Thank you, Lord, she prayed. *Thank you for your love. Thank you for this man.*

A harsh rap on the window made them pull apart. Sandra felt a guilty flush warm her cheeks.

Two grinning faces were pressed against Logan's window. Brittany and Bethany.

"Well, so much for the quiet," Logan said dryly. "Think we should tell them?"

Sandra smiled as she saw the girls come running around to the passenger side of the van. "Something tells me they already know," she said.

Logan squeezed Sandra's hand and gave her a quick wink. As he reached out to press the doorbell, Sandra felt herself praying. Hard.

She felt like a coward for taking up Logan's offer to come with her, but as she stood waiting for her father to answer the door, she was thankful he was beside her.

Then the door opened, and through it came warmth and light and the gentle strains of classical music.

Sandra felt a clench of sorrow at the sight of the slightly stooped man who stood framed by the doorway, folding his newspaper. It had been five years since she'd seen him. He looked older.

Joshua Bachman frowned and took his glasses off as he looked first at Logan, then Sandra.

Sandra couldn't stop herself from pressing closer to Logan, from clinging tightly to his arm.

"Hi, Dad," she said quietly.

Mr. Bachman straightened, his dark eyes hard. "What are you doing here?"

His voice resonated with anger, but Sandra sensed another note beneath that.

"I live in Calgary now, Dad. I thought I would stop by and say hello."

"After all these years?"

Sandra swallowed a knot of guilty remorse. She'd maintained contact, she reminded herself. She'd written him letters. "I never lived close before."

Josh Bachman laughed shortly and slapped his newspaper against the side of his leg. "No. Your letters came from all over the place. Wandering like a Gypsy. Living off the government."

His eyes ticked over Logan, then back to Sandra as if dismissing him. "What do you want?"

His words were like a slap.

Sandra swallowed the sorrow that began to thicken her throat. Logan's hand tightened on hers, and she felt another strength.

"I want to talk to you." She faltered, took a praying breath. "I want my father back."

"After all this time?"

"Yes."

Josh Bachman shook his head. "It's too late, Sandra."

"God doesn't think so," Sandra replied.

He stopped then, looking at her. "You turned your back on God when you turned your back on me. 'Honor your father and your mother that your days may be long.'" He paused. "You didn't honor us much, did you, Sandra."

"I tried, Daddy. I did. But God didn't turn His back on me. He kept calling me and calling me. I know I didn't always live the life I should have." She glanced at Logan, who was smiling at her. "But thanks to Logan, I started listening to God. Now I want to make peace with you. I was wrong. In many ways." She didn't add that he was, as well. She realized that was her father's problem, and he would have to deal with it in his own way.

For now the important thing was that she be reconciled with him.

Sandra's father acknowledged Logan for the first time. "Who are you?"

"Dad, this is Logan Napier."

Logan held out his hand, and to Sandra's surprise, her father took it, albeit reluctantly.

"Can we come in, Daddy?"

Mr. Bachman looked at Logan, then at Sandra. Sandra counted her heartbeats as he considered.

"'Children, obey your parents the Lord, for this is right.'" he quoted from Ephesians. "This is the first commandment with a promise, Sandra. And you went against that commandment when you left this house."

"Yes, but the same passage goes on to say, 'Fathers, do not exasperate your children; instead, bring them up in the training and instruction of the Lord,'" Logan said quietly.

Josh Bachman swung his steely gaze on Logan. "Which I did, young man."

"Yes, you did, Daddy," Sandra admitted. She could tell from the set of Logan's jaw this was not going quite how he hoped it would. "And I was wrong to turn away from you."

She paused, hoping, praying that her father's heart would soften. "But you're the only parent I have. And I'm the only family you have. If you don't let me in, we are both going to be even lonelier. I missed you as much as I missed Mom. Maybe I wasn't always the daughter I should have been. I was wrong. I was selfish. But I still love you. And whatever you do right now, that's not going to change."

For the first time since he had opened the door, Mr. Bachman lost some of his regal bearing. He reached out, catching the side of the door.

Sandra didn't know what to do. She looked at Logan.

"He needs you, Sandra," he said quietly.

She knew he was right, and with a quick prayer went to her father and for the first time in years put her arms around him and held him.

He resisted, almost pulling away from her. But she didn't let go. Couldn't.

Then, with a hoarse cry, he dropped his newspaper and clasped her close.

"I'm so sorry, Daddy. So sorry," Sandra whispered, stroking his head, marveling at the love God had given her to share with this man. Her father's only answer was to hold her, and Sandra wondered why she had waited this long. Then, as she felt Logan's strong hand on her neck, she knew. She needed Logan to encourage her. To help her.

After what seemed a lifetime, Sandra's father drew back, his eyes reflecting a deep sorrow. His gaze flicked over her face. "You look so much like your mother," he said quietly. "I miss her so much."

"I miss her, too," Sandra whispered, touching his hand.

He drew back and pulled himself erect once again. So soon he had drawn his usual barriers of aloofness around him, but Sandra was heartened by their shared moment of togetherness.

"I suppose I should ask you in," he said, some of the starch momentarily coming back.

"We'd love to come in," Logan said, slipping his arm around Sandra's shoulders. "There's a few other things I want to discuss with you, as well."

Mr. Bachman glanced at Logan and then at Sandra. "Well, come in then." He walked away, leaving the door open.

Logan gave Sandra a quick hug, and Sandra leaned against him, sending up a prayer of thanks for who he was and all he had done for her.

Before they stepped through the door, Logan dropped a light kiss on her forehead. “You’re a very special woman, Sandra Bachman,” he said quietly.

“And you’re a very special man, Logan Napier,” she returned.

Then, with Logan beside her, she stepped into her home.

Epilogue

Brittany caught Bethany by the arm. "Sandra and Uncle Logan are going to cut the cake now."

Bethany picked up the long skirt of her pale peach flower-girl dress and ran behind her sister in a most unladylike fashion. She didn't care. Today was an exciting day, and she didn't want to miss a thing.

People stood aside to let them get to the front where the cream layer cake sat in splendor on the snowy tablecloth.

Bethany linked her arm in her sister's, still awestruck with how beautiful Sandra looked. She wore her hair up, tied with a spray of peach and cream-colored roses. Her close-fitting dress had flowing, filmy sleeves that looked like billowing wings. The sleeves had narrow cuffs with shiny beads on them that matched the narrow row of beads at the neckline and the waist of the dress. The skirt was long and just as billowy as the sleeves.

"I still say she looks like an angel," Bethany breathed.

"Except angels don't have brown hair and brown eyes."

"Her eyes look like they're sparkling," Bethany said with a giggle.

"I hope she's not going to cry again." Brittany was talking about the church service, when Sandra walked down the aisle with her father, who looked very serious. Just before Sandra went to Logan, Sandra's dad gave her a quick little kiss. Nothing to cry over, as far as Bethany was concerned.

But Sandra did.

She also cried when Uncle Logan slipped the ring on her finger and then kissed her hand right where the ring was. Bethany thought that was kind of neat, although Brittany was rolling her eyes.

Uncle Logan held up the knife with the ribbon on it.

Bethany had hardly recognized him when he came to the room where they were getting their hair done by Grandma Napier. He never wore such a fancy suit. He called it a penguin suit, but Bethany thought he looked like a movie star. His hair was brushed, and his cheeks were still shiny from shaving.

Now his cheeks were a bit red. Bethany supposed because he and Sandra were having so much fun, laughing and talking to everyone. And kissing each other. A lot.

"Okay, please note that I'm giving Sandra this knife," Uncle Logan announced. "The first test of trust between us as husband and wife."

"Goodness, I'm not about to do any damage with it." Sandra laughed, poking him in the ribs with her elbow.

"Maybe not," Uncle Logan said. "But I don't believe that you can cut that cake in a straight line."

Bethany laughed. Uncle Logan was right. Sandra could never cut anything straight unless it was a piece of glass.

Sandra tilted him a funny grin then looked Bethany's way. Bethany could see her smile change, could see it get softer. She wiggled her finger at both of them.

"C'mon, girls. We're a family now. You've got to help us."

Bethany giggled, and when she and Brittany went over, they were squished between Sandra and Uncle Logan, who had their arms around each other. They all put a hand on the knife and started cutting while lights flashed and people laughed all around them.

Then Sandra's eyes got all shiny, and Uncle Logan reached past the girls.

Brittany and Bethany knew what was coming and scooted out of there just as Uncle Logan pulled Sandra into his arms and gave her a great big kiss.

"When we were trying to get them together, I didn't think there'd be so much kissing," Bethany said with a grimace.

Brittany sighed as she dropped into the nearest empty chair. "But they're married now," she said with a grin. "And it's going to be so nice having Sandra as a mom. Don't you think so?"

Bethany didn't answer. She was looking around the room. Then Brittany grabbed Bethany's arm. "Look. Sandra's dad is all alone."

Bethany glanced in the direction Brittany was

pointing. She could see Sandra's father looking a little bit sad, standing all by himself in a corner.

"He's kind of a funny man, isn't he?" Bethany said, picking up a candy from a dish on the table. She popped it into her mouth. "He doesn't say much and he looks mad a lot."

"I bet Gramma Napier could make him laugh."

Bethany's and Brittany's eyes met. It was as if an electrical charge passed between them.

"Are you thinking what I'm thinking?" Bethany asked, working the candy to the other side of her mouth.

"I think so," Brittany replied.

Bethany jumped off her chair, fluffed up her skirts and started looking around for Gramma Napier.

"Well," Brittany said. "I think we should go with Plan B."

"What's that?"

"I don't know. We'll make it up as we go along."

They giggled and with another quick glance at Logan and Sandra, who were still holding on to each other, still kissing each other, the girls went their separate ways.

They had another job to do.

* * * * *

Dear Reader,

Just like Sandra in this story, I've always been fascinated by stars and the incomprehensible distances between us and them. We've lain outside, watching the stars, watching meteor showers, staring in awe at the Northern Lights, always overwhelmed and awestruck by the part of God's creation we see only at night. I know God speaks to us through Creation, but it is only part of the Word. The final Word is Christ, the Word made flesh, shown to us through the Bible. I pray that you may experience all aspects of God.

Carolyne Aarsen

P.S. I love to hear from my readers.
My address is: Carolyne Aarsen, Box 114,
Neerlandia, Alberta T0G 1R0 Canada.

TOWARD HOME

Come to me, all you who are weary and burdened,
and I will give you rest.

—*Matthew* 11:28

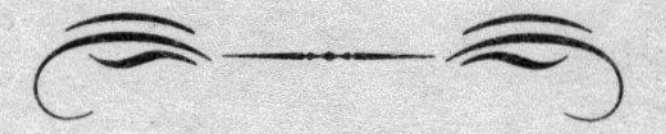

To Ann Leslie Tuttle who helped me shape this book, and to Karen Solem who gave me timely and valuable advice.

Chapter One

"I sure hope *this* is the place." Melanie glanced once more at the wrinkled map her supervisor had given her, then at the unmarked mailbox teetering at the end of the driveway.

Supposedly Helen Engler, her next patient, lived here. It had taken her half an hour with two wrong turns and directions from a young woman out riding her horse to find the place.

She turned into the driveway bordered by willows on one side, swooping poplars on the other. Puzzlement was overridden by happy memories of this place as she finally recognized the driveway. When she used to visit here she had come from a different direction.

It had been fourteen years since she'd lived in the town of Derwin, yet she knew she had been here before. She was also sure that she knew the name Engler. But the name and the place didn't mesh in her memory.

She rounded the last bend into an opening and came to a stop in front of a Victorian-style house.

A deep porch shaded the front and side of the house, its curved pillars creating a sturdy, welcoming place. Gingerbread trimmed the large bay window across the front, echoing the trim above the dormer windows perched along the top floor. Brightly colored petunias and lobelia spilled from baskets hung from the ceiling of the porch, giving it a festive, welcoming air.

But best of all, set alongside the house, flowing out from it and softening the angles, stood a turret topped with a conical roof. The four-sided tower overlooked the yard sheltered with deep green spruce and aspen.

Melanie stepped out of the car, a thrill of pleasure and surprise coursing through her.

It *was* the house of those childhood dreams, Melanie thought with a smile, hitching the strap of her briefcase over her shoulder. The Shewchuks must have sold the house, and now it belonged to the Englers.

Melanie took a moment to listen to the sighing of the wind in the trees surrounding the house, her mind sifting back fourteen years. Her good friend Dena Shewchuk had lived here and Melanie had been envious not only of her large family, but of Dena's house. A home.

The same home her wandering father had always promised Melanie and her mother.

As a child Melanie had woven countless daydreams around this home. She had promised herself that someday she would have a house, a home exactly like the Shewchuks. The memory had stayed with her during the intervening years.

But as she walked closer to the house, reality

intruded on her memories. Blistered paint peeled off the house's wooden siding, dust coated the windows. The weeds choking the flower bed were an ironic contrast to the flowerpots decorating the porch.

She had taken a few steps up the porch stairs when she heard the deep sound of a man's voice. Curious, she walked along the veranda to the yard beside the house.

Sunlight, diffused through the softly swaying aspen trees overhead, dappled the two figures on a lawn that had been hidden from view. A tiny girl about three years of age threw a bright blue ball to a man who sat only a few feet away from her. The little girl wore pale pink coveralls, the man blue jeans and a white T-shirt.

As Melanie watched the idyllic scene, the little girl suddenly turned away, trundling toward the back of the house, her curls bouncing on her shoulders.

"Tiffany," the man called out. "Come back here, sweetie." But the little girl, now gone, didn't come back, nor did she respond.

The man pushed himself to his feet to follow her. From where she stood Melanie caught his expression of pain, at odds with the charming scene she had just witnessed.

He stopped as soon as he saw Melanie, lifting his hand to shade his eyes.

"Hello," Melanie called out. "I'm Melanie Visser. The health nurse. I've come to see Helen Engler."

The man walked up the three steps on the side of the veranda and as he came toward her, Melanie took a small step back.

"I'm Adam Engler. Helen's son." His handshake

was firm, solid, his height on the borderline of intimidating.

The introduction wasn't necessary. Adam Engler had, one time, been as much a part of her dreams as this house and the Shewchuk family.

His once-blond hair had deepened to a sandy color, but he still wore it a little long, curling at the ends. His deep blue eyes that had once sparkled with fun and enthusiasm now looked older. Sadder.

However, they held hers with a faint intensity, his head angled to one side, as if studying her.

He didn't remember her, she realized with a brush of regret. And why should he? When he'd come to her rescue those many years ago, she had been a mere junior high student. He an exalted high school sophomore.

"My mother is in the house," Adam continued. "Just come around the back with me. I have to make sure Tiffany went inside."

Adam half turned, gesturing for Melanie to go ahead of him. As she passed him she chanced another glance, trying to reconcile this older, harder man with the laughing teenager of her memories. To her increasing confusion, Adam looked directly down at her, a faint frown tugging at his sandy-colored eyebrows as if he was searching for the memory Melanie had found.

As they approached the back door, Adam reached past her to pull it open, his arm brushing hers.

Melanie resisted the urge to pull back, flashing him what she hoped was a casually thankful smile before she entered the porch. She blamed her bemusement on an assault of memories. This house and unexpectedly meeting Adam, a young man from a happier time in her life.

She stepped past a small pair of sandals the same size as the running shoes lying haphazardly beside them. They looked lost on the large porch that Melanie remembered chockablock with shoes, boots and the occasional pair of wet socks.

As she stepped into the spacious kitchen, her hungry eyes flitted over the room, revisiting other memories.

The walls were more scarred, the floor more scuffed. The counters that followed the two walls no longer sparkled, the white paint dulled by collected grime.

In spite of the neglect, the room still exuded the same welcoming atmosphere. The bay window with its deep seat still invited a lonely soul to sit in it and look out over the secluded yard.

A feeling of melancholy filled her. Mixed through that was an emotion she experienced only when she thought of Derwin.

Homesickness.

A tiny woman sat at a large wooden table beside the bay window, a walker standing beside her chair. Bright blue eyes looked up at Melanie, magnified by a pair of wire-rimmed glasses. Soft brown hair threaded with gray curled around her smiling face. Beside her chair stood the little girl Melanie had seen with Adam.

"I'm Melanie Visser. I'm sorry I'm late," Melanie said, walking over to Helen Engler. "I got turned around on the way here."

"It is a bit hard to find," Helen agreed, reaching up to shake Melanie's hand. Her handshake was as firm and brisk as her son's. "I'm obviously Helen. And this little angel is my granddaughter, Tiffany." Helen brushed the little girl's blond hair back and clipped a barrette into her curls. "I take it you and Adam have already met." She leaned back in her chair, and her smile twisted into a grimace of pain.

"How long have you been up?" Melanie asked, pulling up a chair beside Helen.

"Only a few minutes. I knew what time you were coming and I wanted to be ready for you. The doctor told me I could sit up for a little while."

Melanie laid the back of her hand against Helen's cheek. She felt a bit warm, but nothing to be alarmed about.

"I told her to stay in bed," Adam said.

"That's okay. She needs to get up once in a while." Melanie opened her bag and drew out Helen's file and the blood pressure cuff.

"But she just came out of the hospital yesterday. Should she even be sitting up?"

Melanie heard the faint note of anxiety in Adam's voice and took it for what it was. A concerned son. "Actually she should," Melanie murmured. "If Helen doesn't move around enough, she runs the risk of developing blood clots, which is far more serious than being a little overtired." She turned back to Helen. "I'm going to take your blood pressure now. Do you mind pushing your sleeve up?"

Helen's blood pressure seemed a little high.

"Have you been taking your medication?" Melanie rolled up the cuff and made a note in her file.

Helen nodded.

"I think we'll need to make a change. I'll contact the doctor for a new prescription."

"The doctor told me this might happen," Helen offered, as she buttoned up her cuff. "He said not to make any sudden changes."

"He's right. Now I'm going to ask you a few more questions, if you don't mind."

Helen answered them in a steady quiet voice, glancing over at her son once in a while.

Adam pulled up a chair and rested his elbows on the table. Melanie didn't look his way as she wrote down Helen's answers, but she felt completely aware of him.

"Gramma sick?" Tiffany clutched the armrest of Helen's chair, her head tilted up to Melanie.

"Gramma had surgery, sweetie," Adam said from his end of the table.

Tiffany frowned, still looking at Melanie.

Melanie leaned a little closer, smiling at the little girl. "The technical term for that is 'owwie,'" she said with a wink.

"Gramma has an owwie." Tiffany nodded, as if understanding this.

"I see I'm going to have to brush up on my medical terminology," Adam said dryly as he got up.

Melanie slanted Adam a puzzled glance, surprised to see the faint hint of a dimple hovering at the corner of his mouth.

"Can I get you a cup of coffee?" he asked.

"No. Thank you."

"But I bet you want a cookie, don't you, Tiff?"

Adam scooped up his daughter as Melanie concentrated on what she was doing. As Melanie and Helen chatted, she tried to ignore Adam rummaging through the cupboard, pulling out a cookie for his daughter.

It was the potent combination of Adam and this house, Melanie thought, blaming her edgy mood on this place. It had occupied so much of her dreams. To see it so run-down, so neglected bothered her.

She turned her attention back to Helen.

"Just to fill me in, how did you break your hip?"

Helen glanced over at Adam, her teeth worrying her lip. "I fell, uh, while…changing a lightbulb."

Adam spun around, dropping the bag of cookies on the counter. "I thought you told me you slipped in the bathtub?"

Helen waved her hand, as if brushing away his anger. "I guess you didn't hear me right."

"I guess you were lying to me."

The tension was rising and Melanie intervened. "Speaking of the bathroom, I need to see what you need in terms of bathing assistance." Melanie closed the file and tucked it into her bag. She didn't know why Helen had lied to Adam about how she'd injured herself and it wasn't really her problem. "Here are some exercises that the physiotherapist drew up for you," Melanie said. "I'd like to go over them with you in a few minutes. You can do the first ones in your bed."

Adam looked over his mother's shoulder, his eyes still narrowed with anger. "Exercises so soon? It's only been a bit more than a week since her surgery."

"It's all about keeping the muscles toned and healthy

and her new hip working. We want your mother to recuperate as fast as possible."

"I'm with you there," Adam said. "I don't need her hurting herself in this house again."

"I'm hoping to be able to get back to my garden. And maybe you can get some work done on the house, Adam," Helen said.

"We won't be here that long." Adam's voice held a note of warning as he straightened, his hands on his hips. "The sooner I get you out of this place, the better."

"It was one little fall. And if you'd been here I wouldn't have had to change the lightbulb. Remember the doctor said no sudden changes." Helen turned back to Melanie. "Adam wants me to move to Calgary. As soon as possible."

Melanie frowned. "What do you mean, as soon as possible?"

"Next week." Helen sat back, her arms crossed over her chest. "And I shouldn't go, should I?"

"It's too early to be thinking of that, that's for sure," Melanie said.

"I told you, Adam." Helen threw him a triumphant glance, which Adam ignored. "This is such a beautiful spot. Don't you agree, Melanie?"

"It's a lovely house," Melanie agreed carefully, sensing from the frown on Adam's face and the pleading look in Helen's that she was venturing into a point of dispute between mother and son. "I always admired it as a little girl."

Helen's face brightened. "Have you been here before?"

"When I was young I used to visit the Shewchuk family here." Melanie couldn't help but smile at the memory and the coincidence of sitting here in the same kitchen she had spent so many happy hours in.

"You lived in Derwin?" Adam asked.

Melanie looked up at him, her mind calling back that silly schoolgirl crush with surprising ease. "Yes, I did. For about fourteen months. That was a while ago."

"And you knew the Shewchuks."

"I was best friends, for that time, with Dena Shewchuk."

Adam tilted his head to one side, as if studying her. "How old were you then?"

"Thirteen." Her first year as a teenager. Her last as part of a complete family unit. Her parents had separated shortly after their brief stay in Derwin.

"I remember you now. You used to come to youth group with Dena."

"Youth group made a huge impact on my life," she replied, pleased that he had recognized her. "Your faith was an encouragement to me."

It was as if someone had thrown a switch. His lips thinned. His eyes narrowed. "That was a long time ago." He turned away from her and walked over to the counter.

"Now I know who you are," Helen said, tapping her cheek with her forefinger. "A lady named Visser was buried here a year ago. Any relation?"

Melanie tuned back to Helen, the mention of her mother bringing a familiar pain, softened by time.

"That was my mother. She loved Derwin as much as I did, and she wanted to be buried here."

"I'm sorry for you," Helen said.

"Thanks." An awkward silence sprang up, broken by the clink of dishes that Adam was washing up in the sink.

Tiffany's entire attention was focused on trying to pick up a couple of chocolate chips that had fallen from her cookie, but she had succeeded only in mashing one of them onto the table.

Melanie reached over and picked the other one up and handed it to her.

"Did you buy this house from the Shewchuks?" Melanie asked when Tiffany took the chip.

"No. Adam did. A number of years ago."

"They were such a happy family," Melanie said wistfully. "I never thought they would move. I always thought that part of the reason for their happiness was this house."

"The Shewchuks were not a happy family when I bought this house." Adam's derision underlined his previous withdrawal.

"Adam, you stop that right now." Helen flashed him an admonishing look, her brief display of spunk surprising Melanie.

Adam ignored her as he carefully wiped Tiffany's hands with a wet cloth. "Come on, Tiff, let's go back outside," he said, tossing the cloth into the sink and holding out his arms for his daughter.

"Don't wanna go." She pouted, pulling away from her father. "Want Gramma."

Adam gently picked her up and set her on his hip. "Gramma is tired," he said, tucking a curl of hair behind his daughter's ear, his head angling to catch her eyes.

Melanie couldn't help but watch the interplay between father and daughter. Couldn't help but be touched by the tenderness Adam showed her. It called out to a basic yearning that had been growing the past few years. A yearning for a family. For a place of her own.

But Tiffany twisted away from him, turning instead to her grandmother. "Want Gramma," she whined, her chubby little hands reaching out to Helen.

Once again Melanie caught the glimpse of pain in Adam's face she had seen earlier, and she wondered at the relationship between father and daughter.

"Gramma has to talk to the nurse," Adam said, pulling her closer. "And we have to work some more outside." Adam glanced at Melanie, as if apologizing for his daughter's behavior. But as their eyes met, some indefinable emotion arced between them, caught their gazes in a gentler snare. Melanie couldn't look away.

Adam broke the connection first, turning to Tiffany, who had given up on her protest. "Let's go, honey," he said quietly, leaving the room.

Melanie glanced down at the papers, trying to compose herself. Her cherished memories were under assault. Adam. The Shewchuks.

Helen leaned over and patted her lightly on the hand. "Are you okay?"

Melanie smiled at the concern in Helen's voice. The patient asking after the nurse. "I'm fine," she said, tilting a grin at Helen. "Now, let's get you settled in your bed."

Melanie opened the door of the bedroom, and as she

let Helen precede her, couldn't suppress her intake of breath. Windows, curved in a half circle in one corner, spilled a profusion of light into the room.

Though the rest of the house looked generally worn down, this room looked like a fairy tale. The walls were painted in a pale buttery yellow and soft organza scarf curtains swathed the windows. Melanie immediately recognized one corner of the room as the turret she had been so entranced with as a child.

"This is beautiful," she breathed as she followed Helen's slow progress to the large maple sleigh bed that dominated the room. A pale-yellow-and-aqua pieced quilt covered it.

"Isn't it lovely? And I made Lana and Adam the quilt as a wedding present." Helen paused, and Melanie could see the glint of tears in her eyes. "You have to excuse my son. He used to be such a happy person. But now he is so bitter. He used to go to church, but he says it's a waste of time. He says he doesn't believe in God, but I know God will still work in his life." Melanie could see love shining from her client's face.

Helen leaned forward, grasping Melanie's hand, her grip surprisingly strong. "Are you a praying woman?"

Melanie smiled at her and nodded. "I can't get through my day unless I start it with the Lord."

"When you pray, can you remember me?" Her gaze was earnest, her bright blue eyes piercing. "Adam wants to move me down to Calgary to some concrete building. I don't want to go there."

Melanie was concerned at the intensity in Helen's voice. What Adam had decided for his mother was between them. But she couldn't ignore the entreaty in Helen's face. "I'll pray for you, Helen," she said, laying her hand over Helen's. It was all she could say.

Helen released her grip on Melanie's arm and slowly sagged back against the pillows. "Thank you, Melanie. Adam is a good son—he just doesn't understand. He used to love this house. But now…he can't be here more than one day. He doesn't visit, and now he wants me to move to Calgary. I was born and raised in the country." Helen clutched her chest, her eyes wide. "I can't live in the city."

Melanie caught her by the wrist, her fingers on Helen's pulse. Elevated. She laid her hand against her burning cheek. Too warm. "I'm going to take your temperature," she said. "I'll be right back."

Her temperature registered a couple of degrees above normal, and when Melanie checked her incision, it showed no sign of infection.

Stress most likely was the cause, she thought.

"You need to relax, Helen," Melanie said, helping her ease back onto the bed. "You just concentrate on getting better."

"Will you talk to Adam about me staying here? He can be stubborn and I don't have the strength to fight him. He says he wants to protect me, but I don't need to be protected."

Melanie nodded, albeit somewhat reluctantly.

"Will you pray for him, too? He's had a tough few years. You used to know him. I'm hoping you can help him, too."

"I'm here to take care of you, Helen," Melanie said quietly. And only you, she reminded herself.

Adam and his daughter were a burden she wasn't ready to take on. No matter how adorable the daughter, or attractive the father.

Chapter Two

"Now it's official." Floyd gave the nail on the for-sale sign one more tap.

Adam hitched Tiffany higher up on his hip, his eyes on the bright yellow sign now firmly attached to the fence in front of the house. He pushed aside second and third thoughts.

It had been Lana's house and Lana's dream. Getting rid of this last tie to Derwin was the smart thing to do.

"Go down." Tiffany patted Adam's shoulder with a chubby hand and Adam turned back to her. Eyes as intensely blue as the Alberta sky above them stared back at him, her expression holding the same serious look it had since she was a tiny baby.

"In a minute, honey," he said softly, giving her a light squeeze. He turned his attention back to Floyd, the real estate agent. "So now what happens?"

"We've already done all the necessary paperwork, listing contract and all that. Now I start doing my job." Floyd set the hammer on the fence post and glanced over his shoulder at the house.

"Handyman's special," Floyd mused. "Though it needs work, it has potential. It's got great lines. I love that tower."

"Down," Tiffany insisted, wiggling once more in his arms.

"You can go down, but don't go into the house," he warned, lowering his daughter to the ground. "Gramma is busy." Busy with Melanie of the amber eyes and the chocolate-brown hair.

The thought came from nowhere and he pushed it back, still surprised at his reaction to Melanie Visser. She had been quite young when she lived here, but already then her unusually colored eyes made you give her a second look. Now she had matured into a beautiful woman.

He had tried to dismiss his reaction to her, but he couldn't dismiss the fact that she was the first woman who had held any kind of appeal since Lana. He wondered if she was unattached.

The door of the house slapped shut. Footsteps echoed on the wooden porch behind them. Floyd straightened and with his thumb and forefinger tugged the lapel of his blazer, pulled back his shoulders in an unconscious preening gesture. Adam's back was to the house, but it wasn't hard for him to guess that Melanie was coming toward them.

An errant scent of soap mixed with a curious fragrance of peaches confirmed his guess.

"Good morning, ma'am," Floyd said, his smile holding a different line than before.

If Floyd had had a cowboy hat, Adam felt sure he would have tipped it.

Adam glanced at Melanie. "Melanie, this is Floyd Wierenga, the real estate agent. Floyd, this is Melanie Visser. The new health nurse."

Melanie gave Floyd a polite smile and shook his hand. "Nice to meet you."

"How long have you been here?" Floyd asked.

"About a month."

Floyd reached inside his coat. "Well, if you and your husband are ever in the market for a place…" He let the words drift away as he handed Melanie a card.

Melanie glanced down at it and then at the sign Floyd had just put up.

"I'm single, but I might be," she said, tapping the card on the palm of her hand.

"That's just great to hear. I know we've got a number of properties that might work out quite well for you." Floyd turned back to Adam. "Pleasure, Adam. Good to see you again." He shook Adam's hand, winked at Melanie and in a matter of moments stepped into his truck and was gone.

Melanie glanced at the card in her hand, flicking it between her fingers, then at the sign. "I'm guessing you're serious about selling the house?"

Adam gave her a puzzled look. "Are you interested?"

She chewed her lip, as if considering. "I love this place," she said softly. "Would love to live here."

"I don't know if it's suitable for a single woman, unless there's someone…" He let the question die the death it should have a few words previously. What business was it of his whether she had anyone in her life or not?

Melanie laughed lightly, unfazed by Adam's blunt question. "No, there's no one as yet. But I've dreamed about this house since the first day I saw it. I can't believe you're selling it."

"It needs a lot of work. And money."

Melanie angled him a quizzical glance. "You sound like you're trying to talk me out of it. Unless you're using reverse psychology."

"I don't work that way." Adam glanced over his shoulder. Tiffany was squatted down, quite content for the moment, her chubby hands drawing in the sand with a twig.

He turned back to Melanie, who stood with her arms clasped in front of her, looking up at the house with a dreamy smile. Why would she want this house? It would be nothing but a headache for her.

"How long have you owned it?" Melanie asked.

"I've had it for about four years. My wife and I lived in it for only one. How's my mother doing?" he asked, forestalling any more questions.

"She's resting now. She just had a bad spell."

"How bad?"

"She spiked a temp for no reason that I could see. She's okay now, though I am concerned about her blood pressure. Make sure you keep an eye on her and if you have any concerns, call me."

Adam felt icy fingers clutch his temple. Not again. "Will I need to call an ambulance?"

"I doubt it. She's not that bad," Melanie hastened to add.

"What about moving her?"

Melanie frowned at him, flicking the real estate agent's card between her fingers.

"To be honest, right now the best thing for your mother is stability. It takes about six weeks for full healing."

"That long?" Adam shook his head. "She can't be here alone six weeks, and I can't stay here that long." He had been getting ready for a long-overdue vacation with Tiffany when he got the phone call from the hospital in Derwin. He'd canceled his plans but not his time off, so that he could be here.

"It doesn't sound like she will enjoy moving back to the city. And I understand you're on holidays."

"Not even I can go on vacation for six weeks." Adam caught Melanie's smile and shook his head. "I should warn you. My mother has her own agenda. She moved out of her apartment in town and in here after our last renters moved out six months ago, hoping that would stop me from selling it." And it had. Until her accident a week ago. "She has this feeling about this house." He glanced back over his shoulder, as if his mother's emotions were creeping up on him and threatening to shove aside his well-laid plans.

"It is a lovely place. I have to agree."

"Well, for now, she's staying, but as soon as she can be moved, she will be. I'd like you to help me prepare her for that."

He didn't want to stay here any longer than necessary.

"I'll do what I can," Melanie said, tucking her hair behind her ear as she glanced up at him.

As their eyes met, he felt it again. The connection to

the past. A connection that called to other times in his life and a deeper hunger that he'd ignored for a long time.

"I appreciate the help," he said, stepping back. As if he needed to create a physical space between them.

For his own sake more than anything. Right now he had enough complications in his life. He didn't need to get his emotions tangled up in a temporary situation.

"Is the asking price negotiable?"

Melanie tucked the phone under her ear as she made a quick note on a pad of paper. She had waited a day after she saw the house, trying to talk herself out of this crazy scheme, but she couldn't.

"It's going to need quite a large cash outlay if you want to finish it off," Floyd continued. "If you want, I've got a few places in town that you might be interested in."

"I could do it bit by bit." Melanie ignored his other offer and curled her bare feet around the metal legs of her kitchen chair. Bit by bit might not cut it. It would be a major project, but how wonderful it would be to see the house transformed. Loved.

"Ideally I'd like to be around to show you the property, but I can't do it until Monday."

"I'm there every day. I could have Adam show me around. Don't worry, you'll still get your commission."

"Of course I will. The agreement I got Adam to sign is ironclad. He can't back out if I have a buyer," Floyd said with a laugh. "Phone me after you've seen it, then, and we can go from there."

As Melanie hung up the phone, she sat back in her

kitchen chair. In comparison to the lovely open spaces of the house, her apartment felt cramped, and instead of trees and a large yard, she overlooked a parking lot. Just like all the other apartments she and her family had lived in, dragged around the country by a father always on the move. Always on the lookout for a chance to make more money doing less work.

By the time they had moved to Derwin, she had been through six schools in seven years.

Harold Visser had promised Melanie and her mother that he was going to settle down in Derwin. Buy a house. Make a home. Go to church with Melanie and her mother.

Though they'd stayed in Derwin longer than most places, in fourteen months they'd been on the move again. But this time her parents had separated and Melanie and her mother had gone their own way.

When Melanie had graduated from high school, she'd become a nurse. She had lived in more small apartments, saving every penny for a place of her own. Thanks to a legacy left her when her father died and thanks to her own scrimping and saving, she now had a sizable down payment for a house.

Melanie fought a pang of sorrow as she doodled an elaborate circle around the Engler house price she had scribbled down. Her dream was supposed to have included her mother. But now Melanie lived on her own, and more than ever she yearned for a permanent place. A home.

And as Melanie opened her Bible later that night, she searched for familiar passages of comfort. She turned to Psalms and read in Psalm 84, "Even the sparrow has found a home, and the swallow a nest for herself, where she may have her young, a place near your altar." Melanie put her finger on the passage and read it again.

Home. It was what she had wanted ever since she had got to know Dena Shewchuk. She had dreamed about owning a home, a place that stayed the same. Even sparrows and swallows look for and desire a home.

Melanie finished reading, then snapped off the light of her bedside table and snuggled into her blankets. She thought again of the house. It was like a dream to think that the one place that represented all she longed for might be hers. If she was willing to make the commitment. And she was. She had a good job now. Though classified as part-time, she was working full-time hours with the promise that it would be turned into a permanent job.

Everything was in place. But if she bought the house, what would happen to Helen?

That thought stopped her. Helen would need another place to live. And if Adam was willing to offer her that, it shouldn't be Melanie's concern.

I want to help them, Lord, she prayed, looking out the window of her apartment into the small sliver of the evening sky that she could see out her window. *Give me the wisdom I need to do it.*

She rolled over and pulled her blankets up around her shoulder. And as she drifted off to sleep, her last thoughts were of wavy hair and blue eyes.

* * *

Adam stripped his leather gloves off and sauntered up to the house, mentally noting the work he still had to do before this yard was cleared off.

Piles of lumber draped with tarps covered part of the yard close to the house. Bricks, once neatly stacked up, now lay tumbled beside the lumber. The lumber was for the rooms he had been going to put in the basement. The brick for the fireplace that Lana had wanted rebuilt.

The clench of sorrow he felt was unexpected and unwelcome. He should be over Lana's death by now. At least, that's what the grief counselor had said.

It was this house, he thought as he jogged up the back steps and yanked open the screen door to the porch. Each time he turned around he was faced with memories of Lana.

The memories not only hurt, they accused.

"Is that you, Melanie?" he heard his mother call from her bedroom.

"Sorry to disappoint you, Mom," Adam called back, washing his hands. "It's just me."

Helen lay in her bed, her hands folded over her chest, her features drawn. Tiffany lay on the floor beside her, coloring with some fat crayons that Adam had bought for her in town yesterday.

"Are you going to make some coffee for Melanie?"

"In a minute." Adam threw the towel into the laundry basket in the corner of his mother's bedroom and carefully lowered himself onto the edge of her bed. "Do you want to stay in bed this morning?"

"I'd like to, but I'm sure Melanie will get me up

when she gets here." She sighed lightly, fingering a fold in the quilt. "Adam, I know you don't like being here. But I still think it's the best place for you and your little girl. You have to think of Tiffany, as well."

"I do, Mother," he said with a forced smile. "I think of her needs all the time."

"But Lana's family…"

"They can come and see her any time now. Eastbar is only half an hour away. Calgary a couple of hours." Adam saw a flash of reflected light through the far window and got up. Through the fly-specked glass he saw a small red car come to a halt in front of the house, and Melanie got out.

In spite of the sorrow he had felt only moments ago, Adam felt a stir of reaction. Even stronger than the one he'd felt when he met her yesterday.

Today her hair swung to her shoulders, catching the sun like melted chocolate. Her loose pants, tied low on her hips, and her flowing cotton shirt couldn't hide the easy grace of her slender limbs.

Beautiful, he thought, watching as she stopped, looking up at the house. A faint smile played on her lips.

What was she thinking about? What was going on behind those unique amber eyes?

He turned away from the window to catch his mother grinning at him, looking livelier than she had a few moments ago. "Lovely girl, isn't she?"

Adam didn't even acknowledge her comment. "Do you still want to wait here for her, or do you want to go to the kitchen?"

"I'll wait here."

"Suit yourself." He crouched down beside Tiffany and fingered a curl away from her face. "Are you coming with me, punkin, or are you going to stay with Gramma?"

"Stay with Gramma," Tiffany replied, not even looking up.

Tiffany's devotion to a grandmother she hardly knew surprised him. Since they had come back to Derwin a week ago, it was as if Tiffany had forged a unique bond with her. His daughter still acted reserved around him and it still hurt. A lot.

He closed the door to the bedroom and went to open the door for Melanie.

She stood on the step, looking over the yard beside the house, her fingers resting lightly on the railing of the veranda.

As he watched, she leaned forward, looking around the yard, her eyes bright, her mouth lifted in a large smile of pure pleasure. And he wondered what caused it.

He opened the door. "Good morning, Melanie."

Melanie jumped, looking guilty.

"Sorry. I was just looking at the yard. It's so lovely."

"You must have a good imagination to be able to see past the piles of lumber."

Melanie just smiled. "I remember it from before."

"So you said. How many years ago was that?"

"Probably about fourteen. I've always loved this place." She glanced back at him over her shoulder. "I phoned your real estate agent last night. I thought I would let you know I'm serious about buying the house."

Adam leaned against the door frame, surprised that his disparaging comments from the day before hadn't deterred her.

"Floyd told you my asking price?"

"He did, and I was hoping, if you had time, that you could show me around the house after I'm done with your mother."

"I can't talk you out of it, can I?"

Melanie frowned. "You're the worst salesperson. No. I love this place and I'd like a tour."

Adam was just going to consent and then look away, the picture of casual, when something in her eyes drew his, held them.

What was it about her that caused this lapse? This appeal that he wished wasn't there? In the past three years he had neither been given nor taken the opportunity to spend any kind of time with another woman. He was a widower with a little girl who needed him.

And now his mother needed him. He didn't have time for any kind of flirtation, casual or otherwise.

Melanie smiled up at him, and in spite of his previous rationalizing, for the first time in years he felt an answering lift in his chest. A lightness in his mind.

"Is your mother inside?"

Adam pulled himself together. Gathered his wandering emotions. "Yes. She's in her bedroom."

"Then I'll see you later?" She turned the statement into a question.

"Yeah. I'll be out back." He held the door open for

her, and just before she stepped through, she gave him another glance. Another smile.

And Adam's heart gave another lift.

Chapter Three

Melanie lowered Tiffany to her bed and gently tucked the quilt under her chin. Tiffany stiffened, then settled down, her eyelids flickering.

Melanie smoothed down a tuft of hair. She remembered putting Dena's little brother to bed in this same room when she and Dena would baby-sit. She could recall so easily the soft, heavy warmth of a sleeping child. Dena had always complained, but as an only child Melanie had loved the responsibility of younger brothers and sisters and the squabbling and laughter that would ebb and flow through the house.

She closed the door behind her with a soft click and walked quietly down the hallway. Her fingers trailed the banister once worn smooth from bodies sliding down it, now sticky with accumulated grime.

She stopped at the bottom of the stairs, listening. She could almost hear the sound of Dena's father's booming voice as he came home from work. The squeal of children all running to be the first to greet him.

Now the house lay quiet, slumbering in the early afternoon. Sun flowed into the kitchen, showing—more vividly than Adam's words could—the neglect of the house.

This house needed a family who cared, Melanie thought, her memories superimposing themselves on the scene.

You're not a family.

The words echoed through a life as empty as this house, mocking her decision. What's a single girl like you doing thinking of buying a house?

Someday she had hoped she would meet someone with whom she could share her life, but her mother's experience had made her cautious.

In the meantime she wasn't going to sit around and wait for the knight she and Dena had dreamed of. She meant to take charge of her own life. And if that meant buying a house as a single girl, then so be it.

She stepped out onto the porch and saw Adam.

He was piling lumber onto a trailer behind his half-ton truck. Melanie knew she should let him know she was there, but her memories kept her in the shadows of the porch, watching.

His back glistened, his muscles working as he picked up another load of wood. His hair, damp from sweat, curled around his face, softening the hard lines.

A faint echo of the yearning she had felt tucking Tiffany in struck her again. But she stopped herself.

He's not the hero from your past, Melanie reminded herself. She knew what she wanted in life. Knew what she wanted in a future partner. Adam was not it, she thought, remembering what Helen had said about Adam giving up on God.

So why did she still feel this strange connection with him?

She cleared her throat, and Adam looked up.

"I was wondering if you had the time to show me around?"

He grabbed his shirt hanging over the side of his truck. As he threaded his arms through the sleeves he called out, "Just give me a chance to check on my daughter…."

"She's sleeping."

Adam's fingers paused over the snaps. "Sleeping? In my mother's room?"

"No. I laid her down in what I presumed was her bedroom. I took a wild guess and figured that she would be the only one who had a quilt covered with cartoon ducks."

"You didn't have to do that," he said, his tone defensive as he came closer.

"Probably not," Melanie admitted, with an attempt at humor and a smile. "But I didn't think she'd appreciate the crick she would get in her neck from lying all twisted on your mother's bedroom floor."

She was rewarded with an absent nod from Adam as he rolled up the cuffs of his shirt. "Where did you want to start?"

"Well, I've already seen your mother's room and…"

"Actually, that's the master bedroom. It was the first room that I fixed up. It needed some structural work, but my wife wanted at least one room done."

His wife. Lana.

"Why don't you surprise me?" she said.

"Not my specialty, I'm afraid," he returned, a ghost of a smile glimmering over his lips.

A smile that did funny things to her heart.

"Well, let's start with the basics," she said brusquely, masking her reaction to him.

Melanie didn't know much about houses, or buildings or construction work, but Adam did. As she requested, he took her down to the basement.

"The foundation is solid, but some of the floor joists need to be replaced." Adam pointed out which ones, pursing his lips.

"Is that a lot of work?"

"Most definitely. And costly."

"Can you tell me how much?"

"Not offhand, but if you want I can break down some of the expenses."

She nodded, as second thoughts began nibbling at her confidence.

"You're going to need to install a new hot water tank. This one is rusted and will probably not pass the house inspection." Adam gestured toward a large squat tank perched in the corner. She and Dena used to hide behind it and scare her brothers and sisters when they would come down to the cold room on some errand for their mother.

"The furnace is not too bad. But same thing again. It's old and will some day need to be replaced. The newer ones are much quieter."

"It always made such a huge rumble when it started

up in the morning," Melanie said with a smile. "It sounded like a plane taking off. You could hear it all the way upstairs."

"Well, that rumble is not what you want to hear." He showed her the cold room, with its familiar musty smell still permeating the wood. It, too, needed work.

"The wiring at least is up to code now," he said, letting her precede him up the stairs to the kitchen. "I had to install a larger breaker box to carry the extra wiring I wanted to do in here. There aren't near enough electrical outlets. Especially in the kitchen and the bedrooms."

"I know. The Shewchuks used to have extension cords all over the place."

"They're lucky they didn't have a fire," Adam said as he held open the door at the top of the stairs. "When I bought the house from them, every outlet was doubled and tripled up. Not a good thing."

Adam stopped in the middle of the kitchen, his hands on his hips as he drew in a sigh. "Now, this is one room I was itching to redo. Those cabinets are simply awful."

"I like the design," Melanie said with a smile. "Turn of the century, aren't they? A fresh coat of paint would make them look better."

"It won't make them work better. They're all out of whack. None of the doors are plumb and most of the drawers stick."

Melanie didn't respond to his negative comment. Instead she walked over to the bay window and sank onto the seat built into it. "I have always loved this spot.

We used to sit here and read and eat apples. Mrs. Shewchuk would be busy in the kitchen, baking and cooking and making our mouths water with all the lovely smells." She laughed lightly, turning to look at the rest of the kitchen.

Adam shook his head as if in disbelief. "You're bound and determined to see past the work this house needs, aren't you?"

Melanie dismissed his comment with a wave of her hand. "And you're bound and determined to show the worst side of this house. If Floyd knew how you were talking, he'd have a fit."

Adam snorted. "Real estate agents have their own language. I speak plain English."

"But it is a beautiful house, don't you think? You must have thought so at one time or you wouldn't have bought it."

Adam only shrugged. "The reality is, this house needs a lot of work. I would be lying if I didn't tell you that. The eaves and soffits need to be repainted. The attic needs a new vent. I could go on."

"You know quite a bit about building." Melanie wanted to stop the list of all the work that needed to be done. He was giving her second thoughts and she didn't want to allow them entrance. For the first time in her life, she felt as if she had found a home.

"I should. I'm a general contractor."

"So you work for yourself?"

He nodded.

"How did you manage to take time off for your mother?"

"I'm technically on my holidays." He glanced around the room with a faint grimace. "Tiffany and I were going to go to Disneyland."

Melanie stifled a shudder. She couldn't imagine how a child as young as Tiffany would enjoy being dragged around a venue as busy as Disneyland. "I think this is a better alternative," she said. "She has a lovely yard to play in. She has time to connect with you and her grandmother."

Adam only shrugged. Melanie figured she had already said too much, so she might as well press her next point.

"I have to confess, besides you showing me the house, I want to talk to you about your mother." *Please Lord, give me the right words,* she prayed. "I know you asked me to help you out. Help her get used to the idea about moving. But she got quite upset when I mentioned it just now. She was running a fever."

Adam angled her a puzzled glance. "How do you make the connection between her fever and my moving? It's probably from her surgery."

Melanie shook her head. "The wound is clean with no sign of infection. She had a temp yesterday, as well. Strange as it sounds, it isn't unusual for this to happen. For stress to bring on a temperature." She folded her arms over her chest, striving to look professional and in charge. She knew Adam wouldn't like what she had to say next. "I think you should reconsider moving her so soon."

Adam shook his head. "And how am I supposed to do that? If the house sells, I'm hooped. I've got a sick mother and then I'm pressuring her to move. Not a situation I want to put her in either."

Melanie could see the sense in it and ventured her next suggestion. "I'm going to be putting a firm offer on the house to Floyd, and I'm willing to wait." Saying the words aloud made them more real and a little more frightening. In spite of what Adam had told her, she knew deep within her being that she wanted this house.

"She so obviously wants to stay here," Melanie continued, sensing he was giving in. "And it is such a good place. It's quiet, it's familiar." Melanie looked around the kitchen. Sure, it needed some work, but it was so homey and comfortable. How come Adam couldn't see that? "I think she'll heal better here, in a place she's comfortable." She pressed her lips together for fear her next words would spill out.

And it would be a good time for you to connect with your daughter.

Adam sighed, shoving his hands through his hair, biting his lip. He did not look pleased and she felt as if she had let him down.

A faint beeping sound broke the silence and she glanced down at the pager hooked to her belt.

"Whoops. Got a message." They were in the kitchen, and thankfully her briefcase and nurse's bag were on the chair where she had left them.

She pulled out her cell phone, dialed the number and was put through to her supervisor. She was asked to cover for another nurse who had called in sick. Her afternoon just got busier, she thought, snapping her phone shut.

She glanced at Adam. "I have to go. The rest of the tour will have to wait until Monday when I'll be seeing your mother again," she said with a touch of regret, slinging the strap of her briefcase over her shoulder.

"Okay." Adam stepped back, slipping his hands into the back pockets of his pants. "What about getting the doctor's approval to move my mother?"

Melanie clutched the handle of her briefcase. "You don't have to take my advice, Adam," she said quietly. "If you can arrange for a stretcher and an ambulance and are willing to pay for that, you can move her any time you want. I'm just telling you what I believe is best for her in my capacity as her nurse. And I'm telling you because I know you care about her and her well-being. After all, that's the main priority here, isn't it?"

Adam held her gaze, then glanced around the room, as if looking for something. Answers, maybe.

"I'll think about it," he said.

Melanie couldn't help but feel a touch of sorrow for Helen, and for Adam, as well. She held his narrowed gaze and slowly nodded her head. It was all she could ask him to do.

As she drove away, she glanced in her rearview mirror. Adam stood on the porch, watching her. Then the trees hid him from view, swaying lightly in the afternoon breeze.

Once again she wondered why he would want to leave this beautiful place.

"Did he say how extensive the reconstruction would be?" Bob Tessier smiled across the office table at

Melanie. For the past twenty minutes she had been talking to Bob, the loans officer at her bank, and she still didn't know if the bank would be willing to lend her the money. But after seeing only part of the house yesterday she knew she wanted to buy it.

"We didn't make it to the second floor and the attic, so I'm not sure what needs to be done there."

Bob Tessier doodled on the notepad, frowning. "I know the bank would like to have an itemized account of the refurbishments necessary so we can better ascertain the value of the house."

Melanie resisted the urge to roll her eyes. The man was in sore need of a thesaurus. "I have a large down payment, which, by the way, is sitting in a bank account here. I have more than enough room to fix the house."

"That is correct. However, we need to secure our portion of the debt. And, I might remind you, your position of employment is, at best, tenuous."

"A position that will be turning into a full-time one after a meeting of the next Health Authority." Melanie smiled to overcome her growing frustration. She didn't tell him she had to apply for it, but her supervisor had practically guaranteed her the job. "But if this bank isn't willing to work with me on this, I can easily set up an appointment with someone at the credit union down the street."

Bob straightened, the implied threat changing his demeanor. "There's no need to do that, Melanie. I'm sure we can accommodate you. However, you must understand that we need to protect our investment. And

I wouldn't be doing my job if I didn't advise you as to all the risks inherent in this purchase."

Melanie didn't feel like arguing with him. Nor, in spite of her threat, did she feel like moving her account. It had taken her a couple of days just to move everything to this bank, order checks, set up her charge cards. Besides, if she did that, Bob Tessier would be hounding her every choir practice they attended together to move her account back, just as he had hounded her to bring it to their bank in the first place.

"So if you would be willing to supply a list of the necessary repairs, I will see that your loan application is expedited." Bob gave her a conciliatory smile. "I have no doubt it will be approved."

Relief tingled through Melanie. Relief mixed with a few more second thoughts based on Bob's obvious reluctance to lend her the money on this project. Buying a house as a single woman was quite a commitment. Buying a house that needed so much work might be one of the more foolish things she had done. Was she sure she wanted to do it?

She thought again of the house, the setting, the peace she felt there. She thought of her apartment. The constant moving.

She thought of her mother and how she had yearned for a place with roots. A place like Derwin, she had often said with a weary sigh.

Yes, she was sure.

"Okay. I can get Adam to draw that up."

Bob frowned. "He's the vendor, is he not?"

"That's correct. But he's also a general contractor."

"I'm a little concerned that his appraisal might not be without prejudice."

Melanie almost laughed. Bob should have heard Adam giving her the tour. If anything, Adam might be prejudiced against the house. "Then get a building inspector to verify." Melanie smiled past her frustration.

"I will agree to that. Once I receive that information we can proceed from there."

"I'll try to get the list to you as soon as possible." Melanie got to her feet and shook Bob's hand. "I'll be in touch."

"Looking forward to it." Bob smiled, still holding her hand, and Melanie carefully smiled back, wondering when it would be polite to reclaim her hand. She wasn't blind. Since she'd joined the choir she had been getting fairly blatant signals from him. Not that she was the least bit interested. But right now she couldn't afford to antagonize him.

"And I imagine we'll be seeing you at choir practice?" he said, coming around the desk to stand by her.

Melanie gave him a vague movement of her shoulders that she hoped wouldn't encourage him without looking rude. "Of course. I go every week." She smiled, then turned to open the door, but Bob already had it open.

"Thanks," she murmured as she walked through the door, her head bent. She was afraid to make eye contact for fear he might follow her out of the room and through the main lobby.

Bob was a good man and a kind man. He had a wonderful baritone voice. He attended the same church she did. And he was single.

None of which made any dent in her feelings for him.

She laughed at herself as she walked out of the bank and into a beautiful summer day in downtown Derwin. She was still possessed of that same silly romantic notion she had created when she and Dena would play in the top floor of the tower of the house.

While Dena's dreams were of some more modern man, Melanie's tended to be more romantic. And her hero was a knight who would come riding up on a horse. A knight worthy of her love and affection.

"Hello, Melanie."

The deep voice behind her sprang into her daydreams. Melanie jumped and turned around, her hand on her chest.

"Sorry," Adam said with a half smile. "Didn't mean to scare you."

He was carrying his daughter easily with one arm, his other hand hooked into a couple of plastic bags. "You were certainly lost in thought. I called you a couple of times."

Melanie looked up into his blue, blue eyes, blinked, then looked away. Having her hand held by Bob Tessier didn't even come close to the impact this man's gaze had on her.

"Sorry, I was just at the bank." Her hand fluttered in the direction of the building behind him. "I was talking to them about the house, actually."

"Really?" Adam shifted Tiffany's weight on his arm.

"Do you want me to take her?" Melanie said, holding out her hands. "You look like you have enough to carry."

"No, that's okay." Adam smiled at Tiffany, giving her a light hitch. "She's not heavy." He spoke with such pride and love that Melanie felt an echo of the yearning she had had a couple of days ago. Had her father ever looked at her with such longing? Such pride?

Tiffany was a lucky little girl.

"Want to go." Tiffany leaned toward Melanie and away from Adam.

Pain flickered in Adam's eyes, deepened the frown on his forehead, and Melanie regretted making the offer.

But Tiffany's forward momentum made it awkward for him to continue holding her, so Melanie lifted her hands higher and took Tiffany out of his arms.

"Actually, it's good I met you. I need to talk to you about the house," Melanie continued, pulling Tiffany close to her as she tried to fill the uneasy silence that followed. They came to the corner of the main street. Across from them was the park, its tall trees and soft grass beckoning.

"We can sit there while we talk," Adam said. "Tiffany could use a break from cement sidewalks and stores. But I don't want to leave my mom alone too long."

His devotion to his mother and his daughter was heartwarming. She couldn't help but think of her father, whose contact with her before he died had been minimal at best.

"It won't take long."

As soon as they got to the park Melanie crouched to set Tiffany down, but she clung to Melanie's neck. "Stay with you," she demanded, her fingers tangling in Melanie's hair.

Adam set the grocery bags on the ground and sat beside her, his knees resting on his elbows. He angled her an aggrieved look, which she guessed had much to do with the fact that Tiffany was on her lap and not his. When his eyes flicked to his daughter, Melanie knew it to be true.

He looked down at his hands, pressing his thumbs against each other. "So what exactly did you need to know?"

"Bob Tessier at the bank wants you to make a list of all the repairs that the house needs done and a possible estimate of the cost."

"Are you sure you want me to do this?"

Melanie lifted her shoulder in a shrug. "You seem to know best what needs to be done. I assured Bob you would be impartial."

"I'll have to write that down to remind me." He pulled a pen out of his pocket, clicked it and scribbled the information on the back of his hand.

"Do you know how bad that ink is for you?"

Adam shrugged. "That's some old wives' tale. I'm surprised a professional like you would bother to repeat it." He smiled at her again, the faint outline of a dimple appearing in his cheek.

"There's been countless studies done on it," she said, trying to keep her expression stern. "You'll be sorry when you're on your deathbed, dying of some ink-related illness, that you didn't listen to me."

"I might, at that," he said quietly.

"Listen? To you?" Tiffany repeated, catching Melanie's face in her hands as if not appreciating being left out of the conversation. Melanie turned to her, smiling at the little girl's serious expression.

"I'm just talking to your daddy." Melanie touched her nose to the little girl's and was rewarded with a bright smile. "Do you want to sit with your daddy?"

Tiffany looked over at Adam, who had straightened as if waiting, and Melanie realized what a tenuous situation she had created with her thoughtless question. Thankfully Tiffany got down and toddled over to her father.

"So you're thinking of buying the house." Adam pulled Tiffany up on his lap. "Why?"

How to explain the emotions the house engendered. The feeling that given the proper care, the house could be a home that welcomed people. "I've always been in love with that house," she said, realizing how silly it might sound. "I think it could be a good investment, once it's fixed up."

"But a single woman like you. Surely you don't need the headache."

"I don't think it would be a headache," she said quietly. "I think it would be wonderful to have a home."

Adam's laugh was a harsh sound. "Trust me, Melanie, that house is no home."

The sharp sound of his reply pulled her out of her reverie. "Why do you say that?"

Adam didn't reply. Simply toyed with his daughter's hair.

"Is it because of your wife?"

His scowl showed her that she had hit a bull's-eye. And a sensitive point. "Maybe" was all he said.

She wanted to know more and was wondering how to ask him when a young woman called out his name and came running toward them, shattering the moment.

"I heard you were back in town." She stopped in front of Adam, smiling broadly. Her blond hair was pulled up in a loose twist, strands artfully framing her face. Her sleeveless shirt barely skimmed the waistband of her low-cut blue jeans. Melanie caught the glimmer of a ring in her navel.

"Hello, Roxanne." Adam politely stood up, still holding Tiffany like a shield.

"It's been ages since you've been around," she said, disregarding his retreat. She slipped an arm around his waist.

Adam threw Melanie an aggrieved glance over Tiffany's head and patted Roxanne awkwardly on her shoulder with his one free hand.

Roxanne pulled back. "The Gerrard family has been asking about you. Wondering when you were going to come around with Tiffany." Roxanne stroked the little girl's cheek, but Tiffany pulled away.

Adam said nothing, his eyes narrowing, his lips thinning. Melanie had heard bits and pieces from the girls at work about the Gerrards, Lana's family. They lived in Eastbar, not far from here.

"They know where I'm staying. They can come around any time."

"I'll tell them next time I see them." Roxanne turned to Melanie as if trying to fit her in the picture.

Adam introduced her, and Roxanne merely nodded, dismissing her with that one curt movement. But as their eyes met, Melanie felt a twinge of recognition.

Roxanne must have felt it, too. "Do I know you?" she asked.

"Melanie used to live in Derwin. About fourteen years ago," Adam offered.

Roxanne straightened, looking from Adam to Melanie. Time hovered and a vague memory coalesced.

Melanie was a young girl again. New to the school. Coming in halfway through the grade eight school year. She was pushed up against the wall of the school, being teased about her clothes, her hair and her makeup by two young girls. One of them was Roxanne.

Melanie was frightened and crying, something the girls thought quite funny.

Then a tall young man came by. He stopped, looked the situation over and, though he didn't know Melanie nor she him, he held out his hand to her.

"Hey, there," he said with a smile and a dimple. "I've been looking for you."

The girls stepped back. Roxanne's mouth fell open as she looked from Melanie to the young man.

And Melanie took his hand and walked away with him.

It was a crazy chance she'd taken then, Melanie realized. She had known nothing about him. Yet at that moment she'd been convinced this young man would not hurt her. That she was safe with him.

That young man was, of course, Adam.

"Don't remember," Roxanne said, dismissing her.

She turned back to Adam. "So you going to go to the community barbecue? I think some of the Gerrards are going to be there."

"I might be in Calgary by then," Adam said, holding Tiffany with both arms, forestalling any more shows of affection by Roxanne.

"Well, if you're still around, come on by." Unfazed by Adam's body language, she laid a hand on his arm. "It's so good to see you back. Don't be such a stranger." She turned to Melanie and gave her a vague "See you around." Tiffany got a pat on the head, and with one last teasing smile at Adam, Roxanne was gone.

Melanie felt a little breathless, both with the energy Roxanne exuded and the memory.

Her knight in shining armor.

Melanie pushed the thought aside. Adam was no knight. He was a widower with enough on his mind.

And she was in the process of buying the house he wanted to sell so he could move to the city.

"Did you need to know anything more from me?" Adam asked, turning to her.

Melanie shook her head. "I have tomorrow off. It's Saturday, but I'd like to come by and see your mother anyhow. Maybe I could get you to finish our tour of the house then?"

"I can do that."

"Go see her." Tiffany pointed to Melanie. Adam obliged, setting his daughter down.

As Tiffany toddled over to Melanie, Adam sat down and pushed his hair back from his face with a sigh. "I wish I knew why she did this," he said softly. He raised his head to Melanie, his hands dangling between his knees. "She seems to prefer any stranger to me."

His pained expression created a responding tug. She had a good idea why Tiffany treated him the way she did, but this time she was going to be a bit more careful about speaking her mind. "She didn't prefer Roxanne."

Adam lifted one shoulder in a shrug. "That's true enough."

"Besides, she might be the kind of child who goes easily to others," Melanie said, choosing her words with care. "I've seen it happen many times." That was true. Some children went easily to strangers. Were only too happy to spend time with other adults. Others made strange at the slightest notice from any other adult. Tiffany was obviously the former.

"Who knows?" he said, rubbing his chin with his finger. "C'mon, baby, time to go."

Once again Tiffany returned willingly to his arms, creating a smile on her father's lips. Adam hefted Tiffany to his hip, then snapped his fingers. "I almost forgot. I was supposed to ask you to come for supper tomorrow night. I tried to phone you, but there was no answer." He took the bags from her, their fingers tangling in the plastic handles. "Just so you're warned, I'm cooking, so you can turn down the invite and my feelings won't be hurt."

Melanie sensed Adam's reluctance at having her visit. She knew he didn't quite trust her assessment of his mother and her care. But the thought of sitting at home alone on a Saturday night was just too forlorn.

"I don't mind finding out what your cooking is

like," she said quietly. "Besides, I'd like to see the rest of the house."

"Then we'll see you tomorrow night."

Melanie nodded. The idea was more appealing than she liked to admit.

Chapter Four

"That was very delicious, Adam." Melanie wiped her mouth and set her napkin beside her plate.

"I'm glad you enjoyed it." Adam had to admit he was quite pleased with his efforts. "I did take a cooking class so I would at least know the difference between a pot and a pan."

"Vital information, indeed," Melanie murmured with a sparkle in her eye.

Again Adam found himself looking at her, holding her gaze, reconciling the young girl he remembered with this very attractive young woman who wasn't scared to speak her mind. And whether he liked to admit it or not, something elemental was happening between them. Feelings he really didn't have time or space for in his life. Feelings he wanted to deny because they seemed disloyal to Lana's memory.

"I have to say myself, it was excellent, Adam," Helen said as well. Adam glanced his mother's way, his cheeks warming as he caught the wink she gave him.

His mother had been at him all day about Melanie, how wonderful she was with Tiffany, how caring and considerate she was. And a good Christian girl.

Not that it mattered, Adam thought, folding up his napkin. He wasn't looking.

"Get down," Tiffany said, pushing herself back from the table.

"You need to go to bed, sweetheart," Adam said, picking her up. She leaned back in his arms, her blue eyes wide as she stared at him as she would a total stranger.

She did that just often enough to remind him she wasn't sure of him. Which always hit him right in the guilt zone.

Once things slowed down with the business, he would be home more, he reminded himself as he walked up the stairs to her bedroom. He just didn't have time right now.

He took his time tucking her in. Playing with her. By the time he left, she was smiling, curled up in her bed, her teddy bear tucked under one chubby arm. He turned at the doorway, looking back at her, the light from the hallway slanting into her room. He couldn't help but wonder what his life would have been like had Lana lived and they had stayed here, in this house, as a family.

It hadn't happened that way, he thought with a trace of bitterness. That was over. He closed the door and trudged toward the stairs. As he walked down the hallway to the kitchen, he heard Melanie's laughter, Helen's responding chuckle.

Melanie had already cleared the table and was washing the dishes, an old apron of his mother's tied over her dress, a tea towel slung over her shoulder. She was wearing a simple sheath splashed with brightly colored flowers. She had put her hair up in a loose topknot, emphasizing her high cheekbones, her mysterious eyes. His mother was sitting in her chair, her cheeks flushed, her eyes bright.

"So then he told me I didn't need to bother coming around with my needles and my advice. Then he turned on the television full blast and I couldn't say anything anymore." Melanie flashed a grin at his mother. "Which is a real punishment for someone like me."

Helen laughed again. "He's a funny old coot."

"I think his problem is worse than simply Alzheimer's, which is bad enough."

"Thank the Lord my mind is good," Helen said.

Melanie glanced over her shoulder at Helen. "And my mind works like lightning. One brilliant flash and then it's gone."

Adam couldn't help but smile as Helen's laugh reverberated through the kitchen. Adam hadn't seen Helen this animated in a long time.

He leaned on the doorjamb, watching, content to simply enjoy the sight of a young, attractive woman in the kitchen of his house. The whole room seemed brighter because Melanie was there. She'd always had that effect, he realized. Even as a young girl she'd had a guileless air about her mingled with an unabashed enjoyment of life. Though he'd been older, she'd still caught his attention.

"Hey, son, if you wait any longer, Melanie will have the dishes done."

Adam felt a little sheepish at being caught staring,

and pushed himself away from the door frame. He caught a towel from the bar across the stove and strode to Melanie's side at the counter.

"I guess the least I could do is dry," he said, plucking a dripping plate from the drying rack on the counter.

"I hope a dishwasher is part of your renovation plans?" Melanie asked, dropping a handful of utensils on the rack with a metallic clatter.

"Absolutely. I figure there's better things to keep a person busy."

"So, Melanie, what keeps you busy?" Helen asked. "Do you ever go out? I can't see that a beautiful girl like you spends much time alone."

Adam was about to give his mother a warning look when Melanie replied, apparently not the least put out by his mother's nosiness.

"Sometimes I work late, updating client files." Melanie dropped a dripping dish on the dish rack. "As for my social life, there's a community barbecue next weekend. I'm looking forward to that."

"You should go, too, Adam."

This time he gave his mother a pointed look.

"You don't get out enough, Adam," she said with a sweet smile, ignoring his frown. "I'm sure Melanie wouldn't mind if you came along."

A heavy silence greeted that remark. Melanie thankfully said nothing, didn't even blink as she continued washing up.

"I can tell you what I wouldn't mind knowing," Melanie said, glancing sidelong at him, "is a decent place to get my car's oil changed."

Adam felt like hugging her. Diplomatic and unfazed by his mother's pitifully obvious matchmaking. "Try Kestrals. They were pretty good last I used them."

"Thanks for the tip." She flashed him a bright smile. "There's nothing a single woman needs more than a good mechanic."

Adam couldn't stop his answering smile. Couldn't stop himself from once again getting drawn into her infectious humor and her easy manner.

"Well, that's the last one." Melanie set a pot on the drying rack, pulled the drain and rinsed the sink out with quick, efficient movements. She turned to Helen. "I should get you to bed and then be going."

Adam felt a tug of regret at the thought of her leaving so soon. "Didn't you want to see the rest of the house?" he asked before he had a chance to think about what he was getting into.

Melanie met his gaze, her features softening. "If that's okay with you, I'd love to. I almost forgot."

He hadn't. In spite of his mixed feelings, his plans, the direction he was pushing his life in, he still found himself looking forward to her company.

He knew it was simple loneliness. An excuse to spend some time with an attractive and interesting woman. Someone from a happier, more innocent time in his life.

"And this, of course, is the top tower room. Or more accurately, turret," Adam said, opening the doorway to the room in the corner of the upstairs.

He stood aside, and Melanie had to walk past him

to get into the room. Her arm brushed his, and the faintest suggestion of his aftershave teased her nostrils.

A distinctly masculine scent, she thought with a pulse of expectation. She moved farther into the room, the light from the hallway throwing an oblong of gold into the room. Dusk had fallen, though she could still see the outlines of the trees outside and the shimmer of the pond.

She walked to the curved windows as fresh memories assailed her.

"This room could use some work, too," Adam said, leaving the door open. "It needs a new light bulb."

"You better change it before your mother decides to," Melanie said, glancing over her shoulder. Adam stood silhouetted in the doorway. She couldn't read his expression, but to her surprise she heard a light chuckle.

"My mother has always had a stubborn streak," he said softly, coming to stand behind her. "And an appalling habit of sticking her nose in other people's business. I apologize for her comments downstairs."

Melanie laughed. "Don't worry. I could tell you worse stories about clients who have a brother or nephew or son who would be just perfect for me." She gave him another quick smile, hoping to ease his obvious discomfort. "But if you want to come to the barbecue, you're more than welcome."

"Thanks for the invite," he said, returning her grin. "If I'm around, I just might take you up on it."

Melanie turned back to the window. "I remember coming here with Dena. We would dress up in her mother's clothes and pretend we were noble ladies waiting for our knights to come and rescue us."

"Rescue you from what?" Melanie could hear a faint note of amusement in his voice.

"Her little brothers," Melanie said with a light laugh. "They would always interrupt our fantasy by throwing lumps of dirt up at the window. We got even, though. We brought up a bunch of balloons that were left over from one of her brothers' parties and filled them with water." She laughed. "They made a lovely splat from two stories up."

"And now?" Adam asked, his voice holding a quiet warmth. "What do you daydream about now?"

A home. A family. A place where I belong. But Adam was not the man to whom she could voice these yearnings aloud. Not anymore.

"Low interest rates and good gas mileage," she said, trying to dispel her awareness of him with light words.

"Lofty ideals," he said, his voice a soft rumble behind her.

"Set attainable goals, my mother always said."

"Your mother was a wise person."

Her mother was a lot of things, Melanie thought as other, sadder memories drifted into the evening. She, too, had loved this house. And she would have loved nothing more than to help Melanie paint and plan and fix.

She missed her mother.

She moved away from Adam closer to the window and pressed her thumb against the latch. To her surprise it opened easily.

She pushed the window all the way open, resting her hands on the windowsill as she looked out over a view that harkened back to happier times in her life.

The ratcheting chirp of frogs laid down a tuneless song counterpointed by the velvet hoot of an owl.

She drew in a deep breath of the soft evening air, trying to imagine herself looking out over this whenever she wanted. It seemed like a dream that she hardly dared cling too hard to, for fear it would get taken away.

"Isn't it peaceful?" she said softly, her voice taking on a reverent tone. "I missed this place when we left."

"Why did you move away, Melanie?"

His quiet question eased past memories and emotions gently into the atmosphere.

"My father was always on the move." Melanie ran the palms of her hands over the blistered varnish of the windowsill. "He could never stay in one place longer than six months. He promised Derwin was going to be a last step. Though we did stay here the longest. Then another idea and a better opportunity came up and we were gone."

"I wondered what happened to you. One day you were at youth group and the next day you were gone."

In spite of the intervening years, Melanie's heart faltered. Memories and daydreams of Adam had taken up a large portion of that first year away. She had never considered that she had been other than a passing memory for him.

"Nice to know I was missed."

"You were."

"And you got to stay here," she said with a wistful sigh. "And end up in my dream home."

"It is a beautiful place."

Adam's brief agreement surprised her. Encouraged further disclosure. "When we moved away, I used to be homesick for this house. For the loving family that lived here."

"The Shewchuks?" Adam's voice held a disquieting note. It reminded her of other things he had said.

"When I first came here you mentioned something about not buying this house from a happy family," Melanie said, half turning to him. "What did you mean by that?"

His face was shadowed, his expression a mystery, save for the glint of his eyes, now a molten silver. "When we bought this house, Mrs. Shewchuk was a single mother, raising what was left of her family. This was about four years ago." He spoke softly, but Melanie could hear a trace of bitterness in his voice. "I'm sorry to bring a shadow to your memories, but this wasn't a happy family when she moved away."

The chill in the room grew with each word Adam spoke. Each word slowly dismembering the dreams she had clung to.

"How could that have happened?" Melanie murmured, shivering again. "Are you sure?"

"Of course I am. When we bought the house, Mr. Shewchuk had been gone for a number of years."

His casual words swept away the fragile dreams Melanie had spun around this house. It had always represented wholeness and completeness to her. She had clung to it when her own father left. When she and her mother were struggling along financially, just the two of them, she always thought of the Shewchuk family and this spacious home and lot. Thought of the fun times she'd had here. Thought of the faith of the family and the prayers she had learned here.

They, too, were now a broken family.

"That saddens me more than I can tell you" was all she said, turning back to the window. "I learned a lot of prayers here, downstairs at the table, and upstairs when I slept over. I thought they had such a strong faith in God."

"For what that's worth. God doesn't care about ordinary people. I can attest to that."

The bitterness that had been merely a trace was now a formidable force pushing against Melanie, his emotions completely at odds with the strong Christian youth she had admired.

Please, Lord, give me the right words. Help me show this hurting man that You still love him.

"He does care, Adam," Melanie said quietly, turning to him, drawn by the deep sorrow in his voice. "He also knows the pain of loss."

"But not of guilt."

That stopped her.

"What do you mean?"

He shifted his weight, dropped his shoulder against the window frame beside her, his silver eyes watching her intently. "I've heard all my life about God's love. His justice. His punishment. But God is perfect. How can He understand the guilty burden of making a mistake?"

Disquiet nudged aside Melanie's calm assurances. "What mistakes are you talking about?"

Adam ran his hand over his hair and clutched the

back of his neck as if holding back what Melanie sensed he wanted to tell her.

She remembered something Helen had said and carefully pressed on. "Are you talking about Lana?"

Adam closed his eyes. Dropped his head back against the wall. Drew in a deep breath.

"I never really wanted to live here," he murmured, massaging the back of his neck. "It was Lana's idea. Her dream. So was getting pregnant. It wasn't in the plan at all. The doctor warned her that there would be complications."

"Why?"

"Lana was a type-one diabetic. Insulin dependent. Pregnancy made her diabetes harder to control. Brittle, the doctor said. I wanted to move to the city, but Lana insisted we stay here."

He lowered his hand, slipped it into his pocket. Held her gaze, his own eyes steady, like a laser.

"When she started going into labor, she also started going into diabetic shock. The ambulance took too long to get here. Then she had to be airlifted to the city. Had we lived in the city, like I wanted, they could have saved her. Tiffany would have had a mother and I would have had a wife."

He spoke with a cold precision, as if each word was a scalpel cutting and slicing.

Melanie could picture the scene so vividly. The rocking ambulance, the intense efficiency of the paramedics as they tried desperately to keep life in this woman as her husband watched.

"I haven't been able to pray to that same God since,"

Adam said. "I don't believe He cares about ordinary people, so I don't think I need to waste His time."

She couldn't stop herself. She reached out to him and touched his arm, pressed her fingers against the smooth material of his worn shirt. She almost told him she was sorry, but those words couldn't wrap themselves around sorrow and deliver it back all clean and sanitized.

"God does care, Adam. He's always waiting for us to come to Him, to give Him our burdens." Her words fell into a silence that seemed to swallow them up.

"I sat and watched my wife die, Melanie." His anger pushed and pummeled her. "I prayed, I cried, but nothing. Nothing." He took a deep breath, turning his head away. "First He took my father, then my wife. I had to take a newborn baby home from the hospital because I didn't listen to my better judgment and God didn't listen to me."

Adam's arm stirred under her fingers, then he pushed himself away from the window. Away from her.

"Let's go look at the rest of the house."

He walked away, his footsteps echoing in the dark quiet. But Melanie stayed behind, trying to collect her scattered thoughts. Impressions that had been turned around. Dumped out and rearranged.

His bitterness was so palpable, it seemed to linger in the room. Her only defense was prayer.

Please, Lord, let him feel Your love. Let him feel Your forgiveness.

Then she followed him down the hallway, going through the motions of looking at the other rooms, nodding sagely when he talked about glazed windows and the R-factor of the insulation. Inside, though, her mind was a swirling chaos of thoughts and impressions.

What dreams had Lana built around this house? What dreams had Adam lost with her death?

"These are the stairs to the attic, if you're interested." Adam had stopped in the center of the hallway, and was pulling on a rope.

Melanie wasn't really interested. Right now all she wanted was to go home and read her Bible. Find comfort in the only constant in her life.

But she had requested this tour. She knew she had to finish it.

A set of ladderlike stairs slipped down as silently as they ever had when Melanie had stayed here. "I think there's a few things here from the Shewchuk family that they didn't feel like taking with them. The renters moved them up here. You might find something there from your friend. I'll go on up first, make sure everything's okay." He easily clambered up the ladder.

Though Melanie's heart felt like a stone in her chest, it was the mention of the Shewchuks that gave her the impetus to follow him up the stairs.

As she got to the top, Adam was waiting for her. She caught his extended hand, his fingers warm and strong around hers as he helped her the rest of the way up.

"Thanks," she said, curiously breathless, the air in the attic even more closed and stale than in the room they had just been in.

"No thanks needed," he said quietly, still holding her hand, his eyes on her.

Melanie gently pulled her hand back. Slowly looked away, far too aware of their situation. She felt secluded in the semidark of this closed-in space.

"There's a switch here somewhere," Adam murmured, taking a step away from her. Melanie didn't dare move, but as her eyes adjusted to the dark she could see humped shapes surrounding her. Boxes piled in one corner, and what looked to be a child's buggy. An old chest.

"Here it is."

The light exploded the darkness away and Melanie had to squint against the brightness.

"I was only up here a couple of times, checking out the insulation of the roof, so I'm not sure what's here." Adam walked away from Melanie, ducking his head as he walked along the length of the attic.

She looked around, the familiar objects bringing a flood of memories. An old quilt that had been threadbare and moth-eaten when she and Dena had played here, now covered what looked to be a stack of old boxes. Beside that was a rusted-out electric fan, an old heater and an exercise bike with the chain broken off that she and Dena had pedaled on each day, trying to bring the odometer to a thousand kilometers.

What was in the boxes that no longer held any interest for Dena's family? Why hadn't they even bothered to come back for them?

"This looks interesting," Adam called out from the other end of the house, his voice muffled by the accumulated detritus of a family.

Melanie stepped around piled-up boxes and old furniture, her curiosity battling with a muted sorrow.

Adam pulled an old dresser away from behind another pile of boxes. It screeched a protest over the old dusty floor. “Looks like it’s in pretty good shape yet.”

“That was Mrs. Shewchuk’s old dresser,” Melanie murmured, running her hand over the familiar scarred wood. “I believe she got it from her mother.” She stooped down, lifting the dainty metal handles now coated with rust. “I always thought it was such a beautiful piece of furniture, but it’s really quite ordinary, isn’t it?”

She tugged on one of the handles, but the drawer wouldn’t move. The one above it was stuck, as well.

“Just needs a bit of gentle persuasion,” Adam said, crouching down beside her. He gave a tug as well, but he wasn’t successful, either.

His knee grazed her knee, his shoulder bumped against hers. She pulled herself abruptly to her feet, creating some distance.

“I guess its mysteries will stay mysteries,” she said with a light laugh, hoping to dispel her reaction to him.

“You can have it if you’d like.” Still crouched down, Adam glanced up at her. “I certainly don’t need it.”

Melanie touched the dresser again, as if making a connection between the harsh present and the gentle memories of the past. Her memories were valid, and no one could take them away.

“It’s just going to sit up here and molder unless you want to wait until you take possession of the house.”

“I’d love to put it back in their bedroom,” Melanie said, her finger tracing a scratch on the surface. “I remember sneaking in there with Dena to look at the old picture albums she had in the bottom drawer."

"Maybe they're still there," Adam said, giving the drawer another tug.

"I'm pretty sure she would take them along with her," Melanie said. She brushed her hands over her hips. "But if you're serious about the offer, I'd love to have the dresser. It's no antique, but it does bring back some fond memories."

"I can move it downstairs for you and take a better look at it. Get the drawers working."

"Do you need some help?"

Adam glanced pointedly at her dress and Melanie followed his gaze. "Guess not," she said ruefully.

"I'll do it some other time." He clambered down the stairs and waited for her at the bottom of the ladder as he had previously at the top. Again he took her hand, helping her down the last awkward steps, reminding Melanie of servants helping elegantly dressed ladies of another era descend from horse-drawn coaches.

It made her feel curiously protected.

And more aware of Adam than she liked. His harsh comment about God still weighed on her mind. It created a distance she needed to maintain.

In spite of her yearning for a family, and her own youthful crush on Adam, she knew that he was not the one to help her dream come true. Not as long as he stayed estranged from God.

"I'd better be leaving," she said as they reached the

kitchen. She slipped her purse over her shoulder and angled him a casual smile. “I’ll see you on Monday.”

But just as she turned, she caught his glance and a glimpse of a deep longing, so brief she thought she’d imagined it.

Chapter Five

"So when do you leave with the little munchkin for Disneyland?" Kyle asked. It was Monday, and the day had not started well.

Adam tucked the phone under his ear, his hands clumsily braiding Tiffany's hair. He wanted to say more to his partner, but his mother sat two feet away from him, so he replied with an ambiguous "A couple of days." He had only a few days to get his mother moved before he left. And he was having no success with that, either.

"I guess there's no way I can talk you out of that?"

"The tickets are bought, Kyle. All the plans are in place." He wasn't going to tell Kyle that he might have to cancel his trip if he didn't find a way to get his mother moved. Whether Kyle liked it or not, Adam needed some time away from him and his relentless demands, phone calls and pressure.

"The reason I ask is that I'm swamped here," Kyle continued, his voice rising. "The bid we put in on the Sarcee mall has been accepted. Conditionally."

"What condition?" He and Kyle had sweated over that bid, sat up until two, three in the morning running the figures through the calculator until he knew them by rote. What was there left that the company wanted?

Just at that moment Tiffany pulled her head away. Adam lost his grip on the phone and it tumbled to the floor.

He bit back an angry retort, let go of Tiffany's hair and picked up the phone. "You still there, Kyle?"

"Yeah. The condition is our liability insurance. What about the house? Is the money going to come through on that?"

"Nothing definite has been signed. I just said I had someone interested."

"Well, we could use the money from that really bad. Give me a call tonight and let me know if you can put off that trip to Disneyland with your girl. I really, really need you here, man. Did you get that bid done on the Anderson home?"

"Still working on it." Adam grimaced at the piles of paper perched on one corner of the kitchen table. He and Kyle didn't need the job, but Kyle liked to cover all angles—put bids in on any potential job.

Trouble was, if this mall deal fell through, they might need the job. Kyle hated missing the tiniest opportunity to turn over a dollar. "Let me know when you can come back to Calgary."

Adam stifled a retort and tried to push down his growing anger with Kyle. He hadn't even agreed to Kyle's request, and resented the implication that all Kyle had to do was ask and Adam would come running.

"I'll see what I can do," he said, keeping his reply deliberately ambiguous.

Adam hung up the phone and turned back to his daughter. Tiffany was running her hands over her head, disheveling the braid he had half done.

"Tiffany, sweetie, don't." He reached for the brush, but she twisted her head away from him.

"Do you want me to do that?" Helen asked, looking up from the book she was reading.

"I think I should be able to manage." Adam followed Tiffany's head with the brush, but succeeded only in getting it tangled in her curls.

By the time he got the brush out of her hair she was crying, her hands working at her eyes spreading her tears all over her face.

Since she'd got up this morning, she had been alternately contrary and cranky, not listening to anything he said. He wondered what she was going to be like at Disneyland. Wondered if he should do as his partner suggested and just forget the whole thing and go back to Calgary.

He picked up the hairbrush.

"Why don't you wait until Melanie comes?" Helen suggested. "She could do Tiffany's hair."

"I'm sure she doesn't have time for that."

"I'm sure she would. Melanie is such a caring person."

Adam made a noncommittal noise vague enough to show he was listening, yet relaying nothing his mother could build on. But he put the brush down and pulled out the container of cocoa for Tiffany's chocolate milk.

The morning had not gone well. He had spent the past hour on the phone trying to organize an ambulance and a home-care worker in Calgary for his mother. None of his phone calls had been very successful. Time was running out, and now Kyle was pressuring him to come back.

"The barbecue Melanie was talking about was on the bulletin. Are you going to go?"

Adam gave the milk another stir, clanking the spoon loudly against the side of the glass, trying to think of a suitable response for his mother. If he could get his ducks in a row, he and his mother wouldn't be here in Derwin on the weekend.

"I asked Melanie if I could go. She said it wasn't a good idea," his mother continued with a light sigh, in spite of Adam's silence. "I remember you talking about her when you were in high school. Didn't you used to like her?"

"I was eighteen and she was all of fourteen, Mother."

Adam would have had to be deaf not to hear the hopeful tone in his mother's voice and blind not to see where his mother was leading. Only, he wasn't following.

Adam didn't deny Melanie's good looks, or her kindness or how considerate she was. Or that he used to think she was cute and spunky. Right now he didn't have the space for a woman. Especially not a woman who spoke so easily of a God he used to believe in but couldn't get close to anymore.

"Here's your chocolate, Tiff." He set the glass in front of his daughter.

"Don't want it," she said with a dark pout, pushing at the glass. Milk spilled all over the table, narrowly missing the papers he was working on.

Impatience burst through him. He closed his eyes and counted slowly to ten. Then he rescued the Anderson quote and the house estimate for Melanie from the spreading brown puddle.

"You said you wanted chocolate milk, Tiff," he said sternly as he swiped at the chocolate mess with a damp cloth.

He rinsed the cloth out and finished the job. Tiffany was now running her sticky hands through her hair, further disheveling it. "Tiffany, don't do that."

"Go to Gramma."

"Wait. I'm going to do your hair again." It would be easier if he got her hair cut, but her long curls were the only part of her that reminded him of Lana. He didn't have the heart.

"I don't think she's going to sit still long enough for you to do a proper job," Helen said.

Tiffany started crying, pushing Adam's hands away as he tried to redo her braids.

He didn't need this, he thought, picking up the elastics Tiffany had thrown on the floor. Maybe Kyle was right. Maybe he should cancel his trip and get his mother settled into the fifty-plus condo he had picked out for her. He could put his daughter back into the day care and he could go back to work where skill saws whined, air hammers pounded, compressors rattled.

It almost seemed peaceful compared to heading off

to Disneyland with a daughter who didn't want to have anything to do with him.

"Hello, everyone." Melanie's voice sounded at the back door and Adam stifled a groan.

Of course Melanie would have to come in the middle of the chaos.

"How are you, Helen?" she asked, setting her bag on the floor beside his mother's chair.

Adam, all too aware of his mother's previous comments, merely gave Melanie a quick nod and turned his attention back to his daughter's mop of curls.

She squirmed away from him. When she saw Melanie she pushed her hands against the table. "Want to go down. Now."

"Just wait, Tiffany. I need to do your hair."

Tiffany started to cry again, twisting her head this way and that. "No. Don't want you. Want her."

Tiffany's words plunged like a knife into his heart. He stared down at her, his hands now hanging idle by his sides as the words his tiny girl had thrown at him reverberated in the sudden silence.

"Tiffany, come to Gramma," Helen said quietly. "Adam, we can watch her while you move that dresser."

As Tiffany clambered out of the chair, Adam looked up in time to see Melanie's gaze on his. He almost cringed at the sympathy he saw there.

He tossed the elastics on the table and left. As his mother said, he had a dresser to move.

Melanie watched Adam go, wishing she dared say something. But though her heart ached for him, she doubted he would appreciate or welcome any advice she could give him.

"Please forgive my son," Helen said quietly, stroking Tiffany's hair. "He's not been having a good morning. He's leaving for Disneyland soon and he can't seem to get an ambulance organized to move me to the city."

"That is too bad," Melanie agreed halfheartedly. Obviously Adam was still going through with his plans. The thought bothered her more than it should have.

"He says he's found one of those fifty-plus places for me to go." Helen twisted one of Tiffany's curls around her finger. "Said I would enjoy it. What do you think?"

Melanie felt torn. She had promised Adam she would help him get his mother ready to move. Yet she fully understood where Helen was coming from. The more excited Melanie got about owning her first home, the more she understood Helen's reluctance to leave. Leave this house. Leave Derwin and the community she was a part of.

She knew how much her mother would have loved to live here.

"I think that for now we need to concentrate on getting you back in shape as much as possible," she said, sidestepping the question and her own opinions.

Half an hour later Helen was sitting back in her chair, slightly flushed from the exercises Melanie had her doing.

"So how am I doing?" Helen asked as Melanie packed up her nurse's kit.

"Truthfully, I was hoping you'd be a little further

along by now." Melanie rolled up the blood pressure cuff and placed it in her bag. "How have you been feeling otherwise?"

Helen sighed. "I want to feel better, but I feel so weak all the time. And I get so many headaches."

"It will take a while for your new medication to help," Melanie said, though she doubted the new medication would fix what was really wrong with Helen. Her problems were emotional rather than physical and the only thing that would cure that wasn't going to happen. "Now, let's get you back to your bedroom." Melanie turned back to Tiffany. "Are you going to come to Gramma's room? Or should we find your dad?"

"Go to Gramma's room." Tiffany yanked Melanie's stethoscope off her neck. Melanie rescued it just before she dropped it on the floor. Tiffany scrambled to her feet and ran over to her grandma's side. "I help you."

Helen wasn't quite as flushed by the time Melanie had her settled in. Tiffany was once again busy with the crayons and coloring books that lay on a small desk that was new to the room.

"You're okay with Tiffany in here?" Melanie asked.

Helen just nodded and smiled down at her granddaughter. "I may as well enjoy her company while I can," she said with a pensive look.

"You rest now."

Melanie crouched down and fingered a curl away from Tiffany's face. She had finished the braiding job that Adam had started, but the little girl's hair had a curl that escaped even the tightest braid. "You be good now for your gramma, okay?"

Tiffany smiled up at her, her angelic expression a direct contrast to the scowl that had twisted her face when Melanie had first arrived.

Melanie stroked her soft cheek, a swift uplifting rush of affection spiraling through her. “That’s a good girl,” she said softly. “I’ll go find Adam and tell him where you are.” She closed the door behind her. The short hallway gave way to the kitchen. Sunshine bathed the room, warm and welcoming. Melanie’s heart thrilled with a sense of ownership. In a few weeks, Lord willing, this was going to be hers. It seemed too wonderful for her mind to accept.

Please Lord, let it happen.

Adam bit his lip as he stared down at the steep stairs. It was going to be trickier getting the dresser down than he had calculated. Gravity and the angle of the stairs were his nemesis.

He worked the dresser as close to the stairs as he dared and laid it on its back, letting it slide over the opening. He grabbed the rope he had tied around it, braced his feet against the top rung of the ladder and eased the dresser down the stairs, slowing its descent with the rope.

The stairs creaked and the rope jerked hard. Then as he watched in disbelief, the stairs gave way, the dresser heaved the rope out of his hands and crashed to the floor below.

Wood splintered. The dresser split and settled.

He closed his eyes, his heart beating against his ribs.

“Adam, are you all right?” Melanie called out from the bottom of the stairs.

"I'm okay," he replied, surveying with dismay the wreckage below him. Why not this on top of everything else?

Melanie was already running up the stairs. She swung around the newel post at the top and skidded to a halt when she saw the twisted wood of what was left of the dresser Adam knew she had prized.

He felt sick.

He dropped down from the attic, using what was left of the ladder.

"Are you sure you're okay?" Melanie asked, looking up at him.

"I'm fine," he said with disgust. "I wish I could say the same about the dresser."

"What happened?"

"Near as I can tell, the stairs gave way." A cold finger of dread shivered down his spine as he spoke. This could just as easily have happened when Melanie was climbing up the stairs the other night.

Melanie crouched beside the dresser, touching it lightly. "Well, I guess we'll get to find out what was in that bottom drawer," she said with a light laugh, tugging at a lower panel that was now awry.

How could she joke about this?

"You're going to get splinters." Once again Adam knelt beside her, taking her hands away from the dresser. "I'm really sorry about this. I feel terrible."

Melanie jerked her hands back, creating a moment of added awkwardness. "Don't feel bad. Please. It was a gift. I didn't know anything about this a week ago." She put her hands on her knees to get up. Stopped.

"What's this?" In spite of Adam's warning, she tugged on a drawer front that had split away. With a creak of loose nails it separated from the sides of the drawer, exposing a cardboard box. Melanie pulled it out and opened it.

"It's full of envelopes," she said, sitting back on her knees as she flipped through the contents with her index finger. "All addressed to Donna Shewchuk. They all come from the same person. Jason Shewchuk. Donna's husband."

"I thought he had left her." Adam frowned, turning the envelope over. "It's not opened."

Melanie took it back, looked it over herself. Then checked out the letters in the box. "There must be about twenty letters in here. And only two of them have been opened."

Adam held out his hand for the box and checked for himself. "He's traveled a few places," he murmured, glancing over the return addresses. "I wonder if they got delivered."

"They're all in this box. Someone gathered them together."

"What are the dates of the cancellation?"

Melanie read a few out. "From what I can see they are about six years old."

Adam tapped the envelope on his hand, thinking. "She had the house rented out for a couple of years while she was trying to sell it. I wonder if they were coming here then and the renters didn't bother to pass them on."

"What are you going to do about them?"

"I'm not sure." He put the letters back in the box and closed the lid.

"It would be nice if we could get them to Mrs. Shewchuk somehow," Melanie said.

"She might not like what's in them."

Melanie didn't reply, but Adam could tell from the wistful look on her face that she didn't believe him. He wished he could understand her eternal optimism.

"Is Tiffany with my mother?" he asked, pushing himself up.

"She's coloring. I think she'll be okay for a little while. She seems quite content around your mother." Melanie got to her feet, brushing the front of her pants. "I was just leaving, so if there's anything else…" She let the sentence drag.

Adam hesitated, looked down at the box of letters, then up at Melanie. "Do you have a bit of time yet?"

"Sure."

He walked with her down the stairs, his steps slow and measured as Melanie sorted through her emotions and reactions to this man.

She shouldn't have come on Saturday night for supper. It had shifted their relationship and called up older emotions and feelings that had no place in the present. And just now, as they'd been sorting through the letters, she'd felt a curious connection and a curious newer attraction.

The screen door slapped shut behind them. Melanie walked over to the railing of the porch. Ignoring the paint flecking off it, she leaned back against the sun-warmed wood, curiosity warring with a new tenderness.

"I'm almost done with the quote on the house," Adam said, his hands settled on his hips. "I'll get it finished by tomorrow. Hopefully."

She wasn't going to ask him how it looked. She had made up her mind that one way or another she was going to have this house. Each visit confirmed her desire, cemented it. In spite of the house's history, it was still the home she wanted.

"I'm also really sorry about the dresser."

"We covered this already," Melanie said, setting her nurse's bag on the porch floor.

"I know how much it would have meant to you to have something from the Shewchuks. I'd like to try to fix it up, though I'm not sure I'll be very successful." Adam shoved one hand through his hair, then looked back at Melanie, his expression intent. "Actually I didn't really want to just talk about the dresser. The main reason I asked you to stay is about my daughter. Tiffany."

Melanie saw once again a shadow of the pain she'd seen in his face before. She thought of the little run-in she'd witnessed this morning.

"I don't know what to do about her. She won't listen to me and, as I said before, she seems to connect with anyone else but me."

"Have you noticed this before?"

Adam was quiet. He chewed his lower lip, looking beyond her. "What I have noticed is she has never spontaneously come to me. Never looked me straight in the eye." He drew in a slow breath, looking beyond Melanie. "She has never called me 'Daddy.'"

The raw pain in his voice twisted her heart, called to a lonely part of her own life. A part that yearned for a man to call "Daddy." Yearned for a man who had been a sporadic part of her life until he died.

"How long would you work each day?" she asked, keeping her voice soft, nonjudgmental.

Adam frowned and tugged at his lower lip. "I had to pull my share of the load. My partner has been in the business for a few years." He looked up at her, his eyes bleak with remembered sorrow. "I had to work fourteen-hour days to catch up. I needed to make sure I could give Tiffany whatever she needed."

And you had a wife's death that you were trying to forget. A guilt you were trying to outrun, Melanie thought.

"It's that kind of business, Melanie," he continued, his arms folded over his chest. "This is seasonal work, and you've got to work when you can. You can't afford to miss out on any opportunities. There's too many other businesses ready to jump in."

"Yet you made the decision to get away in the middle of the summer to take your daughter to Disneyland," Melanie coaxed gently, ignoring his defensive posture.

Adam gave her a crooked smile that lacked any humor or warmth. "The day-care supervisor suggested that I spend some time with her. Said that Tiffany was developing attachment problems. Whatever that means."

Melanie sent up a small prayer of gratitude to the underappreciated people who took care of other people's children and cared enough to get involved.

"Tiffany has had her routine in the city and she has been comfortable with that. And, though it's hard to say, it doesn't sound like you were a part of it. Now—" Melanie lifted her hands in a helpless gesture "—she's around you all the time and she's not used to it."

"So I should probably take her back to her normal routine, is what you're saying, instead of going to Disneyland."

Melanie shook her head, sorrow flitting through her. "Disneyland is not the answer to your problem, nor is it going to be a problem. You could go, but nothing will change if you do. You could go back to Calgary and the same thing will happen. I'm saying that this little girl doesn't know where she fits in your life."

She knew the words would hurt, but hadn't been able to think of a softer way to deliver them.

"But I thought being around her all the time would help."

"Not at a place like Disneyland."

"But I only have so much time."

You have all the time you need, she thought. If you set your priorities right.

But she couldn't tell him that.

"You wanted to talk about Tiffany. You obviously know that things aren't the way they should be." Melanie pushed herself away from the porch railing, unable to keep her distance. "You care about your daughter. Anyone can see that. But now you need to figure out how you are going to be the father that she so badly needs."

"And what about a mother? Doesn't she need that,

too?" The pain was there again in his eyes, and jealousy feathered Melanie's heart at his bleak words.

"She has you, Adam," Melanie said softly, touching him lightly on the arm. "And you're the parent she needs right now."

"So what do I do? She is all I have."

Melanie looked up at Adam and felt a rush of warmth for this man who was so obviously concerned, yet confused.

Adam might not be doing everything right, but she sensed that he was trying. She doubted her father had ever expended the same amount of energy on her needs. Her wishes.

Please, Lord. Help me say the right thing. Help me show him what he really needs.

"I think you need to give her a little bit of space. Let her figure out how she's going to fit in your life." Melanie bit her lip, hesitated, then plunged on. "The only way this is going to work is over a period of time. You said you had your vacation booked—spend those days here. With your daughter. Be with her, but not so intensely involved in everything she does. And at the same time, when she does respond to you, be available for her. Don't call your partner every day. Don't get distracted by your work. Don't do up quotes and make phone calls. Don't let other outside things intrude on this time. And don't take her to Disneyland. It's just noise and entertainment for a girl too young to appreciate it. You won't make a connection with so many distractions around."

Adam ran his hand over his face, then glanced at Melanie. "What do I do with the tickets?"

"I'm sure you could sell them."

"You realize that will mean staying here for the next two weeks. I thought you would want me gone so you could buy the house?"

"I do. As we speak I am arranging financing and transferring money, but you know I won't be taking possession right away. And your relationship with your daughter is more important than this house."

"So why are you trying to get me to stay here as long as possible?" He quirked a crooked smile and Melanie felt an indefinable tension loosen as other emotions gripped her heart at his question.

"Maybe I'm hoping you'll decide to put some of your talents to work and fix up a few things during that time?" Melanie injected a teasing note in her voice to offset her reaction.

"It's actually close to three weeks, but I wasn't going to tell my mother that." He pulled his lower lip between his teeth and looked out over the yard, his hands resting on his hips. "You really think this is going to make a difference?"

Beneath his casual tone Melanie heard the pain in his voice. "It's a start. And a good one." She couldn't help but touch him again, wanting to reassure him. "You care about your daughter and that gives you a lot."

Adam drew in a deep breath, half turning to her. "Thanks, Melanie. I appreciate your honesty. And your advice." He covered her hand with his. She could feel the calluses, the rough skin. The hands of a working man.

His clear blue eyes held hers and Melanie's mind

easily sifted back, remembering a young man coming to her rescue. A man who was now in need of rescue himself.

"I'll be praying for you," she couldn't help but say, drawn to the man he was, the man who now stood in front of her.

Adam blinked, dropped his hand. "For what that's worth," he said, slipping his hands into his pockets.

His words were like a shot of cold water. And in a way she was thankful he had spoken them.

She knew her feelings for him were changing, moving toward dangerous ground. And now she was going to be seeing him every day for the next few weeks.

She hoped she could remember this and other conversations.

She knew it was going to be difficult.

Chapter Six

"So how has it been, working with the infamous Adam Engler?"

Melanie looked up from the form she was filling out to see Serena Davis, a fellow worker, standing by her desk. The expectant look on Serena's face belied the sophisticated air she carried as easily as the tailored suits she favored.

Serena had been an answer to a prayer for Melanie. When she first moved to Derwin it was Serena who had helped her find an apartment, had shown up that first evening at the apartment with a casserole and some friends.

"And what is he supposedly infamous for?" Melanie sat back in her swivel chair, balancing her pen between her fingers.

Serena smoothed a hand over her dark hair, though not a strand of it was out of place, and leaned her hip against the desk as if settling in for a long gossipy chat. "Local boy loses wife. Takes baby daughter and moves his handsome self off to Calgary, cowboy-hat capital of Canada." Serena used her perfectly manicured index finger to tick off Adam's offenses. "Starts construction company. Cuts off all communication with family. Mortal sins in a town like Derwin, where everyone always knows what everyone else is doing. And especially troublesome when said local boy is as good-looking as Adam Engler is."

"I'm sure Adam had his reasons," Melanie said, preferring to err on the side of caution rather than speculate aloud.

Serena laughed. "Bless you for being so discreet, Melanie. I was trying to be facetious. Obviously a bit heavy-handed." Serena fingered the gold chain around her neck. "The other day I was chatting with Sandy Gerrard, Lana's sister. She used to always be checking on Lana. Like a little mother hen. She happened to mention that they haven't seen Adam or Tiffany yet. Did he refer to them at all?"

Melanie blew out a sigh. She should have known this was going to come up sooner or later. In a small town, people not only knew each other's business, they made it a point that other people fill in the gaps in their own information database.

"I guess you'll have to talk to Adam on that," she said with a quick smile.

"Oh, don't get all professional and haul out client confidentiality. That doesn't work in Derwin." Serena tapped her lower lip with her thumb, her eyes on Melanie. "I guess I was hoping you might mention the family to him. Maybe let him know that they'd really like to see Tiffany and him sometime."

"I thought Helen was my patient?" Melanie stifled her annoyance. First Adam wanted her help to get his mother to move, now Serena wanted her to help Adam reconcile with his in-laws. She should have asked for a more clear-cut job description.

"We deal with the whole patient here," Serena tut-tutted, a twinkle in her eye. "And if that means peripheral family relations, then that must be dealt with as well."

"I think that's just an official way to be nosy."

"Informed," Serena corrected. She pushed away from the desk. "Are you coming to the community barbecue this weekend?"

"I don't know. Been thinking about it."

Serena dismissed Melanie's wavering with a flash of her carnation-colored nails. "Do more than think. The new superintendent who is currently reviewing your application for the full-time position you applied for will be coming." Serena pointed at Melanie. "Though you'll probably get the job anyhow, it wouldn't hurt to meet her face-to-face and let her know what an asset you'll be to this health unit."

"Thanks for the tip."

"You'll need the job if you're going to buy that house."

"How did you know about the house?" Melanie dropped her pen on the desk with a clatter that mirrored her faint annoyance. "I haven't even signed the offer to purchase yet."

"We don't have the party-line telephone anymore, but we still have information exchange." Serena gave her a patronizing look. "Coffee shop? Floyd talking to another couple interested in the house? Serena overhearing your name being mentioned?" She lifted her hands in a "what could I do" gesture.

Melanie's heart tripped at the thought of someone else wanting the house. The last time she had spoken to Floyd she was the only one who had put in an offer, but it frightened her to think that someone else was interested. "Thanks for the tip on the barbecue. I'll be there."

"I have my ulterior motives. I'm hoping you might need me to visit Helen sometime." Serena winked as she pushed herself away from Melanie's desk. "Wouldn't mind making Adam's acquaintance again. If you get my meaning."

As Serena walked away, Melanie recalled Roxanne's exuberant greeting to Adam.

Adam created a flutter in many a woman's heart, her own included.

She remembered the touch of his hand on hers. The way his eyes crinkled when he smiled, which wasn't often, and felt her own heart respond.

But superimposed over her reaction were his bitter remarks.

"He's not for you," she whispered, bending over the forms she was filling out. The fact that she was buying his house should serve as enough of a reminder. He was leaving. She was staying.

"Are you sure you don't need a ride home?" Bob Tessier lingered in the foyer of the church as Melanie slipped her sweater on.

"Thanks, Bob. I only live a few blocks away. I prefer to walk."

And I prefer not to give you any ideas.

She tempered her thoughts with a smile as she lifted her hair free from the back of her sweater. "It gives me a chance to practice some of the new parts our choir director gave us."

Bob's smile sagged ever so slightly. "Then I'll be seeing you at the bank whenever you get the information from Adam."

"He said he was going to be bringing the estimate over tonight, so I'll be in some time this week." She pulled her sweater closer around her, gave Bob another polite smile. "Well, I better go. Thanks again for the offer." And before he could forestall her with anything else, Melanie left.

When she came around the building, as was her usual habit, she veered away from the sidewalk leading to the street and toward the tree line separating the cemetery from the church parking lot. The summer evening held a light chill with a hint of rain in the air.

When Trudy Visser's will was read, Melanie had been surprised to discover that she had wanted to be buried in Derwin. It seemed her mother had shared her attachment to the small town.

So now, each time Melanie was at the church, she took the time to visit her mother's grave. It had become a small connection to a parent who had given Melanie everything she could. And it was a way of cementing Melanie's desire to put down roots in this town.

She wasn't alone this time, however.

A single pickup was parked by the trees bordering

the graveyard. As she came closer, she recognized the truck.

And facing his wife's gravestone stood Adam, his cap in his hand.

He bent down on one knee, his finger tracing Lana's name. Then he lowered his head into his hands, closing his eyes.

Was he praying? Berating God? Missing his wife?

Helen frequently fretted that Adam didn't seem to have any interest in women. It had been three years since Lana had died—surely it was time he try to find someone again, she had said, giving Melanie a look rife with innuendo. But Melanie had wisely let the comment slide.

Now, as Melanie watched, Adam got slowly to his feet, his hands working the bill of his cap. His features were twisted in sorrow.

Adam slipped his cap back on his head and Melanie turned away, afraid to be discovered watching him. She walked to her mother's gravestone as a faint jealousy for Adam's devotion to his wife fought with her own sorrow.

She stopped in front of the granite slab and, as always, was unable to connect the memories of her mother with the cold precision of Trudy Visser's name cut into the stone. Though she had witnessed the body being lowered into the grave and had made most of the preparations herself, she still couldn't accept that her mother was no more. She would no longer call her at work. No longer be standing at the stove, cooking up yet another pot of soup, when Melanie would stop by her apartment.

Just as Adam had, she bent and touched her mother's name, surprised at how cold the stone felt under her fingers.

Someday, Lord, I'll see her again. Until then, help me to carry on.

She swallowed a knot of pain as she lifted her face to the sky overhead, as if hoping to catch even a faint glimpse of her mother in glory.

But all she saw was a hawk wheeling on an updraft against a faint wisp of a cloud.

"Hey, Melanie."

Adam spoke quietly, but she still jumped.

"Sorry," he said with a gentle smile. "I didn't mean to startle you. I saw you here, so figured I'd come over and say hi." He looked past her at the stone at her feet. "She died only a year ago?"

Melanie nodded, slowly gaining equilibrium. "She wanted to be buried in Derwin when she died. I guess we both liked it here enough to stay. One way or the other."

"Do you miss her?"

His question caught her off balance. Other than Helen, no one had even mentioned her mother. Though she realized they hadn't been here long enough those many years ago to make a lot of connections, it still hurt.

"Yes. I do," she answered softly, blinking back an unexpected moisture at his consideration. "She was my mother, but she was also my good friend."

Then Melanie felt his hand on her shoulder. Just a light touch, barely discernible through the material of her sweater, but the connection felt better than she wanted to admit.

Since her mother's death she had been all alone, and it wasn't a situation she relished. Nor did she know how to change it. She had no father and no siblings. The various men she had dated all wanted to make their home in the city, and she hadn't found anyone for whom she was willing to sacrifice her dream of living in Derwin.

"It's hard to let go," Melanie said quietly. "I have to confess, I saw you at Lana's grave. I imagine you know only too well how I feel."

Adam lowered his hand, as if mention of his wife created a barrier between them. "That was three years ago," he said brusquely.

Then silence.

Melanie wanted to breach the gap, but was afraid of saying the wrong thing. So she settled for the practical.

"How is the estimate coming?"

"I have it in the truck," Adam said. "I was going to bring them over, but you weren't home."

"Choir practice." Melanie hugged herself again. She risked a quick glance at Adam, disconcerted to find his steady gaze on her. And equally disconcerted to find herself unable to look away.

Adam broke the connection first, taking a step back. Looking away. "I'll get the papers for you." He strode away, and Melanie realized with a sinking feeling that she had done that all wrong, as well. She should have invited him to her apartment. They could have visited over a cup of coffee.

And talked about what? Dead relatives?

Adam came back quite quickly, file folder in hand. He flipped it open, looking down at the contents. "It's all itemized. I would have printed it out, but I don't have access to a computer." He closed it again and handed it to her with a rueful smile. "I tried to be honest and fair. I hope this is what you need."

Melanie forced a smile to her face. "Thanks. I'll look it over tonight."

Adam slipped his hands into his back pockets, rocking back on his heels.

Ask him now.

But he glanced at his watch, the eternal gesture denoting it was time to go.

"If I have any questions I'll call you," she said, beating him to it. "Thanks again." She didn't want to hang around extending the awkwardness of the moment. Like some overeager teenage girl waiting to be asked to the prom.

As she walked away she sighed. She hadn't handled that well at all.

Guess it was another evening in front of the television.

The file folder felt heavy in her hands, and her apartment seemed even quieter than usual when she let herself in. She slipped her coat off, hung it up and dropped into the nearest chair with the estimate.

She paged through it, her heart growing heavier with each line.

And when she read the final figure, she dropped her head back against the chair and blew out a sigh. The number was larger than she had thought it would be.

She had some big decisions to make.

* * *

"This one is a lovely two-bedroom bungalow that I know is in your price range and won't need any work. Basically turnkey." Floyd stopped his vehicle in front of a white picket fence. "I think you might like this one."

Melanie obediently looked at the house beyond the bright yellow for-sale sign tacked to the fence.

She tried to work up some enthusiasm for the tidy white house perched on a lawn so green she felt like Dorothy in the Emerald City. Tiger lilies grew in mass profusion in one corner of the lawn and plump cedar bushes softened the front entrance. It was lovely. And, as Floyd had said, well within her price range. It was only two blocks from the park. Three blocks from the bank. Five blocks from the grocery store and only seven blocks away from the auction market.

Location, location, location.

"It's lovely."

"Now, why do I sense a great big *but* in your voice?" Floyd said with a laugh.

Because it's not the house with the turret. It's not the house that I've been dreaming about since I moved away from here. The house that needs so much work that if I buy it, I'll be in debt for thirty years.

After reading Adam's estimate and doing a little book work of her own, Melanie had realized that if she bought the house she would be stretching herself beyond comfortable boundaries. So she had phoned Floyd, just to give herself a few other options.

"I do have another place out in Eastbar, but I know

you wanted to live in Derwin," Floyd continued. "And there's a larger house on the outskirts of town that is more expensive, but it's brand-new."

"Let's have a look at the new house," Melanie said, turning away from the charming home that just didn't create any zing for her. She wanted to be fair and do justice to this comparison shopping she was indulging in.

The other house was also lovely. Because it was new, the landscaping was minimal. A few scraggly trees were parked on the corners of the lot, held up by guy wires. In a few years they would be fuller and taller.

The first thing she saw was a large two-car garage, its double door like a wide yawning mouth that had gobbled up the rest of the house. The living room, though substantial, looked tiny tucked alongside the garage.

Melanie looked around at the rest of the houses, each as large as the one in front of her, each boasting the same dominant garage. It didn't look like a neighborhood—it looked like a parking garage.

"Did you want to see the inside of the house?"

Melanie sighed. She felt she had to give this place a chance, but she knew it would be a waste of time. The neighborhood looked stark, unwelcoming. At least the little white house looked as if it belonged to a community. It had history and probably its own stories, happy and sad.

And if she bought that house, her payments wouldn't be as steep.

"Let's go look at the little white house again. I'd like to see the inside."

Floyd just smiled.

She got her tour, and she found that the house was even more charming on the inside than the outside. It would be a perfect home for her, she thought, standing in the kitchen, looking out over a large backyard. Not too large. Convenient.

But it didn't give her the same sense of belonging that she felt in the Shewchuk house. Correction, the Engler house.

Was she pinning too much on dreams and wishes that, if Adam were right, were just illusions and fantasies?

"I'll need some time to think about it," she said, turning back to Floyd.

"You've got my number." He smiled at her and escorted her back out of the house.

"By the way," she said as he drove her back home, "you said there was another couple interested in the Engler house. How serious are they?"

Floyd pursed his lips and waggled his hand back and forth. "I think they're like you. They see the work it needs and are having second thoughts. I've shown them the houses I showed you this evening, as well. I'm pretty sure they're going to put in an offer on the house in the new subdivision."

Relief plunged through her, leaving her almost breathless. "So there's no one else interested in it, then?"

"Now that you've backed out, no. No one."

Melanie worried her lower lip with her teeth, thinking. Planning. She was crazy to think about buying the Engler house. Her practical nature told her that.

So why couldn't she get it off her mind? Why did these other perfectly suitable and charming homes not give her the same sense of home that run-down house did?

Floyd stopped in front of her apartment and turned to her. "You're going to go for the Engler house, aren't you?"

"What makes you say that?"

"Eighteen years in the business, that's what."

Melanie sighed, toying with the strap of her purse. "I keep coming back to it. I know it's crazy and maybe not the best investment I could make, but I really, really want that house. These other homes were nice, but they just don't..." She hesitated, not wanting to sound like a complete lunatic. "I don't know, they just don't call to me."

"I'd pay attention to that," Floyd said with a grin. "And if that's the case..." Floyd opened his briefcase and pulled out a few papers. "This is an offer to purchase. I'm not pressuring you, but if you're serious about buying the house, we need to fill one of these out."

Melanie slipped the papers into her purse and walked slowly to her apartment building. This was going to take some more thought. And some more prayer.

Chapter Seven

They fit. Adam felt a gentle rush of accomplishment when the dovetail joints of the drawer slid perfectly into each other. Not even a gap, he mused, running his finger over the joint. Tomorrow he could put the fronts on the drawers, and once the glue was dry he could assemble it.

Knowing he still had the touch gave him more of a thrill than he would have realized.

And his daughter crouched at his feet, happily playing in the wood shavings, created a lingering satisfaction that superseded the fit of the dresser drawer.

The original chest of drawers that Melanie had desired had been shattered beyond repair. While rummaging through his tools and the pieces of lumber he had lying around, hoping to fix it, he had decided to build her a replica. A reminder of good memories. And it would serve the dual purpose of keeping him busy in a place his daughter could be, as well.

But a curious thing had happened as he worked with

the wood. He'd found a satisfaction seeping through his day that he hadn't felt in a long time.

He and his partner specialized in large buildings. Structures of concrete and steel that captured air and space with harsh angles, put together by large pieces of equipment.

But this work he could see take shape under his own hands. As the frame was put together, the drawers took shape, a dormant serenity began to surface. He realized how much he missed working directly with a project, touching it and feeling it take shape as he had when he worked with Lana's father.

"Bess a litto am tonight. Bess a litto am tonight." Tiffany crouched in the shavings at his feet singing the same line over and over. His mother had taught her the song and Tiffany remembered only part of it. What she lacked in repertoire she more than made up for in enthusiasm.

She threw a handful of shavings up in the air, laughing as they twisted down, liberally coating her hair and clinging to her coveralls. Her face was still sticky from the Popsicle his mother had given her, her one braid had come loose again, but she had a look of peace on her face he hadn't seen in a while.

The first morning he'd started working on the dresser, she had stayed with him only a few minutes and then left, wanting to see Gramma. He had gone to the house when Melanie had come, staying only long enough to make sure that Tiffany wasn't in anyone's way. The reassuring words Melanie had given him, and the gentle smile, told him that she understood and approved.

That meant more than he liked it to.

The two-way monitor he'd had installed on the wall by his workbench beeped once. Then again.

He held down the talk button, speaking into the monitor. "Yes, Mother, what would you like?"

"I'm making tea. Do you and Tiffany want some?"

Adam glanced at his watch. Five o'clock. Just about time to quit anyhow.

"I'll be in the house as soon as I'm finished cleaning up."

Ten minutes later he was walking up the steps, Tiffany trailing along behind him with her arms full of shavings that she wanted to show her grandma.

When he bent to take her shoes off, she dropped a shaving on his head, giggling.

"You silly girl," he said, pleasure knifing through him at her spontaneous gesture.

"You are silly," she replied.

Adam held the door open for her as he took the shaving off his head, brushing excess sawdust off his pants. Tiffany stopped, then dropped her shavings on the porch floor. "Mellalie," she called out as she ran into the kitchen.

Adam looked up in surprise. Melanie, who was pouring tea for his mother, looked up, her eyes meeting and holding his.

"I have some papers I need you to sign," she said quietly, setting down the teapot. "Floyd is supposed to be here, as well. I hope you don't mind. Floyd made the arrangements with your mother."

"I'm sorry, Adam," Helen said, shooting her son an

apologetic look. "I forgot to tell you. Floyd said it should be done at his office, but I told him you could do it here."

"That's okay," Adam said, making the required noises. He wished he had known she was coming. He was suddenly aware of the sawdust coating his face and hair, the bits of wood still clinging to his pants. Melanie's pale yellow shirt and khaki pants gave her a cool elegance that made him feel grubby.

Tiffany crawled up onto Melanie's lap, exuberantly relating the events of the day, the wood shavings on her clothes brushing off on Melanie's.

"Tiffany, we should clean you up," Adam said, about to take his daughter away.

"She's fine. Just hand me a wet cloth and we can take the purple Popsicle marks off her face." Melanie smiled up at Adam, and once again he was struck by her beauty.

A beauty, he realized, that was more than the line of her features, the color of her eyes.

A beauty that radiated through her.

The other day in the cemetery he had seen another side of her. Her sorrow had added another dimension to her personality, which seemed to expand, moving slowly, inexorably into his own thoughts.

He turned abruptly away, dampened a cloth and handed it quickly to Melanie. When Adam was finished washing his hands, Melanie had wiped Tiffany's hands and face and was carefully picking bits of wood out of her hair, combing her fingers through Tiffany's tangled curls.

Adam couldn't take his eyes off the two of them. The sight of his daughter on Melanie's lap seemed so right. Like the pieces of the drawer he had just put together, they fit.

Perfectly.

"Isn't this a nice surprise, Adam?" his mother asked, her voice fairly dripping with honey.

Caught, he thought. Staring at Melanie like some love-struck young teenager.

"Very nice," he said, sitting at the spot designated for him, avoiding his mother's knowing look. "I'm guessing the bank didn't have any problem with the estimate I gave you?" He turned his attention to Melanie, who was pouring tea again, steam wreathing between them.

Melanie waggled her fingers in a noncommittal gesture. "I had to practically give them the rights to my life in perpetuity and possibly my first child, should I ever have one, but yes. In the end, Bob said he would start the paperwork on the loan."

Adam didn't care that Floyd hadn't arrived yet. He was more than happy to sit in the kitchen of his house drinking tea with Melanie and his mother as the late-afternoon sun slanted into the kitchen.

Just like a little family.

"Hello. Sorry I'm late." Floyd's booming voice broke in to the little tableau. Adam stifled a burst of annoyance and turned to greet him.

Floyd made his way around the table shaking hands with his mother, himself and lastly Melanie.

He didn't know if it was his imagination, but did

Floyd linger a little longer with Melanie, hold her hand just a little more, make just a little too much eye contact?

"So I brought the papers." Floyd pulled up a chair between Melanie and Adam, flicked open his brief-case, pulled out a set of papers and laid them on the table.

"As you can see, this is a straightforward Agreement for Sale." Floyd set his briefcase on the floor, pulled a gold pen out of his pocket and went over the details of the contract.

Adam listened with only half his attention. Instead he found himself watching Melanie, who was leaning over the agreement her eyes bright with anticipation. He knew how badly she wanted this house.

"So do you have any questions?" Floyd was asking.

"The list of assets that come with the property is laid out somewhere?" Melanie asked.

Floyd pointed them out. "Is there anything missing or anything that you wanted to add, Adam?"

Adam glanced down at the piece of paper and shook his head. Once he signed it, things would be put in motion that would remove this house and this memory from his life. He would have some more money to put into the growing construction business and one less debt to worry about.

So why wasn't he happier?

Melanie leaned past Tiffany still sitting on her lap and signed the paper with a flowing signature that looked like her, Adam thought as he took the pen from Floyd.

It was still warm from Melanie's fingers. Even a bit sticky from the Popsicle stain she'd removed.

He looked at the space he was supposed to sign, nodding when Floyd pointed it out.

Memories flitted through his mind. The endless trips he and Lana had made looking for just the right paint. Piling the lumber up in the yard in preparation for the renovations they were going to make.

Buying the shingles at an auction for a fraction of the cost, hoping they would have enough to do the entire roof.

But in each memory, Lana was just a shadowy figure.

Adam, still looking down at the paper, tried to recreate the color of her hair, the sound of her voice. But he couldn't picture her face.

"Are you okay, Adam?" Melanie asked, her voice breaking in to his thoughts.

He pulled his lower lip between his teeth, looked up at her. Felt the pull of her warmth, her gentle smile. Felt a sudden loneliness that had claws and that clung.

"You just need to put your signature here," Floyd said again, pointing a manicured finger to the line.

Adam pulled himself into the moment, looked back down at the paper and quickly scrawled his signature on the bottom just below Melanie's.

It was done and it was time to move on. If it wasn't for this house, Lana would still be alive.

He handed the pen back to Floyd. Floyd wiped it with the cloth still lying on the table, then tucked it into his pocket.

"Great stuff. So now all we have to do is wait for the financing to come through."

Adam poured sugar into his tea and stirred it absently, listening with half an ear as Melanie and Floyd's conversation moved from business to idle chitchat. Adam kept out of the conversation, ignoring his mother's attempts to draw him in.

His part of the deal was over and he had nothing to say to Floyd.

Floyd, however, had a lot to say to Melanie, amusing her with stories about local people. Floyd's business kept him in touch with a variety of people and he had a story for every person he met.

And Adam didn't like the way Melanie laughed at every story Floyd told.

You're acting like a jealous suitor, he thought, swigging down the rest of his tea. But just as he started to wonder how long Floyd was going to be entertaining them, Melanie got up and set Tiffany on the floor.

"I should be going," she said, idly brushing her hand over the little girl's hair. "Thanks so much for coming out here, Floyd. I really appreciate it."

"No problem. Glad to be of service." Floyd shook her hand. "Adam, it was a pleasure. I'll be in touch once Melanie's financing goes through." He shook Adam's hand, then Helen's. Made a general comment of farewell, patted Tiffany on the head, then gave Melanie one more smile.

Adam felt his irritation growing with each grin Floyd gave Melanie. He walked Floyd to the door, followed by Melanie and Tiffany. As they said a final round of goodbyes, Adam was fully aware of Melanie at his side. Tiffany in front of him.

Like a family.

He felt a twist of sorrow followed by an echo of a previous, equally unwelcome feeling.

Loneliness.

He wanted to be a family. It was what he and Lana had dreamed of when they bought this house. And now, with Melanie beside him, the picture was an imitation of that dream.

Yet as he glanced sidelong at Melanie, he let another dream tease him. This house. This woman.

And what about Lana?

The memory of his wife brought a clench of guilt over what might have been. She was why he was selling the house. The dream was over.

Melanie tucked her blood pressure cuff back into her nurse's bag and made a quick notation in Helen's file.

"You're frowning again. What's wrong?" Helen asked.

"I'm a little concerned about your blood pressure. Has the new medication helped any?"

"A little." Helen pulled her glasses off and polished them, her movements slow. "Adam asked if I could tell you to meet him in the shop this morning. He has something he wants to show you."

Melanie zipped her bag shut, trying to read past Helen's vague pronouncement and complacent grin.

The final sale of the house didn't seem to affect Helen at all. In spite of her blood pressure, Helen hadn't spiked a temperature for a couple of days now and she seemed more relaxed.

"Is Tiffany with him?" Melanie asked.

"She's been spending more and more time with him every day. It's wonderful to see." Helen put her glasses on. "I'm glad you talked him out of going to Disneyland. He's a good father who had to learn so many things the hard way." Helen slowly got to her feet, her bright eyes fixed on Melanie. "And now I'm just going to sit in the front room for a while. I have a book there I've been reading." She gave Melanie a wistful look. "I want to enjoy the view as long as I can. Who knows what the next month will bring? And don't look so sad," Helen said as Melanie put the walker in front of her. "I've been praying every night. And the Lord moves in mysterious ways."

Melanie wasn't even going to ask what Helen's prayers consisted of. It was no surprise to Melanie that Adam retreated to his shop as soon as she came each day. The heavy-handed hints Helen ladled out were enough to make Melanie blush. She didn't want to know what Adam thought.

"Mysterious indeed," Melanie murmured. "I'll stop in before I leave, though. Just to see if you need anything."

"Take your time," Helen said with a conspiratorial wink.

Melanie stopped at her car and set her bag inside before she went to the shop. As she closed the door, she looked around the yard once more. In a month or so this place was going to be hers.

Her first home.

Melanie took her time walking to the shop at the back of the lot, trying to absorb this wonderful actuality. Displacing Helen was the only lingering melancholy.

And what about the son and granddaughter?

Melanie dismissed the errant thought as she knocked lightly on the shop door and pushed it open. Adam had his own plans.

Tiffany looked up and jumped to her feet, scattering the rough wooden blocks she was playing with.

"Mellalie, you are here," she called out, running to her.

Adam stood at the workbench with his back to her, but turned as she closed the door.

It took a moment for Melanie's eyes to adjust from the bright natural sunlight to the artificial lighting in the shop. But in spite of that, she easily caught Adam's gaze with her own.

"Helen said you wanted to see me?" she asked, taking a slow sniff of the wood scent that permeated the shop. "It smells good in here."

Adam smiled at her, leaning back against his workbench. "Brings back memories, that's for sure."

"Memories?" Melanie prompted.

"I used to work with Lana's father building houses and cabinets." He brushed sawdust off his arms as if doing the same with his past as he pushed himself away from the bench. "I've got something for you."

Curious, Melanie followed him to the other side of the shop to a window where a faded blanket shrouded a tall shape.

"I managed to salvage what I could and reuse it," he was saying as he pulled the blanket away. "I tried to follow the same dimensions and pattern, but couldn't match the stain."

He stepped away, dropping the blanket on the ground and revealing a dresser.

It was the dresser he had broken.

"You fixed it," she said with a sense of wonder. She came up beside him. But as she touched it she heard his previous words again and realized what he had done.

"This isn't the old dresser." She pulled open the drawers one at a time, releasing the sharp scent of freshly cut wood. She looked at him, trying to understand. "You built this? From scratch?"

"Pine, actually," he said with a faint grin. A dimple dented one cheek. "I used the same pulls, but I had to sand the rust off a few of them." He pulled out one of the drawers and set it on its side on the blanket. "I took a few liberties with the design. The original didn't have dovetail joints, but it makes for a stronger drawer if you do that."

Something hard and bright flashed within her as he spoke. He had made this beautiful piece of furniture. Had spent all this time replacing something she had yearned only briefly for. Had done all this.

Politeness deemed that she protest. But she couldn't speak words she didn't feel. Adam had made this. His hands had crafted it. As he pointed out other things he had done, his hands touching the silky-smooth wood, Melanie caught an undercurrent of the pride of a craftsman.

She touched the dresser again, trying to assimilate the emotions that threatened to overwhelm her. He had spent hours on this. For her.

"It's beautiful." She slid her hands over the surface, tracing the grain of the wood enhanced by the stain, deepened by the varnish. Even to her untrained eye, she could see that Adam had a gift. Each drawer slid smoothly in and out, their panels so well aligned not a gap showed between them. "I can't believe you did this."

"I'm glad you like it. I enjoyed making it."

She walked around it, still touching it, overcome by a sense of wonder and amazement. She stopped in front of him. "This is the most amazing gift I've ever received."

"Surely you've received gifts before. From your parents."

Melanie swallowed an unexpected knot of emotion. "My father, when he remembered my birthday, always sent money and my mother gave me more practical gifts. No one has ever done anything like this."

She lowered her head, blinking at the moisture welling in her eyes, swallowing against the thickness in her throat.

Adam laid a rough fingertip along her cheek and gently urged her to look up at him.

"I'm glad you like it," he said, his voice low, a soft smile curving his fine lips.

"It's beautiful." She gave in to an impulse and threw her arms around his neck. It was supposed to be a quick hug. A thank-you for something that deserved more than just words.

But as she drew away her hands lingered on the curls of hair at his neck, then rested on his shoulders. He held her by the arms, his fingers rough against her skin, his fingertips lightly massaging her upper arms. Their eyes met and held, a connection almost physical in intensity.

Her flighty pulse stepped up its shallow rhythm. Melanie let her hands slide down his arms as she fought to regain the breath she'd lost. She wanted to move away.

She wanted to be drawn into his arms.

She hesitated, lost in the confused back-and-forth of longing and reality.

His hands lingered on her arms, then he released her.

"Mellalie, come and see my tower."

Melanie swallowed again, sucked in a deep breath, willing her pounding heart to steady as she turned to the little girl who had been playing happily at their feet, oblivious to what had just happened.

"It's very nice," Melanie said automatically. She helped Tiffany place another block on the tower, her hands unsteady and trembling. And what had happened? Nothing. You were just a little overexuberant in your thanks, she reminded herself as she drew in another breath.

"I was wondering if you want me to move the dresser to the house," Adam was saying behind her. "But if you prefer I can bring it to your apartment."

Melanie drew in another breath and turned back to the dresser, touching it again rather than looking at Adam. "Though I'd love to have it in my apartment, it seems a shame to move it all the way to my house when it's just going to come back here."

"I'll move it to Donna's room if you want."

"That would be great. I can go up and look at it each time I come." She granted him an amiable smile. "I wish I knew how to thank you."

"No thanks necessary," Adam said.

Melanie once again touched the dresser, its finish silky smooth. "I'm overwhelmed. I will say it's the most wonderful thing I've ever received. I feel quite unworthy. I don't know what to say."

"You seem to be doing okay," he said with a light teasing tone, as if the moment they had shared hadn't happened.

Melanie drew in a steadying breath. Maybe nothing had happened. Maybe it was just her own silly daydreams and yearnings getting mixed up in this attractive man that had created that moment of awareness.

But as she drove away, she couldn't help but look back. And notice Adam standing in the doorway of his shop, watching her. He was smiling.

Chapter Eight

"I hear that Adam wants to move Helen to Calgary fairly soon." Dr. Leon Drew slipped his hands into the pockets of his lab coat and leaned back against his desk. Melanie had stopped by Dr. Drew's office to ask him about one of his patients. "What's your take on that?"

"It's complicated. Helen wants me to convince Adam to let her stay. Adam wants me to convince Helen to go. I think Adam is resigned to staying for at least another week."

"Adam Engler has had a lot to deal with in the past few years," Leon said quietly. "I don't blame him for wanting to see that his mother is okay."

It was the tone of his voice rather than his words that made Melanie stop. "You're talking about Lana?"

Leon nodded. "Losing her must have been hard. I often wondered if that was why he moved away."

"I don't think he's gotten over it."

"She was such a puzzle to me," Leon continued,

looking beyond Melanie, as if looking into the past. “When she was first diagnosed as diabetic, she was fourteen. She would argue with me constantly. Over her blood sugars, her ketone levels, her diet.” Leon sighed. “It took her a while to settle down. I’m still surprised she went into shock. I thought she had finally accepted her diabetes.”

“Adam seems to think she died because their home was so far from the hospital.”

Leon Drew shrugged. “That could have been a factor. But if she was balanced, it wouldn’t have been. She wouldn’t have gone out of control so fast.”

“What do you mean, ‘if’? Didn’t you know?”

“I wasn’t her doctor when she got pregnant. She was seeing a lady doctor in Eastbar, who apparently was a diabetic, as well.” Leon pushed himself away from the desk. “I better get going myself. I promised my wife I’d be home on time for supper tonight and my day falls apart real quick these days. Say hello to Helen for me.”

“I’ll do that.” Melanie slipped her briefcase over her shoulder, sifting the information Leon had given her and trying to put it together with what Adam had told her.

Something didn’t quite fit, and it bothered her.

Adam pulled into an empty spot beside a small sports car that looked exactly like Melanie’s.

He tapped his fingers on the steering wheel, looking out across the park. People were clumped up in groups talking, kids tearing around. The sun shone benevolently over the small town scene like a benediction.

Was this really such a good idea? He'd been out of touch with so many people it was almost an embarrassment to suddenly show up at a community function.

"Go out and play?" Tiffany asked, leaning forward in her car seat.

He sighed lightly, smiling at the eagerness on his daughter's face. It was for her that he did this, he reminded himself as he got out of the truck.

"C'mon, sweetheart, let's go see if anyone even remembers who we are." He unbuckled his daughter and lifted her out of the seat.

He settled her in his arms, took a deep breath and walked toward the groups of people.

"Good afternoon. Glad you could come." A tall, elegant-looking woman spotted them and walked toward them, her strappy sandals an incongruity on the grass. She frowned as she came nearer, then held out her hands in welcome. "I can't believe it. Adam Engler. Hello. I'm Serena Davis." She spoke the name with a gentle questioning tone. As if he should remember her.

"Hello, Serena." Adam kept the frown he felt from showing.

"You don't remember me, do you?" Serena pouted lightly. "We went to high school together. We had Mrs. Hunter for English 10."

Adam lifted his shoulder in a vague gesture. "I'm sorry."

Serena waved his apology away. "I was only around for a couple of years, then I moved away. From what I remember you were probably too busy with hockey and volleyball."

And Lana.

Her name wasn't spoken, but Adam sensed that Serena had thought it. The sympathetic look she gave him confirmed it.

"Anyhow, come and meet the rest of the people," Serena said, turning.

And suddenly Melanie was there.

She wore a bright orange shirt over a khaki-colored skirt, her dark hair framing her face like a halo.

"Hey, Mel," Serena said, tucking her arm in Melanie's. "I'm guessing you came to say hello to Adam."

Melanie directed a careful smile his way. "Your mom decided to stay home?"

Adam nodded, shifting Tiffany on his hip. "She had a bunch of women over, and I had some shopping to do. So I thought me and Tiffany would stop by."

"I'm glad you did."

A gentle silence drifted up between them, an echo of the moment in the shop.

"Well, I've got to run." Serena patted Tiffany on the arm, giving Adam one more lingering glance. "I'm sure you can take care of him," she said to Melanie. "Don't forget to kiss Janey's baby."

"As long as I don't have to change the diaper," Melanie replied.

"Who is Janey?" Adam asked when Serena was gone.

"One of the secretaries at work. She just had a baby. Do you want some punch? They've got some bowls set up by the pavilion."

"Sure. I guess we may as well start mingling."

"You'll do just fine," she said with an encouraging smile.

Adam took a deep breath, glancing over the crowd, and followed her. They didn't get far.

"Melanie, so glad you came." A plump older woman stopped the little group, smiling at Melanie, glancing over at Adam.

"Adam, this is Lois Tessier, a co-worker of mine," Melanie said, introducing the woman.

"And Bob's mother, don't forget." Lois winked at Melanie. Her perfunctory handshake told Adam exactly what Lois thought of his presence. "Bob was hoping you'd come. He's probably talking golf with his buddies, but I can tell him you're here."

Melanie shifted her stance, putting her slightly closer to Adam. Her body language was eloquent and for a moment he was tempted to put his arm around her. Draw her close as if claiming her.

"So my loans officer plays golf. I'll have to remember that," she said with a bright smile. "But I should go and say hello to a few more people. Talk to you later."

As they walked away, Adam said, "I didn't know you were interested in golf."

"I'm not. But now I know why I won't be starting." Melanie angled him a quick smile, coupled with a mischievous twinkle.

"Hey, stranger."

A hand dropped on his shoulder and Adam turned to the familiar voice. Tall, blond hair worn overly long, mustache and a beard. "Where have you been?" he asked.

Recognition swept away his hesitancy about coming to this picnic. "Hey, Graydon. I see you still haven't found a decent barber." Adam grinned at his former co-worker and old friend with a warmth he hadn't felt since arriving back in Derwin. Graydon had been the only friend of his who had taken the time to come and see him in Calgary from time to time.

Graydon Magrath gave Adam's shoulder a quick shake. "I can't believe you haven't had time to look up your old buddies. Mr. Gerrard was just asking about you the other day. Didn't even know you were around."

"I haven't been back that long," Adam said, clapping his hand on Graydon's. "Been busy at the house, taking care of my mom. Been meaning to call you and catch up."

"I heard about her hurting herself. How's she doing?"

"Not too bad." He turned to Melanie. "You could ask my mom's nurse, Melanie Visser. She would know better."

"I know this delightful woman," Graydon said, winking at Melanie. "I see her around, but when I try to say hi in town, she won't give me the time of day."

"I'd say hi if I met you on the sidewalk." Melanie's tone was wry, but a smile hovered over her mouth. "When I hear someone whistling from their truck, I usually assume they are high school students saying hey to their friends."

Graydon just grinned, slapping his hand on his chest.

"That's me. The world's oldest teenager." Graydon turned to Adam. "You got a feisty one in her."

Adam didn't like the inference Graydon made, but didn't bother to correct him. He suspected that three years hadn't caused much change in his friend. Graydon was always the cliché construction worker.

"So you gonna settle down now, strap on your pouch and come back to work for me now that I'm Gerrard's partner? It'd be like old times." Graydon set his hands on his hips as if he was ready to swing a hammer right that moment.

"You bought out half the business?" This was news indeed.

"He said he wants to keep working but not as hard as he used to. He hasn't been the same since..." Graydon stopped, biting his lip. "Anyway, he said he was getting too old to run after bills and lazy framers. Said I could do that part."

Adam chose to skip over Graydon's slip. He knew what Tom Gerrard felt. "Actually I'm pulling up my last root," he said with false heartiness. "The house is for sale. I'm taking my mother back to Calgary."

"What? That great house?" Graydon lowered his hands. Frowned. "Why'd you want to do that? I always thought you'd come back to your senses and settle down here. And looks like you've got a good start." He looked at Melanie, then back at Adam as if expecting Adam to make a further announcement.

"Melanie is buying my house."

Graydon's disappointment clearly showed in his lugubrious expression.

"I've got a good business going in Calgary," Adam hastened to explain, convincing his friend and himself. "I'm making good money. I've been there three years already. I'm practically settled in there." And in a few weeks his mother would be, as well.

Graydon huffed his disapproval. "Three years is way too long to be building those lousy office buildings and warehouses. No personality in them. No care. You had such a good touch. Why waste it on glass and metal?"

Graydon's words struck too close to the feelings Adam had experienced before. But what could he do? There was no way he could settle back here.

His friend turned to Melanie as if appealing to her to make Adam change his mind. "This man was born to be a fine woodworker. You should see the work this man does. The things he can make wood do. It'd make me cry if I was a woman." Graydon pretended to wipe his eyes. "I get a little weepy just thinking about the waste of God-given talent."

"Actually I have seen what Adam can do with wood," Melanie said, turning to Adam. "And you're right." Melanie didn't state which one of Graydon's outrageous statements she concurred with, but Adam remembered the glint of tears in her eyes when she'd seen the dresser. Her tremulous voice as she thanked him.

He smiled back at her, and the emotion of that moment reverberated between them as strongly as a touch.

"Hey, Graydon. We need you at the barbecue," someone called out across the yard.

"Be right there," Graydon's voice boomed back.

"Okay. I'm going to go fry some steaks," Graydon said loudly, taking a couple of steps back as if giving them space. "You two just carry on. Adam, you owe me about ten hours of conversation and catching up, so I'm gonna get you later."

"More like twenty hours," Adam said with a forced grin, searching for the casual give-and-take he and Graydon always shared. "We'll talk. For sure."

Graydon pointed a finger at him. "It's a deal." He winked at Melanie. "You try to convince him he should stay. Maybe you could find a room in that house for him. And his little girl."

Adam stifled his impatience with his friend's obvious hints. Waited until Graydon was out of earshot before turning to Melanie. "I'm sorry about that. Graydon is one of those bluff, hearty men you see in heavy truck commercials. He's just a lot of talk, but he's got a good heart."

"I know Graydon Magrath," Melanie said with a gentle smile. "I know that he's been taking care of his sister for the past six months."

Adam frowned. "What do you mean, taking care of his sister?"

"Tesha hurt both her arms in a freak accident six months ago at her job. I've been there a couple of times to arrange for home-care relief. Graydon comes every day to help her with her physiotherapy. He's got a heart as big as his voice."

Adam felt a thrust of guilt. It had been over six months since he had seen Graydon. He'd been so caught up in his own problems that he couldn't even take the time to find out how his old friend was doing. "I didn't know that," he said quietly.

"It's not something you get on the phone about."

But Adam couldn't shake off the reality that he'd done wrong by his old friend.

"Let's go get some punch." Melanie touched his arm, as if reassuring him. He gave her a quick smile, thankful for her presence, yet ashamed that she had seen this part of him, as well.

As they moved through the crowd, Adam was stopped again and again, greeted by people he had done work for at one time or had known from his youth. Each conversation, each familiar face was like another gentle barb, hooking into him, pulling him further and further into life in Derwin. A life he had tried to outrun and forget.

Melanie was gracious and charming, ignoring the overt comments and smiling away the curious glances. Everyone got a personal greeting and, in many cases, a light hand on their arm as she asked a few questions about a relative or friend.

They made their way to Janey, who was holding court under a grove of poplar trees, surrounded by a variety of women, none of whom Adam recognized.

Melanie made the appropriate noises about the baby and asked the right questions. When Janey offered to let her hold the baby, Melanie took the tiny bundle of humanity easily, then squatted down to let Tiffany have a close look.

"Baby is cute," Tiffany said loudly, then pulled him closer to give him a kiss.

Adam was about to reach out and stop Tiffany, but Melanie deftly moved the infant aside, at the same time pulling Tiffany to her side to show her from another angle. "The baby is sleeping now, Tiffany," she said softly. Melanie quietly pointed out the baby's eyes, ears, carefully pulled out a diminutive hand and showed Tiffany the baby's fingers, his nails like four tiny beads.

As Adam watched, an older memory surfaced. Tiffany as a baby being held by the woman he'd hired as a nanny. The woman had tried to get him to hold his daughter, but he was afraid. She was so small, so fragile.

Besides, he had told her abruptly, covering up his own fear and loneliness, he was too busy.

Tiffany was now three times the baby's size, talking and walking and growing more independent each day.

He had missed all the steps between the brand-new baby that Melanie held in her arms and the child that Tiffany was now. Regret for those lost years clawed at him. In his rush to outrun his guilt, he had missed those first amazing years of his own daughter's life.

He would make it up to her, he promised himself. Somehow, Lord willing, he would make it up to her.

"Supper is served," Graydon called out from the smoking line of barbecues beside the park's gazebo.

"Guess I should give the baby back, shouldn't I?" Melanie said to Tiffany, slowly getting up.

"I want the baby."

Tiffany was about to grab a corner of the baby's blankets, but Adam caught her hand just in time.

"The baby needs to sleep, Tiffany," he said quietly, squatting down to look at her.

Please don't let her make a scene, he thought, holding her hand and her gaze. Not in front of these people. I know I'm not the best father, but please don't let everyone else know.

Tiffany tugged on her hand once more, but Adam held firm. Then, to his utter amazement, she suddenly stopped.

Relief came in an uplifting rush. Adam smiled at her, and stroked her cheek. "Good girl," he whispered. And as he got to his feet, she lifted her arms.

He settled her on his hip and caught Melanie's gentle smile.

"Good job," she said, touching his arm. "I think you're making progress."

He couldn't help but return her smile, hold her gaze. The moment spun out, fragile as gossamer. Adam wanted to reach out to her. Touch her.

Kiss her.

He blinked and shook his head as if to dislodge the emotions, wondering what was wrong with him.

"Let's go eat," she said lightly, turning and leading the way to the tables.

Adam followed, bemused by his reaction to her, yet unable to find a way around the unalterable facts. She was buying his house and he was leaving a town that would never hold a place for him anymore.

"So you came here with Adam?" Graydon dropped onto the grass beside Melanie, wiping his fingers with a napkin. "That's great."

Melanie took the last bite of her bun and set the

plate down beside her, carefully choosing her reply. "He and Tiffany came on their own. I just happened to meet them at the parking lot."

"*Just* happened?" Graydon's bushy eyebrows disappeared into his hair. "And then you guys sit here all cozy eating supper together. What a cute picture."

Melanie took extra care brushing the crumbs off her pants. She didn't know how to answer that without sounding defensive or flirtatious. So she chose discretion and said nothing.

"I mean, that's okay," Graydon hastened to explain, balling up the napkin and pitching it with a quick snap into a nearby garbage can. "If you came with him, that is." He grinned at her, resting his forearms on his knees. "It's about time Adam got over what happened. About time he started looking around again."

He left her absolutely no avenue out of this quagmire, Melanie thought with dismay. Graydon was determined to think that she and Adam were an item when all they really were was temporary business partners. So she said nothing.

"Oh, boy. I didn't think she would come." Graydon's arms fell as he sat up straighter, his eyes narrowed.

Melanie followed the direction of his gaze, puzzled at his sudden change of subject.

Adam stood in profile to them, holding Tiffany's hand. A young woman faced him, her hand on his shoulder. She looked to be in her mid-twenties, slim and petite with long blond hair.

"Who is she?" Melanie asked, striving to keep her

voice light and vaguely interested instead of avidly curious.

"Lana's sister, Sandy. She lives in Edmonton. Must be visiting her parents, but what is she doing way out here?"

"Her parents live in Eastbar?"

Graydon angled her a curious glance. Nodded. "And how do you know that?"

Melanie shrugged away his regard, her eyes on Sandy and Adam. "I just know."

Sandy stroked Adam's arm with a proprietary air, then she slipped her arms around him, her head on his shoulder. He patted her awkwardly on the back, his other hand still in Tiffany's.

"Friendly town," Melanie murmured with a flicker of jealousy. "Adam seems to have that effect on a lot of women," she said, remembering Roxanne's exuberant greeting in the park.

And their own embrace yesterday.

"Sandy and Adam are old friends."

"Of course they are." And why should you care? In spite of that hug, the two of you don't have a future.

Sandy drew away from Adam, her expression earnest as she spoke. Adam nodded, looking down at the ground, poking it with the toe of his boot.

"I should go and talk to Mrs. Hamstead," Melanie said, pushing herself to her feet. She knew she should do something, anything, rather than watch and wonder at Adam's relationship with his former sister-in-law.

"I wouldn't worry about her," Graydon said with a wink. "Adam never felt that way about her."

"That vague pronouncement makes me feel a lot better." Melanie flashed him a quick smile, then walked toward a group of women sitting in lawn chairs.

She wasn't going to look over her shoulder. She didn't care whom Adam talked to.

In spite of her personal pep talk, just before she reached the group of women she couldn't stop a quick glance over her shoulder.

Adam was leaving.

She turned, watching as he strode through the park, Tiffany settled on his hip. He disappeared behind a group of people, then reappeared beside his truck, opening the side door to put Tiffany in her car seat. But just before he closed the door, he looked her way.

Even across the distance Melanie felt a frisson of awareness. Felt the intensity of his blue, blue eyes.

Then he got into his truck and left.

Chapter Nine

The box was just plain cardboard. Dented in the sides and held together with an elastic.

But since he and Melanie had found it, Adam hadn't been able to get it off his mind. He had set it on the workbench in his shop when he took the dresser apart and each time he worked on Melanie's dresser, the box lay as a quiet reminder, its mystery growing each day.

In this day and age of telephones and e-mail, what would have driven Jason Shewchuk to write twenty letters without a reply?

He dragged the box across his workbench and brushed off the accumulated sawdust, slipped the elastic off, then carefully lifted the lid and pulled out one of the opened letters.

He ran his fingers along the jagged edge, where it had been opened. Then, ignoring second thoughts, he pulled the letter out.

"My dear Donna," it began. "Please don't rip up this letter. Please let me know you got it. I want you to forgive me. I want us to be a family again. I was wrong to leave, but you are wrong to push me away like this. I've tried to call you, but there is never any answer. Please, please call me." And underneath his signature were two telephone numbers and an address.

And that was it. A simple letter, only one page, a few lines, yet in it Adam read regret and sorrow and a longing to make a broken family whole.

Had Donna replied?

He took out the second opened letter and got his answer.

"Dear Donna, I still haven't heard anything from you. Don't push me away because of one mistake. I was wrong to blame you. Very wrong. My life is empty without you and the children. There's nothing. I want to come back, but I want you to let me know that I can."

Adam stopped reading, feeling like an intruder into a very private grief. He carefully folded the letter, slipping it back into the envelope.

Why had Donna ignored this outpouring of sorrow? Why could she not hear what this man was saying?

He thought again of the renters who had been living in the house. They had obviously saved the letters. Why hadn't they forwarded them on?

Mystery upon mystery.

He remembered telling Melanie that Donna might not like what was in them. He could simply throw them away and be done with it.

But the cry of this man's heart, the love he professed for his wife, his children—Adam couldn't walk away from that without making sure, beyond a doubt, that Donna had heard it, too.

He picked up the box and walked to the house, glancing at his watch as he did. Melanie wasn't coming until later today, so he was okay for now.

He wasn't really avoiding her, he told himself. Just giving them both space. Going to the community picnic had been a mistake. Spending time with Melanie at that same picnic had compounded that mistake. And seeing Sandy again had underlined it. The Derwin grapevine was thriving—his mother had heard about it the next morning. Thankfully she didn't press him for more information about either Sandy or Melanie.

Helen sat in the living room, reading to Tiffany. It sounded as if they were in the very beginning of Tiffany's favorite story. They would be occupied for a while.

He set the box of letters in front of him both for inspiration and encouragement. He had Jason's last address. If he still lived there, it wouldn't be too hard to contact him.

Jason didn't live there anymore, but the person who answered the phone knew where he lived and gave him the new number. When Adam dialed it he got an answering machine. He declined to leave a message. What could he say?

But that contact was at least made. Now to get hold of Donna, and he knew where to start with that, too. It took him a few phone calls to get his friend's cell phone number.

"Graydon. How are you?" Adam tried not to sound

overly hearty. He had promised Graydon they would catch up, and his hasty exit from the picnic hardly attested to that fact.

"I'm great, man," Graydon said. "Why'd you leave early? Was looking for you."

Adam hooked a kitchen chair with his foot and dropped into it. "Just had to, Graydon." It was all he could say. Seeing Lana's sister had been unexpected and harder to deal with than he'd thought. Leaving the picnic so abruptly was rude, and Graydon wasn't the only one he had to apologize to.

"Sorry I didn't come to say goodbye," he said now.

"I wasn't the only one who missed you. Melanie was walking around with a fake smile the rest of the afternoon."

Graydon's words gave one more twist to the shard of guilt, yet at the same time gave his heart a peculiar lift.

"She's a wonderful person, Adam. Deserves a wonderful man."

And that was precisely why he had left the picnic, Adam thought with dismay.

He remembered what Melanie had said about Graydon's sister, and this time asked about her. Their conversation eased some of his guilt.

"I have a question for you about Donna Shewchuk," Adam said after a while. "She's been away from here for some time. Do you have any idea how to get hold of her?"

Graydon paused, and Adam could almost picture him twisting one of the ends of his mustache as he always did when he was thinking. "Try Nadine Fletcher, at the paper. Donna used to work there. Why?"

"I found something in the attic that belongs to her. Thought she might want it back."

"Good of you, man. But then you always were a good man. Don't be such a stranger, eh?"

"I'll be in touch." That was a promise he intended to keep, he thought, hanging up the phone. Seeing Graydon was a stark reminder of what he'd once had in this community and what he had lost by burying himself in Calgary. He had missed his good friend. The ease of his company and the history they had shared. Something he knew he and Kyle could never have.

He flipped through the phone book and found the number of the *Derwin Times.* He dialed it and was soon put through to Nadine Fletcher, whom Donna used to work for.

Adam took a pen and scribbled down the number Nadine provided, relief flowing through him. Donna was near Eastbar, which was only half an hour's drive away.

He chatted a moment with Nadine, exchanging a few pleasantries, then hung up, grinning at the number. Melanie would be so pleased.

"Thank you," he breathed. Then stopped. Who was he thanking, anyhow? God?

Melanie smoothed her hand over her skirt, adjusted the collar of her favorite red shirt and took a deep breath. *Please Lord, don't let me make a fool of myself in front of Adam,* she prayed as she got out of her car. Instead she focused on the house.

Her house.

She had spent most of last night looking over paint chips and poring over magazines trying to choose the exterior color and the trim. She had finally decided on a pale butter-yellow for the main color, sage-green for the soffits and eaves and a slate-blue for the shutters. Trying to visualize those colors on the house in front of her made her smile. Excited, even.

She pushed open the creaking gate and walked to the back of the house, looking at it from all angles. Yes. She had chosen exactly the right colors.

She let her gaze slide over the yard. Adam had been busy. The piles of lumber were gone and it looked as if he had even mowed the overgrown lawn. Each day she came, the place looked more and more like the home she remembered.

Her excitement grew. The home that was going to be hers.

The back door was open and as she lifted her hand to knock on the door, she heard Adam talking. Her fingers curled into a fist that she pressed against her beating heart. Why was it surging against her chest at the sound of his voice?

She knew why. Knew she was being foolish.

Soon this would all be over, she promised herself, knocking sharply on the door. She would be living in her dream home and Adam would be out of her life.

"Hey, Melanie. I'm glad you're here." Adam was opening the door, smiling that crooked smile of his.

A smile that made her disobedient heart start up again.

Just a chemical reaction, she reminded herself, smiling back at him. "Why? Is your mom causing you trouble again?"

Helen was finally able to try walking a few steps without her walker. The last time Melanie had come, Helen had secretly told her that Adam was constantly hovering, worried that she would hurt herself again. Though Helen had acted frustrated, Melanie could easily hear in Helen's voice the pleasure at Adam's concern.

"No. She's doing just fine." Adam stepped back, letting Melanie come into the house. "I have some great news."

Melanie set her bag on the chair, willing her heart to stop its erratic beating as she turned to him. What could he be so pleased about? Was he going to stay?

Whoa, Melanie. You are really jumping ahead. "And what is that?" she asked quietly.

Adam caught her by the arms, grinning like a kid. "I finally contacted Donna. I told her about the letters. She hadn't known anything about them."

Emotions tumbled through her, a kaleidoscope of pleasure and hope edged with a faint disappointment that Adam's news had nothing to do with him.

"Where is she? Close by here? Far away? Did she say anything about Dena?" Her excitement grew with each question.

"She lives about half an hour's drive away, north of Eastbar. I asked her if I could deliver the letters to her. And she said yes. She started to cry."

Melanie felt her own eyes prickle. She looked away. This was the second time she'd felt all teary eyed in front of Adam.

"Hey, Melanie. Are you okay?" His hands were still on her arms, his voice quiet, intimate.

"I am," she whispered. "I'm just feeling a little sentimental, that's all." And a little confused.

She wished he wasn't standing so close to her, wasn't touching her. All she would have to do was turn just a half turn, lean a few degrees ahead and she would be in his arms. Again.

The thought was far too appealing, and she carefully pulled away.

"When are you going?" she asked, her voice a little shaky.

"Tomorrow." He was quiet a moment. "Do you want to come? I can wait until you're done work."

Say no, the practical part of her urged. She could easily get the directions and go on her own.

But she wanted to be there when Donna got the letters it seemed she had never seen. She wanted to know firsthand what had happened to the family she had idealized for so long.

"I'd love to come," she said softly, her smile tremulous. "I'd love to see her again."

"Great. I'll pick you up after work."

She heard a scampering sound coming from the front room, then, "Mellalie is here."

Then the sound of running feet and Tiffany launched herself at Melanie. "You are here again," Tiffany said, grabbing Melanie's hand and dancing around her.

"Come, see Gramma. You come, too." Tiffany grabbed her father's hand, and over the top of her head Melanie caught Adam's smile.

"Looks like things are improving in the daughter department," she said quietly as they walked to the front room.

Adam nodded. "My partner wasn't happy with your advice, but it seems to be working." His smile deepened, creasing his cheeks. "We've got a bit of a ways to go, but there's definite progress. Thanks again."

His smile warmed her, and his words of thanks gave her a gentle shiver.

"I have to show you something, Melanie," Helen was saying.

With a guilty start, Melanie turned to her patient.

Then Adam left and Tiffany went with him without one word of protest. Melanie knew she should be pleased that father and daughter were slowly bonding again. But she wouldn't be honest if she didn't admit that the mothering part of her felt a tiny bit jealous.

Pink shirt okay? Did it match the pants?

Should she wear her hair up? Down? Was she wearing too much makeup? What about the perfume? Too obvious?

Melanie dragged her hair back from her face and blew out a frustrated sigh at her muted reflection in a bathroom mirror still foggy from her shower. "It's just a visit to an old friend," she said aloud, as if speaking made the reality more mundane.

But she knew it was the fact that she was going with

Adam that put the flush in her cheeks and the fluttering nerves in her stomach. And created all these indecisions.

She wiped the mirror with her elbow and stood back, inspecting herself critically. She had applied the mascara with a light hand, and the eyeshadow was barely there, just as her mother had taught her.

She remembered her father teasing her mother about the makeup lessons. *Why bother putting it on at all if it's not supposed to be noticeable?* he had said as her mother was getting ready to go to church.

And he'd stayed behind.

Melanie clutched her stomach. *Dear Lord, what am I doing?* she prayed. *I'm starting down the same path my mother went. This can't be what You want for me.*

She remembered Adam's words when they'd been alone in the turret, but his words seemed less a rebellion against God than the cry of a wounded heart. A hurting soul who didn't know where to go anymore.

"You're looking for excuses," she said aloud. Firmly, as if convincing herself. Adam was coming for her and she was going to meet an old friend. Nothing more.

She flicked off the light and left the room.

Her sweater hung over the back of her kitchen chair and as she slipped it on, she gave the apartment a critical once-over. The kitchen counter, though faded and scarred, was tidy, the dishwasher swishing through its cycle. She straightened the candleholder on the kitchen table, brushed an errant crumb off its wooden surface.

She walked into the living room, picked up a

magazine that lay crooked on a side table and straightened a few books on the bookshelf.

A tall book sat between two short books. She was about to pull it out and move it, then stopped.

Fussy old maid, she thought. What are you going to be like when you get the house?

A sudden sorrow, so familiar it felt like a friend, clenched her midsection. She looked around her apartment again.

What was a single woman like her doing buying a house in a small town like Derwin? Was she pinning too much on an old dream she couldn't let go of?

The intercom buzzer sounded, saving her from her roiling thoughts. Adam.

Her heart danced.

"Be right down," she said into the speaker.

She didn't give him a chance to answer, but caught her purse from the hook beside her door, locked the door and ran down the stairs.

He stood in the entrance frowning at the speaker, as if it had let him down, his hands in the pockets of his ever-present blue jeans. These were clean and pressed and the white shirt tucked into them was a bright contrast against his tanned skin.

His sandy hair was brushed, a few curls already springing up around his ears and over the collar of his shirt. Then he turned, saw her and his smile broke free.

Melanie couldn't stop the answering quaver of her errant heart or her own lips as they curved up in response.

She opened the door and for a moment they stood

facing each other, each saying nothing, awareness arching between them.

Melanie was the first to look away, her prayer of a few moments ago slowly seeping back, bringing with it a gentle peace. *Lord, work Your will in my life,* Melanie prayed as she stepped past Adam. *And work in Adam's life, as well. Let him feel Your love. Your forgiveness.*

By praying for him, it was as if she dismantled the miscreant hold he had on her emotions. He was a lonely soul in need of God's love. And in need of her prayers.

"Ready to go?" Adam asked as he pulled the outer door open for her.

"Where's Tiffany?"

"Mom's neighbor was over and offered to stay." Adam let the door fall behind him.

"I have to tell you, I'm a little nervous," she confessed, thankful for the equilibrium her prayer had given her. "I don't know what to expect. Are you sure she won't mind if I come along?"

Adam shook his head as he fished his truck keys out of his pocket. "I told her you'd be coming. Donna was really excited about seeing you. She said that she always enjoyed having you around."

Adam followed Melanie around to her side of the truck and opened the door for her. According to numerous articles in women's magazines Melanie should have felt slightly offended. Especially because she'd been living on her own for some time.

But she appreciated the small courtesy. It made her feel valued. As a single woman she did so much for herself, she didn't mind having something done for her, even if it was as minor as having a door opened.

Adam got into the truck, but before he started it, he turned to Melanie, tapping his fingers on the steering wheel. "Before we go, I know I have to apologize for leaving you so suddenly at the picnic." He paused, his teeth worrying his lower lip. "I should have said something yesterday, but somehow I just couldn't find the right way to do it. Then I realized there's no right or wrong way to apologize, as long as I just do it." He looked up at her then, one corner of his mouth pulled up in a half smile. "Forgive me?"

"Of course I forgive you," she said, stifling the questions that scurried through her mind. What Adam discussed with his sister-in-law was none of her business. Though Serena had given her the background on Sandy's lifelong crush on Adam, it had no affect on her.

She gave him a quick smile, adding to her words of forgiveness, then caught sight of the box nestled in the car seat between them.

"Are these the letters?" she asked, laying her hand on the box.

Adam nodded, then started up the truck and pulled into the street. "I just hope there's nothing offensive in them. I read the opened ones and that was what made up my mind to bring them to Donna."

"Do you mind telling me what was in them?"

He said nothing for a moment, a light frown creasing his forehead. "They were the words of a man still in love with his wife. I couldn't just leave them sitting in the box. Couldn't throw them away." He gave her a quick glance and Melanie was surprised to see the pain in his eyes. She thought again of Lana and realized that though he said little about his wife, he still felt the loss.

"Does Donna know what is in them?"

"I thought it best if she read them for herself." Adam turned the truck onto the main highway leading north out of town. "I don't know how she'll react anyhow."

"I'm going to pray that she will have an open heart." Melanie knew she was taking a chance mentioning prayer, but to her surprise, Adam said nothing.

She leaned back in her seat as the buildings of the industrial park gave way to the open fields. She wasn't often a passenger, so she took the time to appreciate the countryside.

Two months ago, when Melanie had first come to Derwin, the grain in the fields had been just a faint tinge of tender green against black dirt. Now their full heads swayed and flowed in the wind. Tractors cut thick swaths in fields of hay that had been only ankle high.

In a month swathers would be working in the grainfields, getting ready for the harvest and another season.

Summer and winter. Springtime and harvest. The seasons and the time flowed on.

This afternoon she had gone to the bank and signed another set of papers giving the bank authority to check her tax records—yet another step in the ongoing saga of trying to get financing. She hadn't heard anything about the full-time position at the clinic and though she hadn't admitted it to anyone, she was getting concerned. When she'd spoken to the supervisor at the picnic on Saturday, she had practically assured Melanie that the job was hers.

"And where are you?"

Adam's soft question brushed away her concerns. It would all come together—she was just feeling a little melancholy was all. Summer did that to her.

"Just thinking about how nice it is not to have to drive once in a while."

"Don't like driving?"

"I like to look around. Which can cause problems when I'm driving. I usually end up going slower and slower."

Adam smiled. "One of those drivers that I usually pass as soon as I can."

"Mr. Busy Contractor on his way to the next job," she said with a teasing tone in her voice. "Though I notice that you don't have your usual pile of papers on the kitchen table anymore."

"A nurse gave me some good advice about working holidays." He glanced sidelong at her, then away. "For the sake of my health, mind you."

"I'm glad you took it. Tiffany seems a lot more relaxed in your company."

"It's been an interesting time." He waved a hand her way. "We've got a long ways to go, but once we're back in Calgary, things will change."

"That's good."

Back in Calgary. Reality check once again for you, Melanie thought.

And there seemed nothing more to say after that.

Ten minutes later when Adam pulled into the short driveway of a house near Eastbar Melanie's heart quickened with a mixture of excitement and uneasiness. What was Donna like after the sorrows that life had dealt her?

The door of the house opened as Melanie got out of the truck. A woman stood in the doorway, one arm folded across her stomach in a defensive gesture, her other hand cupping her chin. Silver glinted in her dark hair. Dark eyes that had once snapped with vigor and life now held a resigned look.

Then those eyes riveted on Melanie. Held.

"Is that you, Melanie?"

"Hello, Donna." Melanie took a hesitant step toward the woman she had once thought of as her other mother.

Donna blinked, as if to register what she was seeing. Then she flew down the steps, her arms wide. "Oh, my little girl. I can't believe you're here." And Melanie was held close in a tight embrace that she returned.

It had been so long since she had been held in a mother's embrace. So long since she had been supported. Then, as if all the sorrows of the past years returned in one sudden outpouring of emotion, a sob slipped past her thickened throat and another as tears filled her eyes.

"Oh, sweetheart, what things have happened to you?" Donna murmured, still holding her close, rocking her as if to comfort her.

Melanie swallowed, took a shuddering breath and pulled back, wiping her eyes with a trembling hand. "I'm sorry, Donna. I don't know what came over me."

Donna's eyes were shining as well, but she gently pushed Melanie's hair back from her face, smiling a motherly smile. "I think you've had your own burdens to bear." Soft brown eyes held Melanie's, sympathy and sorrow shining out of them. Donna stroked Melanie's cheek, then drew her close and kissed her lightly. "It's been too long and I'm sure we have much to talk about." She looked over Melanie's shoulder, smiling now. "And I'm presuming this is Adam."

Melanie wiped her tears away, hoping her mascara hadn't smudged, then glanced back at Adam, who stood by the truck, a bemused expression on his face.

He shook Donna's hand. "Glad to meet you face-to-face."

She clung to his hand, her eyes bright. "You said you had something for me?"

He nodded.

"Come in. Come in. You can show me there."

Just as Melanie turned to follow Donna, she felt Adam's hand behind her back, helping her along. Supporting her.

Chapter Ten

Donna held the box of letters on her lap, her finger toying nervously with the elastic. "There's how many letters in here?"

"Twenty." Adam set his mug down on the table and leaned forward, stifling the guilt he still felt at reading the letters. "The first ones were opened already."

Donna's fingers ran back and forth over the elastic. "He didn't contact me at all after he left. I waited by the phone. Checked the mail every day, but nothing came. I never knew how to contact him. How to tell him I was sorry."

"What happened, Donna?" Melanie asked. "You were always such a close family."

Donna lifted the elastic and let it go with a snap. "Do you remember Lonnie?"

"He was just a little boy when I used to come here. Your youngest," Melanie said quietly.

"He's a teenager now. He's with a friend. I didn't want him here when you came." Donna sighed lightly.

"When he was little there was a bad accident. On the property. Lonnie fell down an open well hole that hadn't been covered. He fractured his skull, broke his hip and almost drowned." Melanie gasped and Donna pressed her fingers to her lips, as if holding her own sorrow back. "He was in a coma for a month. I had been after Jason for months to get a proper cover on the well, and he told me I should have kept a better eye on Lonnie. We constantly blamed each other, then we stopped talking. For a while it looked as if Lonnie wasn't going to come out of it. Every day I would go to the hospital. Every day we would wait. Pray. The doctor wasn't optimistic, which didn't help our situation any. One day, after an especially bad day, we had a huge fight. Jason said if he was such a bad husband, such a terrible father, why didn't I just ask him to leave." Donna bit her lip. Drew in a shaky breath and gave Melanie a tremulous smile. "So I did. And he left. He'd phone the hospital to see how Lonnie was, but he never phoned here or wrote."

"How could you have sold the house if Jason was gone?" Adam asked. He didn't remember the details of the sale. Only that Donna was the only one they had dealt with.

"I got the house from my father. He didn't care for Jason. One of the conditions of getting the house was that only my name show up on the title. Which caused a lot of bitterness, as well." Donna sighed lightly, shaking her head. "But in spite of all that, we were happy until the accident. Jason was a good husband and a good provider. He never even contacted me about getting a divorce. I didn't want one, either." Donna sniffed and carefully wiped a few tears away. Melanie slipped her arm over Donna's shoulder.

"I have good memories of coming to your place," Melanie said. "It was always a dream of mine to have a home like yours."

"I guess you'll have to find another dream," Donna said softly. "This one is over."

Adam couldn't stand it anymore. "Don't say that. Read the letters and you'll know different."

Melanie gave him a surprised glance.

"I read the first two," he said, refusing to apologize for that. "They are a cry from a lonely heart. Please give him a listen."

Donna blinked again and then, with a decisive movement, slipped the elastic off the box. She lifted the first letter out, glancing quickly at Melanie, who nodded in encouragement.

Adam felt like a voyeur, but he wanted to see this to the end. Wanted to know that Jason would get a fair hearing.

Donna scanned the lines, her eyes flying back and forth. Then slowing. Filling. Her fingers trembled against her lips as glistening tears slid silently down her cheeks.

"What have I done?" she whispered. She put the letter down, disregarding the moisture on her cheeks. Opened the next one and read it once. Then again.

As she ripped open the third one, a cheque fluttered out to the table. Donna turned it over and closed her eyes.

"What have I done?" she repeated. Then she put her hands to her face and burst into tears.

Adam's throat tightened as he watched Donna's sorrow and regret spill over. Listened as she confessed her stubbornness to Melanie.

"You didn't know where he lived, Donna," Melanie whispered, cradling Donna close, rocking lightly. "You didn't get the letters—how could you know?"

"I didn't try very hard," Donna sobbed.

Adam felt superfluous, yet couldn't move away from this open display of honest emotion.

"Why didn't I get the letters?" she cried, swiping at her eyes with a limp hankie that Melanie had given her. "I gave the post office my change of address."

"When did you do that?" Adam asked.

Donna sniffed again. "A few months after I moved away. I just didn't think of it at the time. I just wanted to leave."

"I'm pretty sure the people renting the house were getting them and not forwarding them on." Adam leaned forward, took the envelope of the first one and set it beside the last letter, which was still unopened. "The cancellation dates of the first and the last one are only three months apart."

"I prayed and I prayed that he would contact me." Donna wiped her eyes. "I guess my prayers were answered. Sort of."

"Oh, Donna, I'm so sorry for you," Melanie said, stroking Donna's shoulder.

"Don't be," Donna said, pressing her hand against Melanie's. "I brought this on myself. I pushed him away. Did you know that many marriages break apart when a child dies or when there are problems?" Donna said, her voice quiet. "I used to wonder how that happened. Now I know it's because both parties get stuck in the guilt phase of grieving. The selfish part. And there's nothing left for each other and nothing left for God. If I had just forgiven Jason, let go of my own self-righteous anger, we could have helped each other grieve. And let God heal the broken parts of our lives. But I didn't know how to tell him."

Donna's quiet words sifted into Adam's thoughts and merged with the many careful comments Melanie had made about keeping his burden of guilt to himself. Of not letting it go.

The words spun and twisted through his mind, as if trying to find entrance to a place he had blocked off.

"Now I don't even know how to contact him," Donna continued.

Adam pulled himself back to the moment. "I do," he said, pulling a piece of paper with Jason's number out of the pocket of his blue jeans, thankful he could contribute something practical. He laid it on the table and slid it across to her.

Donna glanced at the paper and pressed it to her chest, her eyes glistening once again. "How can I possibly thank you for what you have done?"

Adam grinned at her. "Send me a family picture."

"We'll see," Donna whispered.

"I'll be praying for you, Donna," Melanie said, giving Donna a hug. "I will pray that the family I've always loved will be whole once again."

Donna hugged her back, then reached across the table to take Adam's hand. "Thank you again, Adam. You were my answer to prayer."

And how could that be? For many years Adam hadn't believed God answered prayer—how could he be an answer to someone else's?

Donna put the lid back on the box as if closing off that part of the evening. "Can I make you some coffee?"

"I'd like that," Melanie said, then glanced at Adam. "Unless you want to go."

He did. He wanted some quiet time, alone, to sort through the thoughts that tangled in his mind. Old emotions, regrets and thoughts came tumbling back and he didn't know where to put them. Though he tried to put God out of his life, He kept returning.

But he knew what Donna meant to Melanie, and for her sake he agreed to stay.

The conversation moved to more practical matters. Adam sat back, sipping his coffee, listening, watching as Melanie described to Donna what she wanted to do with the house, what colors she was going to paint what. Her eyes sparkled, her hands fluttered to emphasize a point, her love for the house radiating from her.

Her expression grew more serious when Donna asked about her parents. Adam's heart contracted as she described the sorrow she'd felt at her parents' breakup. Then as she spoke of the loss of her father, then her mother. Though a faint smile grazed her lips, Adam knew her well enough now to hear the reserved note of sorrow in her voice, the yearning as he realized she had no family at all.

And he understood a little more why she had spun a dream around the house.

"My goodness, I've been talking your ear off and Adam is about asleep in his chair." Melanie laughed a little self-consciously. "You should have said something, Adam."

"I didn't mind," he said with a gentle smile. "I didn't have anywhere else to be."

She held his gaze a moment, as if thanking him for his understanding, then got up.

Before they left, however, Donna gave Adam a hug. "As I said before, I don't know how to thank you," she whispered.

"Like I said, send me a family picture." He bent over and kissed her lightly on the cheek. "Take care, now."

The evening sun shed a soft light on the neighborhood as Melanie and Adam walked to his truck. The soft snick of a water sprinkler laid a gentle rhythm counterpointed by the laughter of children down the street. A young couple passed them, pushing a stroller, smiling a vague greeting as their eyes made brief contact.

It was an idyllic scene, a gentle moment, yet Adam felt a peculiar restlessness as he opened the truck door for Melanie. In the house behind them, all had not been well. He wondered about other homes on the street. How many of them held secret sorrows and pains? As he did.

"You look troubled," Melanie said as he put the truck in gear and pulled into the street.

"No, no. I'm fine." He didn't look at her.

His ambiguous answer seemed to satisfy her. When they got onto the highway, the only sound in the truck was the drone of the truck engine and the light tapping of his keys against the steering column.

The disquiet returned, relentless and unidentifiable. It was as if a crack was opening into the past, and he didn't want to go there.

Snatches of what Donna had said reverberated in his mind, pushing the crack further open—*stuck in the guilt phase of grieving…nothing left for God…let God heal the broken parts of our lives.*

And how was he supposed to do that? He had ignored God so long, how was he supposed to come back to Him?

"Where are you, Adam?"

Melanie's soft voice broke in to his reflections. He gave a guilty start. "Sorry," he said, angling her a quick glance. "I was thinking…" He let the sentence trail off. It had been so long since he'd allowed his mind to stir up old emotions and thoughts he didn't know if he could share them.

"You look sad," she continued, as if unwilling to let him pass her off.

Adam hesitated as the temptation to divulge thoughts long suppressed fought with the need to keep Melanie at arm's length. She was too appealing, too attractive. He couldn't allow himself to be distracted from his plans.

But he was tired of being strong. Tired of trying to keep a balance between what he felt and what he needed. And he was tired of holding his feelings to himself. Being at the picnic had shown him how far he had moved from community and people who cared about him.

"Guilt," he said finally.

"Over Lana's death?"

Adam nodded as familiar feelings, long buried, sifted to the surface of his mind. "It's been a while, I know, but each time I see Tiffany I think how different things could have been if only I'd listened to my own instincts."

"You take too much on," Melanie said. "Lana made choices, too."

"I know, but I don't only feel guilty when I see Tiffany. When I saw Sandy at the picnic I had to think about the Gerrards and what I took away from them, as well." Adam wrapped his hands around the steering wheel as fresh regret assaulted him.

"Maybe I'm out of line," Melanie continued, "but I wonder if it wouldn't be helpful for you to visit Lana's family."

Adam shook his head. "I'm not a part of that family anymore. Best if I just leave them be."

"But your daughter is part Gerrard."

"I let them see her. I would never take that away from Tom and Amanda. But I'm not a part of them."

"I don't think that's true."

Adam frowned at her, irritation flicking through him. She wouldn't let up. The sign for Derwin flashed by and he slowed as he took the turnoff.

He turned onto her street, the trees lining it creating a protective arch over the street and over the houses tucked back from them.

"And how do you know that Tiffany isn't the only one that counts?"

"You were married to their daughter. Surely you are a part of their life."

Adam turned into her parking lot and stopped. "I was. Once."

"What makes you think you still aren't?"

"Why are you sticking up for them?" He wrapped his hands around the steering wheel, squeezing.

"Because I think they need Tiffany, but I think they need you, too."

Adam gave a start. Looked over at her. Melanie was looking down at her thumbs, pressing them together and apart, as if she was nervous. "Why do you say that?"

Melanie dropped her hands, faced him straight on. "Maybe I don't know precisely how family works. Maybe I'm all wrong in my own assumptions, but I can't understand why you want to keep yourself apart from family of any kind."

Melanie's impassioned plea stung. Pushed aside the resistance he had built against Amanda and Tom. Against their pain.

Adam thought again of the invitation Sandy had extended to him and sighed. He wasn't going to be able to quietly leave Derwin without facing his past.

"I think you need to lay some things to rest, Adam."

"Why? I'm not staying."

But even as he spoke the words aloud, he couldn't say them with the conviction he once had. The past couple of days he had found a peace that had been missing from his life.

Working on the dresser for Melanie. Spending time with his mother and daughter.

Even taking the time to visit Donna.

None of these things would have been possible in Calgary. Kyle was pressuring him to get the money for the house to put into a project that would virtually guarantee he would be spending even less time at home than he had.

Adam looked around at the drab concrete block in front of them, the dull exterior broken up by iron balconies. Two floors up a few young boys were yelling out comments to passersby. Rap music thundered out of another window.

He felt suddenly restless and confined.

"Can we get out? I need to walk. A few blocks down, we connect up to a path that follows the river."

By the time Adam got out of the truck, Melanie was outside, waiting for him.

"You didn't even give me a chance to hold open the door for you," he said with a light smile.

"Too independent, I guess." She slipped her sweater on and buttoned it up. "You'll have to lead the way. I don't have a clue where to go."

He turned, and Melanie fell into step beside him.

"Did you grow up in town here?"

Small talk, then. That was a whole lot easier than the larger topics she wanted to discuss. "My dad had a small acreage just outside of town on the north side. It's all houses now."

"What did your father do?"

"This and that. He was a carpenter, handyman. Jack-of-all-trades and master of none was how he described himself."

"So that's where you got your carpentry skills."

Adam smiled. "When he was working in his shop, I used to spend all my spare time there, helping him. The smell of wood shavings always reminds me of him."

"How long ago did he die?"

Adam had to count back. "About four years now. He and my mother married late, so I always had older parents. I think they had more patience with me." He slipped his hands into his pockets, glancing sidelong at Melanie. They had talked enough about him. He wanted to find out more about her. "I know your mother died a while ago. What of your father?"

"He and my mother separated when I was thirteen. It wasn't the happiest of marriages."

"I heard you saying something about that to Donna. That must have been hard."

"It was almost as hard as his death." She shrugged, looking ahead, her expression pensive. "That's why Donna's family was so special to me. That's why family is important, period. You don't really know what you have until it's gone." She angled her head, the faint evening breeze teasing her hair around her face. She brushed it back and tucked it behind her ear with a casual gesture that was artlessly feminine.

His steps slowed as he looked around, simply enjoying the evening quiet, enjoying having Melanie walking alongside him. Their footfalls were muffled by the wood chips strewn on the soft ground of the path. All was peaceful, soft and gentle and his earlier restlessness drifted away.

When they came to a wooden bench overlooking the creek that danced over the stones, Adam suggested they sit down.

Melanie settled onto the bench and stretched her legs out in front of her. "I wish I'd known about this place sooner. I would have been here every day."

"My dad did some work on it—that's how I knew about it." He picked up a branch and pressed his thumbnail into the bark. Still green.

"You have quite a few roots in Derwin, don't you?"

Adam thought about the phone calls he'd made to Nadine to track Donna down. Thought about his friend Graydon. "I had good friends here."

"Good friends stay friends." Melanie angled her head toward him as a faint smile played over her lips. "I've been spending the past few days thanking you," she said quietly. "And tonight's no exception. I want to thank you so much for taking me to see Donna. For bringing her the letters. It was an answer to prayer to see her again." Melanie stopped. Her hand surreptitiously swiped at her cheek.

Another answer to prayer. Did he not do anything on his own? Were all his actions determined by the prayers of other people?

"You're welcome. It was a small thing to do." Uncomfortable with her emotions and her words, he looked back down at the stick he held. Peeled the bark away, exposing the stark white wood beneath.

She lifted her face to his, her smile full, wide. "Thank you again, Adam. You're a good person."

"I wish I could believe that." Adam stripped

another piece of bark away with a jerk, tiny drops of moisture spitting out. He hadn't felt like a good person for years.

"It's true, Adam. I know you're thinking about Lana again. You have to let go of that burden. You're too caught up in her death."

"It's a reality." He dropped the stick, no longer interested in exposing its secrets. "And I have to live with the consequences."

Melanie laid her hand on his arm. "Why don't you let God heal you, bring life to those places of death? He is the God of life. He doesn't blame you for what happened. Why do you?"

He chanced a quick glance her way, and as their eyes met it was as if she drew out from him all the sorrows he had tried to bury. "Why are you doing this, Melanie? It's my past. Why are you trying to go back to it and resurrect it?"

"Because you're carrying over pain from the past and it hurts me to see that."

"Why?"

"Because I care about you," she whispered.

Her words plucked long-forgotten emotions, sending a clear note of longing singing through him.

He couldn't stop his hand from coming up. Touching her face as if underlining with a physical touch the emotional connection they shared. He traced the line of her mouth as her breath warmed his fingers.

Her skin was so soft.

Adam felt his own breath slow, felt time slip away, and he lowered his head.

As their lips met, his hand slid around her shoulders, his fingers tangled in her hair. It felt so right. So good.

She returned his kiss, her hands touching his face.

He brushed his lips over her cheek, her temple, then drew her even closer in his arms, his breath coming out in a sigh.

It was like coming home, having her in his arms. Everything that had been confusion and uncertainty slipped away, replaced by the utter rightness of holding her close to him, of feeling her hair under his chin, her arms around him.

It was as if each was afraid to break the moment with words. He stroked her hair with his chin, content to hold her close. To feel the loneliness that had clawed at him the past few years ease.

Then, far too soon, Melanie drew hesitantly back. Adam didn't let her go right away. Couldn't.

"What's happening, Adam?" Melanie asked, bringing reality back with words. "Where is this going?"

"I don't know." He stroked her cheek with his finger, relishing the fact that she allowed him, unwilling to let the reality of her questions intrude on the still, quiet place they had created.

"Are you still going to the city?"

It was as if she had pushed him into the cold water of the creek below them. Facts and reality intruded into this magical moment. Pressure and a partner who wouldn't ease off. What else could he do?

"I have to, Melanie. I can't change my plans now." He straightened. Lowered his arms.

"And God?"

Adam turned to face the creek. "I don't know where God fits into my life anymore, Melanie. I've been away so long...." Adam couldn't say anything more. Nothing in his life fit as it should. Lana had become a shadowy memory, yet the struggle with her death remained. His work was a burden he didn't want to shoulder.

And God?

Adam had spent the past few years angry at God, pushing Him away, all the while knowing he could not avoid Him.

"He's waiting. Just like Jason was waiting to hear from Donna. He still loves you and is waiting for you to let go of your struggles and your plans and your guilt."

Her words drew memories from the deep places he had buried God. A God whose love he'd once cherished. A God he trusted utterly. Whom he had turned his back on in anger and blame. He'd run so far away, how could he ever come back?

Melanie drew in a slow breath, soft as a sigh. "I don't know where this can go, Adam, if you're not sure. My mother and father broke up because he wasn't a Christian. I don't want that for myself."

Adam rested his elbows on his knees, staring at the water, wishing he knew what to say.

Then, without a backward glance, she got up and walked back to her apartment, leaving Adam confused and bereft.

Chapter Eleven

Tiffany lay curled in her bed, her fingertips resting lightly on her palms. Adam hunkered down beside the bed, resting his crossed arms beside his daughter, his eyes on her sleep-washed face, allowing himself the luxury of just watching her.

The past week had brought about a marked change in her attitude toward him, just as Melanie had predicted. And not only in her. Each day he worked around the yard he could feel the tension that usually gripped his neck and shoulders loosen a little more—and building the dresser had been pure joy.

He smiled, thinking of the satisfaction he'd felt working with the wood. Melanie's happiness when he'd given it to her.

How her arms had felt around his neck when she'd "thanked" him.

The kiss they had just shared.

He put the brakes on his wandering thoughts. That was unknown territory and, according to Melanie, unwanted. He leaned over and brushed a kiss over Tiffany's forehead. She shifted again and her eyes opened.

"Daddy," she whispered, smiling.

Adam's heart contracted with pure joy. She had called him Daddy.

In spite of his previous sorrow, her simple word made him want to pull her out of the bed and dance around the room with her.

"Hey, Tiffany," he said instead, stroking her hair. "Did you have a nice time with Gramma and the babysitter?"

Tiffany nodded. "You were gone? With Mellalie?"

"I was, sweetie. We had to go visit the lady who used to live in this house." He stroked her hair again, combing his fingers through its silky strands, love for his little daughter flowing through him.

"I love Mellalie," Tiffany said, shifting around in her bed. She smiled at her father once more, then her eyes drifted slowly shut.

Adam sighed lightly, his hand still tangled in his daughter's hair. He was worried about Tiffany's attachment to Melanie. What would happen when they left?

And what about your own feelings? What are you going to be thinking about when you're back in Calgary, busy every waking minute? Will you think about her then?

Do you have to go?

The question snaked into his mind and hovered.

Just this afternoon Kyle had phoned again. Had once again pressured him to get the money from Melanie sooner. Had pushed him to come back to Calgary. They were missing a big chance, he kept saying.

Adam got tired just thinking about Kyle. These past few weeks away from him made him realize how little Kyle took Tiffany's needs into consideration. And Adam had let him.

Graydon wouldn't have done the same.

Graydon was his friend. Kyle was his partner. The work that he had done with Graydon he had been proud of. The work he did with Kyle was just another way to make money.

So which one had brought him happiness?

He pushed himself up and stood, looking down at his daughter as his confused thoughts beat in his mind like birds caught in a house.

You don't need to go back. You could stay here. With Melanie.

He closed his eyes to concentrate, to separate fact from fancy.

Melanie wanted someone who was close to God, and he didn't know how to make that step.

"Thanks, Sandy, you've been a lot of help." Melanie clutched the handset of the phone as Sandy's information filled in the gaps of what she already knew. After talking to Dr. Drew about Lana, Melanie had known she had to look further. Thankfully Sandy had been willing to share what she knew.

"I'll have to talk to my parents as soon as possible. Are you going to tell Adam?" Sandy asked after a moment's pause.

"I'm going there this afternoon. But I want you to remember it's not a final analysis and it's only a theory," Melanie warned. "It's just what I've gleaned from talking to her previous doctor and the doctor in Eastbar." And now you.

"But it all fits. It doesn't change anything, and yet I think for Adam, it will change a lot."

"I hope so. And thanks so much for your help." Melanie hung up, hugging herself as she looked down at the notes sitting on her desk.

She wondered what Adam was going to make of this.

But more than that she wondered how she was going to face him after yesterday. The thought of his kiss still made her toes curl.

"You're looking dreamy." Serena dropped into a chair across from Melanie's desk. "What are you thinking about?"

Melanie picked up her pen and tapped it against the loose papers on her desk. "Nothing," she said with what she hoped was an airy tone.

"Let me rephrase that. Who were you thinking about?"

Melanie leveled a wry glance at her. "What did you come here to bother me about? I'm busy."

"Of course you are." Serena rested her chin on her hands, a patronizing smile curving her lips. "Just wondering if you've gotten your interview with the superintendent."

"I'll be seeing her Monday," Melanie said absently, making another quick note on the paper she had been scribbling on.

"You don't sound too enthused."

Melanie pulled herself to the here and now. "Sorry, my mind was elsewhere."

"Like it was a few moments ago." Serena rocked her head back and forth, grinning at her friend. "I think you're in love with Adam Engler."

Melanie's heart skipped in her chest, but she didn't deign to answer her friend. Instead she gathered up her papers with slightly shaky hands and slipped them into her briefcase. "I think you're delusional. There's help for people like you." She flashed Serena a smile, hoping she looked and sounded casual enough.

Serena just laughed. "But there's not much help for you, Melanie. You're too far gone."

Melanie just waved over her shoulder. Serena's comments had hit too close and she didn't want to give her any more ammunition to work with.

"Adam was very quiet last night," Helen said as Melanie got her settled into her chair after her exercises.

"Really?" Just the sound of Adam's name was enough to ignite a soft warmth deep within her. She had it even worse than Serena thought.

Helen slipped her glasses on and adjusted them lightly. "Didn't the two of you go to bring those letters to Donna?"

The two of you. As if they belonged together.

Love and helpless longing swept over her. Her head told her he was all wrong for her, but oh, her heart. It had its own rhythm, independent from her practical thoughts.

"Donna was very happy to get them. I'm really hoping and praying it will help get them together."

"Yes, it's sad to see someone alone who used to be a part of someone else." She sighed lightly. "I still miss my husband, and I know Adam misses Lana. Or at least being with someone." She turned to Melanie and caught her hand. "But I don't think he misses her as much as he used to."

Melanie couldn't stop the blush creeping up her neck, warming her cheeks. She felt as if the imprint of Adam's lips were visible on her lips. Her forehead, her temples.

"Well, once he moves to the city, I'm sure he'll find someone," she said quietly.

"Maybe." Helen stroked Melanie's hand. "You don't like the city, do you?" Helen's blue eyes, magnified behind her glasses, were fixed on Melanie, but Melanie sensed a deeper meaning behind the question.

"I could get a job in a hospital in the city, but I prefer living in the country."

"And you prefer someone who shares your faith." Helen's quiet statement held a tone of resignation.

Melanie just nodded, knowing exactly what Helen was asking her.

"Adam has been through a lot of pain since Lana died. And guilt." Helen clung to Melanie's hand, as if pleading with a judge for the life of her child. "He used to believe in God's love. You can show him the way back."

Her words echoed Melanie's own confusion. Last night as her thoughts twisted and spun, she had prayed, cried. Searched the Scriptures for strength and direction. She knew her feelings for Adam were stronger each time she saw him. And she also knew that each time they were together she tried to find a way to get around the principles and limitations she had placed on herself.

Melanie closed her eyes, praying for wisdom. For guidance.

"I can't be the one to do that," Melanie confided.

"I'm sorry if I stepped out of line, Melanie, but I know he cares for you, too." Helen let go of Melanie's hand. "Can't you help him?"

"Adam has to find the way on his own," Melanie said, holding Helen's longing gaze. "He has to commit his life to Christ separate from any emotions or feelings he might have for me."

Helen sighed lightly. "You're right, Melanie. You're a very wise girl. And I hope my son comes to his senses. Before it's too late."

Melanie could say nothing to that. Her own emotions were fragile where Adam was concerned.

"Are you going to say goodbye to Adam before you go?"

Melanie nodded, thinking of the papers she had slipped into her briefcase. In spite of, or maybe even because of, her personal feelings for him, Adam had to know what she had discovered. For his sake. Only his sake.

Melanie slipped the strap of her briefcase over her shoulder as she stepped out onto the back deck. She took a moment to look over the yard, appreciating how much neater it was since she had first seen it. Adam had removed all the piles of lumber. The bricks. The lawn was mowed and the hedge along the back was trimmed. He'd even cleaned out the flower beds, and under Helen's direction had planted a few perrennials.

Melanie waited for the familiar flush of ownership to come over her. But this time a hue of melancholy colored it.

What was a single woman like her doing, buying a house this size?

No second thoughts, she reminded herself. The papers have been signed. The down payment was sitting in a trust account, waiting for the take-over date. This is what you wanted.

She opened the door of the shop and went inside. The tang of sawdust and shavings hung in the air. A promise of things fresh and new.

Adam was standing by his workbench, his back to Melanie. Tiffany squatted on the bench looking at what Adam was working on.

"So, punkin, what colour should we paint the outside?"

As Adam moved, Melanie could see what he was talking about. It was a dollhouse complete with tiny shutters at the windows, a little porch with a railing.

Melanie felt a surprising clench of jealousy. She had never had a dollhouse, though she had always yearned for one.

"I have pink paint, blue paint or green paint," Adam was saying.

Tiffany bit her lip, shifting her weight from one foot

to the other as she squinted at the little house. "I like pink."

Adam smiled at her. "Pink it is." He lifted her off the bench and gave her a quick hug before setting her down on the ground. As he looked up he saw Melanie.

Straightened.

His eyes lit briefly with a penetrating light that seemed to pierce her soul. Melanie wavered under the intensity of his gaze.

Then as briefly as it had come, the light vanished, he blinked and he was smiling a careful, welcoming smile.

"Well, hi there, Melanie."

Tiffany whirled around at the sound of her name. "Mellalie," she called out, launching herself at Melanie. "Daddy made me a house."

"I see that." Melanie caught the little girl and swung her around.

Tiffany pressed her warm palms against Melanie's cheeks, holding her gaze. "It's my own house, just for me. You come and see it." Tiffany wiggled in Melanie's arms. Melanie let her down and then followed her to the workbench.

"Up, Daddy." She held her arms up to Adam.

Adam frowned down at her. "Pardon me?"

"Up, please, Daddy," she amended with a coy smile.

Adam lifted her up and gave her a quick hug before he set her down on the bench again.

"She called you Daddy," Melanie said quietly, amazed as the realization struck her.

Adam flashed her a self-conscious smile. "Yeah. She just started last night."

Melanie held his gaze, smiling. "I'm happy for you. Looks like things are coming together."

"At least on the home front. I just wish Kyle would get off my back."

Trepidation shivered down Melanie's spine at the mention of Kyle. "If you need the money any sooner, I can give Bob a push," she said quickly, hoping she sounded more relaxed than she felt. As long as the loan was in abeyance, as long as the take-over date was in the nebulous future, she could fool herself into thinking that maybe things could change. "He says he's waiting for an employer's report."

"No need to rush. Kyle needs the money for some engineer reports on a spec project." Adam tucked a wisp of hair behind Tiffany's ear and let his hand linger on her cheek. "He can wait."

Don't read more into that than what he's saying, Melanie thought.

"Lovely little house," she said, stepping closer to the workbench, moving into safer territory.

"I had some time on my hands and thought I would use some of the scraps left over from the dresser. I got the idea from you, actually." Adam pulled the cuff of his shirtsleeve over his hand and wiped off some sawdust from the side.

"You're a lucky little girl, Tiffany." Melanie stroked the little girl's head, noticing that her hair was sprinkled with shavings and sawdust.

Tiffany lay on her stomach on the workbench, busy opening and closing the front door of the house, happily ignoring both of them.

Adam leaned back against the workbench, his arms folded over his chest. A sense of expectation thrummed through the air as their gazes met.

"How's my mom doing?"

"Really well." Melanie fiddled with the strap of her briefcase, her eyes flicking away from his, then returning like a homing pigeon. "Her hip is healing much better than I expected, and I'm sure you could move her any day now."

"That's good to know."

The inane words and conversation were a thin veneer over deeper, stronger emotions. But where could they go beyond the impasse they had reached last night? Nothing had changed in the past fourteen hours, yet for Melanie it was as if everything was different. She knew she was in danger of falling in love with this man.

Adam cleared his throat, shifted his weight. "I, uh, was wondering if you're busy on Sunday."

Her heart jumped in her chest. What did he mean by this? What did he want?

"I'm not. Why do you ask?"

"I got a phone call from Sandy Gerrard today. She invited me to her parents' anniversary party on Sunday." He pulled his lower lip between his teeth as he studied her.

Melanie breathed in long and slowly. "I wouldn't belong there."

Adam pushed some sawdust into a pile with the toe of his boot, then looked up at her, his blue eyes almost piercing.

Melanie was losing herself in his eyes even as he pushed himself away from the workbench. One step and he was in front of her. One movement and his fingers traced the line of her chin. "Please come with me, Melanie," he whispered. "I can't see Lana's parents on my own. It was your idea I see them, so I was hoping you could come with me."

She needed to take only one small step and she was in his arms. One movement and she sensed he would hold her close. She wanted to be held again. Wanted to feel supported and surrounded by strength and warmth.

Instead she took a step back. "Though I'm glad you're taking my advice, I don't think I should go. And I don't think you need my support."

Adam leaned back, his hands clasped around his neck. "You don't think so?" His voice held a tight edge she hadn't heard in a while. "I have only seen Lana's parents a couple of times since Lana died. And each time I've had to face parents who have lost a beloved daughter." Adam stopped. Dropped his head back and blew out a sigh. "It's hard, Melanie."

Melanie clutched the strap of her briefcase even harder, the edges cutting into her hands. "Is it because you feel guilty?"

Adam dragged his hands over his face. "Hard not to when each time I see Lana's mother, Amanda, she starts crying." Adam laughed, a sharp, bitter sound. "I can deal with contractors yelling at me, unwilling employees, demanding bank managers, but a woman's tears unman me. And Amanda's tears always bring back the guilt. Always."

Melanie thought of the papers in her briefcase. “Can I talk to you outside? Do you have time?”

He nodded and Melanie followed Adam and Tiffany out of the shop.

What she had to tell him she wanted to deliver in warmth and sunshine. She hoped it would help him make a decision about going to the Gerrards.

More than that, she hoped it would break down the barriers between him and God.

Chapter Twelve

"Adam, how much did you know about Lana's diabetes?" Melanie asked as soon as they were seated in some lawn chairs beside the sandbox. Tiffany was already busy pouring sand into a pail, singing snatches of a song.

"Quite a bit. I had to in order to help her stay balanced. Why do you ask?"

"What did she ever tell you about her condition? Especially when she was pregnant?"

Adam crossed his arms over his chest, his posture defensive. "Melanie, why are you going into this? What old history are you trying to bring up?"

She had done this completely wrong. She was coming across like a nurse when Adam needed a friend.

She put the papers down and held his steady gaze. *Please Lord,* she prayed, *give me the right words. Help him to understand.* She knew she was going to be talking about someone he loved and she wanted to be fair.

"I had a conversation with an old doctor of Lana's. He made a comment I couldn't let go of. About how Lana resented her diabetes." Melanie fingered the papers, her eyes on his. "I think Lana's death had less to do with where you lived and more to do with how she managed her diabetes before she went into labor."

"What do you mean?" Adam's voice held a definite chill.

Tread carefully. Be diplomatic.

"I understand that Lana went to another doctor when she got pregnant."

Adam nodded. "Some doctor in Eastbar. She would phone here quite regularly."

"Did you know that Lana had missed a number of appointments the last three weeks before she went into labor?"

Adam frowned. Shook his head. "She went to Eastbar twice a week to see the doctor. Sandy always brought her or she'd go herself."

"She didn't go to the doctor, Adam. Nor did she do the daily blood tests she was supposed to be doing."

"How do you know about the blood tests? I saw her daily diary. Her sugars were always good."

Melanie heard the bafflement in his voice, saw the confusion in his eyes.

"I know I'm only supposing that she didn't do her tests," she said quietly. "But Sandy said she found a whole box of blood-testing strips that hadn't been touched. She didn't think anything of it until I phoned to ask her a few questions. Sandy and I both now think Lana fudged the diary just to keep things quiet. Sandy always wondered why her tests were always so good when she'd been hard to control before. If she'd gone to the doctor, she would have been able to prove or disprove Lana's test results with a Hemoglobin A, which is probably why she didn't go."

"Why would Lana want to do that?"

"I don't know." Melanie riffled the papers, uneasy with what she was telling him. Yet she knew she had to continue. "Had she taken care of herself, had she seen the doctor, she might still be alive."

Adam melted back into his chair, his expression one of injured bafflement. "Why did I not know? How could I not see?"

"You couldn't see because she wouldn't let you see." Melanie had to bite back the angry flow of words. Now, facing Adam's puzzled sadness, she felt anew the deceit Lana had been practicing. The chance she had been taking with Tiffany's health and well-being.

Adam shook his head, as if rearranging the new thoughts Melanie had placed there. "So it had nothing to do with living here, or anywhere else for that matter?"

"I'm afraid not." Melanie couldn't stand the isolation of his pain. She reached out, caught his hand. He grasped it between both his, pressing it against his chest.

"Why did you do all this, Melanie?" His voice was hoarse with emotion. "Why did you think I needed to know this?"

Melanie curled her fingers around his, rubbing her thumb over the back of his hand, his skin rough beneath her fingers. The hands of a working man. "I wanted you to go to the Gerrards knowing that it wasn't your fault. That whatever pain the Gerrards may feel was inflicted on them by their own daughter. Not by something you feel you should have done."

Adam clutched her hand against his chest, his eyes like a laser on hers.

"Yesterday I asked you why this matters so much to you and you said because you care." His chest rose beneath her hand in a sigh. "Today you're helping me lay my past to rest. Is it still because you care?"

Melanie held his gaze, unaware that she was drifting toward him until the armrest of the chair dug in to her side. She couldn't lie.

"Yes, I care, Adam. I care about you. I care about the guilt you can't let go of."

"Then don't give up on me yet, Melanie," he whispered. "Give me some time."

And then what? Go with him to the city? Try to convince him to stay here?

But she pushed the questions aside. Prayed that God would give her wisdom and guidance. Because she knew that she wanted to be with him in spite of everything she knew.

Adam lifted her hand to his mouth and pressed his lips on the inside of her palm.

"You've given me much to think about, Melanie," he said quietly. "I just need to sort a few things out."

She nodded, but gently pulled her hand back. She had her own questions and worries, but for today, for now, she was willing to leave them alone.

* * *

Adam closed the door to Tiffany's bedroom. It had taken a couple of stories, a drink and a little talk about Melanie, but Tiffany was finally asleep. He leaned back against the door, his mind a whirling welter of confused thoughts. It was as if the past three years had been uprooted and rearranged and he didn't know where to put his memories anymore.

The guilt he had been carrying had not been his to bear.

Just as Melanie had said from the first.

But why had Lana potentially endangered their child's health? Why, in the last vital weeks of her pregnancy, had she not taken better care of herself?

As his thoughts spun and twisted, old memories surfaced. Lana, shaky from yet another insulin reaction. Him finding chocolate bar wrappers hidden under the seat of the car, under the couch. Like a little girl, she would sneak food that she shouldn't have been eating.

Lana had made some bad choices, and he might never know the reasons.

But in spite of the memories and the questions, he felt as if a huge weight had been lifted off his shoulders. What Melanie had told him gently removed the bitter sting of regret, of wishing he could relive those last moments. He couldn't have prevented what happened. Postponed it, maybe.

The thought, though it comforted, also saddened him. He had given Lana everything she wanted. She'd had so much more than many people. Why wasn't she happier?

He pushed himself away from the wall, and walked slowly down the stairs.

The door to his mother's room was still open, the soft light beckoning. He knocked lightly and opened the door farther.

Helen looked up from the book she was reading and laid it carefully on the bed in front of her.

"Hey, Mom, you can't sleep?" he asked, stepping into the room.

"I'm just doing my evening devotions."

"Mind if I sit with you awhile?" He sat in the chair in the corner of the room and looked around. The soft light enhanced the pale yellow of the walls, creating a gentle haven.

"You look tired, Adam."

"Busy day. Lots to think about."

"Melanie seemed a little distracted, as well. I asked her about her visit with Donna. She was so happy you took her. She said it was like an answer to prayer. How wonderful that God could have used you like that."

There it was again. God in control of his life. "Can God use someone who hasn't talked to Him? Someone who has turned his back on Him?" Where once his words might have held bitterness, now, after what Melanie had told him, they held sorrow. Regret.

"God is always seeking you, Adam." Helen's voice grew quiet while she ran her fingers along the edge of her Bible. "He hasn't turned His back on you, in spite of your bitterness over Lana's death."

Lana.

Adam looked around the room he and Lana had

worked so hard on. Thought of the dreams they had spun when they found out she was expecting a baby. This house was going to be more than a dream—it was going to be a home for them and their child.

And she had thrown it all away.

He sighed lightly and laid his head on the back of the chair. He felt unaccountably weary. As if he'd been running for miles. Aimless miles.

"Do you want me to read to you, Adam?" Helen asked, her voice a soft sound.

It had been three years since Adam had opened a Bible for himself. When his mother would come to visit, she would read to him. He'd just never listened.

But now?

"Sure, Mom. Go ahead."

"This is from Psalm 51." She cleared her throat, adjusted her glasses as she always did. Her own small preparation for speaking aloud the words of God.

And this time he listened. Tried to draw the words into his emptiness.

"'Have mercy on me, O God, according to Your unfailing love; according to Your great compassion blot out my transgressions.'" His mother's quiet, reverent voice touched old memories, drew up old emotions.

"'Against You and You only have I sinned.'"

The words shook Adam. He had not done wrong by Lana. If he had done wrong, it was to blame God for Lana's death. His sin was against God alone.

"'Restore to me the joy of Your salvation and grant me a willing spirit, to sustain me.'"

How long had it been since he had felt joy? Since

he could truly say he was happy? Had he been caught up in the guilt phase of grieving, as Donna had said she had been? Had he wrongly blamed God when it was his own sorrow he hadn't dealt with that was holding him back?

He'd thought he could live without God, but the emptiness in his life attested to the fact that he couldn't. But how to come back? God was all-powerful and not to be trifled with.

"'The sacrifices of God are a broken spirit; a broken and contrite heart, O God, You will not despise.'"

"Is that all it takes, Mom?" Adam asked, lifting his head to look at his mother. "It sounds too easy."

Helen smiled. "It's a beginning, Adam. The beginning of dying to self and living to Christ. You've heard this all your life."

"I know I have. But lately my life has been so far from redemption, I don't know where to start."

"How about praying with me now? And on Sunday, well, there's always church."

"So, girlie. Here we are." Adam set Tiffany down on the pavement of the parking lot and fluffed out her dress. He wiped a smudge of jam from the corner of her mouth and smiled at her. "Are you ready for church, sweetie?"

She nodded exuberantly, her pigtails bobbing up and down. His mother had taken the time to do Tiffany's hair, but had decided to stay home from church this morning. Said she wasn't feeling well, though to him she looked fine.

Adam had wanted her with him when he faced the inside of the church once again.

The last time he'd been in the building was Lana's funeral.

"Restore to me the joy of Your salvation." The words his mother had read last night slipped into his mind. Smoothed the residue of guilt.

"Daddy, Daddy, I see Mellalie."

Funny how the mere mention of her name flipped his heart. He looked in the direction Tiffany was pointing and saw her. She was wearing a dress again, simple yet elegant. It set off her hair. Hair that caught the sun and sent out auburn rays as she stopped and turned toward them.

As their eyes met, Adam felt his breathing slow. Once again he was aware of the sensation of time falling away. He saw her lips move, mouth his name.

Still holding his hand, Tiffany leaned away from him. "Come, Daddy," she demanded. "Let's go see Mellalie."

Adam didn't resist Tiffany's leading, following her easily to Melanie's side.

"Hello, Adam," Melanie said, her voice soft, almost breathless. "So glad you could come."

Adam thought she might say more, might make a comment, but thankfully all she did was crouch in front of Tiffany, unhampered by the narrow cut of her dress. "Hey, sweetie. You look pretty today."

"Gramma did my hair."

Melanie looked up at Adam. "Where is your mother today?"

"She says she's not feeling well."

"Is she spiking a temp?" Melanie got up, frowning as she adjusted her purse on her shoulder.

"I checked, but she seemed fine. Maybe just tired. She said she would catch a service on one of the radio stations."

"And you didn't want to stay home with her?" Though Melanie's oblique question was softly spoken, Adam clearly heard the meaning behind it.

"No. I thought I would come to church today."

"And why was that?"

Adam held her eyes, questions still hovering. "I'm not entirely sure myself."

Her full rich smile sent his heart pounding against his chest. "Well, I'm glad you're here."

He was glad, too. After her revelation and his talk with his mother, Adam needed more than ever the comfort he might find in church and with Melanie.

Tiffany took Melanie's hand as a matter of course and started pulling them toward the church building.

"She's eager to go," Melanie said with a light laugh. "Has she been before?"

Adam shook his head with a rueful glance Melanie's way. "I have never taken her."

The usher at the back of the church greeted Melanie warmly, holding her hand a little longer than was necessary, Adam thought.

An awkward moment followed as they stood in the entrance to the sanctuary. Adam didn't know if he should ask Melanie to sit with them. She had given him no indication of how she felt about what he had asked her the other day.

Thankfully Tiffany resolved the dilemma.

"You sit with us," Tiffany said, tugging on Melanie's hand.

Melanie glanced at Adam and smiled. "I guess that settles that."

Adam smiled back. "Don't mess with a three-year-old."

As they settled in the pew he could see women sidling closer, heads bent, heard whispers swelling.

He knew how it looked. Melanie had obviously been attending church for a while and suddenly one Sunday she shows up with the prodigal son and his daughter.

Like a little family.

He ignored the whispers as he settled Tiffany in between them, avoiding Melanie's gaze, pretending to be engrossed in the bulletin of events. After a few minutes he looked up at the front of the church.

The flood of memories assaulted his equilibrium. Lana's casket buried under a mound of flowers. A picture of Lana perched on top. He clenched the bulletin, fighting the surprising wave of sorrow. It didn't have to happen, he thought.

But this time the guilt that normally accompanied thoughts of Lana's needless death was assuaged by what Melanie had told him.

Lana had made her own decisions, and he and Tiffany had paid the price for that.

"Are you okay?"

Melanie's light touch on his forearm, her voice laced with concern broke through the swirling emotions.

Without stopping to analyze, he clamped his hand

down on hers, his gaze locked on hers, like a storm-tossed ship catching the saving beacon from a lighthouse.

"Is something wrong?" she repeated, leaning a little closer.

He held her amber eyes, unable to look away. "I'm okay," he returned softly, his hand still pressed against hers, her skin soft and warm beneath his. He moved his thumb back and forth over the back of her hand as a gentle peace suffused his soul.

Tiffany slapped her hand on top of Adam's, breaking the moment. "Your turn, Mellalie," she said, nudging Melanie with her elbow.

Melanie blinked, then turned to Tiffany. "Okay," she whispered, laying her hand on top of Tiffany's.

"You can't go, Daddy, so I hafta."

Tiffany laid her hand on top of the stack. It was their little game they'd starting playing at night when he tucked her in. Having Melanie's hands mingled in with his and Tiffany's was true and good.

And where was it going? He had asked her for time to sort out his nebulous feelings. But each time he saw her he knew he cared more.

He pulled his hand back, eliciting a disappointed cry from his daughter.

"Shh, Tiffany. We're in church," he said, bending over her, not daring to look at Melanie.

He knew he had his own obligations. A business that needed him. A mother. A daughter.

Yet each time he was with her, his feelings for her changed. Grew. He had asked her for time and he knew he had to give himself that space, as well. So much had changed in the past two days. He needed to absorb it. Realign his relationship with God.

As people filled up the benches in front of them and beside them, he focused his attention on them. He recognized many of the people, though the names eluded him. Some greeted him by name. Some stopped to chat. Most said something to Melanie, as well.

Thankfully Tiffany sat quietly between him and Melanie, content to scribble with a pencil Melanie had given her on the children's bulletin Melanie had taken.

Adam looked again at the front of the church, this time deliberately remembering the day of the funeral. In spite of what Melanie had told him, he couldn't completely eradicate the emotions that had been a part of his life for almost three years. In unguarded moments he could still feel the hollow clench of regret.

"Against You and You only have I sinned."

The words his mother had read to him braided themselves through his thoughts.

He had come to church this morning on the advice of his mother. And, if he were honest with himself, because he'd hoped to see Melanie.

Was he being fair to her? She wanted a Christian man. Someone who was willing to stay in this small town.

Could he stay here?

The thought wove through his other thoughts, twisting and pulling.

Finally the minister strode to the front of the church, and with a booming voice announced the first song.

The congregation rose to its feet as an overhead screen descended from one corner at the front.

This was new. So was the song. Melanie knew it and sang along.

Her voice carried, clear and true and ringing with conviction. He couldn't keep his eyes off her. A peaceful smile curved her lips, and as she sang, he saw deep love and a strong faith.

He envied her.

The minister wended his way through the liturgy, and when the time came for the children to leave for Children's Church, Tiffany was a deadweight against his side. She was fast asleep. Adam glanced at Melanie, remembering her offer to take Tiffany out, but she noticed, too.

She gave him a careful smile, aware of his withdrawal, then looked ahead.

The minister announced the text of the sermon.

Psalm 51.

A chill shivered up his spine as for the second time he heard God's call to him. The reminder of whom Adam had sinned against.

Not Lana. Not her family. His anger and rebellion had been directed at God.

He drew his sleeping daughter close, as if bracing for an assault.

As the minister preached, his words were a reminder of the call God extends again and again. Of God's sacrificial love.

Adam listened, like a man who had been thirsty so long, he had forgotten what water could do. The message filtered through his confusion, rearranged thoughts that had already been tossed about by what he had learned from Melanie.

"It's not our strength that brings us to God, but the strength of His love. His forgiveness that draws us to Him," the minister said, his voice ringing with conviction. "It is sheer grace. All of our sins from greatest to smallest are an issue with God. And who better to deal with them but a merciful, just and loving Father who wants us back."

"Against You and You only have I sinned.... A broken and contrite heart, O God, You will not despise."

Adam felt all the resistance he had put up against God, all the walls and barriers he had erected in his anger and guilt, slowly melt away, washed like the sand on the beach beneath the slow relentless waves.

He had been adrift. Lost. Striking out at God. But God still called him back in spite of what he had done.

It seemed too easy. It seemed too wonderful.

The organist and pianist struck up the opening chords of the next song just as Adam turned to it one-handed.

"When Peace like a River."

Adam clenched the spine of the book as the words pounded against him just like the sea billows in the song.

They had sung this song at Lana's funeral.

He closed his eyes, clinging to his daughter, as his throat thickened.

And the first tears he had shed since Lana's funeral squeezed from between his eyelids.

Forgive me, Father, he prayed. *Forgive me my anger, my sin, my involvement in myself. Let it be well with my soul.*

Chapter Thirteen

Melanie sang the words of the song by rote, her eyes on the book in front of her but her entire attention focused on Adam sitting beside her.

What in the song had prompted this public unveiling? Had what she told him the other day brought out new grief?

She glanced at him again, then away as he wiped a track of moisture from his cheek. She'd seen sorrow manifested in many forms, yet the sight of Adam, his head bent over his sleeping daughter as tears slid down his cheeks, created an echoing pain.

He looked so alone. She didn't stop to think how anyone around her might see her actions, responding instead to his silent need.

She slipped her arm along his broad back, her hand cupping his far shoulder. He shifted ever so slightly toward her as if drawing from her strength.

The final triumphant words of the song resounded through the building "It is well, it is well with my soul."

She felt Adam draw a shuddering breath, then another, and his head slowly came up. Once again his hand caught hers.

He didn't need to look at her. It was as if they had connected on another level, moved to another part of their relationship.

Then she felt his shoulders straighten, as if his strength had returned. She lowered her arm and drew her hand back.

The last notes of the doxology echoed and faded away, then after a moment of silence the first quiet notes of the postlude drifted down through the sanctuary.

As if suddenly released, voices rose in conversation, papers were shuffled and energy flowed through the building as people moved toward the exits.

Melanie, suddenly conscious of how close she sat to Adam, gently pulled away. An older couple in front of them turned around and greeted Adam, smiled at Tiffany, who still slept.

Melanie felt suddenly out of place and got to her feet. Adam stayed sitting, chatting with the couple. He glanced her way, as if he wanted to say something, but the woman asked him a question and he looked back at her.

"Melanie, how are you?"

The woman behind her tapped Melanie on the shoulder. Freda Hartshorn, another nurse from the health unit.

"Have you heard anything about your job?"

"Not yet," Melanie said, turning reluctantly to Freda. "I'm seeing the supervisor Monday."

"She's a different sort, but I wouldn't worry about it." Freda's eyes slipped away as she spoke, and Melanie knew exactly where she was looking. And she knew exactly what Freda's next topic might be.

"By the way, how's Mrs. Wierenga doing?" Melanie asked, hoping to sidetrack her.

Freda dragged her reluctant gaze back to Melanie.

"She's okay." Freda began walking out of the pew and Melanie followed, hopefully forestalling any questions Freda might have about Adam.

Melanie made the usual small talk, even though she wanted nothing more than to stay with Adam. To somehow offer him what comfort she could give him.

But that would have given people even more things to talk about, more questions to ask. What had just happened had created a subtle shift in their relationship, a movement to an unknown destination pushed along by Adam's ambiguous question the other day. She needed a little bit of distance. Some time to think.

By the time she and Freda had made it out the back door, she finally chanced a look behind her.

Adam and Tiffany were nowhere to be seen.

She made small talk with a few other people, turned down an offer to come for lunch and rescheduled an appointment she had with an older man this week, all the while keeping a friendly smile on her face.

Beneath that, however, her emotions twisted and spun.

A couple of days ago she was in Adam's arms. He had kissed her. And today he had come to church.

She finished up the conversation she was having

with a friendly young teenager who wanted her to help with the youth group.

Then, just as she turned to leave, she saw him. He was working his way toward her through the thinning group of people.

"I'm sorry about that," he said when he finally made it to her side. "I got waylaid by some old friends. Then I looked up and you were gone."

He shifted his still-sleeping daughter in his arms. His smile was careful, almost hesitant, as if bruised by the emotions of the service. "Do you want to go for coffee?"

Funny how that cautiously worded invitation sent her heart soaring.

"I'd like that very much," she said, returning his smile. "What about Tiffany?"

Adam pulled his chin back as if taking another look at his little girl. "Once she wakes up she might be a bit cranky, but if you're around, I'm sure she'll be fine. She seems to have formed quite an attachment to you."

Melanie couldn't stop herself from reaching out and touching Tiffany lightly on one rosy cheek. "The feeling is mutual," Melanie said softly.

In her peripheral vision Melanie saw a movement. A woman stopped beside them. Laid her hand on Adam's arm as she greeted him. It was Sandy Gerrard.

She wore a loose flowing dress today, her shining blond hair tumbling over her shoulders. She turned to Melanie, her attitude reserved. "Hi, Melanie. How are you?"

"I'm good, thanks." Melanie kept her voice casual, but she could sense Sandy's restraint. Melanie suspected it had much to do with the phone call they had shared a few days ago. It must have been hard to relive what had happened three years ago. To raise suspicions over why her sister had died.

So Melanie said nothing more. Not that it mattered.

Sandy's attention was focused intently on Adam, her hand resting on his forearm. "It's so good to see you here, Adam. I usually go to church in Eastbar with Mom and Dad, but I'm visiting a friend. I'm glad I ran into you. Now I can remind you of Mom and Dad's anniversary picnic today."

Adam just nodded his acknowledgment.

"Please come," Sandy pleaded, leaning closer to him. "It's been so long since Mom and Dad saw you. Since we all saw you." Her voice lowered on the last words, and her eyes rose to his.

She's in love with him, Melanie thought with a jolt.

"Your mother is welcome, too," Sandy added quickly. "Is she here today?"

"No. She's not feeling well. And I had other plans." Adam glanced over at Melanie. Was it her own foolish hopefulness or did she read entreaty in his eyes?

Tiffany squirmed in Adam's arms, stretched out and whimpered. She blinked, caught sight of Melanie and reached out to her.

Once again Melanie automatically responded by taking the bundle of warm little girl into her arms.

Too late she saw Sandy's pained expression. "I'm sorry. I didn't think..." Melanie stumbled over her words. "Did you want to hold her?" She tried to hand Tiffany to Sandy.

But Tiffany clung to Melanie, burying her head in Melanie's neck as her damp fingers twisted in Melanie's hair.

"She's always like this when she just wakes up," Melanie said with an apologetic smile. Again Melanie realized how that sounded. As if she, a stranger to the Gerrard family, knew more about the daily habits of their niece and granddaughter than Sandy did.

Trouble was, she probably did.

"You're welcome to come, too, Melanie," Sandy said. She gently touched Tiffany's cheek, then turned back to Adam as if dismissing Melanie. "It's been so long since you've talked to Mom and Dad. I know they'd love to see you."

Adam glanced back at Melanie. "Your parents have quite a few advocates, it seems."

Sandy's smile blossomed. "Then we'll see you there?"

"I suppose." Adam breathed out his acceptance on a sigh, gave Sandy a vague smile and watched her go.

Melanie waited until Sandy was out of earshot. "I don't know if it's such a good idea that I come along," she said, absently stroking Tiffany's head with her chin. "I think it might be best if you spend the time with Lana's family on your own."

Adam turned to Melanie again, his smile gentle. "I don't want to be alone with Lana's family. And I'd like you to come."

She was lost, Melanie realized, drifting into the gentle snare of his eyes. How could she withstand the potency of those incredibly blue eyes, the gentle smile playing over his lips?

Be careful.

The warning wended its slow, torturous way to the front of her mind. Nothing was definite between them.

But today she didn't want to go back to her lonely apartment. She didn't want to spend Sunday afternoon by herself. Again. She wanted to be with Adam. She wanted Tiffany in her arms.

"Okay," she said, pressing her cheek to Tiffany's warm, damp curls. "I'll come. But I'll take my own car."

"No problem. But I'd like you to come with me to pick up Mom. She'll probably come along if she knows you're coming, too."

"I'll see you at the house, then." She carefully handed Tiffany over to her father. Thankfully she went without a murmur.

As Melanie got into her car, she pushed a cassette tape into the deck. The music immediately filled the car, pushing out second thoughts and concerns. Adam had asked for time.

Well, that was exactly what she was giving him.

The Gerrards lived almost half an hour away from Derwin and Melanie was thankful she was following Adam. After a number of confusing twists and turns, the taillights of Adam's truck flashed as he signaled to make a turn into a driveway.

As they pulled up to the house, Melanie's second thoughts clamored for attention.

In the center of the yard stood a white canopy, decorated with streamers and flowers. Older people sat on chairs in the shade of the large poplar trees, younger people hung around the vehicles parked row upon row outside the fenced-in yard. Little children ran around screaming and calling out names of other children. Women scurried between the house and the tent carrying plates and casserole dishes and bowls.

This wasn't the cozy family get-together that Sandy had implied. It was a full-fledged party.

"The Gerrards are quite a bunch, aren't they?" Helen said as Adam helped her out of the truck. When Melanie had stopped by the Engler place, she had half hoped Helen was still not feeling well and would want to stay home. But Helen, looking surprisingly well, had pronounced herself rested and eager to get out, which had made Melanie wonder how "ill" Helen had been that morning.

"Are they all family?" Melanie asked.

Helen sniffed and pursed her lips as she assessed the gathering. "Pretty much," she announced.

"It can be rather overwhelming when you first see them all together like this," Adam said, setting Tiffany on the ground. He tugged the cuffs of his shirt down and ran his fingers through his hair, his eyes on the yard. Pulled in a deep breath.

"You look fine, son." Helen tweaked his collar into place, then patted him on the chest.

"Just watch this step now, Helen," Melanie said as Adam guided her and her walker through the gate. They found an empty chair and settled Helen in.

"Can I get you anything?" Adam asked.

"I'm fine. See, here's an old friend come to say hello."

"Helen, my dear, you certainly don't look like you've just had surgery." An elderly man stopped beside them, his pale gray suit almost the same shade as his thinning hair. He took Helen's hand between his, smiling down on her, his clipped mustache bobbing upward. "Helen, you are as beautiful as you ever were."

A faint flush colored Helen's cheeks as she coyly ducked her head.

She was flirting with him, Melanie thought, trying not to smile.

"Adam, Melanie, this is Mr. Edgar Matheson. Edgar, this is my long-lost son." Helen waved a hand at Adam and then nodded at Melanie. "And this is my health nurse and good friend, Melanie Visser."

Mr. Matheson's gray eyes fixed on Melanie. "You look very familiar."

Memories of her earlier time in Derwin slipped easily back. This very dapper gentleman hadn't changed much since junior high school. "You were my chemistry teacher."

"Ah, yes." Edgar Matheson inclined his head, his eyes crinkling at the corners as he smiled. "How could I forget those unique amber eyes? I remember how a girl named Roxanne used to tease you in class."

"That was a long time ago." Melanie dismissed his comment with a light shrug. "It hasn't created any lasting effects." Nothing like Adam's casual rescue of her after one particularly bad bout of teasing.

"Well, you've certainly turned into a lovely young woman."

"And you, Edgar, are the same unrepentant flirt you

ever were." Helen turned to Melanie. "Why don't you give me that little girl? And the two of you can go say hello to the Gerrards. Tell them that I have Tiffany. Edgar and I have a lot to catch up on." Helen held Melanie's gaze with a rock-hard steadiness that Melanie knew she couldn't shake. If she resisted, Helen would resist back and create an awkward situation in front of an old teacher.

They settled Tiffany on a chair beside Helen. Thankfully she seemed content to sit and page through the books Adam had had the foresight to bring along from home.

When they were out of earshot of Helen, Melanie stopped, about to explain to Adam why he should go alone, when he caught Melanie's arm, pulling her gently aside. A boisterous group of children screamed past them. When they were gone, he didn't let go of her, though, his thumb gently stroking her forearm.

"Do you remember that time I found Roxanne teasing you?" he asked, his expression bemused. "I had forgotten about it until now."

Gentle shivers chased themselves up and down her arm, instigated by his touch, and his eyes delved into hers, as if probing her deepest secrets.

"You held out your hand to me," Melanie said softly, unable to look away from the mesmerizing blue of his eyes. "You said, 'I've been waiting for you.' And then we walked away together. You rescued me."

"And you've rescued me." Adam's smile faded away, and his hand stilled on her arm. Tightened. "This morning in church I felt the sadness I had when Lana died, but this time without the crushing, twisting guilt." He angled his head to one side, studying her face. "I want to thank you for that. I wish I knew exactly where to go from here…."

"You don't need to have all the answers right now, Adam," Melanie said, determined not to let her own loneliness cloud the issues he had to work through. Just because he had come to church didn't mean he was ready for God yet. "You have some things to deal with that will help you decide. Let God work how He will in your life."

"You have such a strong faith," Adam said softly, touching her cheek lightly. His fingers cupped her chin. "I envy that."

As if it moved on its own, her hand rose. Pressed against his as her eyes drifted shut.

Just a moment, she promised herself.

Then she lowered her hand. Looked away.

"I have my own struggles," she said quietly.

Struggles with a confused man I'm finding far too appealing. And a little girl I long to care for as my own. And a house that is growing too important in my life. She stepped back, determined to give them both the distance they needed. "Now you better go and find the Gerrards or they are going to wonder if you ever made it here."

Adam caught her hand. "That sounds like you might not come with me."

Melanie hesitated. She knew she was there only on sufferance. She shouldn't have come. Adam hadn't seen the Gerrards since he had arrived and it wouldn't look good if he showed up with an unknown woman at his side.

"Please come with me." He squeezed her hands. "I don't know if I can do this by myself."

How could she say no? Adam was always so strong. So confident. Now he was almost pleading for her to come with him.

And she was foolish enough to catch on to that and allow him to lead her on.

It wasn't difficult to find Amanda and Tom Gerrard. They stood in the center of a group of well-wishers. Amanda wore a spray of flowers pinned to the jacket of a pale yellow suit. Tom stood beside her, his arm over her shoulders. They were laughing, the picture of joy and celebration.

Envy tugged at Melanie for their happiness with each other and the longevity of their relationship. It was what she wanted more than anything else. To be able to celebrate a thirty-year anniversary with friends and family.

Then Tom turned.

Melanie saw his eyes flicker from Adam to her and his smile disappeared. He nudged his wife, whose face went through the same transformation.

"Adam," Tom said with forced heartiness. "So glad you could come." He held out his hand to his son-in-law even as his eyes assessed Melanie.

Melanie held back while Amanda also greeted Adam with a smile. Also gave Melanie a less-than-welcoming glance.

Melanie understood then what was happening.

Adam had been married to their daughter and it must have been hard for them to see him with someone else. Even though there was nothing more than dreams and wishes that kept her at Adam's side.

Amanda gave Adam a perfunctory hug and then looked away. Melanie could see tears in her eyes.

Adam turned to Melanie and drew her forward. "Tom and Amanda, I'd like you to meet Melanie. She's my mother's health nurse."

"Congratulations on your anniversary," Melanie said, holding out her hand. Tom's handshake was brief. Amanda merely nodded at her.

The other people surrounding them slowly drifted away, leaving the four of them alone.

"I'd like to echo Melanie's congratulations. And wishes for many more," Adam said, slipping his hands into his pockets.

An awkward silence followed his comments. Tom rocked back and forth, looking down at the ground. Amanda chewed her lower lip.

"We met Sandy after church," Adam continued. "She invited both of us to come."

"I see." Amanda glanced quickly from Adam to Melanie as if assessing their relationship. "So you're Helen's nurse. That was nice of you to take time to come with her. You don't need to be with her now?"

"Oh, no. She's doing quite well. Adam and I left her chatting with an old friend."

Amanda's sharp intake of breath told Melanie more than words could what Amanda thought of Melanie's casual linking of their names.

"I see," Amanda said softly, her hard gaze flicking from Adam to Melanie.

"I hear from Graydon that the carpentry business is going quite well," Adam said to Tom, seemingly oblivious to the tension that gripped Amanda.

"Absolutely. Absolutely." Tom grabbed the conversational hook like a drowning man. "We've got more work than we can handle. Graydon is looking at adding on to the shop and upgrading some of the woodworking tools."

While Adam and Tom chatted, Melanie kept her eyes fixed on them, wondering how long she dared stay here, the blatant object of Amanda's displeasure and discomfort.

"Where's Tiffany?" Amanda finally asked Adam during a lull in the conversation.

"Melanie and I left her with my mom."

Melanie almost cringed at Adam's words, echoing her own previously. Amanda's gaze glanced off Melanie, clung to Adam. "We haven't seen as much of her as we would have liked to," she said with a wounded tone.

"You've seen her a number of times already. And you know where we live in Calgary." Adam kept his voice even, but Melanie could sense his withdrawal.

"It's such a long way away," Amanda said, twisting her hands around each other. "You know how I hate driving. Just like Lana did."

"Amanda, be careful," Tom murmured. "Adam doesn't want to talk about Lana."

"She was our daughter. We loved her. Adam seems

content to forget her." Amanda's gaze fell pointedly on Melanie.

Melanie felt the bolt of Amanda's anger. She didn't want to look away, but didn't know how to deal with such blatant animosity and still be polite.

And once again Adam came to her rescue. He moved a step closer to Melanie. Put his arm around her and drew her to his side.

"Lana died three years ago, Amanda. I loved her, too, and I haven't forgotten her, but I know when it's time to move on."

Amanda sniffed and wiped her eyes.

Before she could speak, however, Sandy was at Adam's side.

"Adam, you did come. I'm so glad." Sandy slipped her arm into Adam's other one and pulled him close. "How are you doing?"

"Not bad." His clipped voice gave lie to the words. Melanie ached for him even as she could feel herself slowly being pushed aside.

"I saw your mother and started looking for you. Tiffany is still with her, in case you were wondering." Sandy turned to her parents. "Isn't it lovely that Adam is here?"

"Of course it is," Amanda said with false heartiness.

"Did you have a chance to see what Mom and Dad did to the kitchen?" Sandy asked. "Mom finally got rid of that pink countertop she's hated all these years."

"My feelings weren't that strong." Amanda waved the comment away. But she was smiling now. Sandy's presence had eased the palpable tension.

"I don't know about that," Sandy said with a grin. "Remember how she used to put hot frying pans directly on the counter, hoping she would scorch it?"

Adam didn't reply, but Melanie saw his mouth twitch with amusement at the memory.

Sandy smiled up at him, her gaze affectionate. "I'm so glad you came back," she murmured. "We've missed you."

"But I hear you're selling Lana's house?" Amanda demanded. "That can't be right."

Melanie's prick of resentment was followed by pity for Adam and a new understanding of the role Lana's parents had played in the burden of guilt Adam had carried.

"Melanie is buying it," Adam said.

Melanie's heart did a quick dive at the practical tone of his voice. The juxtaposition of Adam's arm around her while he spoke so casually of her buying the house so he could move on created a flurry of emotions that she couldn't identify.

Where were she and Adam headed? Anywhere?

Amanda's frown told Melanie exactly what she thought of Melanie moving into her daughter's former house. "Why would a single girl like you want to buy that house?"

Melanie stifled her annoyance, reminding herself that though Lana had died three years ago, Amanda, too, had her own sorrow to deal with. "It's a lovely place," she said, determined not to let Amanda's disapproval usurp even the smallest scrap of pleasure she got from the thought of owning that house. Determined not to read too much into the warmth of Adam's arm. She pulled away from him, giving herself distance from him and the emotions he raised in her. "It's going to be a home for me, as well as a good investment."

The practical comment injected a more businesslike tone to a very emotional conversation.

Still, Amanda's breath puffed out in displeasure.

And beside her she could feel Adam's confusion at her retreat.

"I remember how excited Lana was when she first found that house," Sandy said, pulling Adam closer to her.

As if on cue, Tom and Amanda moved closer to Sandy and Adam and away from Melanie, their conversation picking up and roaming over past events shared by the four of them. Events that Melanie had no part in.

And once again Melanie felt as if she was on the outside looking in.

Would they even notice if she left? Would they care?

Melanie brushed the questions away as she waited for the right moment to leave. She didn't need to see the approval that Tom and Amanda so easily bestowed on Sandy and withheld from her, a stranger.

So much of her life had been spent yearning to be a part of a family. As Sandy was.

And what did she have to compare to this family gathering? Her mother's grave in the Derwin cemetery and a father who had chosen to be cremated.

Compared to Sandy and the rich heritage she had in the family surrounding them, she was a pauper.

"I'm going to check on Tiffany a moment," she said to Adam. The longer she stayed with them, the more excluded she would feel. She wasn't an insecure young girl anymore who sought approval from those who spurned her.

Adam made a move to stop her, but was waylaid by Tom, and, without looking back to see Adam's reaction, Melanie left.

Chapter Fourteen

She was walking down the road. He could see her figure moving between the trees that shielded the Gerrard property from the graveled road.

The tension holding Adam's shoulders in its fierce grip dissipated as he started jogging down the driveway. He had left Tom and Amanda as soon as he could, but Melanie had disappeared. His mother hadn't seen her, nor had Mr. Matheson.

"Melanie, wait," he called out as he came onto the road.

She hesitated, then turned, waiting as he caught up.

"I thought you left," he said, breathless with the unexpected exertion. "Then I saw your car was still parked here."

"It's blocked off." A light breeze played with her hair, tossing it about her face. She pushed it back, tucking it behind her ear, her eyes avoiding his.

"Why did you leave?"

She looked away, over the open spaces beyond the

road, as if she might find the reason there. "I knew I shouldn't have come, Adam. I don't belong here."

"I'm sorry about Amanda," Adam said, wanting to reach out and take her in his arms. But so much had happened so quickly, he still wasn't sure what her reaction would be and what would be appropriate on his part. "She's always been an overly protective mother. I suspect that might have been part of Lana's problem, as well. And part of the reason I blamed myself."

"You know better, don't you?" Melanie's eyes were pleading. And once again her hand lay on his arm, warm, hopeful.

Adam let his gaze travel over her face. Her touch encouraged him. He gave in to an impulse and eased a strand of hair away from her forehead. "The psalm the minister read this morning was the same one my mother read to me last night. 'Restore unto me the joy of Thy salvation.' I didn't have that joy because I blamed God. I blamed God because I always thought Amanda blamed me. Because I thought she was right." He caressed her cheek with his knuckle, his feelings for her still a confusion. "And thanks to what you told me, I realized it wasn't true. Lana made her own choices."

Melanie smiled up at him, her lips trembling. "I'm glad, Adam. I'm glad you let God set you free from what you were dragging around."

"God set me free, but so did you." He lowered his hand to her neck, grazing her collarbone with his thumb. Then he slipped his hand around her back and drew her carefully to him, holding her close.

She came willingly into his arms. Slipped her own around him.

Adam sighed into her hair, his chin resting on her head. He knew he was falling in love with her.

And he knew he didn't want to leave.

Melanie drew in a deep breath, smoothed down her skirt and knocked on the office door of the new superintendent.

"Come in," Tanya Docker called out.

Melanie sent up a prayer, and stepped into the office.

Tanya was standing at the desk frowning at a file folder open in front of her.

"Sit down, please, Melanie," Tanya said, indicating with her pen the empty chair on the other side of the desk. She sat down herself, granting Melanie a quick glance. "Glad you could come in." She adjusted her blazer, touched her hair with an absent gesture, her eyes still on the papers in front of her.

"Your work here has been exemplary and your references are very good."

Only a deaf person would have missed the "but" in her voice, Melanie thought, swallowing a knot of fear. She waited, however, still hopeful.

Tanya sighed and looked directly at Melanie for the first time. "But I'm afraid the full-time position is no longer available."

Melanie heard the words, saw the regret on Tanya's face, yet it seemed to take long seconds before they registered completely.

Ice slipped through her veins, deadening her.

"How…" It was all she could get past her suddenly dry lips.

Tanya Docker flipped her file closed with her index finger and folded her hands on top of it. Not one gray hair was out of place, and her blazer didn't even bunch at the shoulders from sitting down. She looked as efficient as she sounded. "Our budget has been cut back substantially, and we've had to take away the full-time position you had applied for."

It was as if a hand of lead pushed down on her shoulders. "When did…" She stopped, trying to catch her composure, and tried again. "When did this information come your way?"

Tanya didn't meet her eye, simply ran her finger slowly up and down the edge of the file. "I found out two weeks ago. This was the earliest I could tell you. I'm sorry. I'm sure it can't be easy."

"I banked on that job." She thought of her loan and winced at her word usage. "I just made an offer on a house…."

Tanya held her hands up as if soothing a troubled child. "I'm sorry to tell you this. I'm sure it can't be easy."

Melanie unclenched her fists. Drew in a deep breath. "Is there anyone else I can speak to about this?" she asked, thankful that her voice sounded more steady than she felt. "The department head? The director of the Health Authority?"

"I'm afraid not. The decision to make the cut was done by the Health Region."

"My current job officially terminates the end of this

week. I don't suppose there's any way it could be extended." It was such a faint hope, and the gentle shaking of Tanya's head extinguished it before it could even settle.

"I'm really sorry, Melanie. You're an excellent nurse. All your reports have been exemplary and I hate to lose you, but…" Tanya lifted her hands in a limp gesture of resignation. "I hope you can find something else on such short notice. We will be giving you a glowing recommendation, of course."

Melanie listened with one part of her mind as realization hit the other. No wonder her loan wasn't approved. The bank had known her job was in jeopardy before she did.

What was she going to do now?

Find another job. Move. But which one would happen first? And how did Adam fit into all of this? Yesterday he had made some faint noises about staying in Derwin. For a brief, luminous moment, she'd thought maybe something would happen.

But now?

"So again, I'm sorry, Melanie," Tanya continued.

Melanie forced herself to smile. To respond. As soon as was reasonably polite she was out the door and then, thankfully, outside.

She made it to her car without stumbling, without tears. When she got inside, she waited for the anger to come. She had wanted this house so long and now the opportunity had been snatched away.

She thought of Adam. Wondered what would happen between them. Because no matter how she looked at the situation, she knew she was falling in love with him.

Yet nothing had been settled. Their relationship was too uncertain. They needed time that neither was going to get. By the end of the week she had to find another job, probably in another town, and by the end of next week Adam was moving back to Calgary.

Could I go with him if he asked?

What if he didn't ask?

She pressed her fist against her forehead, swallowing down the tears of confusion that pressed behind her eyes. *I need Your help to get through this, Lord. Show me what I have to do.*

Her scattered prayer twisted and pulled as she tried to focus, one thought, one idea surfacing with icy clarity.

Her dream house had once again become just a dream.

I'm not going to be living here, Melanie thought, pulling up to the Engler home half an hour later. She had repeated the words to herself again and again as she drove, hoping that by the time she got to the house, reality and thoughts would have meshed.

Her heart still twisted, however, when she saw the familiar lines of the house. In spite of her brave words to herself, she still felt the pull of the house, a sense of homecoming that would never happen.

She didn't have an appointment scheduled for Helen this morning, but her other client had canceled, leaving the morning open. But now, as she parked in front of the house, her emotions were a confusion of disappointment and excitement at the possibility of seeing Adam again.

And even that bright hope held a touch of the bittersweet. Nothing was settled between them, in spite of her growing feelings for him. And his changing relationship with God.

"Melanie, we're over here," Helen called out, waving to Melanie from the backyard. Tiffany was crouching down some distance away from Adam, who looked to be digging in one of the flower beds.

Her eyes clung to him as she walked up to them, her heartbeat as light and precarious as the flight of a butterfly.

He turned as she came near, his smile lighting up his face. "What a nice surprise," he said, standing up. "I was going to leave a message for you, but now I don't have to."

"I wasn't supposed to come today," Melanie said, unable to keep her eyes off him, wondering what his message was. "I got a cancellation and thought I would stop by. It was such a nice day." She was babbling, and she clamped her lips together.

Adam's smile widened. For a moment Melanie thought he might give her a quick hug, but all he did was slap the sides of his jeans to brush the dirt off his hands. "Mom was just supervising some planting. We got some perennials at half price at the nursery this morning. Thought they would brighten the yard up."

Melanie couldn't help but compare the yard to when she'd first come here. Then it had looked like an unorganized garage sale. Now it welcomed you to sit down. Contemplate life. And now Adam was putting in perennials?

“Looks very nice.” She tried to inject a note of enthusiasm into her voice, but without success.

Adam seemed to sense her mood. He angled her a questioning glance but she looked away, watching Tiffany digging up the dirt with her shovel, oblivious to what was going on. Lucky child.

“Well, let’s have some lemonade,” Helen said, turning her walker around. “I just made some. Tiffany, you can come with me to put the glasses out.”

Tiffany dropped her shovel and noticed Melanie for the first time. “Melanie,” she called out, running toward her as she always did.

And as she always did, Melanie dropped down to catch the little bundle of warm humanity. Tiffany smelled like dirt and orange Popsicle and felt like love. Melanie clung to her, a pang of sorrow piercing her. She cared for this little child more than she had realized.

“You’re squishing me, Melanie,” Tiffany complained.

“I’m sorry,” Melanie said, reluctantly lowering her to the ground. Then as she straightened, she realized what Tiffany had said. “She said my name the right way,” she said to Adam.

“We’ve been practicing.” Adam gave Melanie a quick wink. “Thought she better learn to say it right.”

She wondered what he meant by that. Then wondered if she had read too much into his light comment. Then wondered why she wondered.

Her head was spinning.

"So what are you doing?"

"Helping my daddy and gramma plant plants." Tiffany pressed her finger to her orange-rimmed mouth. "It's a secret. For you."

"Tiffany, are you coming?" Helen called from the step.

"I go help Gramma," Tiffany announced, and without a backward glance bounced off toward the house.

When the door banged shut behind her, Melanie turned to Adam, unnerved to find him only inches away from her.

"Hey, there," he said quietly, the timbre of his voice creating intimacy in the open space surrounding them. He grazed her cheek with his knuckle. "I'm glad you came."

His touch weakened her knees and undermined her resolve. She wanted answers, but she didn't know which questions to ask. Once she had asked him what was happening between them and he hadn't been able to answer her. And she had only been able to tell him that she couldn't consider a relationship with someone who didn't want to have a relationship with God.

Yesterday she had seen a different side of Adam. Had sat beside him in church and knew for a fact that he had been touched by God.

And now she didn't know where to go. In the past twenty-four hours her whole life had turned topsy-turvy and she didn't know which constant to cling to.

Only God's love.

She took a deep breath at that gentle reminder.

"I have something to tell you," she said quietly, looking away. She might as well get this part over and done with. "I just found out this morning that I didn't get the job I was hoping to get. I talked to Floyd on the way here. I'm withdrawing my offer to buy the house."

Adam went completely still.

A gentle breeze sifted through the leaves of the trembling aspen and chased a scrap of paper across the yard as the silence stretched out.

"I'm sorry, Melanie," Adam said quietly. "I know how much this house meant to you."

Melanie only nodded, then looked up at him. "It did. I guess it was just a dream after all."

"So now what happens for you, Melanie?"

Was that her call to make? What about Adam? So now what happens for him?

She wrapped her fingers around each other, tilted her shoulder up as she glanced up at him. "I have to find another job somewhere else."

Adam's frown darkened his face. "Where would you go?"

His answer wasn't heartening and she answered with a vague movement of her hands. "Wherever I can get work. I'm going to have to start looking as soon as possible. My job is over this week."

"So soon?"

"What are you going to do about the house?" she asked. She didn't want to talk about herself anymore. It was depressing.

"I'm not sure." He blew out his breath and caught

the back of his neck in a gesture that Melanie now recognized as tension. "My partner phoned this morning asking when I was going to get the money from you. I guess that isn't going to happen."

This was getting more and more awkward, Melanie thought. Each dancing around their feelings, not sure what to commit to. Unsure of where the other stood.

"Melanie, I need to…"

The beeper going off at her side stopped Adam midsentence. Melanie glanced at the number, angry at the intrusion.

It was the clinic. They could wait.

"I'm sorry, Adam. What were you going to say?"

He shook his head. "It can wait. Make your phone call."

It was her supervisor. One of her patients needed her to come immediately. Could Melanie go?

She didn't want to, but her patient's care came first. "I'm sorry," she said to Adam when she'd put away her cell phone. "I've got to go."

"Of course you do." He waited a moment, then, to her utter surprise, bent over and brushed his lips lightly over hers. "I'll come and see you tonight."

More confusion, and yet a promise. He was going to see her tonight.

And as she drove away, her heart sang.

"I don't know if I like the layout." Eileen Olson turned around in the kitchen, her arms folded around her waist, her lips pursed. "We'd need to put all new cupboards in."

"The foundation is solid," Floyd said, "and Adam redid the wiring. Anything you would need to do would be superficial."

Adam stifled his annoyance with Eileen and Floyd. When Melanie had delivered her bomb, his first reaction was disappointment for her. He knew how badly she wanted this house.

Then, on the heels of that came the realization that she was free of this obligation. She could go where she wanted. And that's what scared him.

Then Floyd had called saying that he had an older couple who were interested in the house.

Kyle had phoned this morning asking him about the money and he had put him off. He didn't want to go back to Calgary.

"The living room needs a paint job," Eileen was saying, listing off yet more negatives. "I just don't know." She turned to her husband. "What do you think?"

"We've hardly seen the whole house, Eileen," he said. "I'm not ready to make a call yet."

"Adam, why don't you show them the master bedroom?" Floyd said. "It's one of the finished rooms in the house, and will give you a good idea of what the rest of the house might look like with a little bit of work."

"A lot of work," Eileen added.

Adam was starting to get annoyed. When they had walked around the outside of the house, Adam had been honest, but fair. The exterior did need work and he'd pointed out what needed to be done. He had done the same with Melanie only a few weeks ago.

But somehow when she was looking at it, she could see beyond the blistering paint, the worn-out eaves troughs to what it would look like if someone who cared about it spent some time.

Adam opened the door to the master bedroom and stepped aside as Eileen and her husband, Jerry, entered.

They were silent. Eileen walked around his mother's bed to the windows. She twitched the curtains aside, her mouth still pulled tight like a drawstring purse.

"This is a lovely room," Jerry said, standing in the doorway. "Just beautiful."

"Not too bad," Eileen sniffed.

The room was beautiful and they knew it. This was a waste of time.

But Floyd chivvied them along, bringing them upstairs. Adam showed them the rooms one at a time, growing more defensive by the minute as Mrs. Olson consistently found things wrong with the house.

It was a good place. It would make a lovely home.

"I can't show you the attic. The stairs broke a while ago and I haven't bothered to replace them," Adam said as he opened the door to the last room upstairs. The room directly above his mother's bedroom.

Again Eileen was the first to enter. Again she walked straight to the window. She stopped, her hands resting on the sill, and for the first time she had nothing to say.

Jerry came alongside her. "What a beautiful view," he said quietly.

Adam remembered Melanie standing in the same place. The gentle smile on her face as she'd revealed her memories and dreams to him. Her love for this house and the family that had occupied it. And at that time his emotions had been in such a negative state he'd felt as if he had to disabuse her of her illusions. Let her know that this was not a place to pin so much hope on.

But so much had changed since then. Listening to Eileen Olson talk so negatively about a house that Melanie had yearned so deeply for shifted his own perspective.

He didn't think they were going to buy it, but even if they did, he didn't know if he wanted to sell it to them. Or anyone.

He wanted to keep it. For himself.

The thought dived into his soul and made a home there.

He didn't want to go back to Calgary and Kyle and fourteen-hour work days. He wanted a home for his daughter. And he wanted Melanie in it.

And he wanted it here. In Derwin.

The realization struck him with an uplifting rush of joy.

Eileen turned away from the window and saw the dresser Adam had built for Melanie.

"Where did that come from?" she asked, running her fingers over the top. "This is a fine piece of workmanship."

"I made it," Adam said.

She pulled open a drawer and pulled out some cards. "What are these?"

"Paint chips, it looks like," Floyd said.

"They're labeled." Eileen waved them at Adam. "Did you choose these?"

Adam stifled a flux of resentment. Those belonged to Melanie. "Someone else was thinking of purchasing the house. She had chosen those colors for the various rooms and the exterior."

Eileen shuffled through them. "She has good taste. The colors she has chosen are amazing." She found the one for the room they were in and held it up, nodding. "I think I can visualize what she wanted to accomplish here. Very lovely." She slapped them against her hand as she turned a full circle in the room. "Can I keep them?"

"Of course you can," Floyd said. "The person who picked those out isn't going to be buying the house."

"They were in the dresser," Adam said, flashing a warning look at Floyd. "They belong to the owner."

"I thought you owned the dresser?" Eileen's voice held a peeved note. As if unused to being turned down.

"No. I made it for Melanie Visser. It's hers."

"Well, then, I guess they stay here." Eileen dropped the cards carelessly on top of the dresser and walked out of the room in a huff. Jerry followed.

Floyd waited until they were out of earshot, then turned to Adam, glowering. "What are you doing? She was starting to come around. Why couldn't she have those lousy paint chips?"

"They don't belong to me." They were part of Melanie's dream and he was loath to part with even a small part of it.

Floyd frowned at Adam, his arms folded across his chest. "Okay, Adam. What's happening? My first prospective buyer you almost scare off with a list of repairs that would have stymied anyone less determined than Melanie. Now you're going to ruin a prospective sale over a bunch of lousy paint chips that you can pick up at the hardware store for nothing?"

Adam just shrugged. "I don't think those paint chips are going to swing this deal for you, Floyd." He walked out of the room without a backward glance.

Ten minutes later he was standing on the porch watching Floyd drive off with the Olsons.

He didn't think he would hear from them again.

Tomorrow he would phone Floyd and officially pull the listing off the market, which would release him from the agreement he'd signed with Floyd. The house was no longer for sale. For now, he had other things to do.

And twenty-five minutes later he was standing in the hallway of Melanie's apartment, knocking on her door, his heart keeping heavy time with his fist.

The door opened with a faint creak and Melanie stood in front of him, backlit by the sun coming in through her patio doors.

Adam swallowed at the sight of her, easily calling back yesterday when she was in his arms and he felt as if his life was slowly moving toward a still center.

And now?

How did he start? What questions were his right to ask?

"Can I come in?"

She nodded and stood aside, still clinging to the door like a shield. She closed it behind him and stayed there.

"Floyd brought some people to the house today," he said, stringing his thumbs in the belt loops of his jeans as he noted the piled-up empty boxes in the living room. "Potential buyers."

Melanie's gaze skittered down and away and he caught a glimpse of sorrow. She nodded, leaning against the door as if drawing strength from it. "What did they think of the house?"

"Not much. I don't think they're going to take it."

She just nodded.

The awkwardness that had been so palpable this afternoon was back. He had come here full of expectation, yet now that he stood in front of her, the woman he knew he was in love with, he didn't know how to articulate his feelings. So much had changed.

This afternoon he'd found himself looking with different eyes at a house he had once wanted to dump as quickly as possible. Now he began to see it as a home. For him and Melanie.

"Do you want to move?" he asked, still unsure, still cautious.

As Melanie shook her head, he caught the glint of a tear in her eyes. "Of course not."

"Melanie, I don't want you to leave."

She looked back at him, her incredulous gaze holding his. "Leave what?"

Adam dared to close the distance between them, to gently take her in his arms once again. Like a homecoming.

He drew her close, resting his chin on her head, taking a chance now that she was in his arms. "I don't want you to leave me, Melanie. I don't need any more time to think about it."

She melted against him, her arms slipping around his waist as they had yesterday, her damp cheeks pressed against his shoulder. "I don't want to go, either."

His eyes drifted shut as he held her close. "Thank You, Lord," he whispered.

She drew back just enough to see his face. "You came to church yesterday. And now you're praying." She stopped there, as if hoping he would finish her thoughts.

"I tried to ignore God, Melanie, but He didn't ignore me. Like those letters Jason had sent his wife, the love was there, waiting. I just needed to read it. To listen." He wiped a glistening track of moisture from her cheek with his thumb, glorious happiness welling up in him like a fountain. "I know I'm not there yet, but I also know that if I seek Him, I will find Him." He touched his lips to her forehead, then her cheek.

He kissed her again and held her close, wonder and amazement flooding through him like a cleansing stream that had accumulated drop by drop until this afternoon. When he knew he didn't want to sell the house. He wanted it for himself and Melanie and Tiffany and his mother.

"Are you busy tomorrow night?" he said suddenly. "Can you come for supper?" He had to get some plans in place and for that he needed time.

"Sure. I'd like that." Her smile was all the encouragement he needed. He kissed her again. "Then we'll see you tomorrow." He didn't know if he could wait. But he knew that for the first time in years, his life was moving in a good direction.

Chapter Fifteen

"Where are we going?" Melanie asked. Supper was over, the dishes done and Adam had drawn her aside, telling her that he had something he wanted to say. In private. Just then the phone started ringing.

"I'll get it," Helen said, smiling a benevolent smile.

She knew, Adam thought. But nothing could stifle his happiness now.

"Just follow me." Adam turned to Melanie, took her hand and led her up the stairs, then turned to the left and opened the upper tower room.

He let her precede him and she stepped inside, looking around, unsure of where this was going. The first thing she saw was her dresser—but surely that wasn't what he wanted to show her?

"You moved this up here for nothing," she said wistfully, running her hand over the smooth surface.

Adam caught her hand and lifted it to his lips. "No, I don't think I did." He walked backward, drawing her toward the window. Once there, he pulled her into his arms. "And look, the sun is obliging me with just the right tone."

Pink and orange splashed on the underside of the clouds, reflected in the pond beyond the fenced-in yard.

"Obliging you with what?" Melanie asked. Where was he going with all this?

Adam gently brushed her hair back from her face, his eyes following his hand. His fingers trembled.

"I wish I knew where to start. The first time I saw you, all those years ago, I had a feeling about you. That you were someone special. Now, as I've gotten to know you, I've learned that my intuition was right. You have a beauty of spirit, a generous heart and a faith that I've learned much from."

Melanie swallowed down a flutter of anticipation. He sounded so serious. Intent.

Adam's hand cupped her chin as his wonderfully blue eyes delved into hers. "You've given me hope and encouragement. You've set my feet on right paths. For the first time in years I feel like I'm moving in a good direction. Closer to God, closer to family. Closer to you." He paused, his thumb lightly caressing her chin, his voice growing softer. "I don't want to move away. I don't want you to move away, either. I want to stay here. In Derwin. In this house. With you."

Melanie held his gaze, his last words resonating through all the lonely places of her life and filling them with a joy so great she thought she would burst.

Adam slipped his hand into the pocket of his pants and pulled out a small velvet box.

"I know it's a little soon, but I was afraid to wait."

Melanie's heart did double time as he opened it. A diamond solitaire sparkled back at her from the depths of the velvet box.

"Will you marry me?"

Such simple words. And what a storm they created in her heart. She reached up to touch his face, as if to catch his words and hold them to herself.

Her dream. Come true.

"Yes. I will" was all she could say.

And suddenly she was in his arms, held close to a heart beating in time with hers.

And as they kissed, she felt, for the first time in years, as if she had finally come home.

"A toast," Helen said, lifting up her glass when they eventually came back downstairs. "To Melanie and Adam. Long life and good health. May God's blessing fall on you in all the places of your life."

Adam accepted his mother's blessing with a smile that wouldn't quit. He didn't think his heart could take in one more ounce of happiness. He looked around the table and he raised his own glass. "And I want to propose a toast to the three most important women in my life." He turned to Helen. "My mother. Faithful in prayer and love." Then to Tiffany. "My daughter, a blessing from God that I hope to never take for granted." Finally he turned to Melanie. "And to my future wife. The woman who brought me back home."

Melanie raised her glass and touched Adam's, the diamond on her finger sparkling almost as brightly as her amber eyes. "And to you, Adam. First among men and first in my life. Here's to many years together," she returned, her voice husky. "Many, many years."

Her added words took on a rare poignancy. They both knew what she meant. "May God bless us," he whispered, touching his glass to hers.

Adam looked around the table, unable to stop smiling. He knew he didn't deserve this happiness, but at the same time he had learned how guilt had kept him from enjoying the good things God had given him. He was simply going to allow God to work His way in their lives. And trust that His love would carry them through.

"Did I hear a vehicle?" Helen said, cocking her head to one side. Then she clapped her hand to her head. "In all the excitement, I forgot to tell you that Floyd is coming over."

Voices drifted up the walk, footsteps echoed in the darkness.

A knock on the back door.

Adam turned on the porch light. Floyd stood in profile to the door talking to Eileen and Jerry Olson.

"Adam. Sorry to disturb you," Floyd turned, his smile more generous than it had been yesterday. "As I told your mother, Mr. and Mrs. Olson want to take another look through the house. They're having some second thoughts."

Adam stifled his annoyance. In his excitement he'd forgotten to tell Floyd the house was off the market.

But he didn't want to look ungracious, so he stepped aside to allow them in. He would pull Floyd aside and tell him at the first opportunity.

"Hello, Melanie. Good to see you again." Floyd

reached across the table to shake her hand, his smile even wider. He turned to the Olsons. "Melanie, I'd like you to meet Eileen and Jerry Olson. They're considering buying this place. Helen and Tiffany, you've met the Olsons already?" He didn't give Helen a chance to answer, but turned to Eileen. "Melanie is the former buyer who had picked out the colors you admired."

Melanie threw a puzzled glance Adam's way. He shook his head. He'd explain later. For now they just had to go through the formalities.

"I have to say, I was very impressed with your color combinations," Eileen was saying to Melanie. "Gave me second thoughts about the house. I'm so glad you're here. I'd like to know what else you were planning on doing here."

"Eileen saw the paint chips you had sitting in the dresser upstairs," Adam put in.

Melanie nodded, but Adam could see she was still not sure what was going on.

"I hope we're not interrupting anything," Jerry said, hanging back, obviously uncomfortable.

"Just a small celebration," Helen replied, adjusting her glasses.

Adam laid a quieting hand on his mother's shoulder. The last time the Olsons had been here Helen had taken quite personally Eileen's disparaging comments about the house. Who knew what she might say.

"Really, what are you celebrating?" Floyd asked.

"Adam and Melanie's engagement," Helen said, her voice prim.

Congratulations were murmured, and Floyd gave

Adam a knowing look. Adam was uncomfortable with the attention. He didn't want all these people around during this special moment. He wished his mother had passed on Floyd's message sooner. He would have told Floyd not to come over.

Floyd turned to the Olsons. "So you've seen the house already—would you like to go through it again?"

"I'd like Melanie to show us through," Eileen said. "If you don't mind."

"No. I don't mind." Melanie spoke slowly, a puzzled frown creasing her forehead.

And why wouldn't she be confused? Just moments before he had told her they were going to be making their home in Derwin. In this house. Now she was being asked to show a prospective buyer through it.

"Where would you like to start?" Melanie asked, getting up from the table.

"This kitchen." Eileen waved her hand around the room they were standing in. "What would you do about the cabinets?"

Melanie ran her hand along the edge of the cabinets. "They need to be sanded down and painted. I was looking at a pale cream with sage-green trim."

Eileen nodded, her lips pursed as she considered what Melanie was telling her. "Why not new cupboards?"

"These fit with the decor and I like the country-style kitchen rather than the more modern U shape or island separating the cabinets from the rest of the kitchen. You get better flow between table and counter." Melanie smiled, glancing over her shoulder at Adam. "It creates a more family-centered atmosphere."

Adam felt her gaze as tangible as a touch.

He and Floyd and Jerry followed Melanie and Eileen into the front room. The male entourage, Adam thought. Cut out of the loop because they couldn't interpret the difference between eggshell, cream and off-white.

"I don't know if I like the fireplace," Eileen said, tapping her finger against her lips as they stood in the empty front room. "What were you going to do with it?"

"I had thought of an insert." Melanie walked over to the mantel and straightened a picture of Adam and Tiffany that she and Helen had put up there. Again her hands lingered on the picture, brushed a small bit of dust off the mantel. "That would make it more energy efficient."

"But the mess."

Melanie smiled and waved her objections away. "The ambience of a truly warm place in the house outweighs the disadvantages. Besides, it's a great place to dry up mittens when kids come in from playing in the snow."

Eileen nodded, as if to picture it.

Melanie took them through the rest of the house, pointing out the advantages. The oak newel post and banister that just needed the paint stripped off to show their true beauty. How the light coming in from the window in the landing could be enhanced with the insertion of a stained glass window. Why she wouldn't replace the carpet in the upstairs hallway, but would take down the wallpaper, and how much lighter it would be.

And as Melanie told Eileen her plans for the house, Adam found himself falling in love with his own house. He found resurrected his own plans and dreams for this place that was to be a home.

And he loved her all the more for it. He could picture other children in the bedrooms. See Melanie and himself tucking children into beds, before going downstairs to sit in front of a fire in the fireplace.

A family in a home that he had once wanted to get rid of. But best of all, a family with Melanie at his side.

He wanted the Olsons gone. He wanted to go through the house with Melanie himself. He wanted to dream aloud with his arm around her.

As Melanie was leading them back down the stairs again, Adam pulled Floyd aside. "I have to talk to you."

Floyd gestured for Melanie and the Olsons to go ahead, then turned to Adam. "What is it?"

"The house is not for sale, Floyd. I forgot to phone you and tell you. I'm pulling it off the market."

Floyd shook his head, his smile regretful. "Sorry, Adam. I can't do that. I have an interested party."

"But I haven't signed anything yet."

"You signed an agreement with me, Adam. And I have a party that is serious. Finances aren't going to be a problem for them." Floyd lifted his hands in a gesture of resignation. "You could back me on it and maybe I'd give in. But Olson has a legal right here." And with those heartening words he followed the Olson's into the kitchen.

"Thank you, Melanie, that was very helpful." Eileen looked around the kitchen again, a smile on her face.

"This house would make a lovely home. I think I've fallen in love with it." She turned to Floyd. "We'll take it."

Adam's heart plummeted.

And as he caught Melanie's puzzled look, he wondered how he was going to tell her that for the second time in only two days she had lost this house.

Melanie closed the door to Tiffany's room and turned to Adam standing behind her. "How quickly things change," she said softly, drifting into the haven of his arms. "Just goes to show you that there are no certainties in life."

"I'm so sorry, Melanie." Adam held her close. Pressed a kiss to her head. "I didn't think they were going to buy it. I feel like I've lost your dream for you."

"No. Don't say that." She drew her head back to look into his deep blue eyes. "You've given me better dreams. Better plans. You had said at one time that I was putting too much on this house." She glanced down the hallway at the window she had pointed out to Eileen. "You were right. I made this house my source of happiness. And I should have known better."

Adam brushed a light kiss over her forehead. "I guess we'll have to look somewhere else for a place, then."

"In Calgary?"

"Would that bother you?"

Melanie smiled, then smoothed the frown away from his forehead. "I'll go where you go. Even it if means moving all the way to Calgary."

"I don't think we'll have to do that," he said, stroking her cheek. "I've been talking to Graydon. I think he wants a partner. And I think I want to be that partner." His expression grew serious. "I want to stay here, Melanie, in spite of the memories."

"We can make better ones," she said, her heart soaring.

"I like this one better than the newer one." Melanie looked around the yard of the small house Floyd had shown her previously, trying to imagine Tiffany playing in the backyard. Pansies spilled out of the flower beds along the house and behind them the last few tiger lilies nodded in the summer breeze. "It has a nice big yard and it's close to the school. Tiffany will be able to walk there." She walked over to the apple tree, pleased to see tiny apples developing.

"We could add to the house some day." Adam folded his arms as he studied the house. "It's in better shape than my house is."

"I like the country kitchen."

He turned to Melanie. "The other house was bigger. Are you sure you want this one?"

"I am." She sat down on the bench at the base of the apple tree and looked around the yard with a pleased smile. This would make a lovely home. She felt a momentary pang for the loss of her other dream, but she pushed it aside. She had Adam. Tiffany. Helen.

And God's love covering them all.

She truly needed nothing more.

"This house has personality," she said with a smile.

"Okay, what story is attached to this house?" he teased, nudging her aside with his hip.

"Let's see." Melanie hugged her knees, angling Adam a mischievous glance. "The owner used to be a single woman. Everything she had, she put into this house. It was her dream home."

"Aah. I think I know this story."

"Maybe you do. Maybe you don't. Anyway, one day a man came selling magazine subscriptions. He talked her into subscribing to a magazine about moving back to the land. They fell in love and he whisked her away to a mountain hideaway where she makes cinnamon rolls every other day and is learning to milk a goat."

"Sounds like a fairy story to me," he said with a wry smile.

"Don't be cynical." She turned to him, catching his hands in hers. "There's all kinds of happy endings in real life. Just depends on where you end the story."

"That one I would have quit at the whisking part." He pulled her to her feet. "And this story isn't finished, so if we are serious about this place, I guess we should go talk to Floyd. We have to be there anyhow to sign the Agreement for Sale on my place, so we better get going."

Melanie took another look around the yard, trying not to compare it to the home that had absorbed so many daydreams. It was a lovely place and it would be their home. And she and Adam and Tiffany would make their own dreams in it.

The real estate office was only a couple of blocks

away, so they walked there holding hands like a young couple. Melanie felt a gentle peace suffuse her as they walked past other homes, down a street sheltered by sweeping poplar trees and stately spruce. It was an established neighborhood with history and character.

Thank you, Lord, she prayed. *Thank You for giving me more than I need. Help us to make a home here.*

Floyd was busy with another client when they came into the office, so they sat down to wait in the reception area.

Melanie tapped her fingers together, suddenly restless and edgy, just as she was when she was ready to sign the Agreement for Sale for the Engler house.

She wanted to get this over and done with so she and Adam could get back to their wedding plans. And their plans for their future.

Adam was going to go back to work for Graydon, and had been spending as much time arranging that as they had trying to find a new home.

Melanie had managed to obtain another part-time contract with the Health Authority and she was satisfied with that. She had Tiffany now to take care of, and she didn't want to miss out on any part of her development.

She got up and walked once around the reception area, giving the secretary a vague smile. Other houses were listed on the board by the desk and she took a moment to look them over.

"Second thoughts?" Adam murmured over the top of his magazine.

She shook her head. It didn't matter where she and Adam lived. They would be together.

A shadow fell across the door and Melanie glanced over. Her heart clenched.

It was the Olsons, come to take care of the final bit of business.

Eileen gave Melanie a wan smile, then sat down. Jerry sat beside Adam, said a brief hello and dived into a magazine.

"Well, I see we're all here." Floyd bustled into the room, spilling energy and good cheer into the silence. "Come into my office and we can get the final bit of business cleared up." He stood aside as the Olsons walked down the hallway ahead of Melanie and Adam.

"So what did you think of the house, Adam?" Floyd asked as they settled into his office.

"Melanie and I both like it. Nice location." He shrugged. "What else can I say?"

"So you'll probably take it?"

"Probably."

"Excellent." Floyd almost rubbed his hands together.

He should be pleased, Melanie thought as she settled into the chair. Two sales in one day. Exit one dream, enter another.

"Are you looking at purchasing another place?" Eileen asked.

Melanie only nodded, wrapping her fingers around each other.

"In town?"

"Yes. A lovely little home only a few blocks from here." She had to say more than yes or run the risk of looking ungracious.

"I see." Eileen unzipped her purse, then zipped it up

again. "I understand from Floyd that you withdrew your offer on the house because you didn't get a job you had applied for."

Melanie shot Floyd an annoyed glance. He just lifted his hands in a feeble apology.

"That's correct," Melanie said. "Although I just found out I will be getting a part-time position in a month."

Eileen just nodded.

"So I have the papers ready here," Floyd said, leaning over the desk. "All we have to do is get signatures and the deal is done. Pending financing, of course."

"That won't be a problem," Jerry said. He pulled the paper toward him and skimmed it. He was about to pick up the pen when Eileen put her hand on his.

"Don't sign it yet," she said, sounding breathless. Eileen turned to Melanie. "The house we're buying. You love it, don't you?"

Why is she doing this to me? thought Melanie. She only nodded.

"I could tell that. When you showed us around." Eileen chewed her lower lip, wearing away her red lipstick. "I could tell that you wanted it badly."

Melanie swallowed, then felt Adam's hand on her shoulder. He squeezed as if in encouragement. And it reminded her of what was important.

"It was a dream of mine," she said quietly, looking over at her future husband. "I wanted that house for a home, but I realized that wherever Adam and I will be, that will be our home."

"I think you will be able to do that." Eileen's smile was bittersweet. "I have to confess I didn't want the house at all. And neither did Jerry. Until you showed me around. You made me fall in love with it. And if you could do that, it made me wonder how much that house meant to you." Eileen glanced over at her husband. "Jerry is willing to indulge me, but I know he doesn't really want to live that far out of town."

Hope stirred briefly in Melanie's soul, but she pushed it down. "It isn't that far away," Melanie said, trying again to show them the positives.

Eileen laid her hand on Melanie's. "Bless you, my dear. Still trying to sell it." She withdrew her hand and straightened. "But it won't work." She turned to Floyd. "We're withdrawing our offer. I don't want to buy the house anymore."

Floyd dropped his pen onto the desk with a clatter. "Don't be too hasty," he said. "The house is a great buy. Look at it as an investment."

The faint hope that had stirred in Melanie grew. Filled her as Eileen continued.

"Once Melanie showed me the house I could see the potential. I was starting to see that house as a showpiece," Eileen said with a touch of pride. "Something I could show off to my friends. It could be a good investment and I'm sure we would get a good return." Eileen turned to Melanie with a smile that made the hope blossom fully. "But I know for you it will be a home."

"Thank you," Melanie whispered, engulfed with joy.

"Do you mind, Jerry?" Eileen glanced at her husband apologetically.

"Fine by me." Jerry spoke up. He stood up, obviously wanting to put a quick end to this. "Floyd, sorry about all this, but thanks for your time. Adam, thanks again. Best wishes on your wedding, Melanie." He turned to his wife. "Eileen, let's go." And with those abrupt pronouncements, he left.

Eileen turned at the doorway. "Melanie, send me a picture once you've got the outside painted. I'd love to see what you've done with it."

Melanie blinked, trying to assimilate what had happened, then understood what she'd said. "Sure. I'll do that." She gave Eileen a vague smile, then turned to Adam.

"Did I understand this right?"

"I think so." Adam's smile was as big as hers.

Floyd sat back in his chair, shaking his head, a dazed expression on his face. "I can't believe this. Two commissions. Gone. In minutes. The other Realtors will never believe me." He turned to Melanie. "I don't suppose you'll be buying the little house."

She gave him a look filled with regret and shook her head.

"And you don't need to buy Adam's house." He pushed himself away from his desk, emitting a sigh. "Maybe the Olsons might be interested in the little house." He turned to Adam and Melanie. "Well, thanks for the interesting ride. It's been, well, interesting." He shook Adam's hand, then Melanie's. "And I expect to be invited to the wedding."

"I'm sure we can arrange that," Melanie said.

The walk back to the truck was made in silence. As

if each had to absorb what had just happened. But then, as Adam unlocked the door for Melanie, she stopped him.

"Did that really just happen?" she said, still trying to comprehend it all.

Adam canted his head to one side, studying her. "From the looks of things, I'm back where I started. Can't get rid of it, can I?"

"Do you want to?"

Adam ran his knuckle down her cheek, then cupped the back of her head in his hand. "I want to make a home there. With you and Tiffany. With God as its head. That's what I want."

And as he drew her into his arms, Melanie sent up a prayer of thankfulness and happiness.

"Let's go home," she whispered.

Epilogue

"Did you get the mail?"

"Here it is." Melanie dropped the letters on the kitchen table and walked over to kiss her husband who was washing his hands at the kitchen sink. "You smell like wood," she said, inhaling the sharp scent with pleasure. "Are you almost done with the kitchen cabinets?"

"Just have to put the panels together for the pantry doors and I can install them. Graydon will be happy when I've finished with Mom's house, I'm sure."

"So will your mom. I'm glad she agreed to let us build her a place on the yard. It's nice to have her close by."

Adam dried his hands on a towel and set it on the counter. He drew Melanie into his arms and kissed her lightly. "You look tired, Melanie Engler. How was work?"

"Busy. Thankfully I have tomorrow off. I can get the painting done then." She looked past him out the window.

Helen was bent over in the garden, Tiffany hopping alongside counting the rows of beans. Melanie had to smile. "The garden is looking even better than last year. Mom has quite a green thumb."

"And is only too glad to give it some practice." Adam brushed a light kiss over Melanie's forehead, then picked up the mail.

"Well, well. Would you look at this." He dropped the other letters, pulled out a jacknife from the leather case on his belt and slit one envelope open, then handed it to her with a smile.

"You get to see it first."

Melanie glanced at the return address.

The Shewchuk family.

She pulled out a letter, her fingers trembling with excitement and a touch of nervousness. A picture fell out on the table.

Melanie picked it up, and simply stared.

A family portrait.

She set it carefully on the table and started to read.

It had taken a while, the enclosed letter said, but with some counseling and time and God's grace over them all, the Shewchuks were now together again as a family.

Melanie's eyes prickled as she picked up the picture again. Dena stood to one side, her boyfriend's arm around her. She lived in Vancouver, and she and Melanie had been writing for the past couple of months. But Dena had said nothing about this.

The tears that had threatened rolled freely down her face. "They're a family again."

"Hey, sweetheart." Adam gave her a quick hug,

then laid his hand on her stomach. "We're a family, too, you know."

And that made Melanie cry even harder.

And as Adam pulled her close, she sent up a prayer of thanks to God that so many hearts had turned toward home.

* * * * *

Dear Reader,

Just like the letters that Jason had written his wife, God is constantly trying to call us back to Himself. But like Adam, we wander away, thinking we don't deserve what He has to give us. But when we turn away from God, we rob ourselves. God wants us to lay our burdens on Him. We can't carry them ourselves. Our only true rest comes in Him. I pray that if you are burdened with guilt, like Adam, or if you bear burdens at all, that you will allow God to take that off your shoulders. Allow His love to forgive and heal.

Carolyne Aarsen

Love Inspired®

Maya Logan has always thought of her boss, Greg Garrison, as a hard-nosed type of guy. But when a tornado strikes their small Kansas town, Greg is quick to help however he can, including rebuilding her home. Maya soon discovers that he's building a home for them to share.

Look for

Healing the Boss's Heart

by

Valerie Hansen

Available July wherever books are sold.

www.SteepleHill.com

LI87536